PACIFIC SHOGUN

BOOK ELEVEN OF
THE FALLEN WORLD

Jamie Ibson

Dear Al,
Thanks for all the great
chats and awesome food!
All the best!

Blood Moon Press
Virginia Beach, VA

Jamie

Chris Kennedy/Blood Moon Press
2052 Bierce Dr.
Virginia Beach, VA 23454
http://chriskennedypublishing.com/

Publisher's Note: This is a work of fiction. Names, characters, places, and incidents are a product of the author's imagination. Locales and public names are sometimes used for atmospheric purposes. Any resemblance to actual people, living or dead, or to businesses, companies, events, institutions, or locales is completely coincidental.

Cover Design by Elartwyne Estole.

Ordering Information:
Quantity sales. Special discounts are available on quantity purchases by corporations, associations, and others. For details, contact the "Special Sales Department" at the address above.

Pacific Shogun/Jamie Ibson -- 1st ed.
ISBN: 978-1648550942

Prologue

May 1st, 2065

The *Ship Happens* glided in on inertia alone, bumpers hanging off the side and sail already lowered. The sun was high overhead, but dust and ash from the south muddied the otherwise clear Sunday sky. A man at the rear quarterdeck vaulted over the side of the boat, trailing a rope, and the piles supporting the dock shuddered under the impact. He hauled on the line, and as his feet slipped down the wooden jetty, the sailboat came to a stop. He knelt to tie it off on a cleat, and when he stood again, three uniformed guards were glaring at him from behind submachineguns.

The first grey-clad security officer barked an order at him.

"Teledyne Security! Show me your hands!"

The man did as ordered, unworried and cooperative. He raised them above his head, palms out.

"Turn around! Now, back up until you're off the dock!"

Used to the drill, the man did so and stopped once his booted feet touched sand.

"On your knees!"

If they were sticking to the script, one man would be covering the sailboat, the second would be covering him, and the third was giving the orders. Gloved hands snapped cuffs on one wrist and wrenched the other back, securing his hands behind him. A quick

3

patdown and the contact officer relieved him of his sidearm. He found his ident card in the man's back pocket and passed that off too. A moment later, the too-young NCO moved into view, comparing the ident image to the man on his knees. He glanced up at the man's armor and read the nameplate.

"I'll want that back, Sergeant Nobunaga," the man said.

Sergeant Daniel Nobunaga did a double take when he read the Teledyne clearance codes on the reverse of the card.

"Specialist Hanzo?" he asked and gestured for the contact officer to remove the cuffs. Once his hands were free, Nobunaga offered Hanzo a hand back to his feet. "We didn't think anyone made it out!"

"We very nearly didn't," Hanzo replied. He brushed the sand from his knees and accepted his sidearm back from the contact officer. "I have twelve VIPs in my care, including Vice President Kojima. May I bring them ashore?"

"Of course." Nobunaga clutched at his radio—now fried by the EMP blasts that had rocked the Pacific Northwest that morning—and cursed. "Edson, run back to the CP and get everyone not doing something critical to assist."

The contact officer, a young man with pale blond hair poking out from beneath his cadet cap, ported his TD57 subgun and ran for the command center. Specialist Rikimaru Hanzo, one of Teledyne's top operatives, waved to the other sailboats still offshore. His teammates, Specialists Ayame Kato and Mikael "Kael" Grimstaadt, tacked east to approach the dock. The third officer requested and received permission to head out onto the pier to help secure the sailboats. Rikimaru was glad to see that, despite recent events, the Whidbey Island Air Station security troops were able to think clearly. He looked once again to the south, where the mushroom clouds had blotted out the sun that morning. They'd dissipated as the three small craft sailed northwest from Lynnwood, but their image would be etched into his memory forever.

What now? he wondered. Mikael's ship pulled in behind his, and, once the boat was secure, he joined the uniformed troops on the dock. He took Ranjesh Kumar's hand and helped her onto the dock; one of her stiletto heels promptly sank into a slot between the boards, throwing her off-balance, and she stumbled. Once she'd unstuck her shoe, he guided her off the dock and into the care of Teledyne's Armed Forces.

As the rest of the senior managers filed past, Ayame and Kael joined him at his side.

"What now?" Ayame asked.

"We do our duty. We protect these people and survive."

* * * * *

Part One: Daimyo

Chapter One

Twenty years later

Six of the makeshift fishing boats still burned, Rikimaru saw, as the *Seas the Day* tacked north into Deer Harbor. Rigging and sail floated on the surface, marking where other victims of the raid had already slipped beneath the waves. Master Coxswain Dan Nobunaga released a line, letting the main sail drop, and his ship coasted into the harbor. Nobunaga was tall, about 6'1", with long black hair, now gone grey, that he kept tied up in a traditional chonmage topknot like his daimyo. The beer belly he'd had the day the nukes fell was long gone; it turned out an active lifestyle and a sushi diet were good for his health.

His young assistant, thirteen-year-old Derek Frost, barely topped five feet. He'd emulated his adoptive grandfather and tied his hair up, although Frost was so blond his hair looked bleached. He gathered up the jib sheet so it rested on the foredeck and threw the harbormaster a line of his own.

Rikimaru caught his first whiff of burning rubber, fiberglass, and wood. A grey haze hung over the entire marina, fed by the black smoke from the burning ships.

"Do you have any casualties?" Rikimaru demanded, and Sergeant Edson shook his head no. A lance of Komainu Guardians with their bows and arrows stood near Edson on the pier, ready to board the *Day*, and three more full-grown men heaved on the bowline to force the light sailboat to reverse course and point back out to sea. The six archers hopped aboard, stowed their bows, and took up long oars to paddle the sailboat back out into open water. Derek, Rikimaru, and their six new passengers paddled for all they were worth until they were clear of the dock.

"How long has it been since they cleared the south end of the harbor?" Rikimaru asked. The Komainu lance corporal wore a name-tag that read "Rainier" on her uniform, and she shrugged.

"A quarter glass?" she guessed and pointed to a bare wrist where she might have once worn a watch. "Maybe more, if you didn't see them on your way in."

"Pour it all on, Dan," Rikimaru ordered. "Whatever we can do to make up time."

"You can help by giving Derek a hand with the jib." Nobunaga pointed, and Rikimaru led Rainier forward to where Frost wrangled ropes.

"What can I do?" Rikimaru asked. Derek froze, not comfortable giving instructions to his daimyo, and then he pointed to the rat's nest of brown, hemp ropes in a pile on the deck.

"There are four ropes, I mean, *lines*," Derek stammered. "One for the, uh, port, another for the starboard side, that's left and right in boat talk, one for raising the sail, and one for lowering it."

"And they got all knotted up when you dropped the sail?" the senior samurai asked.

"Yes, Daimyo," Derek nodded. Rikimaru, Rainier, and Derek picked at the jumbled mess and took a step back, allowing the four ropes to drag free so they could tell them apart. It didn't help that there was no way to distinguish between them, but beggars couldn't be choosers.

The *Day* moved infuriatingly slow, considering the rush they were in, but after a minute of careful sorting, the rat's nest of lines came apart, and Derek flashed a triumphant smile. He glanced over his shoulder to confirm the two going back to the cockpit slid through the fairlead loops and passed Rikimaru one more rope.

"And this is the halyard. Heave!" Derek said with a hint of a grin. It wasn't every day a teenager got to order around the second-in-command of their little island kingdom. As Rikimaru hauled on the rope—the halyard—the jib sail rose into place and began to catch the wind.

"Try to keep the ropes straight next time," he said. "We've lost precious time."

The teen's face fell. "I'm still learning, but the important thing is not to mix up the ropes for the sails with the ropes that keep the mast upright. Halyards raise and lower sails, stays hold the mast up, and sheets hold all the sails in place where they need to be to catch the wind. Oh, and watch out for the boom whenever we tack…"

Rikimaru knew what a boom was, of course, and said so.

"Oh, uh, of course you do. I don't think we'll have to gybe, but if we do, I'll warn you so you can get everyone else below decks. A bad gybe could mean someone goes in the drink or gets hurt. I'd better warn the others."

"Perhaps you'd better, yes," Rikimaru said. The boy excused himself and returned to the cockpit at the stern of the ship to lecture Rainier's Komainu archers on the importance of water safety.

"I don't know how you put up with him," Rikimaru said.

"That's because you never settled down to have kids of your own," Nobunaga replied. "It gets easier. Even more so when they're your kids' kids."

"I wouldn't know," the daimyo replied.

Nobunaga rolled his eyes. "Maybe you just need some practice."

* * *

Their quarry, two pairs of sails, sliced through the water ahead, and Rikimaru leaned hard as the wind heeled the *Seas the Day* over. Hanzo was an inch shorter than Nobunaga, which the older man never failed to point out. His Specialist enhancements meant his heavily-muscled torso was even denser than it appeared. He'd been the recipient of all of Teledyne's best nanite enhancements, including nanite-reinforced muscles and bones that made him nearly twice as heavy as he should have been. Like Nobunaga, he had obvious Japanese ancestry, but his parents and grandparents had all been born and lived in the Seattle Sprawl, a region that stretched from Olympia all the way north to Vancouver. "Rick" and Dan were both in their mid-forties now and resembled each other so closely they could have been brothers.

Their sailboat carved sharp furrows of white foam as it raced through the waves, but Vancouver Island was in sight and getting closer. Rick pounded a fist on the starboard gunwale. "They're getting away!"

"We *are* closing on them, fast, but they had too much of a head start!" Dan Nobunaga nudged the bow over and heeled over a few more degrees, but it didn't do them any good. A stern chase was a challenging prospect at best, and although frustrated they were going to escape, a quiet part of Dan's mind was proud they had closed as much distance as they had. But even as fast as they were gaining, the raiders from Victoria were almost in range of the shore, and it was apparent the *Seas The Day* wasn't going to catch them in time. Nobunaga shook his head and eased the wheel back until the deck was closer to 'flat,' and they could tack away, back to the east.

"What are we gonna do, Dan?" Rikimaru scowled. Eight archers were not an insignificant force out on the Juan de Fuca Strait, but close to shore, the raiders had buddies—buddies who might actually have firearms with *ammo*, or ten or twenty or thirty archers. "We can't let them get away with this."

Dan leaned on the wheel and pondered for a moment. He ducked as the sailboat's boom passed over his head, a habit he had developed the hard way after several near-catastrophic incidents almost two decades earlier. The crash of waves and the mocking calls of the seagulls overhead filled the silence as each man got lost in his thoughts. Derek came back from the bow of the *Day* and tucked his quiver away in one of the weapons lockers. He pulled out a rusty tin of beeswax and flopped onto a cushion to rewax his bowstring.

"Lance?" The young 13-year-old offered his tin to the woman in charge of the other five Komainu archers. Melissa Rainier was a fiery redhead in her early twenties, nearing the conclusion of her initial period of service in the Komainu. She was smart, aggressive, and a good leader—that she was a lance corporal while still inside the conscription period spoke well for her capabilities.

Rikimaru was pretty sure that wasn't what caught Frost's attention, though. Rainier kept her red curls tied back in a long braid, and her summertime tan had faded back to freckles over the winter. She refused to be out-rucked or out-run by her male teammates and therefore worked two or three times as hard as they to maintain her strength and fitness. The Komainu uniforms were relatively shapeless and nobody truly looked good in them, but Melissa managed it better than most. The frumpy tunic and pants couldn't disguise how fit and fierce the lance corporal was, and she moved like a panther on the hunt. Rikimaru may not have understood kids, but he'd been a teenager before he'd been a Specialist. Unless he was reading the situation totally wrong, Derek was absolutely *smitten*.

Rainier accepted the tin, and she followed the boy's lead, waxing her bowstring to protect it against saltwater damage. Rikimaru watched the young teen with a bemused smile, and when Derek realized he was busted, he abruptly turned away, searching for something else to look at. He found and glared at the *Buoyancé* as it disappeared over the horizon.

Derek nodded but sulked nonetheless. "I don't see why we don't just go *take* some," he complained. "The Victorians are…*savages!* We could take them in a straight-up fight!" The boy leaned on his bow to take the tension off and slipped the bowstring out of its notch.

"You know why not," Nobunaga admonished. "That's for Shogun Kojima to decide, and until he's declared differently, we will respect his orders."

Derek rolled his eyes and turned back to his duties after tucking the string away in the locker, muttering to himself the whole time. Rikimaru ignored his insolence. Derek wasn't his problem, not for a couple years. Hopefully Dan would have the boy's attitude sorted by then.

* * *

The sun had set when the *Seas the Day* finally coasted into the dock on the west side of Whidbey Island after dropping Rainier and her squad back home at the historic-post-office-turned-barracks at Deer Harbor. Rikimaru left Dan and his protégé to secure their ship and walked alone down the path to what had once been an inn on the base for visiting Teledyne dignitaries. Before Teledyne purchased the station from the failing US Government, it was home to visiting pilots. His feet crunched on the gravel, and he felt every sharp piece of rock through his triple-soled, boiled leather moccasins.

His first duty was, of course, to Shogun Kojima. Their venerable leader had united the San Juan islands in the aftermath of the Fall, and it certainly wasn't his place to question him. Everyone had a place, and everyone had to remain *in* their place. Teledyne and Obsidian had thought they were invulnerable, and look what *that* had wrought.

Kojima believed if they served as a peaceful example to their post-apocalyptic neighbors, they would organize themselves and naturally seek to ally. True, he and Kael and Aya had had to thump a few skulls back in the day, but extreme times called for extreme measures. They hadn't made war on anyone in eighteen years. Those first few years they'd managed to use up the air station's entire supply of ammunition and that of a few preppers as well. Without bullets, they'd had to revise their entire warfighting concept and make it up as they went along.

Twenty years later, if he had to admit it, Rikimaru was beginning to lose faith in Kojima's brand of pragmatic pacifism. Kojima would never initiate hostilities, no matter the threat; they would only use their Guardians—the Komainu militia—to protect their borders and their people. Privately, he agreed with young Master Frost. If the shogun decided to throw off the fetters and allow him to prosecute hostilities as he saw fit, the Victorians would never bother them again.

He winced. To think that *Canadians* could ever pose a threat to his small corner of the Pacific Northwest was appalling in and of itself. Not that Canada had really existed as it had in his grandfather's day. Canada's east and west had been at an uneasy truce since the breakup of the '20s, and that gave the MegaCorps the leverage they needed to assert greater and greater independence. As it was in Canada, so it was in the United States, Europe, Asia, and elsewhere. Over subsequent decades, the significance of national boundaries and citizenship mattered less and less as corporateship mattered more and more.

And then he was home again. He nodded to the two Komainu flanking the doors to the inn. There would be ten more patrolling the grounds in five pairs for a total of twelve. Two lances had duty at night, while the rest of the platoon slept in the duty barracks.

"No luck, Specialist?" Sergeant Carey asked quietly.

"I'm afraid not, Shawn," Rikimaru admitted. "They had too much of a head start and made it back to shore before we could catch them."

"Perhaps next time, sir," the second one, Nora, replied. "I believe Shogun Kojima waited up for you in the *honden*."

The senior Specialist nodded his thanks and turned inside. The interior of the old inn was in desperate need of updating, with fading paint, cracked spackling, and stained, threadbare carpet, not that anyone was making paint, drywall mud, or carpet anymore. The interior was dark, but his enhanced eyes had long adjusted to the night, and he needed no illumination. His moccasins were silent as he padded down the hallway and found two more of the Komainu outside the *honden*, the sanctuary. They admitted him, and he found Shogun Kojima kneeling in front of the large tablet that served as the shrine's central focus, its *kami*. It was a smaller version of two massive stones by Memorial Park; each listed the name of every Seattle Teledyne employee who had died in service to the corporation, and those killed after civilization fell.

It was a very long list.

Rikimaru padded up to the *kami* and knelt beside Kojima, behind and to his side, as was proper. He bowed his head, and after a long moment passed, the shogun spoke.

"I grow tired of adding names to our *kami*, Rikimaru."

"I give thanks that we did not add any today, Shogun. They burned several ships, and they stole the *Buoyancé*, but no one was hurt."

"But the loss of these ships will affect our ability to fish, and therefore feed, our people, Rikimaru. Despite the wealth of the farms on our little islands, the sea's bounty is still where the majority of our people get their sustenance. Losing those ships means losing all that food."

Rikimaru accepted the rebuke silently. It was not his place to suggest he get the stolen sailboat back and more besides.

"But you wish to go *do something*, don't you, Daimyo?"

"I accept your wisdom, Shogun. It is not my place to say—"

"Bullshit." The interruption struck Rikimaru as squarely as a two-by-four between the eyes, and he was stunned speechless.

"For eight years, you were Teledyne's top Seattle operative. *My* top operative. For twenty, you have been my daimyo, my general, my senior warrior, the trainer of my Guardians, and the protector of my backside." Rikimaru glanced up and saw Kojima smirking, an incongruous expression on his venerable, octogenarian face. "And you wish to go kick someone *else's* backside because they dared violate the sanctity of our little community. *Again.*"

"Guilty as charged," Rikimaru admitted. "My place is out in front, between our people and those who would harm them. There are all too many threats in this Fallen World. I should not be chasing them *after* they've done their damage, I need to get out in front. I agree, we have added all too many names to the *kami*. Aya, Kael, and I could go teach these Victorians a lesson they would not soon forget and return with many more sailboats than just the ones they've stolen and burned over the years."

"And that would doom many of them to a long, slow, wasting death by starvation, would it not?" Kojima asked.

"That depends on how much of a fight they put up." Rikimaru's eyes flashed with restrained fury. "More enemy warriors means more food for the rest after we're through with them."

Kojima chuckled but shook his head. "Just because you've never lost a fight doesn't mean you should get cocky, Daimyo. There is always a bigger fish. Piranhas can skeletonize a steer if there are enough of them."

Rikimaru nodded, accepting the chiding again without complaint. "I will meditate here a while yet, Shogun. Perhaps a third way will be revealed to me."

"Perhaps. Good night, Rick."

"Good night, Akihiro."

* * * * *

Chapter Two

Duke Stanley Tremblay thanked his ship's captains and sent them on their way. His hand unconsciously went to the hilt of the saber at his side—the empress herself expected his report, and she wasn't going to be happy with the results of the raid. He spun on his heel, marched up from the inner harbor docks, and crossed the street to the palace. Winter rains had not been kind; two of the letters had fallen off the veranda. Someone had moved the R and the E off the grass for someone else to bolt back into place. The empress had no shortage of laborers. Too many, more like. THE EMP SS was all that was left, and even the E hung off-kilter, ready to succumb to entropy as well.

No matter. Chin up, shoulders back, Duke Tremblay marched past Victoria's handpicked "doormen" and inside the Grand Hall. She had a small army of soldiers, errand-boys, housekeepers, and workers. Or, from another perspective, thugs, slaves, slaves, and slaves. The first made a mess whenever they did their thing, and that created work for those who kept the interior clean. It was a shame she didn't have skilled staff to maintain the exterior, but she didn't venture outside often anyway. The duke swept past one young boy on his hands and knees who scrubbed at a tile with what smelled like vinegar.

It smelled *clean.*

It smelled *good.*

Too much of the Capital Region District reeked of unwashed bodies and rotting seaweed, especially this close to the harbor. Baron

Horton of Oak Bay, whose residence overlooked the Yacht Club, awaited him at the throne room door. Horton had been at his side since the beginning and knew the cross look on Tremblay's face all too well. A bare shake of his head told Horton all he needed to know. He wordlessly opened the door for his duke, then followed him inside. Ahead of Tremblay, his barons of Esquimalt and Hatley stood to the right. Horton joined them, and the trio faced down the other dozen nobles to Tremblay's left. Duke Robitaille of Land's End, to the north, and Duke Armstrong of Goldstream, to the west, waited with their trio of barons each.

The empress sat on her throne, with Sledge, her newest champion to her right. The champion was nicknamed for the enormous war hammer he casually leaned on, and Tremblay tried not to think too much about the damage such a weapon could do to one's kneecaps.

The duke marched to the designated spot at the foot of her throne and bowed deeply. He straightened and met her eyes. As usual, her beauty struck him like a physical blow. Her raven hair was bound up behind her head and held in an intricate bun with long metallic hairpins; she had flawless, porcelain skin and an hourglass figure. Her finery, a Mandarin-collared, ankle-length dress of scarlet silk with golden trim, hugged her curves. The slit was cut high to show off sculpted legs above simple black slippers. It had no sleeves, revealing arms corded with muscle. Tremblay had been invited to her archery range once, where she'd hit targets eighty yards away with a hundred-and-twenty-pound war bow. She was both powerful and *powerful*. If one were to judge her solely by her appearance, she had an ageless beauty that could have been anywhere between twenty-five and fifty, and one did not simply ask an empress her age. Those who'd been around a while knew she'd been an adult when she assumed rulership of Vancouver Island after the nukes fell, so she *must* have been at least forty. Tremblay caught himself staring before it got awkward and spoke.

"Your Imperial Majesty, my ships' captains have returned. The news is not as good as I'd hoped, but it is not as bad as could be either." Tremblay heard a cough that sounded suspiciously like a snicker to his left, but he ignored it. "If I may have leave to report?"

Victoria, empress of the Gulf Islands and queen of the Saanich Peninsula, raised one eyebrow. "Please do, Duke Tremblay."

"Your Majesty, my crews have returned with one of the largest ships from Deer Harbor, the *Buoyancé*. Unfortunately, that is all they were able to commandeer. The militia guarding the harbor spotted my sailors from a hidden observation post and rallied as we approached. The old post office directly adjacent to the docks is their new barracks and the shogunate militiamen responded in seconds. They took my crew under sustained archery fire before they even docked, and they guarded the end of the pier with a pike hedge.

"My crew seized one ship, but it was only after they were underway that they learned the inhabitants stow all their fishing equipment elsewhere. The *Buoyancé* had its mainsail and jib, but no nets, rods, reels, pots, or lines. Two of my corsairs breathed their last on the way out, and militia troops on yet more sailboats pursued them until they reached my fortifications at Ten Mile Point. If we are to seize more fishing equipment, we will need to attack the harbor in a larger force than any one noble can muster."

"I see." Victoria's voice was cold. "One ship, without equipment, isn't going to feed our people, Duke Tremblay."

"Yes, Your Imperial Majesty," Tremblay acknowledged.

"*Weak*," a voice to his left spat. Tremblay ignored the voice, keeping his eyes to the front, but the empress turned her head slightly to acknowledge the uncouth one who'd interrupted.

"Baron Howell? Do you have something you wish to contribute?"

Baron Robert Howell, Esquire, hailed from Sidney, North Saanich. He swaggered forward. "*I* believe the Duke of Craigdarroch is *weak*, Majesty. He's unwilling to commit sufficient troops to guarantee success, has avoided killing the others, was unwilling to suffer casualties of his own, and therefore doomed his task to failure."

"With all due respect, Howell, *fuck off.* You couldn't lead a longboat of Vikings to a brothel and haven't set foot on a sailboat in a decade. *Your* people are starving. The children dig for geoducks in the sand, and the adults brawl over roasted seagull."

"Watch your tongue, Tremblay," Howell spat.

"Or what? You'll challenge me?" Duke Tremblay replied. "That's up to you, you silly twat, dukes don't challenge *down.*"

"Fine. I *do* challenge, Tremblay. Here, now," the baron said with one hand on the hilt of his machete. "Let's do this."

"Well, *this* day just got rather more interesting," Empress Victoria said. "You know the rules; my people work hard to keep this palace spotless. You shan't bleed all over the interior however your little duel goes. Outside, the lot of you!"

Tremblay bowed to his empress once more, came to attention, did an about-face, and marched away. Tremblay's Barons of Hatley, Craigdarroch, and Esquimalt fell in behind him, and the four strode out into the late evening sunset. As the one challenged, Tremblay marched to the south half of the lawn, while Baron Howell, his superior Duke Robitaille of the North, and their assorted hangers-on turned right onto the lawn opposite him. Sledge and Empress Victoria were the last to emerge—Victoria to witness, Sledge as the Arbiter of this latest death match.

Victoria's champion was a young man in his early twenties. He'd tried, and failed, to grow a beard, which ended up being two little braids that barely reached his collarbone, and he had long, fine, blond hair he tied back. The too-small zip-up hoodie he wore showed off well-defined muscles, and some speculated Sledge didn't just watch the empress' back, he likely warmed her bed as well. Tremblay observed he had stopped off at her armory and now had a scattergun slung over his broad shoulders. Tremblay met the champion on the old sidewalk that bisected the field.

"Your Grace, your blade?"

Tremblay had already untied the cord securing his blade in its sheath, and he turned the saber over to Sledge. It was both a functional weapon and a piece of art, truth be told. He didn't know its origin; he'd found it in an empty home in Oak Bay a long time ago. The scabbard was scarlet, with forest green caps and ties. "Prince of Wales Squadron" was embossed on the outside. Sledge examined the sword, and it caught the sunlight like a mirror. "Perseverance" and an unfamiliar crest were etched into the blade. The cavalryman's blade was nearly a meter long, perfectly straight, and had a large, chrome basket hilt. Sledge nodded in appreciation and returned the weapon to the duke, who slipped it back into the scabbard on his right hip.

"Baron Howell, your blade?"

Howell's machete was as rough as the man himself. Tremblay appreciated many of the old classics from the golden age of 2D film, and the ill-hewn hunk of steel Howell handed the champion looked like something an Uruk-Hai would carry. The blade's pair of quillons were poorly forge-welded from raw metal as a crossguard, and the blade was wide and blocky, chipped and scarred. The hilt had several layers of bloodied hockey tape wrapped around it to give it some small cushion. "You're a braver man than I," Sledge murmured and returned it. Howell smiled at the compliment until the implication sunk in.

"You're both nobles, but there are additional rules with her imperial majesty present. As usual, the duel will be one on one; no one else may assist in any way. Begin back to back, walk ten paces, turn and fight. You may use these weapons and only these weapons. The duel continues until one party is victorious. Even stones from the palace grounds are forbidden, not that there should be any *here*. Once I declare the duel over, first aid may be rendered, but not before. Should Baron Howell be victorious, he inherits control of Duke Tremblay's holdings. Should Duke Tremblay win, he may appoint the holder of the Barony of Sidney. Any breach of protocol is addressed with buckshot; there is no appeals process. Clear?"

"Clear, Champion," Tremblay agreed.

Howell rolled his eyes. "Let's get this over with."

Sledge backed up several paces and raised a hand.

"Ten! Nine! Eight!" he counted down. With each number, the duelists took one pace, until Sledge reached one. Tremblay whirled in place, drawing his saber in his left hand, holding the hilt low near his waist. Howell pulled his machete from his belt, turned, and charged. Confusion registered on his face when the duke held his ground, refusing to be cowed by the younger man's aggression. When he'd closed perhaps two-thirds of the distance, Tremblay lunged forward, extending the tip of his saber to meet the baron. Howell recognized the danger at the last instant and threw himself aside rather than impaling himself on the duke's sword. Tremblay backed up a few paces with a chuckle on his lips.

"Well played, Robert. Though, to be honest, it would have been pretty funny had you actually impaled yourself three seconds into the fight."

"Fuck you, old man," the baron snarled, getting back to his feet. "You're lazy and a coward."

"Fuck you, pup," Tremblay replied with a mocking grin on his lips. "I've been called worse by better people than Baron Bridge Club, Ruler of the Retirement Village."

Enraged, Howell closed again and swatted at Tremblay's blade, but the poorly balanced, overly-heavy machete was a poor fencing weapon. A flick of the duke's wrist moved his blade clear of the offending machete and then he slashed downward, opening the back of Howell's hand to the bone. The baron cried out in pain, dropped his blade, and jammed the wounded hand into an armpit. He scrambled to recover his sword, but Tremblay had backed off and given him space yet again. Tremblay noted he'd awkwardly picked up the machete with his right hand and chuckled again.

"See, if you were a man of culture, you'd crack wise about not being left-handed. But since you're an illiterate boor with no appreciation for the classics, I'll tell you this—I'm not left handed either." Tremblay switched his saber to his right and closed with the baron. Howell swiped again, but awkwardly and off-balance. Tremblay slashed, putting Howell on his back foot, and kept coming. Three more slashes had Howell in full retreat until he planted and swiped back with the leaf-spring machete. Tremblay caught the much heavier blade on the *forte* of his own, giving him the best leverage, and shoved the blocky thing away. He punched up in a vicious cross that shattered Howell's nose with the basket hilt and drove a knee into the baron's belly, doubling Howell over. Tremblay bashed him in the back of the head with his pommel, flattening him completely. Tremblay picked up the ineffectual machete and lobbed it away, where it clattered on the remnants of Government Street.

"Any last words?" Tremblay asked.

"Yeah," Howell replied, and he rolled over onto his back. "When you see the devil…tell him I'll be along shortly."

The wounded baron's bloodied hand came out from under his tunic holding a battered revolver. Tremblay didn't even have time to turn away before Howell had fired three shots up into his ribcage. The Duke of Craigdarroch fell back, coughing blood from perforated lungs. The revolver clicked several more times as the hammer dropped on empty cylinders.

"*Damn you!*" Baron Horton cried out, but it was too late. Sledge raced onto the field, but Tremblay gasped his last and went still. The pistol fell from Howell's grasp, and Sledge leveled his scattergun at the bloodied noble on the ground.

"You broke protocol," the champion snarled, "murderer."

"I've served my time in hell already, *Champion*. Go ahead and finish me. Just make it quick." Howell lay back, resigned to the inevitable, and closed his eyes. Sledge paused then shook his head.

"No."

"No?" Howell's eyes opened again. He no longer stared down the barrel of the twelve gauge. Sledge's shotgun hung over his shoulder, and he had replaced it with his war hammer.

"No."

Sledge brought his namesake high above his head and brought it down on Howell's kneecap. Howell howled in agony as the heavy weapon pulped his right knee, then Sledge did the same to his left.

"Stop!" Duke Robitaille shouted and broke ranks to race to his baron's side, but Sledge was quick. He leveled the shotgun again, this time at the duke.

"The duel continues until I declare it over, Your Grace! Until then, no aid may be administered. Do you breach protocol as well?" Robitaille raised his hands in submission and retreated without argument. Howell was keening in agony, and Sledge turned back to him. The champion roughly pried one hand away from Howell's ruined knee, and stepped on it. Raising his sledgehammer once more, he brought it down in a vicious overhead smash that pulverized Howell's shoulder, and then his other shoulder got the same treatment. Sledge turned back to the gathered crowd.

"Duke Tremblay has suffered a murder amid righteous duel. The duel continues until the murderer expires." He locked eyes with Robitaille. "That may take some time. I'd advise you to mount up and return to your home in the north, Your Grace, *forthwith*. The new Baron of Sidney will be along eventually. Barons Horton, Andreychuk, and Clarke, Empress Victoria will speak to you inside."

* * *

"Well, that was catastrophic," Victoria said, throwing her hands in the air. "I swear, some people simply don't have the grace to die with dignity."

"Yes, Your Majesty." Baron Horton nodded. While hardly new to her court, he didn't often get to speak to her in near privacy.

"Well? What do you want to do?" she asked. "By rights, the dukedom of Lower Saanich belongs to one of the three of you. *Please don't fight over it; there's lots of island to go around.*"

"If it pleases your majesty," Andreychuk said, "The Missus and I rather like Hatley Castle. I have no ambitions of Dukedom at this point."

"And my lady and I are quite content in Esquimalt," Clarke agreed. The three looked at Horton.

"In that case…it would be my pleasure to serve as your Duke of Lower Saanich, Your Imperial Majesty?" Horton half-asked.

"Oh for heaven's sake, Don, my name's Victoria. If we're going to work together to sort out Robitaille and his ilk, who seem bound and determined to bully and starve my people through general incompetence, *and* deal with these… Shogunate Islander types on the larger gulf islands, then we ought to at least be on a first-name basis—in private, at least."

"Understood, Your Maj—I mean, Victoria." Horton swallowed hard and knew he was doing a poor job of hiding his discomfort. Victoria turned to the others.

"Thank you, gentlemen. If you have any names to suggest to fill the recently vacated office of Baron of Sidney, please send them my way. Particularly if they're the type who might do well to depose Duke Robitaille. You two may go."

Clarke and Andreychuck bowed their farewells.

"Now, *Duke* Horton, is it my understanding there is no *Duchess* Horton?"

"That's correct, your—uh, Victoria."

"Excellent. You're a handsome man, with a good head on your shoulders and a strong arm. Don't think I don't notice these things—who arrives at my court, remains there for a long time, does right by his people, all that sort of thing. I confess I was rather glad the other two declined the post. So why don't you and I retire to my private chambers so we can discuss matters? Over drinks? You can return to Craigdarroch in the morning."

"I—uh, yes, your—"

The empress pressed her finger to his lips to quiet him. "My name is *Victoria,*" she whispered, then turned on her heel and headed for the rear door, pulling him with her by his hand.

* * * * *

Chapter Three

Specialist Ayame Kato smiled to herself when she heard the familiar clang of metal on metal. Rikimaru was stressed, and any time he was stressed, he went to the base's forge and started hitting things. Thankfully, he was the type who addressed his frustrations by *making* things instead of breaking them. She was...*not*. She slipped through the door to the repurposed hangar and stayed in the shadows by the door. The longer she waited, the better state of mind he'd be in when she delivered her report. She stayed there, still as could be, as her mentor and friend worked with hammer and tongs, moving his unfinished katana from the heart of the furnace to his anvil. He'd stripped to the waist, and she couldn't help but admire the definition of his heavily muscled arms and chest. Sweat dripped from his hair, and soot streaked his face, hands, and back...

She caught herself letting her discipline slip, and for the nth time in twenty-three years, she wished Rikimaru would permit *his* discipline to slip for once. But he wouldn't, damn him, not with someone subordinate to him, and under present circumstances, that was *every* woman in range. Knowing him as intimately as she did, she couldn't imagine any kind of intimate relationship with someone else; anything else with anyone else would feel fraudulent. She wouldn't do that to someone else, or herself, for that matter. Since Rikimaru was ever the disciplined one, that would never happen. He was like some ascetic warrior monk.

But no matter.

Her daimyo pulled the sword from the forge and laid it on his anvil. It was starting to take shape. He'd folded the billet six or seven times, which gave it a gorgeous ladder pattern where the lower-carbon steel mixed with the higher. He'd drawn it out to its full meter length and now had to hammer the blade into its iconic curve. But he still had a lot of work to do, of course. He had to shape it properly, smooth the edge, quench it, attach his *tsuba* guard, and wrap the hilt, but at least it looked like it would be a sword soon.

"What's the damage?" Rikimaru asked between hammer strikes.

Of course he'd noticed her; nothing escaped him.

"Do you want your report now?" Ayame asked.

"Absolutely," he replied and brought the hammer down again.

"One of the senior Komainu on Orcas plots treason."

His face remained stoic and focused, and he brought the hammer down twice more on the glowing sword-to-be.

"Who?"

"Tarl Govnar."

Rikimaru put the sword back into the charcoal forge and wiped the sweat from his brow, smearing soot across his face like camouflage paint. He pumped the double-bellows several times until the upper chamber was full and he had a steady airflow.

"Govnar. Shoulda booted his arrogant ass out a long time ago. I know you've promised them anonymity, even from me, but how solid is your source?"

Do I tell him? No.

"Solid. Hundred percent."

"What's your plan?"

Deep breath.

"I have a team on the island already. There are four definite conspirators and one councillor, Miller, who's *probably* aware. He's going to be a problem. Sergeant Govnar has been keeping his hand close to his chest, so I can't say whether Miller is all the way in on it or not. We're going to take the four after their next meet. Bring them back here for trial."

"What was their plan?"

"They think they'll get a better deal working with the Victorians. My source suggests they'll be meeting to finalize their plan in a couple nights. I'll arrest them once I've personally confirmed the details."

"Well, their timing sucks—but then again, it might be deliberate. I've got to head down to the fort for the newest class grad. How soon will you be ready to go?"

"Dan's going to drop me off tomorrow night and bring me back after the op. Call it five days."

Rikimaru drew the blade from the forge again and, satisfied with the intensity of the glowing yellow steel, laid it across his anvil and began hammering again. Ayame waited, knowing he had to strike when the steel was hot.

"Crap. I may have overdone that a bit." He lifted the blade with his tongs and showed her. The blade had a warp to it that it hadn't had before. "Maybe I've had enough of this kind of fun for one night."

"I'll be fine, Rick."

"I didn't—"

Ayame smirked and put her hands on her hips. "You didn't have to. I can read you like a book, mister."

"So you keep reminding me."

"I should be able to, after two decades."

"Fair." Ayame picked up one of the washcloths hung next to the quenching barrel, wet it, and wrung it out. She leaned in close and wiped the coal streaks off his forehead, cheeks, and nose.

"There. Don't go getting coal dust in your eyes, *Daimyo*. See you soon."

As she left, if she maybe swayed her hips a little more than she normally might…well… maybe half the fun was teasing him.

* * *

Two days later and thirteen miles south, Rikimaru stood, impassive, on the battlements of what had been Fort Casey a century and a half before. Two ten-inch cannons loomed over the training grounds, still standing guard over Admiralty Inlet, despite being decommissioned more than a century earlier. The massive concrete-revetted fortress was one of three used to protect Seattle proper from invasion in the early 20th century. Had he the resources, Rikimaru would have refurbished the enormous, thirty-foot-long cannons and restored them to their former potency. According to the ancient tourist information displays, the devastating coastal artillery pieces could throw six-hundred-pound shells *eight* miles, at fifteen hundred miles per hour. The concrete fortifications had elevators for lifting the shells on trolleys and different elevators for lifting hundred-pound sacks of powder. Each thirty-five ton cannon sat on a giant disc that could raise or lower, allowing them to poke above the parapet when ready to fire and disappear behind cover while reloading.

It shamed him that, despite all the technological breakthroughs the Corporations had made before the fall, these 19th-century cannons were far, far beyond their current capabilities. They couldn't even source powder for a .22.

On the wide-open field behind those battlements, the latest Komainu recruit battalion trained under their cadre. The Komainu leaders were a mixed bag of weapons experts and craftsmen. Looking over the "battlefield," where his teenage recruits were drilling, he reflected on just how far they'd fallen in the twenty years since the nuclear exchange ended the modern world.

Rattan spears and swords clacked and clashed on plywood shields as they practiced attacking and defending. Twenty-one years ago, eighteen- and nineteen-year-olds would have been finishing secondary school, ready to begin trade school or an undergrad. Teledyne would have recruited most of them, funded their schooling, and whisked them away into proper Corporateship. They could have studied 3D fabrication, nanites, or coding, or launched a career in cybernetics, genetics, or the neurosciences. They could have been part of the team developing and improving Specialist enhancements or solved the cyborg or Geno-freak programs' failures. They could have expanded research into JalCom's Juggernauts or reverse-engineered Obsidian's imprint tech.

A few, with the right mix of strength, intelligence, and moral flexibility, could have even been tapped for the Operations Directorate. He had been, and so had Ayame, Mikael, Aster, Bill Wirth, Frost Dancer Ortega, and dozens of others.

But instead, he had five hundred teenagers, drawn from all over the islands, here, bashing each other with sticks.

For the last three months, the recruit battalion had spent its mornings learning the *budo*, the way of war, studying sword, spear, and bow in their lances of six. They spent their afternoons studying *shokunindo*, craftsmanship and artisanry. *Everyone* learned the basics of carpentry; the Pacific Northwest was rich in pines and cedars. Learning to cut down trees safely, prepare them for transport, and turn them into useful things was a vital life skill. Even if they were lucky enough to have a home of their own, they'd need to know how to create and improve the fortifications they'd rely on to protect against Victorian raiders.

One of their primary concerns was fabricating and fixing the log cabins that were now the 'industry standard' all over the strait. Fort Casey was in a constant state of improvement and repair, expanding and improving the facilities until Grimstaadt's second planned training grounds outside Friday Harbor on San Juan were up and functional. After developing a certain degree of competence in carpentry, the recruits—conscripts, really—were parted out for one of their several craft schools or leadership training for those who'd shown maturity. Blacksmiths forged tools and supported the carpenters. The best among them learned to forge blades. Weavers and tailors and seamstresses made clothes from their many sheep, llamas, and alpacas. There was no cotton or denim anymore. Every bull slaughtered for meat contributed to the tanning and leatherwork industries. They were even farming *deer* on San Juan Island—there were so many—for venison and buckskins. The sea-craft types made rope from hemp and turned that rope into fishing nets and lines for the fishing boats.

It was all essential knowledge, and the Komainu program disseminated those skills as broadly as possible. He knew they'd reintroduced conscription and labor parties, but desperate times required desperate measures. It bothered him, but until their physical safety was assured and famine was no longer a spectre on the horizon, no one could afford to be complacent. There were benefits—the Komainu were *very* well fed and were able to stay in whichever community they came from unless they wanted a change. There were no gulags or concentration camps or guards. There was nowhere to run to. And if anyone resorted to banditry, the thousands of retired Komainu would be more than happy to put a stop to it before the active-service types ever got word.

"What say you, old buddy?" Rikimaru asked. "Are they ready?"

"Are they ever?" Mikael Grimstaadt asked in return. "We train them, but there are still plenty who are too sheltered; the violence scares them."

"That's the case in any crowd." Rikimaru nodded. He could pick them out from here—the timid ones who were afraid to give it their all. He could *also* pick out the ones who were enjoying themselves. They'd bear just as much watching as the others.

"Very well, form them up."

"*Battalion!*" Grimstaadt bellowed, and in a few seconds, everyone had stopped and turned to face the two figures atop the battlements. "*Form up!*"

The scattered pairs broke into apparent chaos as they found their platoons and companies, but barely fifteen seconds after the order, four companies of four platoons of five lances each were arrayed across the lawn, standing at ease.

"Ladies and gentlemen, stand easy," Rikimaru began. "As the years go by, I have noticed something. We're now fully into the period where you are all the children of the apocalypse. Not *one* of you here was alive when the civilized world destroyed itself—that you are here *at all* is tremendously indicative of how resilient you and your parents are. Some of you may have lost your parents and had to make a go of it more or less alone. But no more. As of tomorrow, you are all *Komainu*. In ancient Japan, the guardian lion-dogs protected the innermost Shinto shrines! They were protectors of all the Shinto held holy. And now, you too join the ranks of our Guardians. Like everyone else of adult age, you are charged with protecting your loved ones. You will build the walls and sanctuaries that will protect your parents, your families, and one day, your children. Hell, some of you already *have* children." Rikimaru let out a chuckle as some of the recruits glanced at each other in quiet acknowledgment. "And that's a wonderful thing. Ideally, by the time your children are grown, there won't *be* any more Komainu, because by then, they won't have to fear raids and violence, or accidents, or starvation. But that will only come about by hard work, diligent work. Your time in the Komainu may be short, just these next two years, or you may make it your career. I hope a few of you do. Some of you may find the family you never had, and some of you may just want to get home to the family farm.

"You graduate tomorrow. The day after, pack up, tear down, and prep for the spring class. Before you ship out, however, you'll have one more duty to perform. You will be reinforcing the homeguard as we deal with a bit of a situation. We have a few malcontents on one of the islands who would betray us to the Victorians." That caused a stir, and Rikimaru paused as whispers of shock rippled through the recruits. "Samurai Kato will bring the traitors to headquarters in a few days, and we will deal with them. *I* will deal with them. I'm going to kill them, unless they take the honorable way out, because I will not allow anyone to betray you, me, your parents, or your children. Ever.

"I turn you back over to Samurai Grimstaadt for the afternoon, and I'll see you at your parade tomorrow."

* * *

Mount Constitution occluded the night sky; it was an enormous black shadow that seemed to suck in what little light there was to see by. It was dangerous to sail after sundown, even more so without stars and moon to steer by. But Dan Nobunaga was their best sailor, and that's why he insisted he be the one who ferried Rikimaru or Ayame around their little island kingdom, no matter the mission, no matter the hour.

"I'm going to have to anchor here, Aya," Dan said quietly. "Too dangerous to get any closer. You can paddle the ship's boat the rest of the way in; Derek will bring it back."

Dan's protégé scampered forward and released the bow anchor, which spooled out…and out…and out…

"Too dangerous to get closer?" Ayame asked after several hundred feet of rope had spooled out.

"The edge of the island is a frickin' cliff; it drops from fifteen feet to a hundred fifteen in a couple boat lengths. As soon as you're away from the shore, it just keeps going down. I've got no GPS, I've got no *starlight,* and my depth-finder died three years ago. I have best guesses and paper charts, and I'm not going to risk you, me, or Derek getting crushed against the rocks on a moonless night."

"Right," Ayame said. *She* could see reasonably well, thanks to her Specialist's visual enhancements. It was so natural to her, she'd forgotten how poor a normal human's night vision really was. "I'd rather we didn't; if we're crushed against the rocks, I sink like a stone."

"No, because you're wearing your PFD, *right?*"

"Uh, yessss…?" she trailed off and slipped off the flotation jacket she'd been sitting on and slipped it over her shoulders. "Of course I am!"

"Dammit Aya!" Nobunaga hissed. "You *have to* wear those things, you *know* your Specialist density will kill you dead in open water!"

"You're right," she agreed. "It's on now. Clipped in and zipped up, proper-like." She shrugged her shoulders inside the jacket, trying to get it to sit right. They'd only had whatever was available on the ships they commandeered when they fled Seattle, and, despite all her searching, she hadn't found one that fit her frame the way she liked. Even wearing it, it changed her natural buoyancy from "approximately granite" to "barely above neutral, don't exhale too much air." Her musculature and bones had all been enhanced with nanites and other, more esoteric treatments until she weighed closer to two-fifty than the athletic one-twenty one might guess from her appearance.

"So, I probably shouldn't jump down into the dinghy, either, huh?"

"You know better," Dan replied. Ayame could hear the eye roll from across the cockpit.

Once the rear anchor was secure, Derek lowered the small, oar-propelled boat from its clamps on the foredeck and walked it around to the rear. He led the way down the rear ladder and held the tiny, ten-foot dinghy in place as Ayame took her position on the center bench. She hadn't done a lot of paddling, and it was tricky to get into a rhythm, but eventually, she found it and cut through the water toward Doe Bay on the south-east corner of Orcas Island.

"What was it like?" Derek asked a few minutes into the trip. "Before?"

"Before what? Before the world fell?"

"Yeah. You older guys know so much. I barely learned to burn fish over an open fire before the Victorians killed my mom, and I've been apprenticing with Dan ever since."

Ayame didn't have a ready answer. She kept hauling on the oars while she composed one.

"It was faster. A *lot* faster. Information. Travel. Money. Food. Everything. *Everything* maximized what you could get done in a few minutes, in an hour, in a day. Time was the most precious commodity there was. Teledyne and Obsidian were the big two after Delik Unified was knocked out around the time I was born; I don't even remember them. JalCom picked a fight with Obsidian when I was a little younger than you are now and then Obsidian developed Imprint tech. JalCom didn't last too long after that."

"I don't understand, though, what was it *like, Aya*? What was Teledyne?"

"Teledyne?" Ayame exhaled slowly. It was difficult to explain how pervasive the Corporations really were; they controlled everything, and they were everywhere. "Who made your shoes?"

"I did," Derek answered. "Dan got me some salmon skin and showed me how to stitch it onto leather."

"Right. Before, Teledyne would have made them. Your shirt?"

"Uh, I think this one is from Missus Rodrigues. You know, she has that alpaca farm near West Beach?"

"I know the one," Ayame said. "Before, Teledyne would have made your shirt. Your shoes, your underwear. They would have owned the restaurants you ate at, bottled the water you drank, operated the school you attended, assigned you a career based on your aptitudes, produced the movies you streamed..."

"What's a movie?"

Ayame coughed to hide a snicker and shook her head. "Never mind. Entertainment, electronics, food, medicine, education, *every-thing*. They controlled it all, at least here on the West Coast. Corporations had been around a long time, but there were thousands upon thousands of them, and they all competed with each other. Eventually, they coalesced into a few MegaCorps that owned *everything*, and that was the end of countries as a thing. You've seen maps of North America, right?"

"A couple. I can't wrap my head around how big everything is."

"Really, *really* big. Like, if you sailed all day, every day, you could maybe make it to the Upper SoCal Sprawl in a week, week and a half." Ayame did some rough estimation in her head. "It would take another month or so to reach Panama where there was an enormous canal to let you through to the Caribbean and the Atlantic. Then you'd have to sail another couple weeks north again, and now you've reached the very southern-most-point of Obsidian's mainland turf. Another month and you'd reach the NorEast Sprawl."

"That's...huge," Derek said.

"No one sailed that far though. Not unless you made your living driving a boat for some rich Exec type. A jet could zip you across the continent in a couple hours. Breakfast in Seattle and dinner in Philly. Assuming you weren't on a Corporate hit list, no problem."

"*Hours?*"

"Mmhmm. You've seen all the wrecked cars; there were millions of them rolling around. If you left around sun-up, you could drive south from Seattle and get to the SoCal Sprawl by midnight. Flying would get you there for lunch."

"Crazy." The boy shook his head. "What else?"

"When I was seventeen, Teledyne attacked Obsidian. They'd already been grooming me for the Specialist program, not that I knew it at the time, but Teledyne doesn't pay for everyone to get krav maga training, time on the range with pretty much every gun imaginable, acting lessons, or espionage exercises before they can even drive. At eighteen, I signed the contract with the Operations Directorate, and they upgraded my bones, my muscles, my ears, and my eyes. Daimyo Hanzo was my trainer."

"Why did they attack?"

"This is just my opinion. I was still in final training when it all came apart, but I don't think we understood what the Agent program meant, not at first. Maybe the Execs did. I've never asked the shogun, and I don't think I want an answer. All the years and blood and sweat and tears I spent training in Ops? Agents would get those skills plugged directly into their brains. I don't know if the process took seconds, minutes, or hours, but it for damn sure didn't take months and years. They photocopied their special forces staff into Specialist-enhanced bodies and turned them loose."

Derek was silent for another minute as the dinghy cut through the water.

"What's a photocopy?"

This time, Ayame did laugh. "Forget it. They could make a ready-to-rock enhanced-like-a-Specialist soldier faster than you can stitch a pair of salmon-skin shoes. I think that's why Teledyne attacked—our leadership panicked when they realized just how screwed we were. But that's just my theory, so don't go repeating it to anyone. For all I know, someone spilled their double-double on the launch panel." She paused for a moment, remembering the joint misery every proper coffee-drinking adult had suffered through when their caffeine addictions turned into coffee withdrawal. Pure, distilled *misery*. How had anyone functioned before coffee became a thing? "For now, knowing how to make salmon-skin shoes and run a sailboat and burn fish for dinner are way more important than all that other crap."

"Uh, Specialist…"

It was dark, but Ayame could see just fine. The boy was trying to muster up his courage for something; he got formal when he got nervous. She patiently waited for him to continue.

"Is…does…Does Daimyo Hanzo not like me? He seemed really mad when the ships from Victoria got away, and it was my fault the ropes weren't right."

She sighed. "Daimyo Hanzo doesn't understand children." Derek opened his mouth to object, but she shushed him before he interrupted. "And as far as he's concerned, everyone is a child until they've passed Komainu Basic. The best thing you can do to earn his respect is to listen and learn. You made a mistake with the ropes? Don't make that particular mistake again. Experience is nothing but errors made and errors corrected until you know how to get it right the first time. It will be a few years yet before you go off to Fort Casey, and from what I've seen, you're going to be one of the most skilled young men around when you arrive."

The dinghy ground against the pebble shore of Doe Bay, one of the few boat-friendly ways to get onto Orcas Island, and stopped.

"Looks like this is my stop. You be safe, young Mister Frost. Get your skinny butt back to the *Seas the Day,* and I'll see you day after tomorrow."

* * *

The first leg of her hike went practically straight up the side of a mountain. Nobunaga hadn't been kidding when he said Orcas Island was a mountain underwater; Mount Constitution was a mountain above it, too. She felt every one of the two thousand plus feet as she ascended to the peak. The straps on her pack got tiresome quickly. She knew she was on the right path when she reached the shores of the shallow mountain lake halfway up, and then it got *steep.* The stone observation tower at the peak had stood for a hundred fifty years and was probably *the* most secure location in Washington. She reached the edge of the clearing below the tower with time to spare and waited.

Dawn broke—she wasn't sure how much later—and the sun cut gloriously across the hill she'd just ascended. Misty clouds whirled through the space between the strait and Lummi Island and then the mainland beyond it. She hadn't set foot on the mainland in ages, not since their one aborted run into Bellingham twelve years ago. The sunlight was pleasant as beams sliced through the foliage and warmed her bones.

She pulled out a small pocket mirror and angled it to reflect the intense spring sunlight to the top of the stone tower. If it hadn't been sunny, she had other means to signal for her source, but this was the most straightforward and most subtle.

She heard voices from the top of the tower a few seconds later. "Hey, I'm going to go take a leak."

"Whatever man, just don't let no bear eat you!"

"Funny guy."

She slipped deeper into the woods, trusting her top and camouflage tights to help her blend in. Her tights weren't Teledyne Armed Forces issue—they were classic Lululemon yoga tights—but they'd lasted longer and better than everything else. Teledyne had purchased the Vancouver brand of athletic wear ages ago during a major acquisition, but the brand was so well known, Teledyne's execs had kept it alive as everything else changed over to Teledyne's iconic "T" brand. Her top, on the other hand, was a llama wool poncho she'd commissioned ages ago from a farm on San Juan and dyed herself in mottled greens and browns. She had the hood up to hide her face in shadow. A minute later, her source exited the base of the tower and made for the treeline.

"Are we on for tomorrow?" she whispered. To his credit, her source didn't react and pretended to loosen his trousers to pee. He whispered back.

"Yeah. They've been waiting for me to finish my week up here. Relief should get here around lunch and then we ride back down. *Man* it gets cold here at night."

"Your ride home tomorrow's going to be cold, too. Sorry in advance."

"I know. Do what you have to. See you then."

Her source returned to the tower and climbed up the ancient steps. She circled wide around the tower, carefully picking her way around trees and deadfall, until she reached the roadway. With increased density came branches and twigs that cracked like gunshots if she wasn't careful. She listened for the clip-clop of hooves on asphalt, in case the guard's relief arrived early, but detected none. Once she was out of hearing range, she dashed across the roadway, vaulted over a fallen, moss-covered tree trunk, and disappeared into the green beyond.

She jogged at a clip down the remnants of an old cell tower service road until she reached the west side of the mountain and the descent to sea level. Climbing *down* two thousand feet was almost as exhausting as climbing up it. Eventually, she found a decent perch to watch the main road. She pulled her ghillie shelter out of her pack and strung it between some bushes, giving her an unobstructed view.

She pulled one of her favorite old paperbacks about a psychic woman in pre-Corporate Europe battling communists from her pack and settled in for a quiet morning of surveillance, reading, and snacking on dried peach slices. If there was anything she was grateful for in this Fallen World, it was that paperback books didn't take batteries, and some of the great ones had survived.

Sure enough, mid-morning, a dozen Komainu on horseback trotted down the main drag on their way to relieve the troops manning the observation tower. The horses aided them somewhat, but given the switchbacks and long, looping route, she didn't expect her source to pass by for some hours yet. She ate lamb jerky and washed it down with water and continued reading to keep her mind stimulated.

The Komainu on horseback passed by again as she was reading the last chapter. She half-cursed them for interrupting her reading, then she pulled up her monocular—the binos lacked a lens which had shattered years before—and focused on the dozen Guardians riding back into town. Her source was the third man back, riding a handsome brown and white paint with blond mane and tail. She knew where he lived in town, so there was no need to follow him just yet. The dozen troops, two full lances, disappeared around the bend in the road quickly, then she leaned back against the hillside to finish her book.

The sun rose late and set early on Eastsound, saddled as it was between two island peaks, and shadows were getting long when she finally took down her ghillie netting and stuffed it into her pack. It only felt like four o'clock, but she'd been awake for eighteen hours and hadn't eaten much. She unwrapped two of Viktor and Jenny's pressed rice and spiced salmon taco bars and inhaled them. *El Taco Bout It* had been the most successful food truck in the gulf islands before the fall, largely because everything was locally sourced and prepared fresh. The couple ran one of the very few businesses that *hadn't* been a subsidiary of Teledyne; they'd been small enough to escape the Corporate giant's notice. Their spices, fish, beef, pork, lamb—even the rice—were grown on farms on Lopez and San Juan islands. They also made a *fantastic* energy bar that, admittedly, was only good for a day or two but packed a ton of calories into a delicious package. She savored the heat and the flavors, then it was time to go.

Her first stop was Casey and Cassie Morse's hobby farm which was tucked away on the hillside. She knocked at the rear door, and Cassie let her in.

"You made it," she said. "Good to see you."

"I made it." Ayame flopped into a chair, exhausted, and Casey joined them, toting beer from their cold storage.

"Ready for a night on the town?"

"Not dressed like this, I'm not." Ayame groaned and threw back half the bottle in one long swig. "Mariele's?"

"Yep." Cassie nodded. They'd be visiting the Whitecaps Pub in the evening, where the proprietor and brewmistress was a gift from heaven.

"I am beginning to understand why you retired to raise llamas here," Ayame joked.

"Just one llama. One very protective llama, who does a lot of the supervising for us," Cassie corrected. The couple were veterans of Teledyne's Air Division Armed Forces. Casey was a pilot, Cassie, his navigator, but after the nukes fell, there was no further need for aircrew. They remained as solid a team as any Ayame knew, even though their primary gig now was farming. Serving as *Satori* spooks was just a side gig.

Neither had been comfortable with the job at first. They were straightforward, honest people who didn't care for deceit. Ayame had assured them it was mostly a case of keeping their ears open. Shogun Kojima had recognized early on that nobody wanted to make waves; nobody dared to be critical. With so many people isolated by island living, he was nowhere near well-enough informed. The Satori counseled him on the true beliefs, opinions, and priorities of his people. Despite the clandestine nature of their work, their job was to *fight* bullshit and relay honest assessments of the islands' needs. When people bitched, the Satori listened. The shogun would take counsel of this more-honest feedback and announce "a new initiative" (he did so love old corporate buzzword bingo) that just so happened to be in line with what everyone had been whispering and grumping about to each other. Rumors grew that the shogun had *yokai*—spirits who could read minds and steal thoughts—working for him. Ayame encouraged the speculation and cultivated that belief, but the truth was vastly more mundane.

Unfortunately, when they genuinely *did* stumble upon a legitimate threat, rather than merely using intelligence to form good governance, the Satori had to act. Cassie handed Ayame a cloth bag holding a vintage, low-brimmed hat, lambskin kilt, alpaca wool sweater, and matching lambskin vest. Cassie was roughly the same height and shape as Ayame, and they both kept their dark brown hair long, and if it weren't for the subtle epicanthic folds Ayame inherited from her father, they could have been sisters.

Casey disappeared into the front room to give her privacy as Ayame changed. The clothes fit well, and the lambskin was *gorgeous*. "You have good taste."

The women joined Casey, and Ayame picked up a strand of paracord from a side table.

"Good work," she said. Very little Teledyne made was designed to last, and the polymer wrist binders their security forces carried had broken down years ago. Casey, therefore, had been weaving paracord into handcuffs for each member of the arrest teams. A crude joke crossed her mind, but she kept it to herself lest she encourage Casey's particular sense of humor.

"When was the last time you talked to the rest of the team?" Ayame asked.

Casey carefully tucked the cord cuffs away into small, leather, belt pouches as he replied. "Checked in with them at the market last weekend. They'll come by the pub after sundown and have a few drinks. Either we're there, and it's game on, or we're not, and they go home again."

"I need a nap if I'm going to be up all night again. Let me snooze for an hour, and then we'll head into town for drinks."

* * *

The Whitecaps Pub was on the main drag next to Ayame's favorite store on the island, Beth's Books. Nobody was printing new books, but Beth ran a blistering business buying, selling, and trading books all over the islands. She'd recommended the one Ayame carried in her pack, and the rest of that series was calling her name. Not that she'd have time to stop by. This time it was the pub, surveillance, and an *early* morning. She kept the brim of her hat low as she made her way past the billiards room and took a table to the left. Cassie squeezed in next to her, and Casey took a chair opposite them. The proprietor, brewmistress, and tender-of-bar Mariele White nodded to the Morses as they entered and very carefully didn't acknowledge Ayame in the slightest. In what may have been the most cliché, but effective, recruiting effort ever, Miss White, a statuesque Haitian woman who stood six feet tall and had long braids hanging to her waist, had been brought into the Satori by the Morses a decade earlier. Who would ever expect a bartender? *Everyone*, naturally, and therefore, no one. Mariele's insight into who was who and what needed fixing in Eastsound was vital to the shogun's efforts to meet the needs and wants of his people. That the "games" room with its sad old billiards table was the conspirator's chosen rendezvous point was all the more ironic.

Ayame nursed a cider as the pub filled with regulars. Mariele rotated five thirty-gallon kegs, one per week, while the other four fermented from brew day until they were ready. She typically went through a full third of her stock on the evening she cracked the seal—such as this evening—and sold the other twenty gallons over the rest of the week. So, tonight would be busy. Another member of Ayame's team, Kris Smythe, arrived and joined them with a tray of drinks. They joked, caught up, and told sea stories until, finally, one last familiar figure approached Mariele. Ayame's source ordered four glasses at the bar and carried them to the game room.

Showtime.

Ayame withdrew an ancient stethoscope from her pack and slipped one of the earbuds in her ear and hid the second one beneath her collar. She pressed the diaphragm against the vent at her hip that connected to the games room and winced as someone broke the rack of billiard balls with a resounding *crack*. It was low-tech, a far cry from the highly advanced technological mischief she had gotten into on Teledyne ops, but it was subtle, and it worked. She tuned out the din of the crowd when another regular, Dave the Traveling Minstrel, broke out one of his more esoteric instruments—a Greek tzouras—and broke into song. Dave was *not* one of her Satori intelligence agents, if only because that really *would* have been too obvious.

"…dunno, Tarl, I mean, yeah, the Victorians stole that ship, but no one got hurt, and they didn't even get any of the fishing gear." That was Ajay Kumar's voice.

"*This* time. It's horseshit. They just sit there on Whidbey, safe as safe can be, while our asses are hanging out in the breeze. I tried feeling out Rainier, that bitch, and she blew me off. Her lance was the one on duty, and she *still* buys that fucking "Specialists" crap. What's so special about them? Do they specialize in getting good people killed?"

"You and I and everyone else have seen them fight, Tarl," a third voice said. Ayame thought it was Ryu Doraku speaking, but couldn't be sure. "They're inhuman."

"Which is why we need to *drug* them," Tarl replied. "We know they only take the *Seas the Day* around, that Nobunaga "captain" is long in the tooth, and his deckhand is a thirteen-year-old child. I don't care if it's Hanzo, Kato, or Grimstaadt, when the next one arrives in town, we act all friendly-like, slip a little sumthin' sumthin' in their drink, and when they wake up, they're trussed to a steel pole en route to Victoria. One of them should be here soon. The spring graduates are inbound, and they're going to have to come by, fly the flag, tell everyone they're doing everything they can, *blah blah blah*. The same shit they've been doing since you were an infant, Ryu." Tarl's voice was accusatory. "Do *you* have anything you need to bitch about, Carlos?"

"No, Sergeant," the last voice said. There was a meek but sullen tone to his voice; there was something there, but Ayame couldn't just barge in and start asking questions.

"Good. You're up, Ajay."

"Thirteen, corner pocket."

Ayame tucked the stethoscope away and nodded to her team. She took one last swallow of her cider, and all four of them stood as a group. They exited, using the three locals as a visual block so Ayame could slip past the billiards room door unseen, onto the street.

"We're a go. Tarl's plan is to drug me, Mikael, or Rick, and turn us over to Victoria. Follow them home and watch them overnight. Pick them off at dawn and meet at Ship Bay just east of downtown. Kris, you've got Carlos. Casey, Ajay. Cassie, Ryu. I'm taking Tarl myself."

* * *

*M**ore waiting.*
Unlike the night before, it was cool, crisp, and clear. Moonlight reflected off the ocean's rippling waves that gently lapped at the beach.

Three of the conspirators had departed within the first hour, trailed by her team of spies.

Tarl did not.

She hadn't seen Govnar in months, but he was not *subtle*. Mariele typically closed up around 1:00 am. Nobody kept time precisely anymore, but she knew it was closing time when Dave finally emerged, Greek guitar-thing over his back. Tarl was one of the last stragglers. He poured out the front door and stumbled west. On one hand, Ayame was tempted to grab him then and there, as soon as the pack drifted apart. On the other hand, that would mean babysitting the drunken asshole until the sun came up. Maybe he'd puke all over himself, choke on it, and die in his sleep. *That* would solve their problem, and she really couldn't bring herself to care.

She trailed him at a distance since she wasn't sure where he slept at night—or if he'd even make it home. Much to her surprise, he only staggered as far as the former inn—now barracks—half a block west before heading inside. Apparently, he drank so much of his pay away that he stayed in barracks.

Another missed warning sign, but no matter.

She passed the time behind a hedge that ran parallel to the road. The moon was easily bright enough she could read, but she'd finished her current novel earlier. Maybe she *could* stop off at Beth's and trade for the next one?

The sky was beginning to lighten on the far side of Mount Constitution when two figures approached. Kris Smythe was escorting his gagged prisoner, Carlos. Kris had bound the private's hands behind his back, hobbled his legs at the knees, and connected both to a rope. Kris could drag him with if need be. Ayame emerged from the roadside.

"He woke early. He's got duty this morning," Kris explained.

"Good. You can assist," Ayame said and crossed the lawn to the door of the barracks. She doffed Cassie's hat and pounded on the door. Lance Corporal Morton, whom she vaguely knew, and Private Wilkinson, per his nametag, answered. Morton glared at her suspiciously. "Lance Corporal, do you recognize me?"

Morton's eyes widened in recognition. "Y-yes, Samurai Kato," he replied.

"Good. Private Rodrigues will not be relieving you this morning; you'll need to make alternate arrangements in a few minutes. Come out here and take custody of him while I deal with another matter inside. Do not speak to him. Do not answer any of his questions.

You are to ensure he doesn't wander off for the next few minutes, remains in good health, and nothing else. Do you understand?"

"Not entirely, Samurai, but I will do as you order."

"Good."

Kris handed his prisoner's leash to Morton and followed Ayame inside. Upstairs, the barracks' doors bore small slates listing the occupier's names. When she found the slate marked, "Govnar," she nodded at the door. Kris drew out a small truncheon—little more than a stout stick, to be honest—and she tested the door handle. The door was unlocked. She burst into the room with Kris close behind and cleared the room in a hurry. They needn't have bothered. Tarl Govnar was curled up, partially undressed, in the ensuite bathtub. He'd vomited on himself, and more regurgitated beer fouled the tub. She supposed this was some kind of fucked up, drunken stupor mitigation technique of his, but he looked terrible and smelled worse. Ayame took both arms and torqued them up until the unconscious sergeant rolled onto his stomach. Smythe applied the cord cuffs to his wrists and snugged them tight. Govnar started to come to, but he was still hammered, groggy, and uncoordinated. Ayame stood him up in the tub and shook her head.

"You're a fucking disgrace," she spat and buried a fist in his gut. He doubled over and emptied the rest of his stomach. Kris blanched.

"That necessary?"

"This way he won't puke on me when I carry his wasted ass downstairs. I suppose I could have asked you to stick a finger in his throat?"

"Entirely necessary. Very good."

Ayame emerged from the barracks with Sergeant Govnar over her shoulders in a firefighter carry. He was drooling and unconscious again.

"Lance Corporal, prepare to take notes."

"Yes, ma'am," Morton replied and pulled out his notebook and pencil.

"Sergeant Govnar, Sergeant Kumar, Private Rodrigues, and Private Doraku will not be available for duty. They are under arrest. I am taking them to Whidbey for trial; we will be departing from Ship's Bay at sunrise. Please advise your chain of command. You can expect Daimyo Hanzo to be here in a day or two to answer questions, but for now, that is all you need to know."

"Can I ask the charges, ma'am? Lieutenant Chadad will want to know."

"Treason."

* * * * *

Chapter Four

Sunlight gleamed off the polished concrete floors inside the old EA-44 Manta hangar. The wide-open interior gave Rikimaru Hanzo plenty of space to move in and plenty of airflow for the forge. It kept him out of the drizzle that made outside so miserable during the Pacific winters. He'd corrected the bend he'd put in the blade earlier, had refined the edge as much as he could, and was ready to quench it. A long shadow stretched across the hangar from the main door on the east side.

"You didn't sleep again, huh?" Mikael Grimstaadt asked.

"You know I don't like to sleep when she's got an op going on," Rikimaru replied. He slipped the blade back into the furnace for one last heating, and once it was the right color, he quenched the blade in a PVC pipe filled with homegrown peanut oil. The oil flared for a moment, then he drew the blade back out.

Perfect.

He skated a file across the blade to ensure the heat treat had done its job, then let out a deep breath of relief. "Everything alright?"

Grimstaadt nodded and eyed Hanzo's project appreciatively. "That's fuckin' cool, old man." He leaned down closely to inspect the damascus pattern formed by the repeated folds of high-nickel and high-carbon steels. "I'll take two. Oh," he interrupted himself, "they'll be arriving soon."

"Right," Rikimaru replied. He placed the unfinished katana on a rack to cool. Mikael knew where the quenching tube went, Rikimaru put the tongs back on the rack where they belonged, and they pulled the unburned charcoal out of the brick-and-bellows forge together, before allowing the last bit to burn away. Sad to say, but even charcoal was a precious commodity these days. Charcoal was one of the few renewable resources they had, but it was a labor-intensive pain in the ass to produce. "Let's go greet our traitorous saboteurs, shall we?"

"*Saboteurs.* Methinks you give them too much credit, almost as much as the Homeguard do. They're twitchy as fuck, considering we're giving them fucking knives a handful of steps from the shogun."

"Oh ye of little faith," Rikimaru clucked. "I think four Specialists should be able to handle them if they get froggy."

"The old man doesn't count, and you know it." Grimstaadt grimaced and shook his head.

"Be careful who you're calling old man, mister." Rikimaru grinned. "You seem to be throwing that one around a lot."

"That's cause we're old, man." Grimstaadt grinned back. "Tidy up; time to go."

Rikimaru glanced over "his" shop one more time. Everything had a place, and everything was in its place as it should be. He shared the shop with a dozen or more blacksmiths from the Komainu and was determined to set the standard and lead by example in everything he did. There had been entirely too much chaos in the world since it fell, and it was his personal mission to restore a bit of order, beginning with dealing fairly with four treasonous saboteurs determined to fuck it all up.

"Are you seriously going to trumpet us onto the parade square with that thing?" Rikimaru asked when he caught a glimpse of the battered horn slung over his friend's shoulder.

"Absolutely."

By the time they made it down to the dock, the *Seas the Day* had already dropped its sails. Dan Nobunaga threw Kael a line from the stern, and Derek tossed one to Rikimaru at the bow. Ayame looked a bit haggard after sixty hours of nearly-continuous ops, but she could rack out once the trial was over and the mission complete. Her Satori teammates knew their way around a ship and had bumpers over the side and ropes tidied in seconds. Rikimaru lashed down the bowline, then ran to the rear and helped Kael with his. Nobunaga had come in a little hot, and the two Specialists added their combined seven hundred pounds at the stern to anchor the sailboat. It came to a halt with the stern just a little past them, revealing all four prisoners doing their best drowned-rat impressions.

Gags muffled them, and they'd been tied in fetal positions, wrists behind knees and knees at their chests. They'd been dragged, half-submerged, the whole way from Orcas. Rikimaru imagined they were hypothermic and half waterboarded by the wake. He hopped onto the boat and hauled the first prisoner up.

"Ajay." He untied the knots and gave him a moment to get feeling back into his legs. "I'm disappointed."

Ajay Kumar had the decency to look away, ashamed. He stood by sullenly while Rikimaru hauled the other three aboard. Kumar, who was in his early thirties, was shorter than Rikimaru, maybe 5'9", with wavy black hair and a neatly trimmed goatee. Rikimaru made a note to review his file when all this was done. Sergeants were generally in their mid-twenties; he must have been demoted once or twice. Maybe that was the source of his treasonous conduct?

Rikimaru untied the remaining three prisoners and let them stretch so they could regain function in their legs, then they set off for the parade square.

* * *

The Komainu recruits brought up from Fort Casey had moved the archery targets off to one side and set up bleachers for the spectators. An elevated shooting platform for the archers became a dais, with a high-backed chair for the shogun, and a table with four knives on blood-red handkerchiefs rested in front of it. Kojima worked the crowd, shaking hands and exchanging greetings, giving his Homeguard bodyguards ulcers. He didn't travel to the islands as often as he once did, but considering the thousands of survivors in Oak Harbor, he did well to remember as many as he did. Mikael led the way and, upon reaching the edge of the parade square, raised his battered trumpet to his lips and played a credible impression of Rouse to announce their arrival. The crowd found their seats, and the shogun made his way to the dais on the far side of the square. Mikael and Rikimaru marched forward, taking their places to his left and right. Once the two samurai stood in place, Ayame marched her four prisoners forward. At her command, Doraku, Rodrigues, and Kumar took a knee, but Govnar refused. Ayame gripped the rope still wrapped around his chest and kicked the back of his knees while yanking viciously on the line. His knees audibly thumped when they hit the pavement. He winced but remained silent.

"You four stand accused of treason," she began and referred to her notebook. "On November 11th, 2086, Sergeant Tarl Govnar approached Sergeant Ajay Kumar. He was dissatisfied with the shogun's policy of pragmatic pacifism—namely, that we maintained our Komainu militia for defense, but did not engage in offensive operations against the mainland or the Victorians on Vancouver Island. Sergeant Govnar and Sergeant Kumar discussed plans and, on or about New Year's Eve, 2087, Sergeant Govnar brought Privates Doraku and Rodrigues into their circle of conspirators.

"On April 30th, 2087, Sergeant Govnar, Sergeant Kumar, Private Doraku, and Private Rodrigues met at the Whitecaps Pub in Eastsound, where, in the billiards room, they reaffirmed their plan to drug Samurai Kato, Samurai Grimstaadt, or Daimyo Hanzo upon their next visit to Eastsound. In particular, they decided to go overt because of the raid one week ago when Victorians stole the fishing boat *Buoyancé*. Once drugged, they would deliver their prisoner to Victoria, and I quote, "trussed to a steel pole.""

Govnar shot an accusatory look at the other three, but Ayame stopped her recitation and addressed him directly. "Don't look at them, *Sergeant*. I was in the next room, listening. I heard it from your own lips."

"Do you contest these charges?" Kojima asked. Carlos' lip quivered, and he stared at the pavement when he shook his head 'no.' Ryu was silently crying. Kumar shook his head briefly, and Govnar remained defiant. "Daimyo Hanzo, the court is yours."

Rikimaru turned to the table in front of the shogun and picked up a knife. "Ryu, you were born after the world fell. Your mother was pregnant when she fled Seattle, and you were one of the first children born here, at Deception Base. This knife is just as old as you are." The daimyo pulled the slipknot that bound the young man's wrists free, and the young private shook the paracord loose. "This knife is power, the power to resolve this matter, once and for all. Say your piece and turn it on the one you believe responsible for the predicament you are in."

"Honored Daimyo, I failed you," Ryu began, tears streaking his cheeks. "I failed Deception Base and my friends' homes on Orcas Island. I was dissatisfied with life as a 'mere' fisherman and thought I could do more, raiding the Victorians, which the shogun forbid. When Tarl came to me, dissatisfied with the shogun's leadership, I leaped without looking. It was a mistake. I hope my shame can be forgiven."

Rikimaru handed the young man the knife. He cradled it for a moment, then steeled himself and drove the chisel point of the tanto into his heart. He gasped and crumpled forward. Rikimaru leaned in and whispered, "It is forgiven." Ryu nodded once, coughed up a mouthful of blood, and went still. "It *is* forgiven!" the daimyo announced to the spectators and pointed to the *kami* stones in the adjacent Memorial Park. Ryu's name would be added there as one of their fallen, not stricken from the records.

"Carlos Rodrigues, you were just an infant when we fled the city for the islands. Samurai Grimstaadt tells me you were slated for NCO classes in the Komainu, our guardians. There is always a risk, when men and women are given weapons and training, that they will use the power that gives them for ill. Discipline and willpower are just as important in a warrior as strength and cunning. I give you the same power I gave Ryu."

Rikimaru handed Rodrigues the second knife, but he froze, paralyzed by indecision and fear. Ten seconds, then twenty passed. The crowd began to murmur until he finally looked up and met Rikimaru's eyes. "I…can't. I'm scared."

"Tell me what you were thinking," Rikimaru commanded.

"Daimyo…I'm not…smart," he said. His chin fell to his chest, and he stared down at the knife as though he didn't know what to do with it. "Growing up, here in the islands, I always felt dumb, and my friends would tease me. Eventually, I started doing stupid shit for laughs and entertainment. It was better laughing with them than being laughed at. I have always known better than to pull some of the stupid pranks I did, but their encouragement was all I needed. After I joined the Komainu, I thought I might get a chance to do something right for once." Rodrigues' anger seemed to crystalize, and he got to his feet. His voice got stronger, and he pointed the knife accusingly at the man next to him. "I wish, at New Year's, I had listened to my inner voice for once in my life, rather than listening to *his*. Tarl was our leader, Daimyo, but I knew better. I lacked the discipline and willpower to do what I knew was right."

He looked up with new conviction hardening his eyes. "You told Ryu to turn the knife on the one who was responsible, right?"

The daimyo nodded. Rodrigues glared down at Govnar, then his head snapped up. "Does he get a knife too? Or can I just kill him now and be done with it?"

"If you kill him," Rikimaru said slowly, "you're choosing banishment rather than death. You will cross the Deception Pass Bridges and never come back."

Rodrigues didn't hesitate; he turned and dove on the ringleader. The two tumbled, and it quickly became apparent the private was fighting with emotion and not skill; Govnar outclassed him and used the ropes around his wrists to catch and deflect the knife. Govnar took a few shallow, bloody slashes on his forearms but nothing remotely lethal. He kicked Rodrigues in the chest, sending him back, and kept lashing out with short snap kicks at the younger Komainu's shins to keep him back. The two chased each other across the parade square until Rodrigues tripped and the older sergeant pounced. Govnar trapped the knife, and the arm holding it, on the pavement with a shin and smashed Rodrigues in the face with a vicious elbow. Rodrigues' head bounced off the concrete, and Govnar hit him three more times until he bled from his nose and went limp.

The leader of the saboteurs scooped the knife up and awkwardly sawed at the rope around his wrists. When they fell free, he crossed back to the table with the daggers and picked up a second one.

Well, shit, Rikimaru thought. *This day is full of surprises.*

"Save the speeches, Rick, let's fuckin' do this, huh?"

Govnar kept his right hand low, with the knife reversed, and his left hand out and up, with the blade extended. When he slashed with his left hand, Rikimaru exploded forward, smashing his attacker's forearm with the back of his. Deadened nerves caused Govnar to release the knife, which flew from his limp fingers. Rikimaru trapped Govnar's wrist and darted past him, twisting his arm up into a chicken wing. He pivoted sharply and drove his left elbow into Govnar's temple, like Mother Nature's own baseball bat, and the traitor stumbled away, concussed.

Govnar almost tripped when he bumped into Kumar, but he caught himself. He looked down at his fellow prisoner for just an instant, then sliced the paracord cuffs away. The fourth saboteur grabbed a knife off the table. Rikimaru couldn't recall a time where he'd had an accused attack him with two knives; he *knew* he'd never fought two co-accused at the same time.

Protective members of the Homeguard moved forward, making a shield for the shogun with their bodies. Rikimaru caught a glimpse of Mikael, looking nervous, and Ayame, who...did not? The daimyo circled wide in a game of monkey-in-the-middle from hell. He had to keep the two in line. That way, the middle one was the only threat, and the one to the rear couldn't reach him. He could focus on one threat and not get flanked.

"Daimyo, I feel there's something I ought to tell you," Ajay Kumar called over Tarl's shoulder.

"By all means," Rikimaru called back.

"Carlos didn't mention that Tarl had been coercing him, threatening his mother if he didn't cooperate," Kumar declared and drove his knife into Govnar's lower back. Govnar shrieked in pain, and Kumar cut the knife out sideways in a spray of blood and flesh. Govnar collapsed to his knees, keening in agony, and Kumar grabbed hold of Govnar's mop of hair. He yanked his head back and plunged the blade into Govnar's throat and carved out, severing his trachea, jugular vein, and carotid artery in one devastating slice. Govnar tumbled to the pavement, finally silent. Ajay wiped the bloodied knife on the back of Govnar's still-sodden tunic. "And I haven't mentioned, I'm one of the Satori."

Rikimaru shot a look at Ayame, who nodded once, satisfaction written all over her face. Kumar tossed the knife away, and Ayame joined them on the parade square. Rikimaru closed with Ayame's source, still suspicious. "You infiltrated his group, walked into Ayame's ambush, got dragged behind a boat for twenty miles, and waited until *now* to say something?" Rikimaru asked in disbelief. "Are you that hardcore? Or are you that crazy?"

"Both," Ayame replied for him. "Definitely both. Daimyo Hanzo, may I formally introduce my top covert operative, *Lieutenant* Ajay Kumar? Ajay, this is Rick."

Rikimaru glanced back and forth between the two of them. Ayame clearly enjoyed his poleaxed expression, while Ajay looked up at him fiercely.

"I guess that resolves that. If Govnar was coercing Carlos, Carlos should have spoken up, but he's not to blame." Rikimaru waved to Sergeant Major Bridgwater, the homeguard's NCOIC, and pointed to the semiconscious form of Carlos Rodrigues. "Get him to Doctor Marcum in the infirmary, Sergeant; if he wakes up, I owe him an apology."

* * *

"…and that's when I went to Samurai Ayame, Shogun," Ajay finished.

Rikimaru considered Kumar's verbal debrief. "You two have been on this since *December?*" he asked.

"It was a slow boil, but yes," Ayame confirmed. "I had to know how deep the rot went. Govnar kept his own counsel most of the time. Now that I look back over his personnel jacket notes, there are a lot more red flags than I realized, but seeing as these are chicken-scratch, handwritten reports from superiors kept in a dozen different filing cabinets scattered across the islands, I hadn't put it all together. I'm going to have a lot of reading to do to make sure we don't have any more shitheads in the making."

The hangar didn't just house Rikimaru's forge, it was also their primary operations center. Rikimaru wheeled out a corkboard displaying a large map of the region, covered in pushpins in a multitude of colors. They gathered around to pick Kumar's brain, make notes, and update their intel. The pins reminded Ayame of one of the old E^5 games named for the Enlightenment series, noting population centers, industries, resources, Komainu fortifications, concentrations of militia troops, and more. E^5 games were ones where the goal was to Enlighten, Explore, Exploit, Expand, and Exterminate. Some she'd played as a child had gone back to the stone age, and the player guided their faction through to modern corporatism and beyond. Others had been all-in on the post-apocalyptic genre, although none seemed to have gotten all the details right.

"So, in summary, Orcas Island is feeling isolated, vulnerable, and resentful. Two of their little rebellions' leaders are dead, the one who'd been shanghaied into cooperating is in the infirmary with a broken nose and a concussion, and the last was one of the good guys. What do we do about it? If we were on the mainland, I imagine the answer would be, "put them to the torch and be done with it," but that's not an option here."

"Daimyo, they feel like they're an afterthought. Orcas is the most vulnerable to Victorian raiders. San Juan proper can see raiders coming the moment they set sail. It gives the San Juan Komainu plenty of time to rally a hundred archers and distribute the lit braziers, and if the Victorians close to within two hundred yards, our archers can torch their sails with fire arrows." Ajay pointed to a series of islands that began near the tip of the Saanich peninsula and traced a path from island to rocky island, until his finger stabbed Eastsound on Orcas Island. "But if the Victorians launch from the *west* side of their peninsula instead, they can stay behind these uninhabited islands until they're only a few minutes out. By the time we spot their sails, here, it's too late to form a response or intercept them on the water. With respect, sir, Shogun Kojima's instruction that we not respond with punitive raids of our own leaves the Orcas residents feeling very much like we're a speedbump."

Ayame couldn't disagree with her protégé's assessment, but like Rikimaru, she'd be damned if she knew what to do about it. The shogun had been explicit—no offensive operations. Their one attempt had gone disastrously, and they weren't permitted to consider another.

"Let's take a tour of the island and scheme," Rikimaru proposed. "The Victorians are a pain in the ass, but their city didn't eat a cluster-nuke, so for the first time in two hundred years, the old fleet is a threat."

"I think calling them a *fleet* is a bit much," Ayame disagreed. When Teledyne began snapping up all the government military facilities on the west coast, they'd almost been embarrassed to purchase CFB Esquimalt. It was home to five ocean-going frigates that had been refurbed and "upgraded" from time to time since the start of the new millennium. The RCN had three functional coastal defense vessels, with parts cannibalized from three others. Three submarines in the dry dock had, in theory, been upgraded at the time of their purchase, but what was new and exciting seventy years ago *wasn't* now, not anymore. "They're a bunch of feral pirates in stolen equipment. There's not a single one of them who ever swore an oath to the British king."

"Irrelevant." Shogun Kojima spoke for the first time. He sounded…angry? *Offended?* Ayame was stunned. In twenty years, she'd never heard him speak in that tone of voice. She realized her jaw was open and shut it before he noticed. "They threaten our stability, they threaten our way of life. We must honor that threat. You will take this…resentment, this anger, and focus it. Train it. Anyone willing to raise a blade will help *destroy* the Victorian fleet."

Ayame locked eyes with Rikimaru. He raised his eyebrows; he was surprised too. The shogun kept going.

"I had hoped we could resolve our differences with the Victorians in time. But this *betrayal,*" he spat, "makes matters rather more urgent. I, too, have the courage to admit when I make a mistake, Rikimaru," he said with a sad smile. "Ajay, Mikael is commander of the Komainu, our militia forces. The Komainu are the lion-dogs that guard Shinto shrines, and they guard our homes. As commander of the Satori, Ayame is our spymaster. Satori are thus named for yōkai who can read minds, and it is the Satori's job to know what everyone is thinking. Your position within the Satori is compromised after this morning's trial, but to send you back to the Komainu, I believe, would be a waste.

"Therefore, I hereby grant you the title of Samurai, Commander of…" Kojima looked thoughtful. "…Commander of the Onamazu. Onamazu was a giant catfish restrained by the god Kashima, and whenever Onamazu was freed, he thrashed and caused earthquakes. I say, in this case, *I* am Kashima, and I will restrain you no more." The shogun approached the map and drove pins into the smaller, uninhabited islands north and west of Orcas. "We will establish fortifications and concealed observation posts on the rocky islands that have shielded the Victorians from your view. Once our island nation is secure, your marines will seize every Victorian ship they can and scuttle the rest. The Japanese were warriors of the sea once upon a time, and we will be so again."

The shogun rose and bowed to the other four. "I have restrained you for too long; we cannot foresee all possibilities, we cannot anticipate chaos and entropy. A single spark can ignite the mightiest fire. I leave you to plot, to scheme, to plan, and to act. I will not joggle your elbows or micromanage you; the time for that is long overdue. Do not engage in wanton slaughter for slaughter's sake. One can only put up with so much for so long in this Fallen World, before one's patience is worn thin. *My patience has worn thin.*"

* * * * *

Chapter Five

Rikimaru laid out his tools on the table in the *Seas the Day's* cabin and placed his damascus katana next to them. Intrigued, Kumar observed but didn't interrupt. He'd learned, over the last week, that Rikimaru taught by show and tell. If he was patient, the explanation would follow.

"Ordinarily, this would be a terrible place to work, but I fitted everything before we left. Just didn't have time to finish it." He took a small saucepan off the galley's electric range and checked the contents for consistency. Satisfied, he brought it to the table and set it on a coaster. "If you're going to be the Onamazu samurai, you're going to need to choose your weapon. Do you have a preference?"

"I've been thinking about *naginata*," Kumar replied. "But shorten the haft a bit and add a hook. If we're doing shipboard combat, I want something that can chop ropes as well as pirates, but isn't so long we can't swing it indoors. I can choke up on a naginata haft if I need to. The hook can trap ropes or haul someone overboard back up, and in a pinch, a wide blade head could double as a paddle. It ought to be a tool as well as a weapon."

"Seems reasonable," Rikimaru agreed. "Something like that, you can pretty much bang the business end out of leaf springs. Easy, as far as blades go, I mean. Are you sure you don't want a kukri? Your family was Gurkha, wasn't it?"

"Hah, no. They were from West Bengal, right next to Bangladesh," Ajay said. "Gurkha are from the north. I was just a kid when the bombs fell. I'd never been over there. My parents' grandparents were from east India and moved to Surrey in the early oughts. I don't even speak Punjabi."

"My mistake. My aunts and uncles lived on a tiny island with a hundred people on it in Okinawa. My folks grew up in Seattle. They insisted I learn the language, but I've never been either."

Rikimaru slid on his fittings and tested the fit of his handle one more time. It was a snug fit, and he carefully painted the bare metal tang of the katana with the contents of the saucepan.

"Glue?" Ajay asked.

"Glue," Rikimaru confirmed. He finished painting the sticky, caramel-colored substance onto the tang and slipped the wood and sharkskin *tsuka* on. "One of Fiery Tree's stallions broke a leg in that frost we had in January."

"Sad," Ajay said, "but I guess if it's not going to heal and just eat food the others needed…"

"Exactly. Waste not, want not." He unrolled a long, brown, leather lace and began wrapping it around the tsuka, painstakingly folding it and re-folding it until the traditional diamond shapes began to appear as the dark brown outlined the mottled sharkskin beneath. Partway down, he tucked a small, oblong, metal ornament against the tsuka, then continued wrapping. "This is a *menuki*," he explained. "I stamped it from an old Teledyne challenge coin. Reminds me where we came from and how we got into this mess."

"Honestly, I'm more curious about the skin." Kumar said. "I thought mantas were more tropical."

"You remember the shark steaks at the Eastsound barbecue last Veterans Day?"

"Yeah," Ajay replied, then blanched. "*No way.*"

"Waste not, want not," Rikimaru repeated. "Real Pacific leopard shark skin. I've never heard of them this far north before. Most of the skin got turned into sandpaper, but I have a bit more, if I ever make another." He fitted the *kashira* endcap on and slipped the leather through to keep it tight. He tied a complicated knot at the end of the tsuka and tucked the last of the leather under the pre-existing knots. "Done." He slipped the katana into its scabbard and laid it on the table.

He heaved an ancient, fraying hockey bag onto the seat next to him and unzipped it. "You're going to want to take more notes." The daimyo began placing shaped pieces of wood on the table between them. Each one was a work of art—they were painted snow white, and traditional Japanese sketches were etched and inked into their surfaces. Heavy leather straps with buckles indicated they were meant to be worn somehow. Ajay had only seen the Specialists in full fighting gear once; they rarely felt they needed armor. He picked up one of several similar wedge-shaped plates and hefted it. It was lighter than it looked.

"That," Rikimaru said, "is *kusazuri*. Armor for the waist and hips." More armor hit the table. "*Sode*—pauldrons for the shoulders. *Kote*—forearm guards. *Do, haidate, sune-ate*—chest, thigh, and shin guards." Rikimaru pointed to each piece in turn. Kumar examined them and found that the etched plates were backed with some kind of thin metal sheeting with a thin layer of foam sandwiched between. "Plywood armor, aluminum backing, based on the old samurai design. Maximum mobility, minimal tech, functionally useless against firearms, but it allows for sword work and archery, and since its plywood, it's far more effective against blades than it has any right to be. And, most importantly, it floats."

Rikimaru waited for Ajay to catch up on his notes. Another thing the shogun had insisted on was maintaining educational minimums as much as possible—literacy and arithmetic were essential, as were basic problem-solving, first aid, and crafts. Ajay's notes were quick, but he had an eye for detail and spelled out the Japanese terms phonetically as best he could. "This will be the basis for your marines' armor after we're done here. I'll teach you and your top two picks for your Onamazu—it will be up to you to teach the rest. Each marine will have to fabricate their own armor before graduating from Basic."

Rikimaru slipped the first shin guard—*sune-ate*— over the black leg of his pants and cinched the straps tight. They were almost to Eastsound, and it was time for the daimyo to look the part.

* * *

Kael Grimstaadt stood at the bow of the *Drug Money Too*, directly astern of the *Seas the Day* and two hundred meters back. Legend had it the boat had belonged to one of Teledyne's pharmaceutical researchers who'd died in Seattle. The ship's smaller, cheaper sister, *Drug Money,* was two hundred meters behind him, and the rest of the boats were strung out in a line behind them. Rikimaru, Ayame, and the new kid were on the lead ship because, of course they were. His old battle buddy did love to lead from the front, and that was fine—Mikael had always been the lead samurai for the Komainu, but this particular shitshow had kicked off thanks to Ayame's ninja spooks, so she was on point.

Kael's boat driver, Claudia Radcliffe, was from Lopez Island. Twenty years earlier, she had been a stacked, tanned, blonde entertainer who consistently surprised everyone with how intelligent and eloquent she was when she spoke. She'd had all the athletic body sculpting Teledyne could afford, which meant she had grown into a mature, stacked, tanned, intelligent, eloquent, blonde Sergeant Major.

To everyone's surprise but her own, the athleticism necessary for dancing and the athletic mods she'd received translated *very* well to fighting. Her fierce drive, force of personality, and intelligence had tagged her as leadership material early on. She'd spent fifteen years in the Komainu, during which she'd risen to be the homeguard's NCOIC and then retired to captain Mikael's assigned boat. For fifteen years, troops had speculated about why she had never had a boyfriend—or a girlfriend—to the best of anyone's knowledge. Even Mikael had wondered how such a spectacular woman had never found someone special.

Once she was out of Mikael's chain of command, however, it all became clear. Claudia had respected the fraternization rules the entire time she'd served, never betraying a hint of anything less than absolute professionalism. So Mikael was therefore shocked and delighted when *she'd* propositioned *him* the evening of her retirement party. She'd wrangled captainship of the *Drug Money Too* shortly thereafter, and she spent her days sailing, maintaining her (tan-line-free) tan, and jacking up Komainu recruits who needed sorting out. Okay, so maybe she wasn't *entirely* retired, but rank had its privileges.

Dan Nobunaga cut his speed and cleanly brought the *Seas the Day* across the end of the pier. Dan was easily the best sailor in the fleet, but Claudia was a close second. Rick, Aya, and Kumar jumped over to the pier, then made room for everyone filing in behind them.

Yep, Rick's got his samurai armor on. Good. He didn't feel quite so awkward in his own getup. He knew Kojima, Rick, Aya, and a bunch of the rest of Teledyne had really gotten into the Feudal Japan thing after the end of the world, but as their token white guy, he kind of wished he could have channeled less Japanese Samurai and more Norwegian Viking. Sadly, Kojima insisted that marauding Scandinavians didn't instill the proper sense of order and discipline, which was fair enough. Hostile corporate takeover jokes to the contrary, Vikings weren't known for their calm demeanor and selfless sense of duty.

Claudia slowed her approach and followed in Dan's wake. Mikael gave the word, and his Komainu recruit lances lined up in their stacks along the starboard edge of the deck, with him at the leading edge. As the bow of the boat crossed the edge of the pier, Mikael stepped off and kept moving. Two heartbeats later, the first lance corporal was right on his heels, and a moment later, the second junior NCO and the first private stepped off next to each other. The rest of the privates followed, two at a time, jumping across the tiny gap Claudia had left between the boat and the pier. They naturally went from two ranks to two columns thanks to the boat's forward momentum. It was pretty slick, honestly, and considering how difficult it was to dock the sailboats and get them going again, hot unloads like this were essential recruit training at Fort Casey.

To Kael's relief, his two lances managed the maneuver cleanly, and no one went in the drink. Rick nodded his approval, and the sixteen of them marched down the dock to Eastsound. There was a greeting party, and Councillor Miller kicked things off, as Ajay predicted.

"What is the meaning of this?" he demanded. "This looks like an invasi—"

Kumar buried a fist in the man's too-soft belly, and the chubby councillor folded like an origami crane.

"*Mister* Graham Miller, you are hereby removed from council," Rikimaru pronounced. Mikael was watching the rest of the Eastsounders, and he wasn't happy with their reaction. Two were impassive, another smirked, and the last let a flash of anger cross her face before she regained control. *They'd known something was up.*

"The island will vote at the next meeting to have you replaced, but you will never be part of our leadership again. I have detailed reports on your part in the troubles here a week ago. I have further reports that show you *knew* Carlos Rodrigues was a victim of coercion and failed to act as your title, office, and honor demand. If you wish to appeal, I have a knife with me, and we can work this out right here, right now," the daimyo finished. He offered the red-faced councillor a knife, hilt first, but Miller was so stunned he couldn't speak. As he tried to relearn how to breathe, Kael's Komainu lances spread out to flank the delegation, revealing that two more boats had unloaded their troops as well. A full platoon, thirty-eight Komainu, now occupied the pier. It was a show of force, which was ample enough to cow Miller into accepting Rick's declaration without arguing.

"You're soft, and you're *fat*. That's a rare thing these days when everyone around you is calloused, rough, and ready. My team and I will be addressing the island's security vulnerabilities, likely until the autumn, and I'm going to suggest you find a crew to work for because you *certainly* don't want to work for me. Make sure you can trust them because it would be the easiest thing in the world for someone to put a knife in your gut and dump you overboard."

Miller stood shakily and glared but said nothing. Kael suppressed a laugh when Rick took a half step toward him, and the tubby man fled.

* * *

"This is the saddest lighthouse on Earth," Ayame said and visibly shivered. They'd anchored at the mouth of Active Cove, a thin, C-shaped bay on the west end of Patos Island. The island had once been entirely Teledyne Parks & Recreation: Patos Island Park, and a lone building—the lighthouse—rested at the western-most end. "I hate it here."

"Oh, shit." Kael blanched. "Right. You don't have to go ashore," Kael said and gave Ajay a subtle shake of his head. "We've got this. Why don't you oversee Waldron?"

"Appreciated," Ayame said and went back below deck. Ajay looked at Mikael, but this time the head shake was clear, and Kael put a finger to his lips. With the anchors set and half an hour or so before she had to leave to deliver Ayame to the next minor island south, Claudia stretched out on the foredeck in a black bikini and sunglasses and let the troops handle the busywork. Kael took one last moment to appreciate his lady's form, then boarded the *Drug Money Too*'s dinghy, which groaned under his enhanced density. Ajay paddled the short distance to the rocky beach where the advance party was ready to help them out of the boat. The rest of the company—newly graduated recruits, senior conscripts, and their volunteer veteran leadership—were likewise boarding small craft and paddling ashore. Some were already dragging tool chests onto the rocks and helping their fellow troops out of the boats.

Now that Aya was out of earshot, Kael pointed to the lighthouse. "Before the world fell, this little chunk of rock was cared for by a volunteer organization. It fell apart when the nukes dropped, and it was, quite literally, months before Ayame traveled out here to find out what had happened to the Patos Island Lighthouse. A family of three had been out here camping. Their ride home never showed up."

"It never…?"

"They'd packed a couple cases of bottled water, but nowhere near enough. Per the note we found, they were expecting pickup on May second. Mom and Dad stopped drinking on the fifth to stretch the supplies for their little girl. Mom died on May tenth. Dad, the twelfth."

"Oh, my god." Ajay physically recoiled at the thought.

"Young Miss Briona Alderdice left us a note, tied rocks to her hands before she was too weak, and threw herself into the sea. She'd seen how horrible her parents' deaths were, as they wasted away, surrounded by water but unable to drink any of it. She chose to end her life on her own terms. Ayame found the note and two desiccated bodies laid out, hand in skeletal hand, in the foyer of the lighthouse. She's never been back. Briona, Alexavier, and Hayleigh Alderdice are etched near the top of the *kami* stones at Memorial Park. The first of many. Sometimes taking matters into your own hands is all you can do in this Fallen World."

Ajay remained silent for a moment. "This is Patos Island, what the hell is a *Patos*?"

Kael cocked an eyebrow at the abrupt change of topic. "It's Spanish for *duck*. Some Conquistador type named it that three centuries ago. Probably the same guy who named San Juan and Lopez."

"Can I make a suggestion?" the younger man asked. He regarded the Komainu work party, who were taking measurements and staking out construction plans on the barren, western tip of the island.

"Of course."

"Fort Alderdice has a nice ring to it."

Kael nodded in appreciation. "That it does. Good call, *Samurai*. Now, let's get to work, and keep your eyes peeled for anyone you want to steal away for your catfish marines. They may not realize it, but they're already in selection."

"Yes sir," Ajay said, then went to help one of the lances haul their tool chest up the beach.

* * *

"**A**lvarez!"

"Hai!"

"Cobb!"

"Hai!"

"Cross!"

"Hai!"

Ajay "Akuma" Kumar read from his list of names for several minutes, until concluding with "Zabrowski!"

"Hai!"

"All those I named, when I dismiss the remainder, fall back in. Everyone else, to your duties—*Dismissed!*"

The gathered ranks of Komainu marched off the "parade square"—the Eastsound market parking lot. The majority of them were from Eastsound or elsewhere on Orcas and broke off to return home, or to their barracks, or down to the dock to catch a ride back to Lopez or San Juan and return to their regular duties. A curious few remained, however, to watch whatever was going on with the rest. Akuma took note of who stayed—it wasn't like it was a secret, and being curious and taking the initiative to remain was a good sign. Forty-two of the Guardians remained, and with puzzled looks at each other, fell back into formation.

"We're announcing a new initiative," Akuma began. He rather liked the nickname; Terry Cobb had accidentally hung it on him while stumbling over his name. *Akuma* was Japanese for demon, and when Rikimaru overheard the error, he made sure the name stuck.

"You all know Shogun Kojima declared me samurai, but during the last two weeks' construction, we haven't discussed *why*. Daimyo Hanzo is our top general. Samurai Kato is head of the Satori, or as some prefer to believe, the shinobi. Samurai Grimstaadt is head of the Komainu. As of now, I am samurai of the Onamazu marine raiders, and I'm looking for a hardass bunch of troops. I want people who have the stones to take the fight to the Victorians, who will soak up punishment and ask for more. We are going to do more PT, more weapons drills, run faster, fight harder, and kill more pirate raiders than *everyone else combined*." That caused a bit of a stir in the ranks, but a stern glare quieted them instantly. He continued, "The Onamazu was a giant, earthquake causing, catfish who needed a *god* to keep him restrained. Well, the shogun isn't going to be holding us in check, and we're going to go pick a fight. We're going to inflict a lot of casualties and torch a lot of boats, but that also means we're going to take more casualties.

"For that reason, the Onamazu will strictly consist of volunteers. Komainu don't go looking for scraps, but we do. After the last week of hard labor and construction, I'm offering you bunch of rowdies the chance to form the core of the Corps, as it were." He began to pace as he delivered his pitch. "PT will increase! We're going to run and do pushups and crunches and climb ropes and swim in the, yes, horrifically frigid ocean! Ask me how I know! The only construction you will be doing is making and maintaining your weapons because we will be too busy kicking ass to worry about log cabins and goat fences! Daimyo Hanzo and our top smiths—some of you are already counted among them—will teach us how to forge our own weapons and how to maintain them, and we will do this *ourselves*. You've all seen the samurai's plywood-and-lamellar armor; *everyone* will be making their own. We'll be going into close combat a *helluva* lot more than the regular Komainu, and as marines, twenty-something plates of plywood will act as a life jacket if, and when, someone falls overboard. Expect to be sweaty, tired, freezing, battered, and bruised. Bruises now are better than bleeding later." He let that sink in for a moment.

"If anyone here does not wish to join the Onamazu, you may march off now and rejoin your Komainu platoons. You may release from the Onamazu at any time *during* Basic, but upon graduation, you will swear an oath, and that will make you Onamazu for life— once you're in, you're all the way in. Anyone who wants to release may do so now."

When no one moved, he stopped pacing and faced them directly.

"With that in mind, who here is going to be a *marine?*"

"*HAI!*"

* * * * *

Chapter Six

"Well, well, gents, what have you brought for me this fine day?"

"Bit of flotsam, washed up down by the ol' Ferris Wheel in a busted one-man sailboat, boss," the first peon replied. The boss couldn't remember the peon's name; it didn't really matter. One was no different from another; they were infinitely replaceable, and none of them was worth two turds in a leaky bucket. The 'flotsam' in question was a pale, chubby man whose face was beet red, likely from being strung up by his ankles. His eyes were wide, and surprisingly, even redder than his too-round, too-fat face.

"A *tubby* bit of flotsam," the boss repeated. He kneeled so they were eye to eye, and he took the too-fat face in his hands and squished the cheeks together as though to test how pliable they were. Tubbo whined, but the gag kept him from interrupting.

Peculiar.

Nobody was tubby in the Sprawl. Nobody liked grilled seagull or rat burgers enough to get fat, not a chance. For that matter, Tubbo was *old*, too. Fifties, maybe sixties, meaning he would have been in his thirties or forties when cluster nukes gutted everything south of Pike Place Market. A couple more scattered here and there rendered huge chunks of the Sprawl uninhabitable. Someone in his thirties was an old man in most zones, and if the gangs didn't get them, then tumors would.

CRACK!

The boss slapped the fat man, rattling his brain and eliciting a muffled scream. The swingarm he hung from rotated with the force of the blow, until he was looking straight down at five hundred feet of air. Far below him, he saw the dead grass, dirt, and concrete of the park at the base of the Space Needle. The boss didn't know why it was called that, it was neither needle-shaped, nor did it have anything to do with space that he could tell. The only relevant thing at the moment was that there was a *lot* of space between the fat man's head and the ground below. He swung there, an overweight pendulum suspended over the edge of the needle's observation deck, but only for a moment. The boss reeled him back in. He was blubbering now, muffled by the gag, which pissed the boss off even more.

"Shh!" he urged. "Stop that, *stop that*, STOP THAT!" he bellowed. He took hold of the man's collar and slapped him again, making sure he took the full impact rather than swinging back out into open space. The man shrieked behind the gag and erupted into tears. The boss rolled his eyes in exasperation.

"Shut *up*, you greasy, ponderous, pathetic twat; I've barely even *hit* you. If I take the gag off, do you promise to stay quiet and answer my questions?"

"Mm-hmm?"

"Good. That's a good Tubbo. Just suck it up, buttercup." He reached out and slipped the gag upward, so it rested around the man's neck.

"Now, what's your name?"

"Gra-Graham Miller?"

"You don't sound very sure about that, Gra-Graham Miller."

"Graham Miller, sir," the man repeated, this time without the stutter.

"Graham Miller, you have intrigued me. You see, my colleagues and I are what you might call *thin*. Not emaciated, not quite, but there are plenty out there in the zones who are very *definitely* emaciated. But they're weak, and they'll be gone soon, and I can't rightly say I care about them one whit. Still, I could stand to have more meat on my bones. It's cold here in the winters, Graham Miller, without an insulating layer of *chub* to help keep warm. To see such a fine, *healthy* specimen as you makes me wonder—*where are you from, Graham Miller*, that you've managed to stay so thick and well-insulated?"

"Or...Orcas Island, sir," Miller whined.

"And how did you come to wash up on *my* waterfront?"

"I, they, uh..." He swallowed hard. "They kicked me out. I took a little CL-14, only good for one or two people, really. There wasn't any hope they'd let me live, and, but, uh...I haven't sailed since I was a boy."

"*They?* Who are *they* who kicked you out?"

"The...shogun and the daimyo. Kojima and his pet brute, Rikimaru."

"The...*shogun?* Is *that* what Kojima calls himself these days?" The boss laughed. His peons glanced at each other; they hadn't heard him laugh like that in quite some time. "Akihiro Kojima is *Shogun* of Orcas Island?"

"Well...not just Orcas," Miller said. "Orcas, Lopez, San Juan, Shaw, and Whidbey. The shogun lives on Whidbey, and that's where they send all the food and all the troops. They left us to fend for ourselves against the Victorians from Vancouver Island!"

"Akihiro Kojima. Will wonders never cease?" The boss chuckled again, but there was no life in his cold, dead eyes. "Is Rikimaru's little bestie, Mikael, still running around with him? I haven't tangled with them in *decades*."

Miller nodded, pathetic and desperate. "Mikael Grimstaadt and Ayame Kato. The three of them are Kojima's heavies. They murdered two of my allies in the militia in a kangaroo show trial and banished me." He sniffed.

"Tell me, Graham Miller, do the bridges still connect the mainland to Whidbey Island? I haven't been up that way since before the world fell." He gestured to his wire-thin raiders. "We've been down here, trying to scratch out a living in Seattle. Well, I should say, *they* have. I only got here a couple of years ago, myself."

Miller nodded vigorously. "Yes, the bridges are both still up."

"*Good*. Thank you for your service, Graham Miller. It's a shame we can't keep you around, too many mouths to feed as it is." He spun Miller around so he could look out over the endless miles of urban ruin. Hazy smoke hung over the city, and skeletal ruins clawed up to the sky like bony concrete fingers from an undead corpse. "When you meet the devil, you tell that overachiever that Stephen Gaunt says he's made his point, and he can bloody well quit showing off."

Gaunt shoved him back out over open air and threw the ratchet clear of the pulley's locking teeth. Miller's scream dopplered away, only to be replaced by the whizzing of the cable as it unwound faster and faster. The cable *thrummed* when it snapped taut, but only for a moment. Gaunt looked down over the edge of the observation deck and wrinkled his nose.

"I could have *sworn* that cable was five hundred feet! That looks more like…four-ninety. Oh well. Tell you what boys, get down there, untie his legs, and collect that mess in a tarp or something. We'll have one last Pike Place barbecue tonight, then *everyone* marches north to Mount Vernon."

* * * * *

Chapter Seven

Once upon a time, Master Sergeant Marcus Eriksen had been a medieval reenactor. His job had been in real estate, but the flexibility of a realtor's schedule allowed him to carve out time for weekends away where he'd bash fellow "knights" with rattan swords and spears. He was a young, charismatic salesman who also made a decent living forging and selling real blades to anyone at an event. From a personal point of view, the worst part of the whole "end of the civilized world" thing had been missing out on Pennsic 100, which had been set for July of 2071.

Aside from missing the greatest two-week party of the century, the nuclear exchange hadn't affected him *that* much. His hometown of Anacortes was untouched by the bombs; it was the secondary and tertiary effects that really fucked things up. Nobody was buying real estate anymore. If someone wanted a patch of dirt, they took it—no mortgages, no loans, no buyers, no sellers, and worst of all, no commissions. No banks, for that matter. He found himself utterly without work, so he did what he had to, to survive. For the first month, survival involved living aboard his cabin cruiser, the *Always Be Closing*, frying up whatever fish got hooked on his line overnight, and trading the rest to his friends nearby.

Then the Teledyne Specialists arrived in Anacortes and explained that, despite the end of the world, they were still in charge. More importantly, they were looking for people with a very particular set of skills, skills that most people would have considered hobbies at best. Skills like "bashing people with swords and spears" and "hand forging blades." He took pride in the fact that *he'd* taught the daimyo how to work a forge, and he could best Samurai Grimstaadt one time in three, *despite* the Specialist's enhancements. He'd even met a handful of Specialists who'd attended Pennsic; the umpires and referees had made an exclusive combat class just for them. It was small, it was elite, and it was a *huge* draw.

When they'd formalized the Komainu, Marcus was their go-to for teaching blacksmithing. He was part of the original cadre and received promotion after promotion as the Komainu grew until he was finally granted the title of Master Sergeant. Like a Laurel in the Society, a Master Sergeant was someone recognized for their skill at an essential trade, in his case, working the forge, making weapons of war. Despite the years he'd spent working and teaching the craft, his true love was, to be honest, bashing people with swords and spears. Thus, he'd requested that he rotate back onto "the line," and they'd reluctantly agreed. He had more time in than any of the platoon commanders, so they'd made him boss of platoon Fox Two Five, and Fox Two Five guarded the eastern land approach to Fidalgo and Whidbey Islands.

The *horde* marching up Highway 20 suggested he'd get to bash more people with swords and spears before the day was out. The sheer size of it also suggested it would be the last bashing he'd ever get to do. He'd only seen that many people all together at once at Pennsic. Easily hundreds, maybe a thousand? So many, he couldn't begin to count.

Their "fortifications" at the crest of the Swinomish Channel Bridge were laughable in the face of that many raiders; they were going to be overrun, swept aside by the tide of invading humanity. He lifted his binoculars and scanned the leading edge of the mass of humanity. They were dirty, filthy even. Most of the ones he could see were armed with little more than clubs and sharpened sticks to use as spears and wore little better than tattered rags. His observation post's altitude let him look deeper into the formation, and much further back, he saw trash-can shields, rough-looking blades, hammered from salvage, and even some rudimentary armor. They were unkempt and bearded, with scraggly hair. He didn't see a single woman among them.

"Put up the flare," he ordered. He had two lances with him on the bridge. The other four were scattered across three other OPs along their border; he'd have to send runners to collect them. Lance Corporal Mario DiPaulo didn't delay; he reached for the old boating flaregun, slipped in one of their red flares, and fired it straight up.

"Good. Mario, your lance needs to grab their rucks and shag ass. Send pairs to bring in the other OPs and get the rest of the platoon back here on the main drag. I want one lance every two hundred meters. As soon as that mob is in range, we're going to loft half the arrows we have, torch the barricades, and run. Each lance dumps half their arrows, then runs to the end of the line. Yes, that'll be roughly a klick at a dead sprint, uphill, but either we embrace the suck, or we die. We make a fighting withdrawal to Sharpes' Corner and see if we can't draw them north to Anacortes."

"Roger that, Master Sergeant," DiPaulo said. He turned to his lance, gave them their orders, and took off at a dead run.

"What are you thinking, Master Sergeant?" Lance Corporal Karisa Kesting asked.

"I'm thinking we have to buy the rest of the Komainu enough time to lock down the bridges at Deception Pass," Eriksen replied. "If they get into the forests there, we're utterly fucked."

"About what I thought," she admitted. A flare blossomed to the northwest, white this time. She looked relieved, a little. The white flares were to rebroadcast the distress signal without confusing it with the original. Another popped far to the south over Dugalla Park.

"Having said that...help is on the way. We don't have to kill *all* the bastards, we just have to slow them down as much as possible. And that we can manage just fine."

* * *

Rikimaru rode the waves as the *Seas the Day* bobbed up and down, keeping his binoculars steadily fixed on the ancient ferry terminal. The tide was changing which was always an exciting time to be on the water, as the currents flowed from "out" to "in," but he paid them no mind. He'd acquired sea legs a long, long time ago, and now they merely made reconnaissance slightly more awkward. He had distant, but decent, seats to watch a beating in progress. One of the scrawny Victorian survivors was on his back, clutching his hands to his head, trying to protect his face. A much larger man in a torn, red hoodie laid into him. He kicked the skinny one in the ribs and head as everyone watched, and no one intervened. The larger man straddled the smaller, took hold of both forearms, and bashed the back of his head into the deck. He hoisted the man up—he was strong enough to heave him into the air—and carried him to the railing.

They were on top of the sixth deck up, ninety feet over the waterline below. Arms and legs flailed as the larger man tossed the smaller one overboard and he hit the water with a great splash. When the smaller man resurfaced, alive and somewhat intact, Rikimaru raised the glasses again. The brute in the red sweatshirt made a show of dusting his hands off, then rejoined a group of similarly dressed toughs. A smaller man in a black leather jacket fist-bumped him and passed him a bottle.

Rikimaru jotted down the last of his notes and addressed Derek, who'd been sitting next to him, reading over his shoulder and squinting to try to make out the details Rikimaru had observed.

"At Dan's leisure, get us home to Whidbey. It's going to be dark by the time we get home unless we leave now."

"Aye, Daimyo." Frost scampered off to help Dan prepare for sailing home. Rikimaru joined Ayame, Akuma, and Kael below. Each had noted their observations independently and then compared notes to see what was the same and what they'd missed. "I counted twenty-two on the *Spirit*," Akuma said, "and three dogs. Six light sails are moored off to the east side, each with dinghies tied up alongside. They look like the only functional fishing boats in the area. They're sheltered from the weather there, but we could almost certainly use Goudge and Coal islands as cover to approach from the east, scramble up the hillside, and torch them from land with fire arrows, or steal them."

"You haven't been out this way before." Ayame shook her head. "One of the largest marinas at the north end of the peninsula is tucked in behind Goudge. Hundreds of slips, hundreds of boats. One jetty alone probably berths sixty of them."

"Why haven't they been sailing them then?" Akuma asked.

"Because they don't know how to launch a sailboat without a motor," Rikimaru replied. "And the cabin cruisers' fuel went bad about the time you were…four. It would take some major industry to produce enough high-proof alcohol to run those engines, and marine motors drink fuel by the gallon."

"Anything to add?" Kael asked. He handed over the scratch pad with their consolidated notes, and Rikimaru scanned it.

"The one in the ripped red hoodie is the enforcer, not the boss," he said and summarized what he'd witnessed. "If we're going to come back here, we can cow most of them by taking out the guy in the black jacket, and the redshirt. With the brains and the brawn gone, you're in charge just like that. Otherwise, it looks good."

"Have you given any more thought to your training program?" Kael asked Akuma.

"Task-specific PT," the junior samurai replied and flipped to a different part of his notebook. It was covered with notes and diagrams and went on for several pages with information on rank structure, promotional criteria, pay, and so on. "I have the advantage of working with pre-trained recruits, thank *you*. I'm going to be one of the Komainu's first construction customers. I want an obstacle course set up at the south end of Blind Bay on Shaw. That will get us out of Orcas' western hills and everyone's hair. We'll train on Shaw since there's hardly anyone on the island and it's central. Once it's up and running, we'll run the obstacle course every morning—climb up and down cargo nets and ladders, walk along beams. We'll get them used to being off-balance and being able to run around on a ship without going in the drink. We'll swim twice a day, in armor, across Blind Bay. It's a bit more than half a mile across, and they need to learn to trust the armor to keep them afloat. We'll give them dummies to bash and stab and attack. We'll conduct regular checks of their weapons for rust, which is going to be a major issue since we have precious little stainless steel. And we'll work a lot at night. I'll want to use your Komainu as training opposition force, once we're up to speed on cutting-out expeditions. Commandeering a harbor full of boats is an art, not a science, and since we aren't making new boats, the fewer we burn, the better."

"Sounds reasonable," Kael agreed. "I hope you aren't going to pillage my NCO cadre *too* heavily."

"Ideally, once the catfish-god marines have addressed the issue of raiders, your NCOs will be out of a job." Ayame grinned. "A good offense makes—"

"*RICK!*" Dan Nobunaga shouted down into the hold. "*GET UP HERE!*"

The other three chased Rikimaru out onto the deck. They'd been making good time during the briefing and were approaching the channel between Orcas and Shaw Island. The skyline around them was filling with paraflares, and one glowed red to the southeast on the far side of Shaw. Rikimaru calculated their heading and narrowed his eyes. *Deception Pass.*

"You said your marines-in-training are in the western Orcas hills?"

"*Hai.*"

"Dan, swing us into Deer Harbor."

"Aye, aye, Rick," their captain replied, and Rikimaru turned back to his junior-most samurai.

"Akuma, rally all the Komainu not already dispatched to the smaller islands and get them aboard ship. Send them on as soon as the boat's full; don't wait to set off as a group. Try to flank them at Bowman Bay."

"By your orders," Akuma replied. The paraflares were an "oh shit" advisory of a major threat, and that it was coming from Whidbey or Fidalgo Island was capital-B Bad. Without knowing the nature of the threat, Rikimaru had to be unfortunately vague and trust Akuma to expand intelligently on his orders. Dan swept their sailboat across the dock, and Akuma leapt clear and landed unsteadily on the dock. Dan peeled back into open water, with Akuma already shouting orders to the harbor's Komainu detachment. When they returned to the channel, Derek already had the jib sail up and was making fast everything on the deck. There was a stiff breeze, and the boat began to heel in the water.

"If you could all put on your PFDs," Dan said. "I'm hoping we can get up to twenty knots, and we'll be near forty degrees to the vertical when we do. It'll start to get a bit dicey."

* * *

The waiting was probably the worst part. Any significant fighting was a long, drawn-out process—Marcus had heard once that much of soldiering was long periods of boredom followed by short periods of intense battle. (Or, "activity," or "terror," depending on how one felt about the whole thing.) He did his best to bury his fear deep. *Never let them see you sweat,* they said in leadership school.

"They—they've passed Tom-n-Jerry's; that's the five-hundred-meter marker," Private McPhee said. His skin was pale, and his eyes were wide.

"Excellent," Eriksen said. "How's the fire coming?"

"Ready," McPhee replied. He stoked the barrel full of desiccated tree limbs again, sending sparks flying above the flames blazing out of the old drum.

"Good."

Eriksen waited another thirty seconds, then nocked an arrow to his longbow and flexed his broad shoulders, which had been toughened by years of hammering in his forge. He pointed his bow high, almost forty degrees to the horizontal, and when his fingers brushed the anchor point on his cheek, he loosed it. The incendiary arrow flew away on a near parabolic arc, and he lost sight of it for a moment. Three and a half football fields away, the shaft lanced out of the sky and struck one of the horde. His fellows' responses were clearly audible, even at that range, and the front ranks broke into a jog.

"I'd say that'll do. On my mark, troops!"

He fitted another arrow, lowered his angle slightly, and drew.

"Loose!"

The seven arrows flew, but this time, he couldn't track their flight. Shooting so few seemed pathetic in the face of so many raiders, but it wasn't like they were saving the arrows for anything else.

"Nock! Draw! Loose!"

"Nock! Draw! Loose!"

By the time the raiders were halfway up the long slope of the bridge, they'd slowed, clearly running out of steam. Marcus supposed these brigands probably hadn't had much opportunity for something like cardio.

He didn't know where the raiders were coming from or how far they'd marched, but if they were from nearby, Fox Two-Five's patrols should have spotted them long before now—a horde like that didn't just spring fully formed from nothing.

By the time they reached two hundred meters' distance, Eriksen only had three arrows left. He nodded at McPhee. The young private tipped the burn barrel over with a branch, sending flaming debris and sparks flying. McPhee rolled the barrel the short distance to their barricade and knocked more of the flaming deadfall free of the can.

"Nock! Draw! Loose!"

The raiders reached fifty meters, and Eriksen fired his last arrow, this one nearly level with the asphalt. It took one of the first, fastest raiders in the throat, and he collapsed, gurgling.

Teach you to be first in line, asshole.

"Fall back!" Eriksen bellowed, and all seven of the Komainu Guardians turned and fled. Two hundred meters wasn't all that far away. They weren't above water any longer, but they were still near the crest of the bridge. They reached Lance Corporal DiPaulo's reconstituted lance, and Eriksen ordered Kesting to keep going. He'd be damned if he was going to keep running and leave his troops behind.

"Nock! Draw!" Eriksen ordered, and another six archers pre-pared to fire. "Loose!"

The flaming barricade had, indeed, slowed the raiders, but the flames weren't nearly widespread enough to stop them. A few had managed to get around it somehow, and they used hand weapons to knock the flaming barrel over the edge of the bridge. It hit the chan-nel below, sizzled, and sank. That let them clear more of the barri-cade, and although the horde was slowed, they weren't stopped.

"Loose!"

* * *

Lance Corporal DiPaulo cheered when Eriksen finally caught up. For more than two kilometers, his troops had leapfrogged back through each other. Six lances of six, with Eriksen as their commander, meant thirty-seven Komainu had fired twenty arrows each. More than seven hundred arrows had been loosed at the mob. *Some* of them had to have hit.

Eriksen smiled. "Now, all we have to do is run another three klicks to Sharpes', keep them from falling *too* far behind, and get them to chase us down to the waterfront instead of going after the bridges."

"Easy, peasy." DiPaulo was struggling to catch his breath after his two one-kilometer jogs between firing lines.

"That's what I want to hear. We're leaving them behind, though. We need to cut the pace. Scout-pace and conserve your strength! We're not into the woods yet."

For a hundred paces, they marched at an easy, regular pace they could maintain, *had* maintained, for hours. After one hundred paces, Eriksen broke into a jog, and the rest of his platoon followed his lead. The horde's vanguard was still in sight and had flowed out to fill the wide-open, four-lane highway. A hundred paces later, he slowed to a brisk walk again. They continued alternating between marching and jogging for fifteen minutes, eating up another two and a half kilometers.

"I don't think they *have* ranged weapons," DiPaulo said when they again fell back into their more-leisurely marching pace. "They would have opened fire before now, wouldn't they?"

"I didn't see any," Eriksen said. "But assumption is the mother of all fuckups. We need to keep them in sight, so they see us, but we can't let them get any closer. Tighten up!" Eriksen ordered loudly. A couple stragglers jogged to catch up, sucking wind hard, and he winced internally. He went to the head of his platoon and began walking backward to address them face-to-face so he could look them in their eyes. "Our job, right now, is to delay as much as we can. We're going to try to sucker them into heading north toward what used to be Anacortes. *If you fall behind, we can not wait for you.* The lives of everyone south of the pass depend on our buying them as much time as we humanly can. *Do not—let them—catch you.*"

They reached the roundabout at Sharpe's Corner a few minutes later, and Eriksen ordered them to take a breather, drop their rucks, stretch, and hydrate. He pulled his binos out and scanned the horde's vanguard. One of the filthy creatures caught sight of him, flipped him off, and drew a thumb across his throat. The raider tapped another one, pointed, and a small group of them broke into a jog. He counted five. "Grab your packs, everyone," the Master Sergeant ordered, then looked at the copse of woods on the north side of the highway. The trees were thick, and although the copse was relatively small, the invaders couldn't tell that from their position. He reconsidered a moment and lifted the binos again. The five invaders racing ahead of the pack were armed with clubs.

"Change of plans, Guardians. I'm going to mime an argument with Lance Corporal DiPaulo. Everyone will run into the woods, "abandoning" me. When they get close, you cut them off, and we take them out. That ought to goad the rest into chasing us north."

To his credit, DiPaulo thought for a moment and then shoved Eriksen. Eriksen went with it and pushed him right back. DiPaulo turned and fled into the woods, followed by the rest of the platoon. Eriksen affected the defeated, abandoned soldier and dumped his ruck at the center of the roundabout. He drew his langseax from his harness. It was a simple blade, one of the first he'd made since the world fell, but he'd taken particular care with it, and they'd been through a lot together. He'd forge welded several layers of leaf spring steel together, drawn it out into a long rectangle, and sharpened one side until he could shave arm hair with it. The hilt was antler, originally well-textured for gripping, but worn smooth with two decades of use.

"Your buddies leave you all alone?" one rasped when he got close enough to talk.

"I told them to go on," he replied evenly. "I was slowing them down."

"Heh." One chuckled, but then he froze. He was close enough to the roundabout to see that the forest didn't continue—it was just a nub of land barely two hundred meters wide.

"Lucky for him, we're not very good listeners," Kesting said behind them as she strode from the bush, sword in hand.

"None of us are," DiPaulo chimed in at her side. The raiders' faces fell when they realized the men and women with swords had suckered them; they held little more than sticks. Eriksen forced the issue, unwilling to waste more time, by closing with all five bandits. He held his blade high, but across his body, to hide his reach. When he was close enough, he slashed down, aiming for one raider's hand and club. His prey had little choice but to attempt to deflect the blow, which was precisely what he wanted. As the club came up, his blade knocked it down, and he reversed his slash, opening the raider's throat in a welter of spray. Kesting and DiPaulo rushed them from behind, and the rest of the platoon followed and hacked the invaders down in seconds.

"Rucks! Move!"

Their ambush had undoubtedly caught the attention of the foremost members of the horde, who broke into a run, and Fox Two Five did likewise. They loped north along the highway in a burst of speed but hadn't even gone half a klick before McPhee called out from the back of the pack.

"Master Sergeant? They aren't chasing us anymore!"

"FUCK!" Eriksen snarled and turned. The road had curved north, but it was all open water to their right, and from their vantage point, they could clearly see the roundabout and copse of trees. Twenty or thirty of the raiders had broken off from the main group to give chase, but the rest of the host, steadily marched on, turning south toward Deception Pass.

"Who among you is the fastest runner?"

He already knew the answer as he dug out his paper map of the region.

"I am, Master Sergeant," Kesting said, without hesitation.

"I should have sent you south from the roundabout instead of playing bait, dammit. It's *another* nine klicks to the bridges. I need you to run your absolute best 10K, overland, and get to the bridges as fast as you can. Take one of the bicycles, get down to the barracks, and give them a full update. They *have* to know what's coming, or they're going to get overrun."

She looked like she wanted to protest, and Eriksen understood. She was a good leader, slated for promotion as soon as a spot opened, and she wouldn't want to leave her lance behind. But she also knew this was more important, and her troops would slow her down.

"Understood. Good hunting, Master Sergeant." Kesting cut left, scrambled down the ditch, up the far side, and opened up her stride, disappearing into the woods beyond.

"And we're going to have to follow," he said to the rest. "Bounding ambushes, Guardians. Fighting withdrawal. When we find a decent spot to hammer a few, we'll peel a half lance away to slow up our pursuers. Everyone have rope?"

Rope was an essential item for log-based construction, and the hemp farms on San Juan made top-quality ropes, given the circumstances. Standing orders were that every Komainu carry several lengths of the stuff in their rucks, 'just in case.'

"Good. We can lay hasty tripwires as we go and pounce when they fall. Let's move."

* * *

Lance Corporal Karisa Kesting's heart pounded in her chest. She didn't know exactly how long it had been since she'd abandoned—no, *raced ahead*—of Fox Two Five, but it had to be forty minutes or more. She'd followed the old powerlines south along the edge of Mount Erie, trying to minimize her elevation changes. She vaulted fences or kicked them over where the boards were rotten and disintegrating. She'd burst from the treeline on the north side of Lake Campbell, which helped her orient herself immensely. Rather than backtrack to where the highway went south past the eastern edge of the small freshwater lake, she'd taken advantage of the decent side road to really open up. Then it was south again, back into the trees and scrabbling up steep embankments across from Roger Bluff, before she vaulted one last fence into the old Wolfermann place. That was good. Roughly knowing "south" was one thing. Landmarks were entirely different. Now she knew exactly where she was—almost to the pass.

When she emerged onto the cracked old highway, there was no sign or sound of the raider horde. She summoned one last burst of speed and pounded up the cracked pavement until the road opened up to show just how much altitude she'd gained since leaving Two Five behind.

The first classes of Komainu had lined the center of the two-lane bridge with wrecked automobiles ages ago. They'd dragged hundreds of cars made useless by EMP or low-tech but out of fuel, into place. They stripped the vehicles for parts and spiked their tires. The wrecks were parked hedgehog style, fortifying the bridge against any foot traffic. It dramatically limited the amount of space one had to walk, run, or ride, and the angle of the cars meant defenders could stand with their backs to a vehicle. That made any attackers vulnerable since they had nothing behind them but a thin railing and a hundred-fifty-foot fall to frigid ocean or jagged rock.

She raced down the west side of the bridge, waving to the two-troop Komainu detachment that held Pass Island. "Raiders!" she gasped when she reached them. She was in luck—sort of—she'd done Basic with Christoph, and she recognized him immediately, although she didn't particularly care for him. "A ho-horde of them, hundreds, easy, maybe a thousand or more. Marching this way. We put up…a flare."

"We saw it," Christoph said. "Are you sure, though? *Hundreds?*"

"*I am fucking well sure, Private,*" she snarled. Christoph had always had a chip on his shoulder; it drove Karisa nuts. She'd noticed it as far back as Basic. If she'd passed along information or orders, or any other woman did likewise, he questioned them, always seeking "clarification" from higher. If it came from a man, though, it was 'yes sir, no sir, three bags full sir.' That she was a Lance Corporal while he remained a Private probably chafed him, but fuck him. For now, all he had to do was deliver the message. "Two Five just fought a two-kilometer fighting withdrawal, *burned* the barricades behind us to slow them further, and tried to sucker them north. It didn't work. I have no idea if my platoon is alive right now; they were being chased by a secondary force that broke off from the rest. Now, either you get on that bicycle, race downhill, and bring backup, or you can wait here for the raiders to show up while *I* get help."

"Okay!" Christoph threw up his hands. "Okay, I'm going."

Of course you are. You aren't about to stick around, not with an invading force bearing down on us.

He took the old pedal bike and sped away. Hopefully, he wouldn't blow a tire on the way down and eat asphalt. On the one hand, that would be a Very Bad Thing. On the other hand, she would pay a month's wages to see it happen.

"Do you, uh, want some water, Lance Corporal?" the other Komainu troop asked. The younger girl, who wore a single chevron, offered her a canteen, and Karisa drank from it deeply.

"Thanks...?"

"Medici. Private Sabrina Medici."

"Much obliged, Sabrina Medici. How long have you been on this bridge?"

"Uh, our shift started at noon, so..."

"I mean, how long have you been posted to Fox Two Three?"

"Oh, this is only my second week." She blushed. "I just graduated from Fort Casey in the last class. I got trained as a weaver, and I'm hoping the folks at Crystal Hectares will hire me once I'm done here."

"I see. Look, Sabrina, this is a no-fucking-shit emergency; you understand that, right? There are hundreds of raider scumbags marching this way right now. You and I and *maybe* the remnants of my platoon are the only ones between them and everyone on Whidbey." Karisa rummaged around in her pack, pulled out her binoculars, raised them to her eyes, and looked out to sea.

"When you put it that way, it sounds like Christoph was the smart one."

"Not at all. For example, I know for a fact that Christoph sucks at semaphore. Do you know your semaphore?"

"Absolutely! I'm good with languages—semaphore, morse, even braille."

"Good. Grab your flags because that's the *Seas the Day* down there!"

"Who?"

"Daimyo Hanzo's boat! We have to get their attention!"

Medici hurriedly grabbed two large Teledyne flags. The ultramarine blue had faded over the years, but the chrome shield and stylized, split "T" were still clearly visible. She waved the flags back and forth over her head while Karisa watched through her binos. When she had the daimyo's attention, Karisa dictated.

"Raider—that's 'R D R,' XL, Mainland Location 2."

Medici did as ordered. Rikimaru repeated back the letters he received, and through her binos, Karisa saw him grab a duffel bag and strap his katana to it.

Oh. Right.

"He got the message!" Karisa said, and as young Private Medici put her flags away, Karisa muttered to herself. "I can't believe we're going to use this thing…"

There was a bicycle, and there was a winch. It was the sketchiest winch Karisa had ever seen, but then again, it was one of the *only* winches she'd ever seen. The bicycle was set in a frame, and the rear sprocket was used to turn the crank. The winch raised and lowered a hardy rope, almost two hundred feet long, that ended in a kevlar five-point harness. That harness was one of the only ones in the entire San Juan Island chain. A weight hung from it to ensure it would unwind to the maximum length of the rope and not just flutter in the breeze. The rope went from a storage barrel, through a fail-safe channel that prevented the rope from slipping backward, through a block and tackle that reduced the difficulty of winching up any appreciable weight, and then to the harness.

It was insane. She didn't know of anyone who'd actually used it. But fortune favored the prepared, and the daimyo had insisted that, given the vital nature of the bridge as *the* chokepoint protecting Whidbey Island, there had to be some quick way to get from sea level to bridge top. "Here goes," Karisa said, and she unlatched the rope from the holdfast and began unspooling it over the side of the bridge.

"Is he…is he going to *climb* it?" Sabrina asked.

"No," Karisa said. "I'm going to get on that thing and *pedal*. Christoph should have already briefed you on how this thing works."

"He…doesn't really talk much," Medici said. "He's kind of an asshole." Karisa laughed and nodded her head.

"Didn't take you long to figure that one out, huh? Look, assholes like him are around. Living well and being successful is the greatest revenge against dickheads like that. That he won't be here to brief the daimyo will chap his ass, but you saw how quickly he jumped at the chance to get out of here, huh?"

"Yeah," Medici agreed.

"Let's just say, not everyone bought into the whole mystical lion-dog guardian thing. He's just treading water until he can get out. His folks have rice paddies on San Juan, and he'll be off to play rice merchant soon, assuming we survive."

Karisa unwound enough rope that the weight of it alone pulled it down. There was a breeze, so the rope swayed, despite the weight at the end, but the boat's captain seemed to know what he was doing and brought the ship into irons, so the wind didn't catch the sail. Daimyo Hanzo caught the rope with a hooked pole from the bow of the ship. It took him a minute to secure the harness around his limbs and waist, then Karisa felt two sharp tugs on the rope, and she started pedaling. She had to use the bike's highest gear—Lord Hanzo certainly didn't *look* heavy, but he was a long way down. The ache in her legs from the afternoon's running made her weak, but unlike her mad dash across Fidalgo Island, she could fall into a steady piston-pumping rhythm. *Much* better.

"He's almost to the underside of the bridge!" Medici warned her, and Karisa slowed her pace somewhat. Another minute of pedaling, and the shogun's top warrior clambered onto the bridge deck, hauling a black hockey bag behind him. He took in the two Komainu before him and nodded to the Lance Corporal.

"Well done, Karisa. Now, let's never do that again."

Karisa Kesting didn't know the daimyo knew her by name, and she was a bit taken aback. "I'm good with that, Daimyo Hanzo."

Rikimaru set down his duffel, and Karisa updated him. He raised his eyebrows at her description of the horde but didn't challenge her report. "Christoph rode down to the base to bring up the Komainu," she finished. "Marcus' platoon went north to try to draw them away to Anacortes, but the raiders just sent a chase force. The main group is still on its way here."

"They're *chasing* a platoon?" he repeated, and Karisa nodded in confirmation.

"Uh huh. There's a *lot* of them."

* * * * *

Chapter Eight

Breaking contact was the hardest part of the whole clusterfuck. Sure, "no plan survives contact with the enemy," but there's Murphy's Laws of Combat and then there are disasters.

Master Sergeant Marcus Eriksen was in a fucking *disaster*.

His troops were running on empty. The first three ambushes they'd sprung had worked well—they were following Karisa's trail, more or less, including a few of the thick board fences she'd kicked through, rather than climbed over. A short length of rope, strung at shin height, with some foliage or vines draped over it, was enough to trip up the first raider or two through a gap in a fence, then his guardians would leap from cover and hack into the raiders with their choppers. Then, it was back to running again.

He should have known they'd catch on. He'd let them get into his decision cycle, and on the fourth ambush, the raiders flanked his troops. They'd brained McPhee before anyone realized what was happening, and then they were into it. At last count, his thirty-six troops were down to twenty-six—they simply couldn't maintain the pace.

He had a last, desperate 'out,' and had worked out the details with his three remaining lance corporals on the move. The dusty parking lot on Pass Lake was the hiking trailhead. With water on one side and steep hill on the other, the trail was the only way through. Shoulder to shoulder, Marcus, DiPaulo, and five more of his platoon

109

held the line. Everyone behind them was hastily making Swiss harnesses out of their ropes, tying each other in at the waist, legs, and shoulders, and hiding their rucks in the bush. If they lived through this, they could come back for them. If not? Well, it wouldn't be their problem.

The raiders chasing them slowed the moment they saw the wall of Komainu and their blades. They didn't have blades. The largest among them shouldered the others aside. "I'm going to rip off your head and shit down your neck, Islander," he snarled.

Eriksen snorted. "Really? That's your go-to? Get over yourself, Duke Nukem."

The raider frowned for an instant, his confusion evident, but then he decided he didn't care and raced forward, leaving the rest of his warband behind.

"Hold," Eriksen warned. The bigger man roared and closed half the distance in a few long strides.

"Hold!" Eriksen urged them again. This asshole was *big*, the biggest raider they'd seen yet. He raised his club—a tree branch, really, as big around as his biceps, to smash the Komainu line, and Eriksen darted forward, diving below the tree trunk and slashing low. Eriksen's langseax bit deep into the brute's unprotected shins, and his roar turned to a scream of agony. His legs collapsed, and he fell heavily to the ground, where DiPaulo brought his blade down across the back of the big guy's neck. The lance corporal and others advanced, staying tight with their master sergeant.

"Who's next?" Eriksen growled at the raiders, and they retreated a few feet, unwilling to face the sword line. Someone tapped DiPaulo's shoulder, and he came off the line to prepare his harness. That left only Eriksen, and someone tapped him a moment later.

"Do you really think this will work?" DiPaulo asked in a low voice so only Eriksen could hear.

"I think this is the only chance we've got, and some chance is better than none," he replied. He wrapped the rope around his waist and tied it twice at his belt buckle. He put the trailing ends between his legs, then hiked them up so they were snug at his groin and up his backside to his kidneys, where DiPaulo helped tuck them around the waist loop. He squatted, adjusted the rope so it wouldn't cripple him if he moved wrong, and tightened the rope ends until he could tie them in a proper square knot to stop it from loosening. The trailing ends crossed between his shoulder blades and then back down to the knots on each hip, completing his Swiss seat.

DiPaulo checked him over, and he checked the junior NCO's. Movement beyond DiPaulo caught his attention—he'd been so busy tying in, he'd let security lapse. The raider force that had been marching down the highway had finally caught up and were barely two hundred meters distant.

"God *damn* it," he cursed. "FOX TWO FIVE! MOVE NOW!"

The Komainu holding the line against the smaller warband about-faced, bolted across the parking lot, then across the highway, and followed DiPaulo up into the trees. The raiders had clearly been playing for time, and now that their fellows had caught up, the chase was on again. Marcus' lungs burned, and his legs ached as he and the rest of his platoon scrambled up the embankment, dashed from tree to tree, and steadily gained altitude as they raced south. It was dark in the trees—the sun was setting—and Marcus bashed his forehead on an unseen branch. He cursed but kept going. One of the new privates was lagging behind, and despite his earlier admonishments,

Eriksen slowed to buy the young trooper some time. He'd lost too many young men and women today, and that shit was going to *stop*.

He angled wide and slowed his pace a bit, letting the fastest raider close on the hapless private. There was a slight clearing ahead, and the moment they entered it, Eriksen sped up to catch the raider from behind. One savage chop at the runner's calf hamstrung him, and that was enough. Eriksen caught sight of more shadows racing through the trees. *None of them stopped for their wounded comrade*, he noted. It did seem they were running ragged though; there were fewer of the raiders, and Fox Two Five was leaving them behind.

Finally.

The shadows thinned, and they were at the forest's edge. They weren't going to just break contact, they were going to break legs. The foremost runners in the platoon had already looped their ropes around stout pine trunks, then DiPaulo emerged from a bush, rope in hand.

"After you, Master Sergeant," the Lance Corporal said, and clipped the rope and one of their precious carabiners through the rear of Eriksen's harness. Marcus began to object, but DiPaulo stopped him. "You've led us this far, but the troops need to know this bit of insanity works. If you fall to your doom…we'll make a valiant last stand here," he said with a mischievous grin. He knew it would work…

*One small step for a man…*Marcus thought and threw himself into open air. The rope fed through his biner, cinching down on itself and acting as a brake until his feet touched the asphalt fifty feet below. He rolled to absorb the impact, then rose to his feet and shrugged out of his harness. The biner was *hot.* Lance Corporal Bourbon followed him down and then more of his platoon erupted from the trees on more ropes. *One catastrophic fall for the raider vanguard.*

A single figure approached from the bridge's edge. Marcus had a hard time making out the details in the dying light; the trees were already casting stark shadows. He wore black pants, a black shirt, and white armor strapped to his shins, thighs, waist, chest, shoulders, and arms. His long, black hair was tied up in a samurai topknot, and a long, curved sword rode on one hip.

"Master Sergeant Eriksen," Daimyo Hanzo said in greeting. He helped DiPaulo remove his harness, then untied a private who'd gotten stuck. "How good of you to drop in."

"Two minutes, maybe three," Marcus wheezed. "Hundreds, easy." The rest of his platoon followed him down, DiPaulo being the last. They yanked the ropes down behind them, leaving nothing for the war party to find.

"Well done, Master Sergeant," Rikimaru said quietly, then pointed to the island that joined the two bridges. "Go! Form up on Pass Island, pike hedge both sides of the foot path, and get the archers ready to support." Marcus was almost exhausted, but Hanzo caught his sleeve. "You know about the final protective fire, right?"

"Yes, Daimyo."

"Get Karisa to check below the bridge and confirm everything's sited correctly."

* * *

Rikimaru heard them before he saw them. The raiders who'd chased after Fox Two Five erupted from the treeline, and their howls of rage turned to whoops of terror mid-air. They leaped without looking, and since there were no ropes, they fell to the asphalt highway below with a sickening *crunch*. Rikimaru ended their suffering with the tip of his katana. He glared at those above him who'd lagged far enough behind that they had time to realize something was wrong. They retreated from the precipice and followed the cliff face until it became an easily-navigated embankment.

The daimyo was a supremely patient man, and it bothered him not a bit to wait, surrounded by the broken, bleeding bodies of the enemy. When the raiders emerged around the distant corner of the highway, he eased into a guarded stance, his left hand holding his scabbard, his right hand on the hilt. They were an undisciplined mob. They didn't work well together, coordinate their attacks, or even arrive at the same time. The first carried a stout length of wood with a crude axe head made from a rotary sawblade. Rikimaru let him approach, unperturbed, until the last moment. In a flash, he stepped aside and drew his katana in a single smooth motion that took the raider's arm off at the elbow. The bodged-together axe tumbled and bashed the raider in the leg, and he collapsed, screaming, clutching his ruined stump. Rikimaru darted between the offending raiders in a lethal dance, deflecting attacks and carving a swath through the thugs, leaving nothing but dead and dying bodies behind him.

The last stopped short, having taken stock of the remnants of his former associates. He hefted an ancient, spiked baseball bat that still read, under all the bent nails and organic matter, 'Louisville Slugger.'

This half-savage thug probably doesn't even know what Louisville was.

He did, however, have something approximating a batter's stance, as though he wanted to tee up Rikimaru's head and swing for the bleachers. The flaw in his plan became clear when Rikimaru's katana slashed into his lead leg, parting meat from bone, without his having realized he was in melee range. He collapsed, and Rikimaru drove the chisel tip of his katana into the man's heart to finish him quickly. Bloody pieces of a dozen men littered the road, and the daimyo's snow white armor dripped red blood so dark it looked black.

* * *

"I have a new appreciation for your readiness drills," Ayame said. Dan had practically beached the *Seas the Day* at the airbase, and the two were now racing to catch up. The Homeguard remained in place, surrounding the inn with the shogun inside; Sergeant Major Bridgwater had roused his entire force, tripling the guard, and had had the foresight to pack the samurai's weapons and armor for them. The rest of the Komainu stationed at the base, one full company of infantry armed with bows, spears, and swords, were scout-pacing their way along the beachfront on their way to Highway 20, where they'd begin their ascent to the Deception Pass bridges, almost two hundred feet above sea level. Despite their armor and weapons, the Specialist's blistering pace meant they were about to pass the mid-point in the column.

"I'm rather pleased," Mikael agreed. "It *is* rather impressive, isn't it?"

They slowed a couple hundred yards later, having caught up with Fox Company command.

"Captain Hayes," Mikael greeted the OIC. "Your initiative is appreciated."

"Any idea what we're looking at, sir? Our messenger from the bridge wasn't terribly helpful."

"Raiders coming west along Highway 20. The scouts from the bridge signaled us with semaphore: 'Extra Large, but not enough specifics.' Rikimaru is already up there. We're going to catch up, but the faster you can get the troops into position, the better."

"Understood, Samurai. We'll get there soonest." The company commander turned to platoon Fox One One's commander. "Double time, pass the word."

"Sir," the lieutenant replied, but Mikael and Ayame were already racing ahead.

Feels good *to stretch the legs and cut loose,* Mikael thought. The shogun's "pragmatic pacifism" had made them strictly defensive, and honestly, Mikael missed it. He'd been enhanced for combat against the worst JalCom and Obsidian could throw at them, but the Shogunate's Komainu hadn't had a decent scrap in months.

They reached the Deception Pass bridges in record time, and Mikael spotted the scouts who'd signaled the *Seas the Day.*

"It's a fucking *huge* horde of raiders, Samurai," Lance Corporal Kesting said. "I cannot be any more clear than that. Hundreds, easily. Fox Two Five shot itself dry, twenty arrows each, and they didn't even notice. Then they chased us, non-stop, from the channel bridge. Master Sergeant Eriksen is holding Pass Island, and Daimyo Hanzo is at the far end of the bridges. He had me check that the, and I quote, "Final Oh Shit plan" was in place, and I've checked. It seems to all be prepped and ready; it just needs to be armed."

"Very good. As soon as the rest of the Komainu arrive, tell Captain Hayes we'll want three platoons on Pass Island and another in reserve here at this end." Mikael gestured to the old tourist parking lot and the information-booth-turned-storage bunker there. "Dig out the barrels of arrows. If this horde is as large as you say, we'll need 'em."

"Yessir, already done. The rest of Two Five hauled them up earlier."

"Good work, Lance. Pass along my orders to Hayes when he gets here."

"Sir."

The Specialists crossed the first bridge, reassured Master Sergeant Eriksen that more help was actually coming, and pressed forward. Rikimaru cut down the last of another human wave and wiped his katana blade on a ragged pair of shorts. "Hey," Mikael said quietly to Ayame. "Remember that old tune we used to listen to in the dojo when we were scrapping?"

"I do." Ayame grinned. "Rick!" she called, and they raced to join him.

"One for the money!" Ayame half-sang as she unfurled her *manrikigusari*. The five-pound flanged mace head hung from six feet of linked chain, giving her an enormous lethal radius. Mikael made sure to give her enough space to work her magic.

"Two for the show!" Mikael sang and drew the wakizashi/tanto pair he favored. The shout-out was enough to communicate with Rikimaru the plan, and he chimed in next with the punchline:

"Three to get ready! Are you ready, motherfuckers? LET'S GO!"

The three Specialists raced forward, slamming into the front ranks of the mob. The host filled the road from the cliff side to the treetops. Mikael batted a club aside and drove his tanto up under a raider's jaw. Ayame crushed one face, then another with her mace-and-chain before their foes had any clue they were in range. Rikimaru darted one way and leaped another, the blade of his katana flicking in and out in a silvery arc, slashing a wrist here and a throat there, piercing lungs and hearts with every movement. Most strikes were lethal, but even those that weren't were crippling. One lucky brute clubbed him in the leg, but the plywood armor held, and Rikimaru reflexively lashed out with his full strength, decapitating the one who'd dared hit him.

Mikael didn't have the outright leverage with his short wakizashi and tanto dagger to cleave through necks in one slice, so he stuck with what worked. Slashes to inner thighs opened femoral arteries, faster than the eye could see. He slipped his tanto between ribs, opening up lungs and hearts, killing in seconds. Slashes to wrists and forearms severed essential tendons. He even punched a guy so hard his neck broke. The three Specialists formed a wall of whirling death and destruction, each taking a section of the front nearly twenty feet wide and filling it with dying raiders and dismembered body parts.

Then Rikimaru went down. A slippery spot on the ground cost him his footing, and an enormous raider, head and shoulders taller than the rest, barreled through a smaller pair and leaped on the daimyo's chest. He raised both fists high in the air to hammer fist the Specialist, but Ayame flung her ball and chain with pinpoint precision and smashed the brute in the jaw. That was enough of a distraction for Rikimaru to violently bridge up and throw the larger man clear. Mikael kicked a barbarian raider hard in the chest, caving it in and sending him sprawling. Then he dropped his wakizashi like a guillotine across the massive brute's throat and ended that threat. Rikimaru kipped up to his feet, only to take a makeshift axe to his breastplate. He tore it free and flung it into the horde, but the press of bodies was getting to be too much.

"Tighten up!" Ayame shouted, and the three steadily backed away until they reached the bridge and the barricade of rusted vehicles. Ayame jumped onto the hood of an old Ford pickup and sent her manrikigusari rocketing out at blinding speed. Rikimaru backed down the west half of the bridge, with Mikael on the east.

Mikael was struggling a bit. The next wave of raiders came armed with long, spiked clubs and shields, or the closest thing to assegais he'd seen—short spears with jagged blades wrought from salvage strapped to the tips. Since he was using a wakizashi instead of a full-sized weapon, he had to stay fast and mobile, lest he be overwhelmed. He ducked under one jabbing point, forced another one up with his wakizashi's guard, slid his tanto along the haft of a third, and hacked deep into the raider's hand, forcing him to drop the polearm.

A hot, burning sensation scored his ribcage, and he lashed out blindly, cutting the wooden broom-handled assegai in half. He buried his tanto in the offending warrior's eye socket, then pulled the spear tip from his side and clamped his elbow down tightly on the wound. The weapon hadn't penetrated deeply—the spear tip jammed between his ribs—but he was bleeding, and it would take a bit of time for the nanites to stop the flow.

* * *

Two hundred meters to their rear, Captain Scott Hayes hailed Master Sergeant Eriksen.

"Fox Two Five, I relieve you!"

Eriksen breathed a deep sigh of relief. "Fox Six, I stand relieved." He rolled his shoulders and neck, then pulled his canteen from his harness.

Empty. Lieutenant Josh Moon noticed and passed Eriksen his own, full canteen. The master sergeant accepted it gratefully and drank. To his left and right, fresh members of Fox Company tapped his troops' shoulders and took their places on the line. His surviving lance corporals gathered their troops, checked injuries, and refilled quivers. Hayes and Moon arranged their company—three ranks of spear hedge at the center, archers on the flanks. Master Sergeant and company bowmaster Auren Marsh estimated the range. She nocked, drew, loosed, and watched the arrow soar across the void between Fidalgo and Pass Islands until gravity asserted itself, and the arrow plunged into the mob. She had the range pretty well figured out. Using her angle and draw as their guide, Lieutenant Moon bellowed commands to the archers on both flanks.

"Nock!"

There was a two-second pause, as the archers set their arrows to their bowstrings.

"Up!"

There was another two-second pause as they mimicked the angle MSgt Marsh had used.

"Draw...LOOSE!"

A bare half-second after Marsh found her anchor points on her cheek, she and seventy more archers volleyed their arrows in a high arc that came down far beyond the edge of the bridge where the Specialists fought their desperate fight. This time, the volley had a visible impact Master Sergeant Eriksen could appreciate. Raiders screamed, collapsed, and died. One of the larger ones bashed a smaller goon in the head and picked up the limp form to use as a human shield against the next volley. Eriksen shook his head in disgust.

"Nock! Up! Draw! LOOSE!" Moon continued.

"How can I help, Captain?" Eriksen asked. He'd been a sweaty, haggard mess when he leaped from the clifftop and met Rikimaru roadside. Now that he'd cooled down from the extended run, he was a freezing cold, haggard mess. Sunset was chilly, and there was a noticeable breeze on the bridge deck. Hayes beckoned him onto another wrecked car to survey the battle. A scream dopplered away from them as someone on the left path fell from the bridge. Although the sun was already halfway below the horizon, they had enough light to see him fall nearly fifty yards and splatter apart on the rocky shore.

"Shit," Hayes said. "That means they've already fallen back twenty or thirty meters onto the bridge. We need to ease the pressure. Moon! Rapid rate!" Hayes counted the barrels of arrows they'd prepositioned, knowing this was their first fallback point. "Eriksen, get a tally of our arrows and assign your troops as porters. If I know the samurai, they'll trade distance for time. If we're forced back, I don't want to leave any weapons, ammunition, or anything else useful on this island when we fall back to the next."

"Yes sir," Eriksen said and strode back to his platoon. "DiPaulo! Kesting! On me!"

* * *

The raider he'd kicked over the ledge had held a shield. That suggested a number of things to Rikimaru, the least discomfiting of which was, *the first hundred of them were just...meat shields.* No sane general would throw away unprotected troops when he could lead with an armored shield wall. Would he?

The next thing that worried him was that no one was behind the guy he'd booted over the ledge. He knew, because he'd been able to count to three in his head as the raider screamed before he came to an abrupt end. He took a couple of deep breaths—it seemed the axe to the chest earlier had maybe broken a rib—and stepped out from the nook where he'd held the line against the raiders. At the end of the bridge, a tall, lean figure in a button-up, collared shirt, a thin, blood-red tie, and grey slacks stood at the fore of the army. The stranger was—to be precise—only the second person Rikimaru had seen wearing a tie in two decades.

"Rikimaru! Rikimaru Hanzo!" the figure shouted. "You've killed quite enough of my men today, Rikimaru. Come here, and let's discuss matters." His accent was British, and his voice crawled inside Rikimaru's brain, stirred old memories, and grabbed him by the pit of his stomach.

"*Kael needs a minute,*" Ayame whispered. "*I quote, 'stall for time, until the bleeding stops.'*"

"*He's a damn fool,*" Rikimaru replied. "Does that voice sound familiar to you?"

"No." Ayame shook her head, but on the far side of the pile of wrecks, Kael answered.

"Yes, but I hope to God I'm wrong. How...how does he know your name?"

Rikimaru didn't know the answer to that question, but every instinct he had was screaming trap. "If this goes sideways, go with the FPF plan and protect the base. *At all costs.* Wait here."

"Come *out*, Rikimaru. I don't have all week!"

Rikimaru emerged and stepped carefully along the narrow walkway, avoiding the largest puddles of blood and other, more odiferous bodily fluids.

Gaunt.

Of all the evil Obsidian had ever unleashed upon Earth, Stephen Gaunt was...well, he was in the top three. Bottom three. *Worst* three. And he'd marched an army right up to Rikimaru's front step.

"What are you doing here, Gaunt?" Rikimaru spat. The Agent's white, collared shirt had evidently been washed and re-washed, and probably re-washed again, but blood was hard to remove. Combat boots poked out from beneath the cuffs of his slacks, and a plain skinning knife hung from his belt. "Last I checked, you were in Utah, and that was before the bombs fell."

"Oh, Rikimaru, it's so *good* to see you again," he replied, his tone condescending and snide. "Yes, I was in Utah, but I rode out the end of the world in Vegas! 'Twas really quite glorious. A shame we can't do it again, I'd've taken more souvenirs! Then I headed north, to SeaTac by way of Oregon. It's been twenty years, after all, and it's a long walk. I've had the north end of the sprawl under my control for a year or so now, but you know what they say…amateurs study tactics, professionals study logistics." He paused and gestured widely to the barbarian horde at his heels. "My *associates* are sick and tired of rat burgers and grilled seagull. The whole city's a bit of a mess—we can't drink seawater, there's not enough fresh water to go around, the harbor is too polluted for crabs or fish. To be frank, it's appalling. And 'ere you are, quietly hoarding the ocean's bounty all to yourself. I'm *hurt*."

Gaunt's associates, the horde, or army, reminded Rikimaru of an orc warband more than anything else. They carried rough, misshapen shields hammered out of car doors or some other thin metal, rusty cleavers, and machetes. They were filthy, with matted beards and ratty hair, missing fingers, teeth, eyes…

"They don't look much like fishermen, Gaunt," Rikimaru said. "They look more like the type who'd burn a village and then rape the women by firelight."

"Hah, this mob?" Gaunt laughed, and for a moment, he seemed to consider it. "I suppose it would be more romantic that way. No, I just came to see if the rumors were true. Rumor had it that a few old Teledyne troops had made themselves warlords of the islands. And 'ere you are."

"Enough chit chat, Gaunt. Are we going to do this?"

"Quite," he agreed and his hand flashed. Rikimaru dove into cover behind a wrecked Mitsubishi, and the knife Gaunt had thrown sailed into the void and splashed in the ocean far below. When Rikimaru re-emerged, he held his katana at the ready, and Gaunt laughed. The raiders charged them again. The stygian flood of humanity's worst wretches streamed past their Agent warboss, and the battle began anew.

* * *

Somewhere around midnight, Ayame heard shouting behind her. She risked a glance backward and realized they had retreated all the way to Pass Island, the near-vertical, rocky island that divided the two bridges that constituted Deception Pass. Her black, plywood armor was dripping—a bit of the blood was even hers. The archers who'd been supporting them the whole night had already fallen back to the far side of bridge two, putting them out of range of the host. They needed a rest; few had the endurance to draw and fire hundred-pound recurve bows continuously for so long.

"Go!" Kael shouted from her right, and the thicket of spears to their rear parted a bit to let them slip through and grant them a reprieve. Apparently, Kael had lost his tanto and had replaced it with a bizarre, little weapon taken from some raider along the way. It was sort of a spear and sort of an axe, but the head was an intact rotary saw blade wedged into wood and tied into place. He swept the space in front of him, and Ayame winced. It wasn't worth a damn for stabbing, but the teeth bit deep when he slashed with it and left ragged wounds behind. Dead raiders were pitched over the sides by their still-breathing brethren, but wounded raiders clogged the channels, got in the way, and slowed things down. One asshole had actually been savage enough to throw his wounded over the side, but he'd earned his comrades' ire and found himself hoisted over the edge, very much alive and screaming, in short order.

Ayame couldn't understand what drove them forward—why they just kept coming—but as the three Specialists ground away at the front ranks of the marauders, falling back inch by bloody inch, she caught sight of a proper shield wall three-quarters of the way back. These raiders had large shields, rectangular like Roman scutum, and Gaunt was beyond them. They were literally *shoving* those in front of them forward and striking down anyone who tried to turn or flee. This wasn't quite as voluntary as she'd assumed. Perhaps they didn't know she could see them, given that it was night, but Gaunt would have—should have—known the Specialists had enhanced vision to go with their nanite enhancements. It was a clear night, hardly a cloud in the sky, and that meant she could operate just as efficiently at midnight as at noon.

The struggle was fighting all night. She was tired; they'd been fighting for *hours*. How many? She wasn't sure. Five? Six? Seven? They blurred together. She was hungry, she was thirsty, she was hot to the touch, and her nanites were burning energy like a blast furnace.

"The Komainu are set! On three!" Rikimaru called from below her, to her left. He deflected a rough chopper up with his katana and drove a knee into a raider's groin. Even Ayame winced, and the attacker doubled over to retch.

"Three!"

As one, the three Specialists turned and fled. Despite their injuries and exhaustion, they were still faster than the raiders, and they slipped through the gap in the pike hedge. The Komainu closed up behind them to hold the raiders at bay. Shield bearers, ranked spears, and archers supported them and kept the pressure on. Ayame collapsed and breathed deep gulps of air for a moment.

Master Sergeant Eriksen emerged and knelt next to her. "Here. Food and drink."

Logistical support from the base must have made its way up the hill, because Eriksen offered her a battered canteen cup of cool water and a plate of food. She poured half the water over her face and wiped away some of the blood and fleshy bits that had dried there, then she threw back a long swig. The scent of the tantalizing spices of a half-dozen tacos from El Taco Bout It wafted her way. She crammed half of one into her mouth.

"Mmmh," she groaned in pleasure. Fish tacos as war rations, with rice, beans, salsa, hot peppers, and goat cheese, were pretty hard to beat.

To her rear, she heard more shouting, so she scrambled to her feet. The Komainu were engaging the raiders, and she hastened to get back to the fight.

"Wait!" Eriksen said. She glanced back at him, and he shook his head. "Samurai...we've trained for years for this. Let them do the fighting while their champions fuel up. If you keep going as you have, you're going to collapse. Then they'll either kill you or capture you, rape you, and *then* kill you."

She saw the wisdom in that. "Maybe even in that order," she agreed and wolfed down another combat taco ration. Rikimaru was likewise stuffing food down his gullet and stretching his shoulders.

"You alright?" she asked.

"I think they busted a rib a couple hours back." He interlaced his fingers behind his back and flexed his arms, hard. His chest *popped*, and he gasped in relief. "Much better."

Kael joined them; he had ditched his wakizashi for a round, wooden shield of polished, lacquered planks and a spear, and he handed Ayame the same. "I shoulda had these to begin with," he said ruefully. He pointed to a slash in his gambeson and the wound behind it. "A shield would have been handy. Are we ready for round two?"

"The question is, are we ready to go to round ten?" Rikimaru asked.

* * *

"This is absurd," Gaunt complained. "How many of you unskilled, untrained, barely sentient savages does it take to kill one Specialist?"

"Uh, there's *three* of them, sir," one of the nearby unskilled, untrained, barely sentient savages whined. Gaunt shoved the snivelling, cowardly wretch back with his truck-door shield, and he rolled his eyes. Hard.

"So you *can* count. Very good. And, yes, once one of the Specialists is dead, I'd want another one dead, and then the third, but since you have altogether failed to kill anybody despite our ongoing, continuous losses, I am simply hoping for *one*."

The sky to the east was beginning to lighten, and the fighting had gone on far too long. He hadn't had many chances to engage a Specialist in honest battle; that hadn't been his style. Before Teledyne's incompetents destroyed civilization, he'd *ambushed* plenty. Plenty fell under his knife—the marvelous thing about imprints was how easily one received a new face and new body. They never saw him coming. When his quarry had had a particularly vicious rep, he hadn't used a blade; he'd used a customized 8.6x70mm Timberwolf sniper rifle and popped them from two klicks out. Obsidian had even authorized an airstrike once and accepted the collateral. Replacing that bridge had been expensive, but killing two trucks full of Teledyne's finest in a single hit had been priceless.

Gaunt moved forward, shoving past the shield wall and stalking up the left path. The Specialists had fought for every blood-soaked inch and carved far too many of his minions into bloody chunks.

Speaking of which, there's one of the wounded oafs now.

The man had been badly lacerated across the belly and was crawling on his hands and knees to the rear. Gaunt wrinkled his nose at the stench; they'd punctured this man's bowel. He was a dead man, but he didn't know it yet. Gaunt tossed him over the side of the bridge into the darkness below.

Am I not merciful?

The man's scream ended abruptly, but Gaunt had already put the faceless peon out of his mind. He'd noticed this about himself a long time ago—he suspected it was part of why Obsidian had made an imprint of him. It wasn't just that he was one of the most dangerous men in the world. He saw people but didn't perceive them to be people. Faces were blurred, irrelevant, and forgotten. Very few people made a strong enough impression on Stephen Gaunt that he remembered them. Stephen tended to sort people into one of two categories—targets or peons. Targets were to be dealt with; peons were to be used and abused as necessary. From that perspective, Specialist Hanzo should be honored; Gaunt remembered his name *and* his face. That made Hanzo a Big Deal in Gaunt's mind.

Years ago, conventional wisdom held that civilization was "nine missed meals" away from collapse. That was the trick—starvation gave one time to think about the coming hunger, to grow desperate, to resort to eating something—anything—they wouldn't have even considered a week before. Or, to grow desperate enough to kill, to feed ones' loved ones.

Not that Gaunt knew much about *that*; he didn't have family or loved ones, but he understood it intellectually. No civilization collapsed because people drowned en masse—that was ridiculous—and they weren't in some kind of space habitat so air wasn't an issue. Shelter? Shelter was practically unnecessary in the Pacific Northwest. Before the nukes, the Olympia-Vancouver sprawl had accumulated an enormous number of parasitic bums and hobos precisely because it *didn't* get too hot or too cold, even for the homeless. A lack of fresh water pretty much meant the end of the world was over and done in a handful of days for anyone who couldn't hydrate. That was another thing; Gaunt wanted to know how these Teledyne fools, normally inept at everything save destroying modern civilization, had managed to keep their population hydrated. The survivors in the ruined sprawl drank a lot of dirty, fouled water, and many of them had shit themselves to death when dysentery reared its ugly head.

Of all the basic needs—food, water, air, shelter—an absence of food created the perfect balance of "critical need" and "time to panic," letting savagery set in. Yet these bastards had been quietly hoarding food, while Gaunt and his minions suffered! Stephen very much preferred to hit his targets up close. The shock, the anguish, and the pain in their eyes when they realized what was going on was simply *delightful.* The power to hurt was the greatest power of all; most people could be manipulated into doing practically anything to avoid pain. Sometimes, they would choose physical pain over emotional hurt, but that was simply a different lever, a different tool in the same toolbox.

Hanzo cared about these people, and for the all-powerful, there was nothing more painful than seeing the ones they cared about hurting. He would hurt Rikimaru, and his little girlfriend, and his little boyfriend, until they all begged for death.

Then he'd grant it—but only at each other's hands. Gaunt couldn't imagine anything more delicious than making one of them finish the others off, as 'mercy'.

Rikimaru's shadow, Grimstaadt, held the east footpath to Gaunt's left, while Rikimaru's plaything, who hadn't even finished her training as a Specialist, held the right. Rikimaru was nowhere in sight, but there hadn't been any kind of cheering, shouting, or celebrating that suggested someone had gotten lucky. Therefore, Rikimaru must be hiding behind his thicket of spears. With only two Specialists on the line, now was as good a time as any.

Grimstaadt had fallen into a rhythm, working with a shield and spear to keep Gaunt's halfwit—*quarter*wit—raiding force at bay. Gaunt pulled one of his two stilettos—the Fairbairn-Sykes fighting knives he'd preferred since forever—and ducked low to use the bodies of his raiders as concealment, which would keep the Specialist from seeing him until it was too late. Grimstaadt's spear tip erupted from the back of the peon in front of him, spraying Gaunt with gore. *Perfect.*

Gaunt leaped past the dying fool and wrapped one hand around the spear shaft. Grimstaadt's eyes widened when he realized who he faced, and Gaunt buried his stiletto in the face of the Specialist's shield with a hammer blow. That gave him the leverage he needed to bash Grimstaadt backward with the shield and rip it from his grasp. He cast the shield aside and pounced, driving his second stiletto between Grimstaadt's third and fourth ribs.

The Teledyne operative's eyes bulged in shock and pain, and Gaunt drank it in. He didn't find much worth living for in this Fallen World, but that pain, that horror?

That made it all worthwhile.

* * *

"N o!" Ayame screamed. She dropped her shield and spear in favor of her preferred weapon, sacrificing the shield's defensive capabilities for sheer, bloody-minded offense. She leaped from the far walking path and soared in a high arc. As she descended, her manrikigusari streamed above her, and she snapped it down just before she crushed the roof of an old Chevy pickup. Gaunt bounced backward, narrowly avoiding the flanged mace head. Rikimaru burst through the shield wall and saw Ayame advancing on Gaunt, and Kael crawling on his hand and knees. Kael's right hand clutched his ribs, which were streaming blood. Rikimaru scooped up his old friend and fireman-carried him back to the shield wall.

"MEDIC!" Rikimaru shouted, and Master Sergeant Eriksen's head snapped up. He, Lance Corporal Kesting, and a private Rikimaru didn't know came running.

"Punctured lung," Rikimaru said when he saw the frothy blood coming from the wound. "I need to get back out there. Karisa?"

"Daimyo?"

"Make ready for final protective fire," he snapped. "When I give the order. *No matter what.*"

Kesting nodded. "We will, Daimyo."

Eriksen and his medic got to work on Mikael, and Rikimaru got back to the battle. When he joined Ayame, Gaunt had already backed off. He was outside Ayame's threat range, and she kept whirling and snapping her ball and chain to keep him off-balance. His army had fallen back behind him, and when he saw Rikimaru return, he smiled from the top of an old Escalade. He clasped his hands behind his back like he was giving a speech. One of the few Komainu archers who still had ammunition fired an arrow at him. He leaned slightly to one side and allowed the arrow to pass inches from his head.

"This is your fault, you know," he said. "This whole…end-of-the-world mess. Teledyne launched the nukes. *Kojima* held the codes."

"Bullshit," Rikimaru snarled.

"Why would *I* lie, Rikimaru?" he asked.

"Because you'd stab a man in the gut just because it's a miserable way to die, you sonofabitch."

"True," he conceded. "But also true: I had a run at stealing the codes from Kojima before our little op in Salt Lake. We weren't into outright warfare just yet, and they needed an operative who could be rational, a man like *you.* There's a reason they didn't send your man

Mikael to Utah; they didn't trust him to let bygones be bygones and get the job done. Tell me, when you fled the city, did you or did you not get more notice than anyone else?"

Rikimaru didn't have an answer. It had been twenty years, and he couldn't be sure what he knew and what he only thought he remembered. He did know he needed the bridge clear of friendlies, and if Ayame knew what he was planning, she'd refuse. "Ayame, check in with Marcus and Karisa and see to Kael." He pointed to the rear, and Ayame backed up. "Stephen and I are going to settle this once and for all." She snapped her ball and chain at one of the savages who'd been creeping forward, then disappeared behind the Komainu spear wall.

Something, or someone, had crushed the roof of the truck and his footing was poor. He stepped down onto the truck's hood, katana in hand. Gaunt brought his hands in front of him, loosely holding a long, thin knife in one hand.

They closed, and despite Rikimaru's reach with the katana, Gaunt deflected the sword with his much-shorter dagger, slipped closer, and buried it to the hilt in Rikimaru's side. Rikimaru snarled in pain, and Gaunt instantly danced back out of reach.

"That's for the gut quip, *Specialist,*" he spat and produced a second knife identical to the first. "Now, are you going to run home to mummy? Watch us sack your little island? Put it to the torch and carry off Kojima's head on a pike? Or are you going to work for *me* now? Everyone has a price, Rikimaru. What does your loyalty cost?"

The sun was cresting the mountains on the mainland far to their east, and the first sunrays cut across the bridge in a flood of blinding orange. He detected movement at the far end of the bridge and orange rays reflected off something, but Rikimaru didn't know what he was seeing. It was another host, except this one carried a banner, a vicious, fanged Japanese catfish at their fore! The Onamazu marines lowered their spears into a deadly thicket, trapping the raiders on the bridge.

Everyone has a place, everyone in their place.

My place is out in front, protecting my people from the likes of Stephen Gaunt.

"Final protective fire, now!" Rikimaru shouted.

The explosions began at the north end, sundering the bridge supports, dropping girders, asphalt, wrecked vehicles, and raiders a hundred and fifty feet down onto the rocks and into the ocean.

A curious look crossed Gaunt's face as the explosions drew nearer. He looked *impressed.* The south bridge detonated and fell in a twisted wreck to the sea below. Rikimaru plummeted out of sight along with it, lost in the smoke and debris.

* * * * *

Part Two: Ronin

Chapter Nine

"**N**o!" Ayame screamed, but the explosions rippled down the length of the bridge in a span of a few short seconds. The sundering charges began as staccato pops that crescendoed as they raced closer. She lost sight of Akuma's marines in the smoke and flying debris and then turned away as Rikimaru, her mentor and friend, disappeared in a flash of smoke and chaos. She glowered accusingly at young Lance Corporal Kesting, who'd detonated the charges. Kesting was rapt by the explosions, but Eriksen caught the look of fury on Ayame's face and moved to intercept her before Kesting noticed.

"*Don't you dare, Aya,*" he hissed. "*She was doing as he ordered.*"

"*Don't you 'Aya' me,*" she snarled back. "She *killed* him!"

"Maybe," Eriksen snarled back. Captain Hayes joined them but listened without interrupting. "People *die* in this Fallen World. The daimyo knew that, and neither he nor we saw any other way to stop that…maniac and his army. This was his "oh shit" plan from the moment we met him at the base of the cliff."

A wet cough behind them interrupted Ayame's retort, and her eyes locked on Mikael, who was reclining against an empty barrel of arrows. A dressing was taped over his ribs.

"He's right," Mikael croaked. "Rick—"

"*Shut. Up.*" Ayame snapped. "You're going to make it worse! For that matter, what are you still doing here?" She shot an accusing glance at Master Sergeant Eriksen. "Get a stretcher crew and get him

137

down to the clinic! Send runners to wake Doctor Marcum and his staff!" When Eriksen opened his mouth to object, Ayame snapped, "NOW! DO IT NOW, DAMN YOU!"

Eriksen turned to task his exhausted platoon, but Captain Hayes interrupted. "Belay that, Master Sergeant." Ayame rounded on him, but Hayes ignored her for a moment. "I have troops who *haven't* been on the run since yesterday dinner time; they're "only" on hour twelve or so. March your platoon back to the barracks and prepare for a hot wash AAR. Lieutenant Moon!"

"Sir!"

"Form work parties! Assign your best medic to Samurai Grimstaadt. Monitor his vitals and chest seal for pneumothorax. Have one party lash together a hasty stretcher and get him to the clinic. Send your fastest runners, plural, to collect Doctor Marcum, everyone he'll need for the clinic, and any supplies they'll need."

"Sir!"

Moon began barking orders and delegating tasks, and Hayes turned back to Ayame. "Samurai Kato, would you walk with me a moment?"

She knew she was visibly shaking as they walked down the road a ways from the ruined remnants of the bridge. She didn't know what Hayes wanted, and she was on the ragged edge of losing her shit completely, so she clamped down with every ounce of discipline she had. Walking helped.

"Ma'am, I'm sorry for countermanding you, but I'm not sorry at the same time." Hayes had guided her away from Fox company, who were busy at the ruined edge of the bridge, even though they had neutralized the threat. "Under our chain of command, Samurai Grimstaadt is my senior, and Daimyo Hanzo and Shogun Kojima are above him. You are, if I may be blunt, the spy-mistress and master of spooks, but you are not within my chain of command. Similarly, Master Sergeant Eriksen and Fox Two Five are not under your command either."

She swallowed hard. Her role as samurai of the Satori had indeed left her isolated from the Komainu. Soldiers weren't spooks, and vice versa, and didn't integrate well with them. She'd never considered how quickly that might go to hell in circumstances where Mikael was critically injured and Rikimaru was…

Oh dammit…

She wiped unbidden tears away and took a deep breath to lock down her emotions.

"Fair," she allowed. "You're correct, and I apologize for my outburst."

"Having said that…have you considered that, if Samurai Grimstaadt does not survive his wounds…that makes *you* our daimyo?"

"*What? No—*"

Hayes raised his eyebrows. "Mikael and Rikimaru were Teledyne's senior Specialists, and Shogun Kojima naturally placed them as generals of Teledyne's surviving armed forces. Rikimaru was senior to Mikael, so Rikimaru was the senior commander and Shogun Kojima placed Mikael in charge of the Komainu. However, you are OIC of Intelligence—the Satori—and with both of them out of commission, our senior intelligence officer would naturally fit into the top slot."

"I can't be *Daimyo!*" she hissed.

"You can, and you will," Hayes replied. He'd guided her to a footpath that passed down the face of the cliff and under the bridge. He pointed across the pass, beyond the ruined bridge to Pass Island.

It jutted straight up out of the water, sheer cliffs on three sides, and the surviving raiders still occupied it. Not everyone had been on the bridge decks when the charges blew, and that meant they had a problem. "You're a, forgive the term, spook and not used to commanding troops. You have cells of intel officers, agents, spies, and sources. Ninety percent of what you guys do is acting and relaying information. Command is a kind of acting too, but there is only one show you have to put on. 'All Is Well and Things Are Going According To Plan.' Obviously, all is *not* well, but you cannot, under any circumstances, allow the troops to see you sweat. You're a *Specialist*, and that means you're damn near a superhero to these people."

"I'm just a—"

"Stop. You're selling yourself short. You're quicker on your feet, and you run faster, fight harder, and soak up punishment that would kill any ten of us mere mortals. They honed you to a razor's edge, and as of twenty minutes ago, you're the most lethal human on two feet within a hundred miles. Maybe more. The only reason my people were still holding the line when the sun came up, was because you three Specialists held the line against hundreds. Hundreds. You fought all night after being up all day. Gaunt is a nightmare made real. I was a junior NCO in the Teledyne Armed Forces before the nukes fell, and we had standing orders to call in an *airstrike* if Gaunt showed his face. He was Obsidian's own woodchipper, personified. That he didn't kill any of you outright is miraculous, and Rikimaru recognized the threat he posed; *that's* why he blew the bridge."

"It feels like there should have been another way," Ayame complained.

"But there wasn't. Cheating—ambushing him—was the only way we were going to take him out. Now. I understand you have a new samurai leading the marines on the far side of the pass. They're in need of some leadership and direction—none of them could have known the bridge was about to blow. You might begin with figuring out how you're going to get over there, sort them out, and deal with the surviving raiders." He gestured toward the wreckage of the bridge. While some of the beams poked out of the water, the water was so dark, it was impossible to see what lay just below the surface. "I don't see anyone sailing through that pass to get to the eastern, accessible side of Pass Island any time soon, so you're going to need to tackle that. I suppose you could just post a guard and watch them until they're starving and mad with thirst…"

"I—shit."

"Ignore your heart and start using your brain, Aya," Hayes said with a twinkle in the corners of his eyes. Ayame nodded and replied with the rote response.

"If Teledyne wanted me to have feelings, they would have issued them to me."

"Exactly. Let me handle the clusterf—uh, charlie-foxtrot above. They don't call us Fox Company for nothing. Mikael will get the very best care available. Doc Marcum knows his stuff, and you Specialists are hard bastards at the worst of times. But you have to look at the big picture, and rallying your Onamazu marines needs to be priority one." He pointed to the far side of the pass. "If you're puzzled about what to do next, just ask yourself, *What would Rikimaru do?* and dial it up ten percent."

"Thank you, Scott, you make some very good points," Ayame said before clearing her throat and turning to squarely face him. "Captain, I'll need one boat crew to get me across to my marines on the outer passage. My marines and I will clear Pass Island, then we'll need another set of crews to pick us up at the downslope when we're done. We'll return to Whidbey after I've sent the remnants to Hades, and we'll plan our next steps then."

"Much better, Samurai," Hayes agreed. "I'll have them meet you by Cranberry Lake's western tip?"

"That will do," Ayame said. "Carry on, Captain."

"Yes, ma'am," Hayes said. He strode back out to the road and began barking orders.

* * *

The sun had risen above the horizon, and it warmed Ayame's bones. It got cool at night, and despite her exhaustion, she found she was restless. Edgy. She clamped down on the fidgeting and got a grip. She waved to the *Master Baiter* as it neared the shore. The ship was a good thirty-feet long, and though it wasn't one of their fastest cutters, it was in good repair. The boat driver had two crew with her, who moved with a sense of urgency as the small blonde at the wheel shouted orders. Ayame splashed into the seawater, cursing the cold now that she'd begun to warm up, and scooped up the thrown line. She looped the rope around her waist, tied it off, and started hauling herself in. Everyone knew the samurai by their white, plywood armor, and everyone knew the Specialists were barely buoyant when wearing their full gear. Without the help of the plywood, Ayame would have sunk like a rock, and the ocean floor dropped off precipitously. A bare hundred meters west of Pass Island, the ocean bottomed out at thirty fathoms which was deeper than the height of the bridge above sea level.

"Welcome aboard, Samurai!" Coxswain's Mate Dana Parkes said and offered her hand to help Ayame aboard. The Coxswain's mate was a young blonde in her mid-twenties, maybe five-foot-six, muscled from years on the water and tanned from the same. Her age meant she was likely just a child when the bombs fell. That she drove a boat meant she'd finished her first tour with the Komainu, volunteered for sailor training during her re-enlistment, and was now into her "open-ended" engagement.

"Thank you, Cee-Em," Ayame replied. "They briefed you?"

"Meet Samurai Kato at Cranberry Lake, aye. Rendezvous with Onamazu marines at Bowman Beach, aye. Wreak terrible vengeance on the survivors on Pass Island, aye," she finished with a feral grin.

"That about sums it up. Let's be on our way."

* * *

When the *Master Baiter* rounded the point into Bowman Bay, fifteen sailboats were moored near the beach where the Lighthouse Point Trail nearly dropped to water level.

"When we get to shore, I want you to get with the other coxswains," Ayame said. "We'd have to sail all the way south to Clinton and back north again to get at the lowest part of the mountain. That's nearly a hundred fifty klicks, and that's too far. Nor do I want to sail back to Cranberry Lake, march to the far side of the pass, and take the small handful of fishing boats we have in the inner passage on an island assault. So, I need a tally of how many spare ropes you have and their lengths. We're going to climb the west side of the island, using the trees as cover."

"That's...hardcore," Parkes said. "Get a tally of all the spare ropes and how long they are, aye."

When they neared the rest of the marine boats, a familiar face greeted Ayame. She splashed into the surf and went ashore. "Ayame!" Akuma shouted with audible relief. "Thank Shiva you're here. We were holding them on the bridge, and then the first blast…well, it took a moment to remember we'd rigged the bridge with charges. But once we realized it was deliberate, I put a scout up a tree. They saw our troops holding the Whidbey side, and figured someone would be along shortly. What happened?"

"We fought all night, Ajay," Ayame said, and her face fell. She summarized the night's fighting. "…and then Rikimaru ordered us to blow the bridge. He, and Gaunt, and most of the rest of the army went into the water—those who weren't killed by the blast outright. Mikael's going into surgery; I have no idea how complicated it is to repair a sucking chest wound, so…you and I are all that are left, for now."

Akuma gulped, and his eyes were wide.

"I—shit…"

That brought a bit of a grin to Ayame's lips. "I said the same thing to Captain Hayes not an hour ago when he was giving me the *Chin up, harden up; you're a goddamn samurai now start acting like it* speech. So, chin up, harden up, Akuma, you're a goddamn samurai, now start acting like it. Whenever you're not sure what to do, just ask yourself, *What would Rikimaru do?* And dial it up ten percent."

"Aye aye, ma'am," Akuma agreed. "I have forty-four Onamazu marines in fifteen boats ready to sally forth and kick ass. Your orders?"

Ayame told him her plan, and his eyes went wide.

"That's…hardcore," he said.

"That's what we do," Ayame agreed. "Get me your strongest climbers. They're going to follow me up the embankment until we don't need the ropes anymore. I will hold the line as your climbers set the ropes. It won't go fast, but it'll get done. The instant the ropes are set, send your troops up. At the top, we'll form up and push hard until the only living thing on those mountains are squirrels and catfish."

"Oorah, Samurai," Akuma said and turned back to his troops. "Strongest climbers! Front and center!"

Three young men, built like linebackers, and one girl, who looked more like a gymnast, presented themselves.

"Will they do?" Akuma asked.

"They will. Here's what we're going to do, marines…"

* * *

Coxswain Parkes was a *great* boat driver, as it turned out. With the four marine volunteers aboard, she sailed south and cut in toward the southern edge of the ruined bridge. Girders and twisted debris stood above the water, and Ayame checked their depth charts. The water here was nearly a hundred feet deep. She assumed the wreckage must have gotten twisted and piled up on itself—it didn't seem possible it could be resting on the ocean floor and still be above water. But there was no telling what lurked below the surface, and one girder could rip the bottom out of a boat faster than they could react. As much as she wished she could simply mount the island at its lower, eastern edge, it wasn't worth the risk.

As Parkes closed with the mangled debris, the surviving raiders jeered and shouted at them and threw rocks. They were poorly aimed and weakly thrown, and they fell well short of the boat. The Coxswain heeled the boat around to cut north; their mainsail's boom snapped viciously as she threw the boat through the turn. She followed the edge of the island's cliff side shore until rocks ground against the underside of the *Baiter*. There was *one* shallow spot where the stones were small and round and the ground was flat-ish before it dropped precipitously away into the depths again. This had been their destination, and that was Ayame's cue. She jumped from the boat into the seawater once again, going in just up to her knees. Privates Sam Alvarez, Terry Cobb, and Reid McIvor, and Lance Corporal Melissa Rainier followed her into the water. Their combined eight-hundred-some pounds off the boat was enough to lift it clear of the rocks, and Parkes sailed on.

The lowest handholds were too high for the marines to reach. That was no problem for Ayame, though. She checked her footing on the slimy rocks, crouched, and jumped. She caught hold of a thick cedar, which was growing precariously out of the side of the cliff face, and hauled herself around it, so she was between it and the cliff face. She unclipped a biner from the back of her harness and set it down with four rope bags hanging from it. She looped the first rope around her perch and lowered it to the marines below. Her climbers swarmed up the rope, and she wasn't surprised when Melissa Rainier was the first to reach her. Melissa had long, lean muscles, and her mass was probably only two-thirds the males'. Maybe even half. She scampered up the rock face like a spider monkey, aided by the rope, and quickly reached Ayame's perch.

She wanted five climbing paths for her marines; that was all the cliff face could accommodate. Each of her pathfinding climbers would take a rope up with them, tying it to trees and branches, whenever the terrain allowed. With a rope bag clipped to their harness, they let out enough that the ropes would reach their beachhead, and then they climbed.

Midway through the climb, one of the men swore, and Ayame risked a glance down. A handhold had come loose under Cobb's grip, and he pinwheeled his arms as he fought to keep his balance. When he concluded his balance was well and truly lost, he committed to the fall and kicked out, hard. He fell nearly forty feet back to the water's surface, turned a half-somersault in the air, and hit the water feet first. Ayame held her breath until he bobbed back up to the surface, and for once, she was thankful for the underwater cliffs. If the water had been shallow, he'd have broken both legs or worse. Cobb swam back to the rocks, crawled out, and flashed her a thumbs up. He checked his rope, arranged it in his bag, and started climbing again.

Ayame kept climbing until the rocky cliffs finally flattened out and she had rock under her feet again. She stayed low, hiding in the shadows of the enormous cedar trees, hoping to escape the raider's notice for as long as possible. A few minutes later, Melissa Rainier joined her.

"Rope's tied off, Samurai," the Lance Corporal whispered.

"Good. Stay low and out of sight. Do what you can to guide the others and then the assault force."

"Aye aye, ma'am," Rainier said and crept away, back into the brush.

McIvor checked in next, and she sent him back to his ropes too. Then Alvarez. Cobb joined her last.

"First three marines are climbing, Samurai," he said. "Well, three and the one who started climbing my rope the moment I gave them the go-ahead."

"Good. Stay low and help the others."

"Ma'am," Cobb replied. As he crept off through the underbrush, he bashed his head on a low-hanging branch. Ayame heard the tree rattle and a muffled curse. Just when it seemed the sounds had gone undetected, a murder of crows took off from the upper branches, cawing at the top of their lungs. That drew the attention of the raiders, then one shouted.

"They're here!" He raced through the brush toward Cobb, who was holding his head, blood visible on his fingers.

"*Shit*," Ayame said as she moved to her left. The lead raider came within range, and she snapped out her manrikigusari. She crushed the man's temple with the flanged mace head and sent him flopping to the ground, twitching. Among the trees was a terrible spot to fight with a chain weapon—she couldn't whirl it in circles to hold them at bay. She needed to get into the clear.

"Cover the clifftop!" she shouted and raced forward from her hiding spot to intercept the last of the raiders. There looked to be thirty or forty of them; they'd been trapped on the island when the bridges on both sides blew, and they were *mad*. This bunch was better armored and armed than many of the limitless mob she'd fought on the front line. Whereas the dozens of 'warriors' she'd fought on the bridges had been mostly armed with sticks or axes or other rough hand tools and dressed in ragged scraps, these wore metal plates strapped to their arms, legs, and chests. They carried shields—one had the remnants of a Mitsuyota logo from a truck door, while others were rough plywood. They moved together, interlocking their shields and using their spears to keep her at a distance.

They watched her manrikigusari warily; they knew it had reach, but no idea how much. Now that she was on the road, she had space, and she swung the mace in a dizzying pattern— overhead, around her waist, at arm's length—shifting the pattern every second or two just to keep them guessing. One of the raiders edged closer to her, looking to hit her from the flank, and she whirled the mace overhead and let the chain slide outward to its full length. She expanded the circle wide enough to encompass a thin tree trunk. The weighted head accelerated as it rounded the tree, and she bashed the brave one in the back of the head. She laughed as the man collapsed, head leaking red and grey, and she snapped her chain back in close.

"Just go!" one of them urged. His shaggy mop of ginger hair and beard made him stand out from the rest, who all wore scruff in shades of brown or blond. "She can't stop all of us!"

She let the mace fly again, this time aiming squarely for the man's plywood shield. The mace head smashed through an upper chunk of it, peppering him with splinters, and he flinched back.

"She doesn't have to!" Melissa Rainier snarled from her right flank. She emerged from the brush with the rest of her Onamazu lance. The marines weren't equipped with shields, but they did have the hooked naginatas, or what they were calling "boarding pikes." They weren't pikes, precisely, but the Onamazu were marines, not historical reenactors, and didn't particularly care. The polearms were shorter than regular spears so they could be used in ship-to-ship combat. The blade at the end of the shaft had a single cutting edge, and the backside of the blade featured a U-shaped hook.

Rainier was proving to be one of the keenest of the newly formed marines. Her lance had several trained blacksmiths in it, and they had spent the first day in the forge as a team, putting the new weapons together. They'd spent all their spare hours in the days since practicing, and it showed.

Private Torino angled to flank the right-most raider and slipped his 'pike' sideways under the spear shaft. His target didn't know where the threat was coming from—the troops to his front or the one still out of range just to the side. Torino rotated the weapon so the hook went upright, caught the spear, and yanked it aside. Private Pynn did likewise to the next raider in line to prevent him from covering the vulnerability. A third marine ducked low and hooked the top of the raider's shield, pulling him forward and down, then Rainier darted forward and chopped down. Her chop split the man's skull; he collapsed, and the raiders shouted angrily. The ginger-haired raider tried to lunge forward with his spear, but a quick upward strike from the haft of Pynn's pike sent the spear point skyward. Ginger retreated as he got his weapon under control again, but by then, the whirling threat of the manrikigusari forced him back to a 'safe' distance.

"Left flank!" Akuma shouted, and he joined the line, Alvarez and his lance in tow. Lance Corporal Wilson's troops arrived with standard Komainu weapons—short swords and shields—and he arranged his troops to anchor their right flank. Ginger looked less and less confident as the marines added reserves to their skirmish line, and looked warily to his left and right flanks. That moment of distraction cost him when Ayame let her ball-and-chain fly again. It smashed into the plywood shield, but that had been her target. He yelped and dropped the shield and clenched his left hand tightly under his armpit. She'd smashed the mace head into the spot between two bolts that indicated where the grip was. As she'd suspected, the grip was just a leather strap which offered no rigidity or protection. The crushing impact left him defenseless. Then she followed with her manrikigusari, which she swung at full extension, smashing him in the face and knocking him backward.

The Onamazu marines crashed through the hole in the raiders' shield wall and swarmed over and through the front ranks, ripping shields away, chopping with their hooked naginatas, and running them through with their swords. Ayame wove between the raiders, finding little pockets of resistance where the skilled enemy held her troops at bay. She brought her manrikigusari crashing in from an unexpected angle, crippling or killing the target, then she moved on. She spotted Cobb as he and his lance corporal dogpiled a raider. Cobb throat-punched the bandit with the edge of his shield, shattering the enemy's trachea. He bounced up to his feet, and rejoined the line again, guarding their flank. They chopped at each other, hooked naginata versus spear and shield, without either side making much progress, until McIvor and the rest of his lance joined them. These bandits weren't soldiers; they were raiders with no sense of cohesion, leadership, or teamwork. They didn't stand a chance.

After a few more breathless minutes of fighting, a cluster of four raiders was all that remained. Although they still held their shields and spears, they were shoulder to shoulder, backing away from the marines who surrounded them. They moved down the close side of the road, keeping the wrecks to their right to secure their flank as best they could. They backed onto the bridge, and the ground fell away below them until they reached the only bridge support on the little island straddling the pass. "I don't suppose...you'd accept our surrender?" one tentatively asked. He was smaller than the other three and skinny, and he looked ridiculous in his soccer shin guards, stained and ripped hockey shorts, and bare football shoulder pads. *Pad*, singular, in truth, since it bore only one pauldron. A too-large, three-quarters motorcycle helmet bobbled on top of his head, and goggles hid his eyes.

"Why should I? You and Gaunt's horde," she spat the word with venom, "marched up here, intent on robbery, rape, pillage, and plunder. Gaunt killed one, maybe two, of my oldest, best friends. To stop Gaunt, we finally had to destroy the bridges we've maintained over twenty years of peace with the mainland. So you tell me—would you be feeling merciful?"

"When you put it that way…" the raider said, with fear in his voice, "I guess not." One of the other raiders, much larger than the speaker, lunged forward with his spear, but Alvarez caught it on his shield and deflected it. Lance Corporal Wilson drove his blade into the man's guts, and he collapsed.

Ayame whipped her manrikigusari in a circle above her head, then she let the chain whistle out and bashed the scrawny man in the side of his helmet. The helmet shattered, and the raider went sprawling. The last two raiders roared in anger, but Akuma and a lance of six marines raced forward, shield-slammed them, and sent them back into open space where the bridge used to be.

Ayame went to the edge and looked over. Twisted iron wreckage skewered one of the raiders, and judging from the exit wound, he was dead. The ripples of his partner's splash showed where the second had gone into the water, and though she waited, he didn't surface.

She returned to the relative safety of the island. Her troops hadn't survived the battle unscathed—two of her marines had been speared and would need to recover. Private McIvor was the only fatality, with a wound to his throat.

The scrawny man was down but not dead. He dropped his spear and his shield, and tore his ruined helmet off. He spat blood on the concrete, and when Ayame dragged him to his feet, his goggled eyes were unfocused. "Just...kill me quickly and be done with it?" he pleaded.

"You're..." Ayame stared at him. "You're just a kid?"

* * *

Shogun Kojima's face was etched with worry lines when Coxswain Parkes pulled her sailboat up to the old airbase dock. Ayame and Akuma were the first two to disembark, and Ayame took the junior samurai aside for a moment. "Get your marines squared away in the old hangar—take care of first aid, weapons, and gear, in that order. Get the forge going. Let them kibitz and chat. Your job is to listen and take notes. Consider it an informal hot wash after action report. Get them all to tell their war stories—what worked, what didn't. Brainstorm what we're going to do now that the pass isn't."

"Will do, Aya," Akuma said. He waited on the dock for the rest of his boats to arrive, and Ayame went on ahead. As she approached Kojima, he wordlessly turned and retreated into the privacy of the *honden*. She followed.

"Congratulations on a well-fought battle, Ayame," the shogun said once they were inside.

"Then why does it feel like we lost?" she replied.

"You are confusing the sting of losses, with that of losing a battle," Kojima replied. "We most certainly suffered losses, but that was no defeat. Consider how many of our young men, women, and children would be dying or dead, if not for you and your fellow samurai. Rikimaru was a creature of duty who went to his death knowing his place was between our people and those who would do them harm. We will miss his courage and leadership, but what I will miss most is his dedication to our fellow survivors. Teledyne's motto once was 'knowledge is power.' Power, it can be said, corrupts, and absolute power is…well, it's actually pretty neat." Ayame did a double-take when the shogun's words registered, and he flashed her a small smile. "That was a joke, Aya. Don't think you kids have a monopoly on dark humor."

Ayame rolled her eyes. "Kids? I'm *forty-one*."

"As you say. Rikimaru was the best of all of us, I believe. His sense of duty tempered the…power, his infinite capacity for violence as a Specialist. He placed this small community and his responsibilities to us ahead of his own personal gain. God knows he could have removed *me* at any time. But despite our many disagreements, I never feared he would seize control. I'm not sure I deserved him."

Ayame pondered the shogun's words. From her earliest days as a Specialist trainee until after the nukes dropped and the world fell, she'd never heard Rikimaru contradict the shogun. *Not once.* Rikimaru's sense of duty had also prevented them from ever moving past 'colleagues' into a more intimate relationship. She felt tears again, unwelcome and unbidden.

Kojima gave her a moment to let her emotions out, then cleared his throat. "All is not lost, Aya. Mikael is already out of surgery. He will be fine, in time."

"He is?" Ayame blinked, surprised. "He will?"

"Yes. The nanites bought us enough time to get him down the hill to the clinic and Doctor Marcum. He had further injuries we didn't know about—he'd been nearly hamstrung, at one point, and he had another eight cuts and wounds, two of them serious. Since we didn't have proper anesthesia, Mikael grumped afterward that we should have spared him the surgery and thrown him into the Pacific instead. More dark humor, I think." Kojima smiled a small, brittle smile. "You can go see him if you wish."

"I will, Shogun, thank you."

"Once you have checked in on Kael, continue your preparation and development of the Onamazu program with Samurai Kumar. You and he will be our operational commanders in the field. An army of that size should never have been able to sneak up on us with only a few hours' notice. The Komainu will need to increase their patrols of the Puget Sound, of Possession Sound, of the remnants of Everett and Marysville, and all the rest. I'd like to try to reopen trade with the survivors in the Tulalip Reserve and canoe or kayak patrols up the Stillaguamish and Skagit Rivers as far as the highway. Once Kael is well enough, he will administer those patrols, and we can discuss future operations. And Ayame?"

"Shogun?"

"I miss Rikimaru, too."

* * *

"Hey, Grim," Ayame said from the doorway. "You look like shit."

"Hey, Aya," Mikael Grimstaadt croaked. "Go fuck yourself, huh?"

156 | JAMIE IBSON

Ayame smiled broadly, but her eyes were shining, and a tear threatened to escape. The clinic was the old medical aid station for the facility, but it was not, and had never been, a proper hospital. Mikael was lying on a bed in one of the side rooms off the main clinic, which accorded him some slight amount of privacy. A tube ran from his side to a bottle on a tray below him. Another hose connected that bottle to a second one filled with water. Yet more tubing connected the second bottle to a third, then ran out of the third, letting them control the suction exerted by the primitive device. The first bottle was the largest, and there was half an inch of blood at the bottom. "Doc Marcum says you're going to be okay, eventually. You had me scared."

"I told Doc Marcum you guys should have thrown me to the sharks," Grimstaadt replied. "You have any idea how awful it is to have surgery for a sucking chest wound without freezing or anesthetic?"

"Not a clue." Ayame shook her head. "I've heard it said that a sucking chest wound is Mother Nature's way of telling you that you were too slow."

"True," Grimstaadt said ruefully. "True. I don't recommend the experience in the slightest. One star: would not get shanked again."

"I had a boyfriend as a teenager who thought the same," Ayame said. "It didn't work out."

"The relationship? Or the shanking?"

"Yes. He kept getting stabbed by ex-girlfriends. I finally took one out when she attacked us at the zoo. Then I ditched him. I wasn't going to go through his life as his bodyguard and troubleshooter. They found him face down in Salmon Bay a month later."

"Harsh," Mikael said. "Wait, you were still a teenager?"

"Yep. I'd gotten a part-time gig with Teledyne as an admin clerk, but taking out insane ex-girlfriend number three barehanded caught the operations directorate's attention, so I suppose it was for the best. Now, rest up. You're going to need to be tip-top to replace all the Komainu we're stealing away, mister. Marines gotta come from somewhere."

"Yo ho ho." Mikael chuckled, but laughing even a little bit set off a coughing fit. Master Sergeant Sparks, one of the senior medical staff, rushed into the room, but Grimstaadt weakly waved an arm. "I'm fine, Paul," he said, a broad leer on his face. "Just imagining Aya here in a pirate blouse, tights, and knee-high leather boots."

"I *should* have thrown you to the sharks, you lech," Ayame replied, but she was smiling, nonetheless. If Grimstaadt was well enough to wisecrack, he'd recover soon; she was sure of that. "Don't make him too comfortable, Sarge. Otherwise, he won't ever want to leave."

"Can do." Sparks smiled and checked the suction tube sutured to the Specialist's rib cage. "Man, that's gonna be gnarly when we take it out."

"I don't even wanna *think* about it," Grim complained. Ayame gave him a gentle hug and headed for the door. Behind her, Grim asked, "Can I get another pillow?"

She smirked when Sparks' replied sternly, "No."

* * *

Back at the hangar, Akuma had his Onamazu marines laying out their kits for inspection and repair. The short time they'd been allowed since founding the unit meant nobody had a full set of armor yet, nor did they all have standardized weaponry. Akuma was examining one of the hooked polearms they'd fought with on top of the pass when Aya walked in. The hooks weren't forged as part of the blade—at least, not yet. The chopping end was similar to a Viking seax—a single, straight cutting edge—nothing fancy—with a thick spine. They'd drilled holes at the rear of the spine to pin the hooks in place.

"What's the opinion on the hooked naginatas?" she asked quietly. She hadn't been convinced of their utility until she'd seen them in action, and if the marines didn't care for them, they'd find some excuse to go back to the sword or spear and shield of the regular Komainu.

"ONAMAZU! WHAT'S THE OPINION ON THE HOOKED NAGINATAS?"

"OORAH!" the marines roared back. Four were holding theirs when he asked, and they slammed the butts of the polearms into the concrete floor of the hangar in unison.

"We like them," Lance Corporal Melissa Rainier replied, a ferocious grin etched on her face. "We like them a lot."

"Good!" Ayame replied. "While I have your attention, well done on your first actions as Onamazu Marines. Without any training in naval assault or high-angle ascent, you managed both and outperformed my wildest dreams. That bodes ill for our enemies."

"Oorah!" Cobb shouted from the back, and everyone chuckled at his enthusiasm.

"Oorah, indeed," Ayame agreed but grew somber. "Having said that, we lost Daimyo Hanzo in the fight, and with him, roughly a quarter of our entire fighting strength." Whispers and pointed looks rippled through the troops. They hadn't been there, not at their end.

"Steady up!" Akuma ordered, and the Onamazu braced themselves at ease. Ayame recounted the fight on the bridge, concluding with Rikimaru's ordering the bridge destroyed, and his disappearing in the smoke and chaos of the explosions.

"But...he's a Specialist," Rainier objected. "Shouldn't that mean he's okay? You guys are, like, almost invincible!"

"No, that's exactly why he's *not*," Ayame disagreed. "Without some kind of floatation equipment, he, myself, or Specialist Grimstaadt sink like rocks. Our nanites do make us tougher, stronger, faster. But the pass goes down beneath the waves even further than the bridge was above them. That's a long, *long* way for a rock to sink. Any time any of us sail, we have to be *very careful* not to go in the water. If it's shallow enough, we can hold our breath—for minutes, even—and try to walk to shore, but for any kind of depth, a rapid descent like that would crush us with the water pressure."

"You're...risking your life every time you step into a boat?" Akuma asked. Even he was shocked.

"No one ever said being a Specialist was safe," Ayame said. "And, let's be honest, neither is being a Marine. Or a Komainu guardian. Or, hell, a *civilian*, for that matter. Nothing is safe, anymore. One of the purposes of the Komainu was to create a structure where *everyone* could learn to *defend* themselves. Against raiders, like we fought at the bridge today. Against pirates and thieves from Victoria. Against thieves, brigands, or scum hidden within our borders." She raised her voice again. "Unfortunately, we're too small a group, and going on the offensive against hostile neighbors means we have too much to do in too little time. I want each of you to take a moment and think of three people—active or released—you'd want at your back, to your left, or to your right. Siblings, maybe, or friends. You were all chosen, hand-picked, based on your can-do attitudes, aggression, intelligence, and fighting know how. Samurai Akuma and I don't know, *can't* know everyone on every island well enough to headhunt potential marine recruits from across the entire Shogunate. But we need to get our numbers up to a serious fighting force in a hurry. No one's getting re-conscripted—this is entirely voluntary—so don't think that's the case. But if you have an older brother, older sister, cousin, or best friend, and you think they might be interested in finally getting out there, kicking ass, and taking the fight to the Victorians, your recommendation is enough for us to make them a pitch. If you each name three friends, and even half of them say yes, we'll be at full company strength in no time."

Rainier came to attention and raised a fist to ask a question.

"How soon, Samurai?"

"I want to be seizing boats and burning docks by next week."

"I have some names for you," she offered, and Ayame prepared to take notes.

* * * * *

Chapter Ten

When Dyson, Katie, and Sid crept down to the beach, there were bodies strewn *everywhere*.

"Ew," Katie whispered under her breath. She picked her way carefully around the dead men—they were *all* men—and spotted a breathing hole in the sand, indicating a gooey. Sid followed her, but she smacked him with her digging stick and made him find his own.

"What happened?" Dyson asked. Dyson was older than the other two and a little bit taller, with unkempt brown hair. He liked to think he was the leader, but Katie knew he was a scaredy-cat. He was poking one of the dead men with a tree branch. Katie had guessed right and came up with one of the gooey clams. She threw it in her bucket and joined Dyson. In the darkness, their injuries were hard to make out, but this guy's head had been crushed. His skull was all misshapen above one eye, and fluid still leaked from one ear. The dead guy next to *him* was missing a chunk from his thigh—it looked like something had bitten him. Either he'd been attacked by a *bear* somewhere, or a shark had had a nibble.

"Dunno, dummy," Katie said. "D'you think the tide brought them here?"

"Oh, for sure," Sid said. Sid didn't know anything about tides or the ocean. He wasn't even very good at fishing. The big jerk was always stealing bites from Katie's food, and if he hadn't been taller than she was, she would have hit him with her digging stick like she meant it. She didn't like him, but at least he didn't try to hurt her like some of the adults did. Adults were *mean*. But as long as the three of them stuck together, they usually found enough food to get by, and Miz Waylan would give them *fresh* to drink.

The lighter it got, the worse things appeared. Dirty, sandy lumps all up and down the beach were more dead guys. They hadn't been there yesterday morning, so where had they come from?

Katie decided it probably was the tide, and Sid agreed because she was right. Sunlight breached the horizon and bathed them in brilliant rays of warmth. Now that she could see better, she went into the water until it was up to her waist and used her clear-bottomed bucket to scan the sand by her feet. The bucket was part of the reason she was so good at clamming for gooeys. She could go deeper into the water and find them where no one else could because no one else could see through their buckets.

There! She spotted another gooey's breathing tube thingy and excavated it with her digging stick. She scraped sand and pebbles away, over and over, until she got deep enough to pull the clam free. The gooeys looked gross—kinda like penises—but after they were skinned and cut open, they looked like any other fish meat. They even tasted good. She kept scanning the sandy bed, then let out an *eek!* that she quickly stifled. Her bucket's much scratched, but still pretty clear bottom had revealed a hand and arm beneath the waves. She took the arm and gently tugged. It was still attached to a submerged body, so she pulled it behind her until the water grew too shallow. The dead guy's legs were still in the water, but another big guy, wearing some kind of white armor, lay in the way. She tried to drag that guy out of the way, but he was super heavy. She gave up and hauled the floater further down the beach, then let a wave carry him to shore.

"Wait!" Dyson whispered. He had his spear-stick with him. Dyson was proud of it, but Katie couldn't see why. He'd just sharpened the stick and then re-sharpened the area behind the point until it was barbed, like a massive fishhook. She let out another *eek!* when she saw his prey—a dogfish shark that had been nibbling on the dead guy's leg. Dyson crept into the water and then stabbed it with his spear!

"Hah!" he shouted in triumph, then glanced around to make sure no one had heard him. He didn't see any adults on the beach, so he dragged the still-wriggling dogfish out onto the sand. It was almost as long as Katie was tall, its gills pulsed in and out, and its mouth snapped as it slowly drowned in the open air.

"Shark's good eatin'," Sid said with a big smile.

"How would *you* know?" Katie asked. "Not that you helped."

"I had shark once," Sid protested. "I did!"

"Uh-huh," Katie rolled her eyes. "Okay, Mister I'm an Expert at Everything."

"Quiet," Dyson said. He wasn't looking at the dogfish anymore; he was looking back up the beach.

"Don't tell me to be—" Sid argued, but Dyson punched him in the tummy and clamped a hand over his mouth. "*QUIET!*" he hissed in Sid's ear. "Go for the bushes! Adults are coming!"

The three kids scampered off the beach, but when she reached the safety of the piles of driftwood that separated the Homes Zone from the beach, Katie realized her bucket was still down by the dead guy and the dead shark.

"What in the *hell?*" the first adult said. "Hey, Mac, come take a look at this!"

The speaker was, as she'd suspected, Jeremy. Marchand had given Jeremy and Mac this little chunk of beach two weeks ago. It wasn't fair—it was their beach—but the baron had given it to the adults and Jeremy and Mac had chased them off it four times already. The last time Mac had chased them, he'd said they were getting too big and taking too much, that he really would hurt them the next time he caught one of them because he didn't like starving anymore than they did, and it weren't like they were *his* kids.

"Hoh-lee sheeeit," Mac said. Sure enough, he and Jeremy came into view, looking up and down the beach at all the dead guys. "You up fer some long pig, Jer?"

"Man, fuck you," Jeremy replied. "We ain't that hungry yet."

"Well, no, but there's a *lot* of meat there, an' if ya do it up right…"

"Dude. *Dude! Seriously.* It was just that one time, alright? To hell with those savages, I ain't ever going back there, and I ain't ever eating nobody again less there ain't nothing left to eat." Jeremy was skinny, like *really* skinny, but he wasn't starvation-level skinny. He wore a tattered pair of badly salt-stained pants and a broad-brimmed hat to cover his balding head, and his shaggy beard was greasy and gross. He had a spear-stick with him, and he poked a couple of the dead guys. Then he froze. "Aw man, those fuckin' kids been down here ag'in."

"They what?" Mac replied, then followed Jeremy's gaze over to the bucket and the dead dogfish. "Oh, dammit. They can't've gone far."

Jeremy approached the bucket and shook his head in frustration. "Yeah, it's them, awright. Three gooeys right here, the lil bastards." He tossed the clams to Mac, who tucked them in a ragged canvas bag he wore over one shoulder. "We've tried ta warn ya!" Jeremy shouted down the beach. He turned Katie's bucket upside down on the sand and stomped on it, hard. The plastic shattered under his boot heel.

"No!" she cried, then clamped both hands over her mouth. It was too late.

"I figured," Jeremy said, hands on hips as he glared into the bushes. "Git out here, you."

Katie meekly emerged from beneath the piled driftwood, head down. "Where's the rest of em? Ain't you always runnin' aroun' with them two boys?" Jeremy demanded, but Katie wasn't a rat. She shook her head and crossed her arms in a childish symbol of defiance. Jeremy looked mad and grabbed her by her hair. "Now, girl! You tell me where they are! I know you don't come down here alone!" Katie cried as he wrenched her hair viciously and shook her, but she refused to answer.

"*Let her go,*" another voice said behind them.

"Huh?"

Jeremy swung around, dragging Katie with him. The big guy, the heavy one wearing the white armor, wasn't dead and had gotten to his feet. He was unsteady and swayed like he was drunk or having trouble standing up.

"Back off, man, this don't concern you," Jeremy said. Mac was creeping up behind him, using the crash of the surf to hide his footsteps.

"Look out, mister!" Katie cried, and the man in the white armor...*moved*. One moment he was standing next to the dead dogfish.

The next, he'd rolled aside, scooped up Dyson's barbed fishing stick, and slashed with it. Mac stopped and raised his hands to his throat. He coughed, and red streamed between his fingers and down his chest. He dropped to his knees, staring at his bloodied hands, then fell face first onto the sand.

"Motherf—" Jeremy snarled. He let go of Katie's hair and took two steps forward, then she shrieked as the barbed spear erupted from the middle of Jeremy's bare back. He collapsed too. Katie's eyes were as wide as clamshells. She was no stranger to violence; she was nine! But the dead dude—or, the not quite as dead as she thought dude—had killed Jeremy and Mac faster than she could follow.

"Uh, thank you," she whispered. The man in the white armor took a step toward her and dropped to one knee. He slumped to one side and lay there on his back, staring at the sky, taking huge, deep breaths. "Are you okay?" she cried and ran forward.

"No," he said. "I'm not." He lay there for a moment. Katie worried he might have actually died that time, he was so still, but then he untied some straps on his armor and shrugged out of the upper parts. He poked, prodded, and checked his torso, wincing and hissing. Dyson and Sid emerged from their hiding spot and crept close.

"What can we do to help you, mister?" Katie asked.

"Can you check with one of the medics? I'm going to need to tape up these ribs until they've healed. Maybe some crutches? I think my ankle's sprained too." He stuck a finger in one ear and wiggled it, opened his jaw and closed it a couple of times, then tugged on his earlobe again. "And I might be deaf in this ear, or it might just be waterlogged."

"Uh, medics?" Dyson repeated. "What's a medic?"

"We don't have any crutches, mister," Sid said. "I can try to find you a tree branch, though."

"No medics?" the man repeated and sat up with a groan. "No crutches?" He looked around—took a really good look around—and leaned back again. "What island are we on?"

"Um," Katie said. "I…don't know."

"Where do you live, then?"

"We move around a lot but usually just down from Miz Waylan's. Mostly."

"That's not helpful. Parents?"

"No." Sid shook his head.

"No parents? You're children. Who looks after you?"

"Miz Waylan, mostly," Katie answered. "But she does that for a lot of kids. And, only until our fourteenth winter. After that, we're on our own. That's one of The Rules."

"What's your name, little girl?"

"I'm not little, I'm *nine*," Katie answered fiercely. "But my name's Katie. Dyson is the big one with the brown hair, and Sid is the one getting you a walking stick. Who're you?"

The man accepted a stout tree branch from Sid and nodded his thanks. He slowly got to his feet, rolled his head and shoulders, and patted himself down again. "Call me…Ronin," he replied. "Who is Miz Waylan? How far is she from here?"

"I just *toled* you, she looks after us kids," she said. "She's not too far." Adults could be so dumb sometimes. She pointed in the general direction of the house, but then remembered the gooeys she'd dug up. She reclaimed her clams, and the bag Mac had tucked them in, from Mac's cooling body. She gave Dyson back his fishing stick, and kicked Jeremy in the groin.

"That's for breaking my bucket, you big jerk face. I'm glad you're dead," she spat. She tied Mac's bag's shoulder strap much shorter so it would sit properly on her tiny frame, then marched out to the road, made a right turn, and took the weird Ronin man to introduce him to Miz Waylan.

* * *

Something is very wrong with this picture.

Rikimaru had lived in the San Juan Islands for twenty years. He'd patrolled every coast. Komainu should have been cleaning the beachfront of all its dead. They should have had a funeral pyre burning.

They should have noticed him.

Where the hell *was* everyone? The pre-fall street signage was all standard, white text on a green background, so that was no clue. The more he hobbled along, the more he realized this particular patch of sand was alien to him.

If there *was* a beach where orphaned kids got roughed up by adults over geoduck fishing rights somewhere in the Shogunate, he'd've known.

Ergo, he wasn't in the San Juan Islands anymore. How long had he been out?

The little girl marched steadily ahead, passing old houses, abandoned and overgrown. Rusty fences surrounded some yards; rotten wooden pickets lined others. Adults he didn't recognize emerged from homes that looked abandoned. The strangers stared wide-eyed at the four of them walking down the middle of the street.

Everyone was skinny, some even skinnier than the two he'd killed on the beach. The girl turned down a small two-lane road that went beneath a multi-lane overpass. Rikimaru hobbled after her. The 'crutch' wasn't helping all that much, so he threw it aside. He'd just have to limp.

"Katie?" he asked. "I can't keep up, my ankle's injured. Cut the pace, please."

"Okay, Mister Ronin. Miz Waylan's is just up ahead."

"I can go get her!" the boy, Sid, said excitedly.

"No!" Katie shouted at him and planted her hands on her hips. "*I* want to do it."

"But—" Sid started to argue, and Rikimaru rolled his eyes in exasperation. *Kids.*

"I'd rather we all arrive together. I don't want Miz Waylan to think something's wrong."

"Mmkay." Sid kicked some loose rocks on the street and pouted, but he'd have to get over it.

A large house at the end of the street was clearly in much better shape than several of the neighboring residences. Neat rows of garden boxes divided the well-tended yard into lanes. It looked like carrots were sprouting in many of them. The house was rough, like every other house on the street, but the windows were intact, and when Rikimaru turned his head, his undamaged ear picked up the sounds of children playing inside. Katie scampered up the porch and threw the door open. "Miz Waylan! Come quick! We found someone!"

An elderly matron came to the door, towed by Katie. "Oh my. Yes, I suppose you did, young lady. Can I help you, sir?"

"I hope so," Rikimaru said. "It's a long story, but I washed up on the beach not far from here and came to as some men were accosting the girl."

"Jeremy and Mac," Dyson helpfully supplied. "They were really mad. They smashed Katie's bucket and grabbed her by her hair. Jeremy had his harpoony thing, and he was going to hurt her, but then Mister Ronin saved her!"

The woman looked Rikimaru up and down with a gimlet eye. She took in his wounds, his armor, and the splash of color where Jeremy had bled on him before he collapsed. She cocked a single eyebrow and fixed him with a look.

"I'm not from around here, but where I'm from, ma'am, we don't let adults hurt kids," Rikimaru said. "Not that I'm sure where here is, ma'am."

"You're full of it, 'Mister Ronin.' How can you possibly not know where you are?"

"I washed up on the beach, ma'am, far as I know."

"It's true," Dyson agreed. "There are lots of dead people down on the beach. They all washed up overnight. Like, more than *this* many!" he said, holding up both hands, fingers splayed wide. "We thought Mister Ronin was dead too. But he saved Katie when Jeremy grabbed her."

Sid and Katie were nodding as Dyson explained, and she rolled her eyes and turned back into the house. "You can come in, Mister Ronin, but don't expect to stay long. I help *children*. Adults have to fend for themselves."

Katie led the way in. There was a living room to his right, and he recognized the old Teledyne-branded polymer furniture, covered by ratty, threadbare blankets. The woman had a wood stove in her kitchen, venting out the back wall. Sprigs of dried herbs hung from strings, and she took some down and tucked them into a little mesh ball. She poured water from a kettle into a rough clay mug, popped a small block of honeycomb in, and added the tea strainer.

"Start at the beginning," she commanded the children and took a sip from her mug. Katie, Dyson, and Sid recited their adventures down at the beach.

"...and then Ronin was all, *Leave her alone*," Dyson said, trying for a deep, impressive voice, but failing. "Mac was sneaking up on him, but Ronin killed Mac with my harpoon! Jeremy had a harpoon too and went after Ronin, but Ronin took him out, bam!"

"And then you hobbled here, Mister Ronin?"

"Yes, ma'am." He hadn't said a word or prompted the kids to add anything to their story. He didn't want her to think he was making up the story or that the kids were lying on his behalf. "Adrenaline's a funny thing. I didn't notice how bad my ankle or my ribs were until after the danger was past. But I'm a little bit wrecked right now. I think, with some bandages and a bite to eat, I'll be fine in a couple of days."

Miz Waylan took another sip and eyed him suspiciously.

"Tell me about before you woke up on our little beach. Explain to me how come there are, shall we say, ten or more dead people on the beach?"

"I'm not sure I can, ma'am. I was unconscious for most of it. Raiders attacked us, and we were fighting for control of a bridge. But one of the raiders was very dangerous. A veteran of the Corporate Wars."

"Do tell," Miz Waylan said. "One of those accursed Specialists, I'm sure? You're old enough. You must remember what it was like during the wars?"

Rikimaru cleared his throat. "I do, ma'am. I used to work for Teledyne myself. But this one was an Obsidian Agent, one of their worst. To stop him from getting to our civilian population, we destroyed the bridge, but I was still on it. That's the last thing I remember before waking up on the beach."

"I see," Waylan said after a moment's thought. She stood, crossed the room, and pulled an old, faded map book from a shelf. She returned to her seat and flipped through the pages until she found what she was looking for. Her head came up, and she again fixed her stare on Rikimaru. "I'm going to have to ask you to leave, Mister Ronin, and never come back."

"But!" Katie exclaimed.

"Don't interrupt, Katie," Waylan shushed her. "You see, you're in Sidney right now, Mister Ronin, on what we used to call Vancouver Island. The only bridges of any significant size anywhere near here were Vancouver, which suffered multiple cluster bombs during the attack and is mostly a radioactive hole; Seattle, which suffered even more; or the ones connecting the mainland to Anacortes and Whidbey. In the days, weeks, and months after those warmongers ruined two thousand years of progress, the residents of Deception Pass and the surrounding islands *cut Vancouver Island off.* For two decades, they have callously sunk the few boats we had and limited us to fishing in whatever water we could row or wade out to. Vancouver Island used to be Teledyne property, too, Ronin. I used to work for them. *Everyone* did. Sidney was a nice, quiet retirement village with beautiful views and beautiful homes. The speed limit was thirty— that's kilometers, mind you—and the most excitement we ever had was taking the ferry to the mainland. But after the nuclear exchange, our pleas for help went unanswered. Whoever was in charge over there didn't just ignore us, they hung us out to dry. The empress has been making do ever since. Starvation is rife here, and it is *your* people's fault. There is the door, sir, you may use it."

Rikimaru stood, stiff and slow. "I humbly apologize for intruding, Miz Waylan. You're doing good work here, ma'am. I don't know the first thing about raising kids. You have my respect." He hobbled out the front door and didn't look back.

* * *

Rikimaru mentally slapped himself as he made his way back down the street. Of *course* he was on Vancouver Island. The morning of the battle, the tide had been running out as the sun came up—it would have flowed west at high pressure through Deception Pass and then gotten all jumbled up passing between the islands. The most surprising thing was that he was alive. He should have gone straight to the bottom, crushed and drowned in thirty fathoms of Pacific saltwater. He'd have to think about that one. *Had he become less dense, somehow? Were the nanites wearing off?*

The last thing he remembered before ordering the bridge sundered was Gaunt stabbing Mikael and Ayame dragging the wounded samurai clear. Were they alive? The Shogunate believed he was dead, that was certain. Hundreds of bodies would have been in the water—ninety percent of Gaunt's forces, alive or dead, strewn about the old ironworks, then dumped into the outgoing tide en masse.

Miz Waylan's words played on his mind, too.

How the hell was he going to get home?

He passed a still-legible street sign—he noted Waylan lived on Rideau Ave—and next to it, a faded, rusty Neighbourhood Watch sign. They'd walked right past it, and he berated himself. If he'd been paying attention, he would have seen it and immediately deduced his location. Even after corporateship became more important than citizenship, the West Canadians had retained their spare u's.

Waylan's words bounced around in his head, enhancing the seed of doubt Gaunt had planted in his mind about the shogun. He'd served the shogun honestly and dutifully for decades. It didn't make sense that Kojima had rebuffed the Victorians if they'd reached out for help. *He* would have been the one doing the rebuffing, and he knew he hadn't done anything of the sort.

"Mister Ronin?" Katie's voice behind him surprised him. He was beginning to suspect his hearing really had been damaged in the blasts, and that didn't bode well for his situational awareness. He turned to face her and was shocked when the little girl ran up to him and hugged his leg.

"Thank you for saving me from Jeremy," she said. "I'm sorry Miz Waylan was being a big jerk. She's very strict, but she tries to grow enough food for us, at least until we're old enough."

"I understand," Rikimaru said, stiffly. "I don't want to get you in trouble, though."

"I'm kinda in trouble already," she admitted. "I told her she was being mean, that you hadn't done anything wrong, and that you just needed help."

"No need to get yourself in trouble on my account," Rikimaru said. "I'm an adult. I can take care of myself." Honestly, though, he was impressed the child had stood up for her convictions. She had spirit.

"Too late!" she said in a sing-song, mischievous voice. "Whatcha gonna do now?"

"I think I'm going to head back down to the beach," Rikimaru said. "I like the look of some of those driftwood shelters. Then I'm going to figure out how to get home."

The look on the little girl's face told Rikimaru what she thought of his leaving, but she didn't object outright. "I know a spot where no one's gonna bother you," Katie said. "Follow me."

Rikimaru couldn't help but smile as the precocious child led him back down the road, back under the overpass, and down to the beach where he'd regained consciousness. "This is where we started?" Rikimaru asked.

"It is!" Katie replied. "There's a shelter there." She pointed to the spot she'd been hiding when Jeremy and Mac first came down to the beach. "And no one's gonna see."

"They won't?"

"Well…you killed Jeremy and Mac, you big silly. It'll be a few days before anyone else tries to jump their claim, and if you're here, well, you can scare them off. Or kill them too. Whichever."

It did make a very limited amount of sense, but he had to assume the dead guys had friends who would miss them. That this little girl was comfortable with him killing the two thugs on the beach was disturbing, though.

"Do you know where Jeremy and Mac lived?" he asked.

"Mmhmm." Katie nodded. "They had a trailer down at the Park'n'Ride. Lotsa people live there. It's a couple minutes' walk."

He pondered, for a moment. How much trouble was he in, really? Could he ask a favor, a potentially dangerous favor, of this child? *A lot. And, yes.* "Would you get in trouble if you went to see if Jeremy or Mac had any tools at home? A knife? An axe? Anything like that?"

"I can do that, sure!" Katie beamed at being given such an important task and raced away south.

Rikimaru bent and twisted, examining his armor plates. The plates and lamellar had saved him multiple times during the battle—they were a mix of plywood and foam cushioning or polymers salvaged from the base's machine shop. The plates bore scars from his battle on the bridge—some he remembered, some he'd ignored. An axe chop here, a sword thrust there—the armor had more than proven its worth. Despite his fatigue, he decided to keep the armor on. He couldn't afford to be taken unawares, and his hearing was pooched.

He turned to the dead littering the beach. Bald eagles, or as he called them, vultures with better PR, were already ripping into the bodies and feasting on the meat. Once upon a time as a child, he'd attended an "Eagle Fest" east of the Vancouver sprawl, where hundreds of eagles had gathered upstream to prey on salmon after they'd spawned. He'd been fascinated when a junior bald eagle, only a year or two old and lacking the white feathers of his elders, spent fifteen minutes clawing and tearing at one salmon. The ultra-tough salmon skin refused to yield to the bird's talons, but the bird persevered. Young Rick had cheered when the eagle finally got at the pink flesh inside—and then yelled at the opportunistic elder birds that swooped in to steal the fish from Junior after he'd done all the hard work.

These eagles weren't having any difficulty ripping into the dead and had already made one helluva mess. He chucked a rock, and the birds scattered. The scavengers had already gouged faces and limbs, and one guy, whose arm was sheared off cleanly above the elbow, had already been eviscerated. They'd torn into intestines and opened up bellies full of bile and partly-digested food that had cooked in the spring sunshine. The stench was *foul*. No matter. He'd done worse, plenty of times. Hell, he'd probably killed a bunch of these men himself. The missing arm looked like it had been taken off with his katana.

His katana!

"Shit. SHIT!" he cursed. "I spent *weeks* on that blade! One fight. *One fight,* and now it's at the bottom of the ocean! *Damn it!"* He kicked the nearest body in frustration and immediately regretted it as pain lanced up his leg. He screamed, wordlessly, venting his frustration and anger with his breath. His legs gave out, and he leaned back against a driftwood log and covered his eyes with his hands.

It's fine.

It was a good blade, served me well through my one and only grand battle. I can make another.

All I have to do is get home. Work the survival scale, work the priorities.

Food, water, shelter.

Health, security.

Go from there.

He regained his feet and searched each of the dead. Once he had thoroughly checked them, he dragged them down to the water's edge and laid them in a neat row. Rigor mortis had set in, stiffening them, and nature was already hard at work recycling the bodies. In addition to the eagles, maggots and other bugs had hatched and were feeding on the rotting carcasses. The raiders' clothes were mostly rags, ripped, torn, and ruined with time. Only one wore shoes. He did find three pocket-folder knives and claimed those. The shoes were too small, but the laces might be useful. One raider's clothing was leather of some sort, not cheap, disposable synthetic textiles, and he cut the pants away to salvage the material. After yanking on the leather to ensure it wouldn't tear, he cut a long strip and wrapped it tightly around his injured ankle. The additional support helped.

Eighteen of Gaunt's dead barbarians lay there in rigid poses when he finished cleaning up 'his' beach. While doing so, he saw a barrier of driftwood logs, a bunch laid end-to-end, and recognized it as some kind of marker. A property marker, perhaps? Something to declare where the dead Victorians' turf started and ended? That would make a certain amount of sense; otherwise, the beachfront would have been utter anarchy.

Then again, maybe it was.

The tide would carry the bodies away that night to be fish food, or at least to be someone else's problem. An old class he'd taken in basic forensics bubbled to the surface: the fact that the bodies were still in rigor mortis indicated no more than forty-eight hours had passed since they'd died. Given it was sunrise when he awoke here, he estimated he'd been unconscious for just the one day. What a difference that one day made! Regardless, another mystery solved— he knew where he was, and now he knew when he had arrived. That was enough, for now. It wasn't even noon, and he was exhausted. He gingerly sat down, crawled under the driftwood, and dozed off in minutes.

* * *

The daimyo jerked awake, feeling a presence nearby. He jumped to his feet—or tried to—but his body refused to cooperate. Instead, he groaned, rolled onto his side, came to his knees, and found himself face to face with the young girl, with her inquisitive eyes and stringy, muddy, black hair.

"I got the tools 'n stuff, Mister Ronin," Katie said, and she proudly displayed her collection. Rikimaru despaired.

One set of scratched-to-hell diving goggles.

One long stick, with ten feet of white cotton string and a hook.

One fish bat.

One rusty filleting knife.

One rusty axe head pinned to a short chunk of pine limb that would undoubtedly break the first time he thought about hitting something with it.

"That's it?" Rikimaru asked in disbelief. Katie's proud smile turned into a frown.

"They had a solar still, too, for making water, but that was too big and heavy to take," she said, pouting. "And the other adults would have asked too many questions."

"I meant no offense, little one," Rikimaru said.

"I'm *not* little," she exclaimed. "I already toled you!"

"Yes you are. You're tiny, even for your age. Your legs are as big around as my wrists. Clearly, they aren't feeding you enough." He found himself flustered by this fearless child as he heaved himself onto a log. "I apologize, Katie. All I meant was, I'm surprised that was all *they* had, not that you hadn't acquired enough of their stuff. Is this pretty typical?"

Katie brightened and nodded. "Pretty much. Everything's rusty and old, and stuff breaks all the time. That's why Dyson just sharpened the end of his fishing stick. Making one with a metal tip is way too much work, and then it just falls apart."

"Any kind of fire starter?"

"Nuh-uh." She shook her head no. "Miz Waylan keeps wood shavings and beeswax to start a fire, but one of her firestarters costs a whole day's food."

Rikimaru took one of the pocket knives and cut and tore the dead men's clothes until he had several square feet of fabric. It was sodden from the rain, so he laid it out on the driftwood to dry. He wouldn't be able to light it yet—the cloth needed time to dry.

"What do you do for food?"

She unslung the bag she'd taken off Mac's corpse and laid it out.

"These are gooeys," she said, hefting one of the—he had to admit—obscenely phallic clams. She examined the filleting knife quickly, rubbed the pad of her thumb along the edge of the blade, and decided it would do. She began by whacking the shell on one of the logs, hard, a couple of times. She used the filleting knife to cut into the clamshell, then cracked it off, and pulled out the meat. Rikimaru had eaten geoduck often, but it had been a decade or more since he'd watched someone prepare it. He tended to just sit down to a bowl of clam soup, chowder, or raw sashimi. Katie was something of an expert.

The contents of the clam looked like an alien from outer space. She deftly sliced away one collection of (ahem) parts, trimmed the base of the siphon, then ran the blade lightly up the outside of the siphon to part the wrinkly skin. She dug her fingers in and pulled, peeling the skin away from the inner meat. It took a bit of doing, but in a few seconds, she laid the siphon down again and cut it in half.

"This is how gooeys eat," she explained. "One tube sucks seawater in to eat…whatever they inhale, and the other spits it back out again. So there's always sand and junk inside." Rikimaru could, indeed, see dark specks of sand and debris inside, and he nodded in understanding. She carried the meat down to the water's edge and tossed the guts to the flock of eagles. They squawked and fought over the bits, but she ignored them. After rinsing the meat in the water, she returned and proudly displayed the pale yellow-pink meat. She sliced the base of the siphon into a thin disc and popped it in her mouth. She passed the rest of the meat to Rikimaru and got to work cleaning the next one.

"This is *good*," he said between mouthfuls. And it was. The meat was almost crunchy and had a salty/sweet taste. Most of the time, his geoduck sashimi was drowning in herbs and homemade soy sauce, which hid the flavor.

"Thanks," Katie said, as she cut the second shell open. "That's why Jeremy and Mac were so mad. They weren't very good fishermen, but gooeys are easy to find."

"What else do you do for food around here?" Rikimaru asked, eyeballing the cluster of eagles tearing strips of flesh from the dead raiders.

"Ew. No," Katie said. "Eagle's *nasty*. If it eats dead things, it tastes like dead things. There are rabbits *everywhere* on the other side of the highway. Sometimes, we can bop them with rocks and scoop a couple. Miz Waylan grows vegables, mostly carrots, and tomatoes, and cabbage."

"What about rice? Bread? Corn?"

Katie looked at him, puzzled.

"No? Whazzat?"

Rikimaru's eyes widened.

"Rice? Little white or brown…pellet things you boil in water? Bread is…bread. Don't you know what bread is? You make sandwiches with it." Katie just stared at him blankly. "You've never even *seen* those?"

The little girl shrugged. "Nope. When I'm thirteen, I wanna claim a house and dig a garden, see if Miz Waylan will give me some of her seeds so I can grow vegables too. Mostly, I eat fish, gooeys, rabbits, and vegables. Or stew. Miz Waylan makes stew a lot, too."

"Aren't you hungry all the time?" He cursed himself silently for the ridiculous question. Of course, she was.

"Of course, I am," she said, very matter-of-fact. "But, maybe, since Jeremy and Mac are gone, and this is kinda *our* beach now, we can catch more fish, and I won't be as hungry anymore?" She turned and left Rikimaru to go wash her geoduck meat in the surf. Rikimaru rose to his feet, stiff, sore, and still hurting from the broken ribs and twisted ankle, but he limped down the sandy beach.

O, how the mighty have fallen.

"How about you teach me how you find these gooeys, and I'll see what I can find?"

Katie's face lit up, and she passed him her digging stick. They walked up and down the beach until she spotted one of the little divots in the sand where the clam's siphon was exposed. She quickly dug a trench leading to the siphon but left the siphon itself encased in sand.

"Those jerks broke my bucket," she said. "Normally, I'd wash the sand away and follow the siphon down."

Rikimaru thought about the problem for a moment, then returned to "his" shelter. The shallow curvature of his *sode* pauldrons meant they could scoop and hold water—but more like a dinner plate than a soup bowl. He returned to the waterline, scooped up some seawater, and presented it to the little girl.

It took multiple trips, but Rikimaru kept her supplied with water, and she patiently rinsed away the sand, until the gleaming white shell was just barely visible.

"And now, you just grab it and pull it free," she said. Rikimaru got down next to her, grabbed hold, and wrenched the clam free.

"Wow, that's *huge!*" Katie said in awe.

"Feels like ten pounds or more," Rikimaru said. "We make a good team."

She smiled at the praise and hefted the clam up to the shelter for him as he limped after her. This time, Rikimaru followed her instructions from memory. When he'd cut the guts away, washed the siphon, and sliced the breast meat into strips, they dug in.

"And, with that," Rikimaru said, "I need to rack out. I'm still pretty banged up, and I'll heal faster if I sleep."

"Rack out?" Katie repeated. "Whazzat? "

"Sleep, Katie. I need sleep."

"I can keep fishing if you want. I'll share," she offered.

"This is your beach too," Rikimaru said, but she shook her head no.

"You killed Jeremy and Mac. I didn't help, so it's yours."

"Okay…" Rikimaru said, puzzled. That sounded suspiciously like a rule, not just a nine-year-old being bizarrely generous. "In that case…yes. You and those two boys are welcome here at any time. If you're going to keep fishing, please keep the noise down." She looked at him expectantly. He had never been one for effusive praise, but talk was cheap, and his approval seemed to motivate her. "Thank you for all your help, young lady. Means a lot."

"You're welcome! How're you going to start a fire?"

"Watch," he said, "and learn."

First, he made a ring of rocks on a clear spot just outside the mouth of the driftwood shelter. Dried grasses, twigs, and other kindling went into the middle, and he gathered up sticks of all diameters and put them aside. One chunk of driftwood was rectangular, and the length of his forearm. That would do nicely. The polycotton cloth he'd cut from the dead raiders had dried as they fished. Now, Rikimaru sliced it into thin tatters and spread the threads wide until he just held a fluffy square of cotton, smaller than the palm of his hand. He laid the fluff down on a driftwood log and dusted it with a pinch of sand. He rolled the fluff up into a ball, twisting the material up into a ball, with the sand stuck to it, inside and out. Then he sandwiched the sandy fluff between the log, and the rectangular driftwood.

He rolled his piece of material between the driftwood, tightening it even more until it was a hard, compressed mixture of cotton and silica. Satisfied, he placed the small now-grey mixture back where it had started, then leaned on the board and started rolling it back and forth as quickly as he could. Barely twenty seconds passed before he could smell the burning. Ten more, and wisps of smoke tinted the air. He removed the board and scooped up the smoldering fabric, gently blowing on it to encourage it to catch flame. It glowed, sparked, and then ignited. Rikimaru gingerly placed it down with the kindling and gently blew on it until it caught.

"That's...*amazing!*" Katie said. "Can I try?"

"Next time," Rikimaru said. "We only have so much fabric, and if you do it wrong, the material's wasted."

"I won't waste nuffin," she protested.

"You did a good job with the gooeys, so I'm inclined to believe you, but we can't waste anything. For now, I'm going to build up this little bit of heat and then I'm going to crash."

* * * * *

Chapter Eleven

Sergeant Shawn Carey gratefully accepted a cup of tea from the proprietor of Oak Harbor Tea (formerly, Oak Harbor Coffee) and rejoined his troops outside.

He enjoyed this part of the job—foot patrols through their few urban areas gave him a chance to get to know the local businesses and spend a bit of coin. There wasn't much in the way of luxuries to be had guarding the Naval Air Station's headquarters. It was a mark of trust that his platoon was even considered for the job, supplementing and backstopping the Homeguard, but the job itself was miserable.

"So, what do you say, Sarge?" Ian asked. "You gonna go for that new Marines thing?"

Carey sipped his tea for a moment and composed his answer.

"No."

He sipped again. Ian, Scott, and Ben looked at him expectantly. They knew better than to interrupt.

"First, swimming across Blind Bay strikes me as cold, wet, and miserable." He eyed the nearby sign for Flintstone Park and pointed east across the inner bay to where the docks met the waterfront. He sipped again. "It's about that far, and that's a long, bloody swim. Not my cup of tea, as it were. But second and more important, since they blew the bridge and all those raider bodies hit the water? Sharks been having a frenzy. One guy, fishing in Skagit Bay? A shark tipped his boat and took his arm off at the elbow. He's lucky to be alive."

"Ouch."

Ben nodded in understanding. "No kidding. They say killer whales don't kill people, but you couldn't pay me enough right now to go swimming in that. The Onamazu are a bunch of maniacs."

Ian looked puzzled. "How'd the guy survive getting his arm taken off?"

Carey shrugged. "He had a necktie, of all things, and used it as a tourniquet. The shark must have found something else to munch on because the guy dragged himself to shore. I don't know him, but someone's taken him in until he recovers. Probably family or something. He'll need a while, but he should survive unless infection sets in. Sharks don't floss, you know. All kinds of nasty things in their teeth."

Scott shook his head. "Kinda sad, in a way. How do you go back to fishing, less an arm? He can't fight. He's going to be pretty useless for a lot of trades. Almost be better if the shark had taken him outright."

Carey held the door to the High Tides Bookshop, and his half-lance headed inside. They had a few coins in their pockets, and the bookshop always had a good selection. "You gotta do what you gotta do. But yeah, between the cold, the wet, picking fights with the Victorians, and not getting chomped by sharks? I'll take foot patrol in Oak Harbor every day of the week, thanks."

* * *

When Rikimaru awoke, embers were still smoldering in the fire pit he'd built, and the sun was coming up. He crawled out of his hideout and stretched—he was already feeling a little bit better. The muscle aches were gone, his ankle was much better, and his ribs hurt a little less. Katie'd disappeared after saying she needed to find Dyson and Sid again.

He rekindled the fire and added larger and larger sticks until he could put a log on that would burn for several hours.

For now, he was focusing on healing, and healing required more food. Before he risked his hide any further, he needed to be well again, and that meant fueling the nanites that coursed through his arteries. They reconstructed damaged tissue at the cellular level, toughening muscles and reinforced structures like ligaments and bones.

He shuddered at an ancient memory that arose unbidden. Some of Teledyne's earliest Specialists had gotten experimental nanite treatments to increase their muscular strength, but the science geeks had failed to strengthen their tendons and ligaments. The first Specialists were crippled immediately when their new musculature tore away from their skeletons. "Obligatory secondary superpowers," Kael had called them. The first volunteers were repaired, but what happened in the early months very nearly killed the program off until the eggheads devised a way to strengthen the connective tissues.

That hadn't made him invulnerable, though. The battle of Deception Pass had been the single most taxing event of his life, bar none. He'd been in conflicts that had lasted longer, but most of those had been mobile skirmishes between Obsidian and Teledyne forces all over North America.

And he'd had guns.

The Whidbey airbase didn't have enormous stores of small arms ammunition, and they lacked the necessary powder and primers to reload, so once they'd used the ammunition up, it was gone. Barring an expedition to the sulfur hot springs far to their north or to the caldera of Mount Baker, they couldn't even produce black powder, never mind modern propellant.

That said, if he ever made it to the interior, he still knew the codes for accessing their clandestine bunkers, and those were chock full of rifles, ammunition, and prepackaged, long-storage food. But they'd never built bunkers here, in the heart of Teledyne country. Why would they? He was surprised to find himself wishing Obsidian had tucked away some similar secret facility nearby that he had yet to discover.

How times change.

He'd never really studied the depth charts of the coast off Sidney and wasn't sure how quickly it dropped off. Time to find out, he supposed. He put another bit of fluff on the fishing hook, as the cheapest, saddest, most pathetic lure he'd ever seen. He stripped down to his underwear, hung his pants and shirt to warm near the fire, adjusted the mask, and waded into the surf armed with the "fishing rod" and the filleting knife. The tide was higher today, and once it was up to his thighs, he ducked underwater to see what the terrain was like. It was cold, but he'd been chilled before, and if he could survive the trip here, unconscious, there wasn't anything to fear.

He had precisely no buoyancy, as he'd expected. It must have been his full armor that kept him afloat. He hadn't ever tested that, come to think of it.

Duh.

His improved lung capacity gave him plenty of time to move about underwater, marveling at the schools of fish that darted to and fro. Sunlight carved brilliant beams through to the sandy bottom, which went a long way out. Bull kelp waved back and forth in thick, green, underwater forests, and Rikimaru went for those first. He cut a dozen of the rectangular, green 'leaves' from the closest of the kelp formations and took them back to shore. It was basically salty Pacific sea lettuce, so he ate a couple handfuls and left the rest to dry by his clothes.

He went back out into the water, found a bare patch of sand on the bottom, and sat. Not moving conserved oxygen, and he wouldn't scare the fish. He occasionally exhaled a bit to relieve the carbon dioxide buildup, and he was pretty comfortable. He leaned the long fishing pole out in front of him and let the current carry the fluff and hook out on the braided line.

He jerked the line occasionally to make the fluff dart and move, and seconds ticked away. He exhaled a bit of air and wondered how long he'd been holding his breath. His personal best was about eight minutes, but he'd practiced for that. Seconds became minutes, but none of the fish seemed interested in his sad, little lure, so he stood up and walked back far enough for his head to breach the surface.

"Mister Ronin?" Katie squealed from the shore. "Were you down there the *whole time?*"

"I was fishing," he replied. "I can hold my breath for a long time. I'm going to go back in, I'm not done yet. Don't worry. I won't forget to come up."

When he went back under the water, he started tapping his left hand, about once a second, to keep time. He walked a little further, a little deeper, and cleared his ears to relieve the pressure.

Twenty seconds.

He was only fifteen or twenty feet down when he came to a drop off that went down maybe twice that far. Whole schools of fish darted back and forth far below him.

Forty seconds.

He sat a couple feet back from the precipice, rocking with the waves, and lowered his stick so the lure hung almost on the bottom.

Sixty seconds.

A minute twenty.

A low, broad-headed fish with brown scales eased out from between the bull kelp and pounced! Rikimaru tugged on the hook to set

192 | JAMIE IBSON

it and almost lost the rod when the fish panicked and tried to swim away. He got to his feet and slowly forced the fish up above the shelf. He wrapped his hand around the line so the fish couldn't whip back and forth and turned for shore.

One fifty.

He increased his stride and was just starting to feel the burn in his chest when his head broke the surface.

"Hey!" Katie called from the beach. She was crouched next to the fire, nibbling on something.

"Can you bring me the fish bat?" The little girl leaped to her feet and searched the shelter until she found the short, wooden club. Rikimaru met her by one of the larger, flatter driftwood logs and laid the fish out. It was twitching and twisting now that it was out of the water. He held it still with one hand and accepted the bat in the other. Two swift strikes to the head dispatched the fish, and Rikimaru let go of the braided line. It was a big thing and ugly as sin, but fish meat was fish meat.

He gutted the fish and showed Katie how to trim away the gills. She smiled and asked for the knife. Rikimaru passed it to her, and she surgically cut into the fillet half an inch from the end, then cut down to but not through the skin and started working the knife up the meat, cutting the skin away.

"If we don't know how to make food, we don't eat," Katie said. "That's what Miz Waylan says. Everyone helps in the garden, everyone cleans the vegables, and everyone cleans the fishies."

"Do any other adults help you?" Rikimaru asked.

"No, Mister Ronin," Katie said, "they're selfish."

"That's right," a male voice said, and Rikimaru snapped his head around. His hearing *was* screwed up. Five men marched up the beach, but he hadn't heard a thing. The one in the lead was skinny, with loose, ragged clothing hanging off his spare frame like a scarecrow. He was dirty, with a scraggly beard and unwashed, greasy brown hair. A scar bisected his face from his forehead, down the bridge of his nose, and out onto his cheek. He reminded Rikimaru of one of Gaunt's raiders.

Scarface stepped over the logs demarking the 'property line' and hefted a stout length of wood in his hands like a club. "Selfish. Because every bite one of these brats steals is another bite closer to starvation for the rest of us." The speaker eyed the fillets on the log. "It's worse when it's an adult that starts thievin'. You're new to the area. I'd remember a big lad like you, so maybe you don't know how this works. This beach here is MacDonnell and Dickson's hunting grounds. You fish here without their permission, an' they'll gut you like that lingcod there. Leave you to the buzzards."

"This…MacDonnell and Dickson. Would that be Mac and Jeremy?" Rikimaru asked. Scarface's eyes tightened in suspicion, but one of his buddies nodded behind him. "That them?"

He pointed to their corpses, which were next to the others at the waterline.

"*Bastard!*" Scarface cursed and ran across the soft sand. His steps were awkward as the sand sank beneath his feet, and that gave Rikimaru plenty of time to prepare. When Scarface lifted the club high over his head to bash Rikimaru, the Specialist drove a fist into his belly.

Scarface retched, folded in half, and dropped to the ground, clutching his abdomen. Rikimaru snatched the club from where it fell and whipped it down in a vicious chop, braining Scarface and silencing his efforts to breath.

"The…the Baron'll hear about this!" one of the followers said.

"By all means," Rikimaru said. "Run off to whoever that is and cry to him that the stranger on the beach, whom you outnumbered five to one, was being mean to you. Run along now, I'm hungry, and this fish isn't going to cook itself."

The four looked at each other in fear, and Rikimaru took a single, aggressive step toward them. That was enough to send them running back down the beach. This whole Ronin act was kind of fun. After two decades of cultivating his daimyo persona, he didn't have to remain upright and proper and maintain decorum at all times anymore. He wasn't the shogun's general, he was a masterless samurai, beholden to no one. He could tell assholes they were being assholes—he didn't have to sugar coat it, and he didn't have to filter his snark. It was incredibly liberating.

Rikimaru glared at them until they left the beach, then went back to his lingcod fillet. He was pleased to see Katie had already sliced up the meat into easily skewered cubes and threaded several onto sticks for roasting.

Clever girl. She never let the knife get out of arm's reach.

* * *

"Uhh, Mister Ronin?" a small voice called from up the beach. Rikimaru recognized the two young boys who'd been with Katie the morning before and waved them forward.

"Help yourself." He gestured to the roasted fish sticks, and the boys' eyes went round.

"Really?" the shorter one asked. Sid, if Rikimaru remembered correctly. Sid was the shorter one, with sandy blonde hair and a narrow, weaselly face. Dyson was taller, with unkempt, curly brown hair, and he already had scars visible on his face and arms, though he couldn't have even been Derek Frost's age. All three looked weathered and worn. Katie was the smallest of the three and had wavy black hair that looked like she'd never cut it.

The boys fell upon the fish skewers and devoured three each, then licked the sticks clean. The lingcod had netted him almost thirty pounds of fish meat, so there was plenty for all of them. Rikimaru wrapped a squarish chunk of it in some bull kelp and made a sea lettuce wrap.

"So, tell me about this 'baron,'" he said. The boys exchanged looks and then looked at Katie. Katie rolled her eyes and finished chewing.

"Baron Howell was a *jerk*." Katie spat, and the boys nodded. Their cheeks were stuffed. "Like a total butt. He was mean, and he hit people all the time, and he took some of everything everyone caught and kept it all for himself and his friends. He didn't care how hungry someone was or how old they were. He just took it. He and his friends hurt anyone who tried to say no."

"And the new Baron is even worse," Dyson said once he'd swallowed his fish. "At least Baron Howell was lazy. He only came around a couple of times a week; his friends would normally be the ones out taxing everyone. But Baron Marchand is way worse. He lives on the top floor of the Pier Scraper, where he can watch everything that goes on at the market, and everything that happens on the waterfront. He killed all of the old Baron's friends and hung their bodies from lampposts for the crows. If you go a bit up the coast, you'll find the scraper. You can't miss it. The bodies line the street."

"It's super gross," Sid added. "They've got maggots and flies and stuff. The crows and the eagles and the rats and the coons rip bits off, and it splatters all over. They fight over food as much as we do."

"How far away is that?" Rikimaru asked. "I've never been to Sidney before."

"Not far," Dyson said, but he had no frame of reference to mark time or distance. "When you reach Ear-oh-kwoiz park, you're halfway."

"What happened to the first baron? Baron Howell?" Rikimaru asked. "Did Marchand kill him too?"

"No one knows," Sid said it like it was some grand mystery.

"Some people say Baron Marchand killed him for the position," Dyson said, rolling his eyes at Sid's dramatic efforts. "'Cuz that's how it normally happens."

"Some people say the *empress* killed him," Katie continued. "Or her champion. Others say Duke Robitaille had him executed for one thing or another. There are, like, nine stories about what happened."

"Duke Robitaille doesn't like Marchand either," Dyson said. "That's why I think the empress killed Howell. Barons come in two types. They're the Duke's bestest buddy, or they're looking to take the Duke out and get promoted. Marchand isn't the Duke's buddy."

Rikimaru chewed on his fishkabob for another minute. It was sad how desperate the kids were to eat and how grateful they were that'd he'd deigned to share. This rampant starvation? This was exactly the kind of thing Shogun Kojima and he had opposed from the first mushroom cloud. If you could keep people fed, you kept barbarism and panic at bay. Contrariwise, starvation bred desperation.

"So what's to stop someone from taking out this Baron Marchand?" he asked.

"Just he and his friends," Dyson said. "All barons wind up with a bunch of friends who will protect him and get protected in turn."

"Except that one of his friends is normally the guy who kills him later," Katie added. "According to Miz Waylan, *Baron Howell is the first baron who wasn't whacked by one of his inner circle*," she quoted. "We don't even know where Baron Marchand came from. He just showed up one day and said he was in charge."

"How did you know Baron Howell wasn't in charge anymore?"

Dyson and Katie exchanged a look, and Sid spoke up. "The new baron, Marchand? He kinda had Baron Howell's head on a stick. Like, a big one. That was super gross too."

Rikimaru digested that for a moment. If that was how Marchand operated, he couldn't afford to take naps on the beach anymore. He'd have to find somewhere anonymous and secure to sleep, or risk falling asleep and never waking.

The whole situation was screwed up; adults were willing to hurt, or worse, *kill*, children because starvation was that rampant. If the authorities were so screwed up they did likewise, then maybe he needed to tear down whatever passed for governance and force a hard reset.

But then again, he'd only been here for thirty-six hours, and he'd spent half of that unconscious, so…he'd give them a chance. *One* chance.

"Do you kids sleep at Miz Waylan's overnight?"

"No, we—" Sid began, but Dyson interrupted.

"Uh…nearby." He glared pointedly at Sid, whose mouth closed with an audible *clop*. Sid went back to chewing.

"If you don't want to say, that's alright." Rikimaru smiled as kindly as he could. From what he could tell, these kids had only ever had one adult they could trust. "I get it. You're vulnerable when you're asleep, and you can keep on the move when you're awake. I just wanted to know how to get a message to you if I need to. Miz Waylan wouldn't be too pleased to deliver messages on my behalf. So…" He scanned the beach and spotted a large, flat rock about the size of a dinner plate. He got to his feet, picked it up, and moved it up near the driftwood shelter. He held it in one hand and picked up a roasting stick with a charred tip. "If I need to speak to you guys, I'll write you a note on the underside of this stone with charcoal, and you can meet me wherever I've gone."

"We, uh," Dyson stammered, "don't…"

"None of us learned our letters, Mister Ronin," Katie said. Rikimaru's features tightened, and with a massive contraction, he hurled the stone so far out into the water, they couldn't see it splash. "Woah," Sid gasped. "That was awesome." He scanned for another rock and presented it to Rikimaru. "Do it again?"

Rikimaru did as requested. Once again, the rock sailed out beyond the whitecaps and disappeared, swallowed by the ocean like it had never existed. He didn't like to lose his temper. Most times, he kept it under absolute control, but both his discipline and his patience were slipping. Starving, illiterate children, whom he didn't know how to handle, murderous adults, whom he did, warlords who ruled through fear and violence…no wonder the Victorians had fallen so far, so fast.

The rocks gave him an idea, though.

"Okay, you don't know how to read or write. Long term project. It's harder when you're older, but that can't be helped. What about weaving? Katie's good at cleaning fish and geoducks, so you've been taught some essentials. Do you know how to make baskets out of bull kelp?"

"Yeah," Dyson replied, "but all this stuff on the beach is dead and dry." He picked up a strand of dried, brittle bull kelp and cracked it with two fingers. "We can't make anything with this."

"No problem," Rikimaru said. "Go ahead and eat your fill, just don't eat so much that you get sick. Be right back."

He put his acquired diving mask back on and walked into the surf. He soon reached the kelp forest and pulled half a dozen of the tall stalks free from the ocean floor. He emerged from the water a minute or two later and laid the bull kelp across a driftwood log. With the filleting knife, he sliced the rubbery green strands of seaweed away from the central stalk, then separated each two-inch-wide strand into thinner ones. Finally, he laid them out in a grid pattern.

Sid took to the weaving immediately but had trouble keeping the weave tight with the slippery material. Rikimaru watched with some slight amusement as Katie tried to help, but the stubborn, young boy refused her assistance until the entire thing fell apart.

He didn't say a word, but when Sid glanced up at him, Rikimaru looked at him expectantly. The boy tried to weave the leaves together again, and this time, when Katie tried to help, he accepted her advice, with much more success.

Next, Rikimaru braided more strands from the bull kelp's stalk to make a drawstring. Once that was ready, he set a half clamshell in the bottom to give the pouch some structure and rigidity, then tied it off like a homemade Crown Royal dice bag. He selected half a dozen granite stones, worn round and smooth from the beach, and tucked them away in his seaweed ammunition pouch.

He stood and stretched. The food had done good work, feeding the nanites that repaired his broken body. He thought he might even be getting some of his hearing back. It was mid-afternoon and time he got off the beach.

"Come on down here any morning for a bite to eat," he said. "But I'm going to head into town and wander for a bit. See how much of a disaster this place has turned into over the last twenty years. I won't say, 'Stay out of mischief,' but I will say, 'don't get caught.'"

"We don't," Dyson said with a mischievous grin, but Rikimaru frowned and shook his head.

"Don't get cocky, mister. You guys got busted yesterday morning. You'd have been in a world of hurt if I'd been completely dead, instead of only mostly dead."

Dyson sullenly accepted the rebuke. "Yessir."

"Don't be like that," Rikimaru replied. "Overconfidence will get you in trouble in this Fallen World. All I'm saying is be careful."

As he said the words, it occurred to Rikimaru that, perhaps, having washed up on the beach in Sidney, surrounded by potential hostiles, and almost certainly being believed dead by Ayame and the others…he might be in a bit of trouble himself.

* * *

Rikimaru had several hours before the sun set. The kids wandered off, bellies full, and he chided himself for not doing anything. But he knew he was still vulnerable, and discretion was the wiser course for the time being. He wandered up and down the street, a few hundred feet in each direction, and he saw a few people down on the beach at a distance, but everyone kept to themselves. No one wanted to talk to the tall stranger in the black clothes and white armor, so he returned to the beach. The moon was up, almost full, and at last, the tide was high enough that it was carrying the dead out to sea.

Let nature recycle them there.

Once the sun sank behind the treetops to the west and the shadows grew long, he racked a number of heavy logs in an even pile and hid most of his resources in a hollow beneath them. He put his armor in a neat pile and left everything but his pouch of rocks and a knife. He rolled a four-foot-wide driftwood stump in front to prevent easy theft. Then he was off.

He'd taken stock of the neighborhood in his limp to Miz Waylan's, and many of the houses seemed uninhabited. Sidney had once been a quiet little town full of quiet little houses. Teledyne retirees had been a good seventy percent of the population, and management execs in summertime cottages made up another twenty. One of the cottages would be ideal. The odds of finding a house that *hadn't* had its door kicked in by some desperate, starving survivor (or desperate, starving miscreant for that matter) were virtually nil. That was fine. He wasn't looking for a bunker stocked with weapons and food, just a quiet hideaway where he could be ignored.

The homes with backyards that backed onto the beach were dilapidated and overgrown, and they generally oozed neglect. He passed a few adults, skinny and malnourished, who hugged themselves and hurried in the other direction.

He came upon an entire neighborhood that was little more than charred ruins. One of the houses had caught fire, and the flames had spread to the others. He couldn't begin to guess how long ago— years, judging from the weeds growing through the ashes. Then he found a green space, inland from the beach, and beyond it, a multilane highway that paralleled the beach.

The sound of a rustling bush made him pause, and a skinny black cat emerged from it with a rabbit in its fangs. Rikimaru's fingers dipped into his pouch of rocks, but the cat disappeared back into the shadows after a quick glare.

"Good idea," he whispered after it. If he could kill a couple rabbits, he could use the soft fur as insulating lining. He wasn't above killing cats, for that matter, but they kept the vermin under control. Rabbits were good for little more than skinning, eating, and making more rabbits.

A bit further up the road, the greenspace turned into another suburban neighborhood. Doors were missing, fences were knocked over, and windows were smashed or outright gone. That proved to be helpful, as conversation floated on the air, informing Rikimaru which houses were occupied. It seemed his ears might be recovering, after all. He locked eyes with a shadow in a second-story window, then the figure retreated into the inky blackness inside.

Best to keep moving.

He rounded a bend in the roadway and, two houses later, found a well-trodden walking path. It cut between houses to a gravel trail that paralleled the crumbling divided highway that bisected the peninsula. Without any specific destination in mind, he traversed the drainage ditch and crossed the highway. He found trees and low lying scrub obscuring the far side. He threaded his way through the thicket and exited onto a huge soccer pitch, repurposed to be a garden.

He crouched at the southeast corner of the broad, rectangular space, which was big enough to place two football fields side by side. Rusty uprights marked the field's original purpose, but now the gridiron had numerous furrows running east to west for crops. Rough wire tomato plant stands lined several of the furrows, and there were grape trellises further north, then more low-lying green plants that could have been anything. At the north end, two rows of evenly spaced trees made a small orchard. At the far north end, beyond the trees, loomed a large building. The moon gleamed off the ancient, faded signage, that identified it: *Tel dyne Parks & ecreati n Co munit Cen*

.

A sharp *crack* to his right shattered the night, and he froze.

"Bloody hell, Evan, that was loud. Was that a stick or a gunshot?"

"Fack off, Derek, you fink I'd waste a shot wifout sayin' nuffin? Jus' gimme a minnit, I gotta take a piss."

The two voices were close by, maybe thirty or forty feet away. Rikimaru couldn't move into the open space of the garden without being seen, and if he slipped back into the thicket, they'd hear him. Worse, it sounded like they had *guns*. More movement caught his eye on the far side of the garden—two more people, whom he took to be guards, and one of them appeared to be carrying a long gun.

Rikimaru was more than familiar with the Steiner doctrine: A stealth mission remained a stealth mission if no one was left alive to report in. Hell, he'd run more than his fair share of ops with exactly those rules of engagement. He suspected the garden was there to keep the baron and his thugs fed, but he didn't know for sure and wasn't about to start killing the guards on a mere hunch. Splashing to his right confirmed "Evan" was taking a leak in the bushes, so if Rikimaru remained patient, they'd be on their way. The two guards moved toward the rec center at the north end of the field. Rikimaru again scanned the area and didn't spot anyone nearby, so he gingerly crept from the woods, stayed low and slow, and padded after them. Civilization had battled to keep the edge of the green space neat and even, but civilization had lost. He moved from bush to shrub to tree, keeping something between him and the guards until they reached the north end and turned left into the mini orchard. That was far enough. The green space became a parking lot, and he darted between the old dumpsters and broken-down cars until he could scramble onto the roof of the building.

Once he was on top of the building, he saw a ramshackle tower and crow's nest they'd built at the south end. The black of the structure against the night sky had rendered it invisible earlier.

If Rikimaru were in charge of this setup and had troops with guns and ammunition, he'd put his best rifleman up there, so they could pick off anyone in the garden below with ease. The crow's nest was so small, the sniper would be solo up there. Any occupier would have a clear view of the entire garden. If they'd had starlight goggles, he'd be dead already.

The ladder was rickety and poorly made, just a series of two-by-fours hammered together. For that matter, so was the crow's nest. Climbing up would take away his element of surprise, so Rikimaru bent low, flexed his knees, and leaped.

The guard hadn't even registered that he had an intruder in the crow's nest with him before Rikimaru snaked an elbow under his chin and clamped down hard. The guard struggled, but with his jaw clamped shut, he couldn't get much more than an "mmph" out before the pressure on his carotid arteries rendered him limp and unconscious.

As he'd suspected, a rifle leaned in the corner of the crow's nest. It was a compact bullpup, with faux-wood polymer and a stubby magazine in the mag well. Someone had applied pipe clamps to attach a poorly adapted camera tripod. He could get rid of that later.

The unconscious guard, a blond kid with a punk undercut and fauxhawk that reached his chin, wore a black load bearing vest three sizes too large for him. The vest had six magazines in mag pouches, so Rikimaru threw it over his shoulders and lashed a cord around the guard's wrists.

The guard came around after a ten-count, and bleary eyes locked on Rikimaru's face despite the dark. He took a deep breath, but Rikimaru's hand shot out and clamped onto the man's throat.

"Your one chance to survive this night relies on what you say and do in the next thirty seconds," Rikimaru hissed. "Nod if you understand." The guard's eyes were so wide and so white, they practically glowed. He nodded vigorously. "Good. You're guarding a garden, that much is obvious. Whose garden is it? Who gets the food produced here?"

A confused look crossed the guard's face for a moment. "You...you're not from around here, are youurrk?" Rikimaru squeezed and held on until the instant just before the guard lost consciousness. Again.

"You weren't listening. Answer my questions, or I'll find someone who will. *Whose garden?*"

"*Marchand*," the guard squeaked. "*Baron Marchand.*"

"And he makes sure you and your fellows stay well-fed in exchange for protecting what little food grows on this rock. That true?" Rikimaru hissed.

"Yes," the guard whispered. The Specialist squeezed his throat a little tighter.

"And your orders are to shoot anyone hungry enough to risk stealing from the Baron's vegetable patch?"

"Yes," the guard squeaked. Rikimaru had heard enough. Using food as a means of exerting control over his people? The guards keeping themselves, and only themselves, fed? Marchand was a classic third-world dictator, one each.

And what are you? a small voice at the back of his head asked. *The Shogunate uses conscripts and the threat of violence to enforce the shogun's rule too, you know. How are you any better?*

He buried that question deeply and placed one finger to his lips in a quiet "shh" motion.

"Thanks for the tip. Stay here, silent, until I'm out of rifle range, or you won't live to see the sunrise."

* * *

The guard lived. "Ronin" didn't hear any kind of hue and cry for a good hour. When it came, the response from the others was quick, and he counted six of them onsite, protecting the garden. Meaty thwacks suggested the guard from the tower was getting tuned up by the others at which point Rikimaru crept away southbound.

He found a quiet, abandoned house that suited his purpose in a wholly abandoned neighborhood south of what had been the Victoria International Airport. If he'd guessed correctly, he wasn't all that far from Miz Waylan's *or* the little chunk of beach. Plywood sheets barricaded the ground floor doors and windows, but whoever had fortified the place hadn't thought to do the upper floors. He jumped to the second story balcony and slipped in through the unprotected door. He slept more securely knowing he'd hear anyone trying to get in long before they busted through the plywood if they'd somehow followed him.

As dawn broke, the ache in his ribs was mostly gone, and his ankle was good as new. He'd search for a sailboat, today or tomorrow, and offer the kids a chance to come with him. He couldn't fix all the problems this island had created for itself, but he could do right by the kids.

It took him some time to figure out where he was, and where 'his' beach was, so the sun was well above the horizon by the time he arrived, and he had visitors. Not just the kids, either. They were there, but they sat, heads down, on the driftwood stump hiding his armor. Five thugs surrounded them, and four more glared at him as he came down the path. Each had a club or a baseball bat with nails driven into the business ends. The leader carried a cheap, decorative katana with blue cord wrapped around the handle. Rikimaru guessed it was a flimsy, stamped, decorative thing and he'd probably never had to hit anyone with it.

"The baron wants a word, stranger," the first began without preamble. A couple of his thugs were big, but this guy was merely average, for a Victorian, and positively scrawny by Shogunate standards. He wore a ragged undershirt and too-big jean shants torn off just below the knee. The katana had no scabbard, so he'd tucked it through the belt holding his pants up.

"So bring him on out," Rikimaru retorted. "What, is he hiding behind that rock? Going to make some grand entrance? Or maybe you're going to call him on a phone or something?"

Sid looked at him quizzically. "What's a—"

"Shut it," the goon behind him snapped and cuffed the back of his head.

"You're coming with us," Thug One said. "My boys will stay here until we get back and make sure the kiddies stay…comfortable."

Well, shit.

Rikimaru was out of practice; *of course* these thugs would use the kids as hostages. Things at home had gotten so close to stable, he'd forgotten how shitty people could be. "Lead the way." Rikimaru caught Dyson's eye, and he waved a finger at him. "Stay out of mischief, mister; don't give these guys any grief. I'll be back. You're going to be fine."

The kids nodded and studied their toes as Rikimaru and his escort left the beach. They turned north on the main drag and traveled in silence along the same route he'd taken the night before.

Rather than detouring into suburbia and across the highway, they stayed close to the waterfront until they reached Iroquois Park, which must have been the landmark Dyson referred to the day before. They walked a few more blocks, then they reached the scraper on the pier. It was…underwhelming. It was, indeed, taller than any other building around, but six floors did not a skyscraper make. Bodies in various states of decay hung from lampposts on the sidewalk, and out front, a partial skull was mounted on a pike in a flag stand.

"Charming," Rikimaru said. The skull's lower jaw was gone, and long, ratty hair clung to the skull in chunks where it hadn't been torn away by weather and scavengers.

"The old baron," Thug One said. "Before we had a change in management." He led the way inside, where they tromped up flights of emergency stairs until they reached the top floor.

Thug One opened the door to the penthouse, and Rikimaru stepped through. The entire eastern wall was open to the elements, and the apartment bathed in the morning sun's rays. A lone figure stood on the balcony with his back to them, looking out across the water. He was dressed in a tattered, black and yellow tabard over chainmail and high leather boots. His short, dark hair matched the black of his clothing, and he wore a *much* nicer sword on his hip than the blue katana carried by the escort party leader. It even had a proper scabbard. The basket hilt and straight blade suggested it was a cavalry saber. Even the scabbard was noteworthy, with near-pristine scarlet paint, green ties, and green fittings. A rusty POS could have been inside the scabbard, but Rikimaru doubted that very much.

The goon squad spread out and joined the other guards. When the baron turned, Rikimaru saw that the warlord was young, but his face bore scars from fighting, and his eyes held years his face did not. His tabard bore a yellow "B" on a black background in the center.

"Neat. That stand for baron, so you don't forget?" Rikimaru asked. He had no interest in pageantry or spectacle; he simply wanted to get this over with so he could go home.

"Silence, trespasser," Marchand snarled. "Thou art in *my* territory. Territory I hath assigned to two of *my* subjects, subjects *thou* hast murdered. I should strike thee down where you stand."

Rikimaru put his hands out to his sides to show that they were empty. "First of all, you sound ridiculous, like some drama class nerd channeling bad Shakespeare. And second, you're welcome to try. Better men have tried and failed."

Thug One strode forward and drew the souvenir katana from his belt. He raised the blade to strike, but to Rikimaru's finely honed skills, he moved like an elephant and telegraphed like an amateur. He swept his attacker's lead foot out from under him and caught the descending wrist. Rikimaru yanked the guard forward, twisted his wrist painfully backward, and ripped the katana from his grasp. He booted the falling thug in the ribs but pulled his kick so he didn't shatter the man's ribcage.

The other guards were too stunned to react, and Rikimaru snapped the katana over his knee. Or, he tried to, but the metal was so soft and flexible, it bent rather than broke, and he was left holding the metal prop with an eighty-degree bend in its spine.

"Anyone else?" Rikimaru asked as he threw the blade, and it clattered in a corner. He returned to an at-ease position, with his hands clasped behind his back. Marchand faltered for a moment, and Rikimaru continued. "I didn't ask to come here. No one was more surprised than I was to wash up on your beach, *not* dead." He eyed the tabard. "But where I'm from, it's not …chivalrous, to beat children for the crime of starving. Your so-called subjects—dirtbags more like—attacked three kids. I intervened. Then, the dirtbags' friends came stomping in and got more of the same. How does one become nobility around here," he asked, "when it just means you're King Turd of Shit Mountain?"

That was too much, and Marchand drew his saber and pointed it across the penthouse.

Yep. Way nicer.

"I won the right to this seat by righteous duel," he snarled. Marchand's pretentious, affected accent was thinning, but not all the way gone. "I proved myself the better warrior, and Empress Victoria granted me the right to hold this seat."

"And what? These 'guards' just swear fealty to whoever's in charge?" Rikimaru asked, gesturing to his escort.

"Of course," Marchand replied as if it were the most obvious thing in the world. "I keep them fed. I keep them armed. If one thinks he might do better, he may challenge. I have never lost a duel, though, and one day I might become Duke of these lands. If, by chance, a challenger proves himself the mightier warrior, then I've no right to keep the title. The empress demands strength from her dukes, and the dukes demand strength from their barons. I was the strongest."

"I challenge you then."

That gave Marchand pause. "You *what?*"

"I've been killing people for Teledyne longer than you've been alive, kid. Now, how do we do this? I assume it's a duel to the death. Pistols at dawn? A fencing match atop the Cliffs of Insanity? Twister? Battleship?"

Marchand looked the older man over. Rikimaru knew what he'd see. Salt-stained pants and shirt, a leather belt, fish skin moccasins, and no weapons. Salt and pepper hair bound up in a topknot and a few days' stubble. Despite how he'd disarmed the earlier guard, this trumped-up warlord with delusions of grandeur wouldn't see a threat. Better, the baron wouldn't see the seaweed ammunition pouch, since it hung off the back of his belt nor would he see the egg-shaped stone he'd palmed.

Marchand grinned wickedly. "To the death, yes. I normally don't duel in mine own apartments—I hate having to get the blood off the furniture—but here and now is fine."

"Very well, then," Rikimaru said. His arm came up, and the stone flashed across the intervening gap like a bullet. It struck Marchand squarely in the forehead, and his head snapped back under the impact. The ornate sword clattered to the floor, and Rikimaru crossed the penthouse in an instant. Before Marchand recovered, the Specialist front-kicked him in the chest, and this time, he didn't pull his kick. The baron's ribs shattered with an audible crack, and he sailed over the balcony's railing in a flash of yellow and black. He tumbled six stories to the ground and crashed to an abrupt halt, impaled on the pole holding dead Baron Howell's crumbling skull.

Rikimaru whirled to face the rest of the guards.

"Does anyone here challenge me?"

The rest of the guards numbly shook their heads and jointly stared at Thug One. The man who'd escorted him to the pier with the cheapo katana was in slack-jawed shock. He took a deep breath.

"No, Baron."

"Good! Day three, and I've had to kill someone every day before lunch. At this rate, I'm going to conquer this entire fucked up island by June. You—" he pointed to Thug One. "I don't know how things are done here. Does this "empress" count assassination as a duel?"

Thug One shook his head, again. "Barons maintain a household guard. If a Baron is assassinated, the Duke, his household guard, and the other two Barons' guard forces will march on the remaining household guard, and they are executed. If a Duke is betrayed, his own Barons similarly march on the household guard and slaughter them. Ascension by duel is endorsed, but murder begets massacre. Near certain fratricide is the only stabilizing force; it's the only way to be sure."

Rikimaru wasn't quite sure it would work that way in practice, he could already think of a couple of ways around that, but these men were all young—the oldest couldn't have been more than a toddler when the bombs fell. Maybe they just accepted that was how it was?

"Of course, you could be lying; I don't even know your name yet, so you'll forgive me if I don't take you at your word. But if what you're saying is true, the only recognized—I hesitate to say 'lawful'—way for authority to transfer is by personal combat?"

"Yes, milord. Except, if a noble dies outside of a duel, the empress or her delegate may appoint the successor. And, they call me Axton."

'Milord' would take some getting used to, he supposed.

"Well then, Axton, as…'Baron,' I have two orders I wish carried out immediately. First, send a runner to my little patch of beach. Bring the three children here, *unharmed*. If they are not entirely well when they arrive, I'll carry out a near-certain fratricide of my own, and that'll be that. Second, send more runners, as many as necessary, to collect whoever counts as household guards. I want everyone out front as soon as can be managed. I want to meet each one of you, and if anyone wants to object, we can deal with it right away, up front. We'll meet downstairs."

"Where shall I have the men assemble, milord?"

"Look for the dead guy in the goofy yellow coat. Move now."

* * *

The children arrived unharmed, as promised. Rikimaru was relieved. If anything, it proved that some of these thugs weren't amoral scum, so that was a start. Thirty-seven men counted themselves among the recently-departed Baron Marchand's household guards. By dinner time, that number had winnowed itself down to thirty-one. Rikimaru didn't hold anything back and killed each challenger as brutally and efficiently as he could, barehanded. The rest were suitably cowed by Rikimaru's superior martial skills and fell into line like good, little minions.

"Axton and…you." Rikimaru pointed to a battered, bruised young man in the second row he recognized. "Remain here. The rest of you, next order of business! Six of you will collect driftwood on the beach, I don't care who, and lay it out to build a funeral pyre. Considering how many people the previous asshole hanged here, it'll need to be a big one. The rest of you will cut down those bodies and take Baron Marchand's corpse and drag them down to the water-front next to the driftwood. We can't bury them all, but *I* am in charge now, so I am making this a clean start. I won't have any more of these death cult terror tactics or dead bodies hanging around, rotting and attracting vermin and disease. It's gross, it's stupid, and it's

PACIFIC SHOGUN | 213

cliché. Move now." When they didn't react immediately, he deployed his command voice.

"NOW! MOVE NOW! WITH A SENSE OF URGENCY! GET THESE BODIES DOWN! I WANT TO SEE FLAMES BY SUNDOWN!"

Twenty-nine pairs of legs dashed madly off in all directions, sometimes colliding with each other. Two remained.

"What's your name, guardsman?" he asked the one with the injuries. In the daylight, Rikimaru could see he was skinny and in his late teens, and his long, sandy blond hair hung down past his chin. He wouldn't have been out of place in a Seattle Neo-Grunge band from the 2030s. But now, he was just…grungy.

"Th-th-th-Thor, sir," he stammered.

"Like the God of Thunder, Thor? Or ith that a lithp?" Rikimaru demanded. The subject of his ire straightened his back, braced his spine, and enunciated.

"Like the God of Thunder, sir!"

"That's better." Rikimaru leaned in and lowered his voice so Axton couldn't hear. "*You got those bruises when you reported to your superior that you'd been ambushed and disarmed, didn't you?*"

"*Yes, sir,*" he replied.

"*Who beat you?*"

Thor looked around, and pointed to one of the failed challenger's cooling bodies. "*Evan.*"

"*Good. I waited at the south end of the garden for a good hour, just to see how long it would take you to raise the alarm. Intelligence is a survival trait. This bodes well for you.*" He waved Axton over and spoke in a normal tone again. "We'll be organizing things a bit more formally from here on out. Congratulations, Sergeants."

Thor's eyes bugged out a bit. "I'm no sergeant, sir," he protested.

"And I wasn't a baron when I woke up this morning, but here we are. The best leaders are the ones who lead by example, don't ask their people to do anything they wouldn't do, and follow orders of their own. You'll have me backstopping you. I want you each to be crew boss over nine guys. I need a third sergeant, and I don't know the rest of the guards. Find me one."

"Derek Roberts, Milord," Axton suggested. Thor nodded. "He's the one what pulled Evan off me. Said I'd taken me lumps, and we'd see the thief soon. I suppose he was right."

"Good, done. Introduce me once the work's all done. Tomorrow, we're going to get organized because this 'ragged edge of starvation' shit has got to stop. It's counterproductive. Either we all eat together, or we will all starve separately. Let's go."

Three of 'his' troops were coming back from the little marina next to the tower with armloads of torn sails. Rikimaru beckoned for one, then picked a lamppost with a tattered, thoroughly bleached skeleton hanging from it. He climbed the pole barefooted and cut away the rough twine noose suspending the skeleton. It collapsed into a loose pile of bones when it struck the pavement, and Rikimaru dropped down. He gathered the bones in one of the ragged canvas sails. One of the tarp-fetching guards offered to take it, but Rikimaru refused. He needed to set the right tone and the right example from the very beginning. He carried the bones down to the beach where a pile of logs was already beginning to form and laid them reverently down to be added to what would eventually be a raging bonfire. Then he returned, sail in tow, to repeat the process another half dozen times.

Removing Marchand's body from the pike proved to be a messy affair. The Baron's body had hit at an angle such that the spear tip pierced his lower left back and exited the upper right. He hung there like a butterfly pinned to a display case, arms splayed wide and head tilted back. If Rikimaru was any judge of anatomy, the spear tip had almost certainly pierced his heart and killed him instantly. Now they were trying to figure out how to lift him off the spear. The body was still several feet off the ground and had hit with such velocity, the impact had bent the crossbars until they were more like fish hooks. The body was stuck.

"Allow me," Rikimaru said. He lifted the pike, body and all, straight up from the base. The base was a good twenty- or twenty-four inches tall, so lifting him straight up was nontrivial. As soon as the shaft cleared the base, he set the butt down next to it. He tipped the pike over until Marchand lay on the ground, then braced, flexed, and increased pressure until the stout hardwood shaft cracked off as close to the dead man's chest as he could manage. That gave him enough play to pull the lower half of the pike free, and he threw the ruined weapon aside to burn with the rest. He stripped off the chainmail—it was costume shit that provided almost no proper protection, but they could probably reuse it somehow.

Then Rikimaru took the former baron, rolled the body into that same canvas tarp, and dragged it down the hill to be cremated with the others. He then sent a messenger to Miz Waylan, requesting that she prepare a list of needs, and letting her know he would try to fill them. If she lacked space, there would be room on the third and fourth floors of the Pier Scraper for her and everyone she wished to bring.

Two hours later, roaring flames soared high into the sky, and it occurred to Rikimaru that his Komainu, the guardians watching from their hidden OPs on Stuart or San Juan Islands, might wonder what the Victorians were up to.

* * * * *

Chapter Twelve

The *Ship Happens* scythed through the water, almost silently. Akuma knew Dan Nobunaga could have gone faster and heeled the sailboat over ever harder, but it wasn't just Dan sailing tonight. Most of the trailing coxswains were new to combat operations, and the Onamazu Marine commander didn't want to lose anyone or leave them behind. Parkes was about the only one who was comfortable with the whole "sailing through the sea in the pitch black of night" thing. Nobunaga had impressed upon him that keeping a tight formation in the pitch black was hard. Dan had taken out the marine coxswains for nighttime sailing training over the last few nights, but they still had a lot to learn. Right now, sailing at top speed would be a disaster. Eventually, they might dye their sails black to lessen their outline, but not until everyone could handle such operations in near blindness.

They'd passed what the charts called Cordova Bay, but there wasn't much of a bay to be found, just a gently curving shoreline. The depth charts showed a safe channel just past Ten Mile Point, but there were a handful of underwater hills that came as close as three fathoms to the surface, so Dan had to stay well out from shore.

A low rock jutted above the surface, a patch of black-on-black illuminated by crashing whitecaps. Barely. It was Jemmy Jones Island, one of the underwater hills whose peaks were just barely above the waterline. It was also his landmark to tack west.

"Signal the turn here, Master Frost," Nobunaga ordered quietly. Derek slipped one of the opaque covers off their candlelit lantern. The blackened covers were mirrored on the inside and kept anyone onshore from seeing the already dim light. He kept the cover off for a twenty-count, then slipped it back on. It was the closest thing they could do to approximate a turn signal. "Make ready, Samurai."

"Hai, Captain," Akuma replied. At Dan's signal, Frost loosened the lines and let the sails luff, so the wind no longer carried them. They glided into Cadboro Bay on momentum alone.

Ajay's heart hammered in his chest, even more than the night he knew he was to be jumped and arrested by Ayame's Satori. That had been easy compared to this. All he'd had to do then was not fight back, then embrace the suckage that was hypothermic waterboarding during the ride back to Whidbey. Leading his marine raiders into their first cutting-out expedition, to reclaim what boats they could and burn the rest, was an entirely different matter.

Never let them see you sweat, Kael had told him. Easier said than done; he wasn't a Specialist. Maybe he'd just meant "worry" because they'd already seen him sweating and bleeding right there alongside them in training. He'd been there on Day One, he'd been there for the battle of Deception Pass, and he'd been there ever since. The PT, the frigid swimming, the fighting—they all scored him points with the troops, especially because he wasn't one of the superhuman Specialists. He was normal, and he was fallible, and he was right there with them every miserable step of the way.

Starlight and the barest hint of sunrise behind them illuminated the light grey of the Royal Victorian Yacht Club's breakwater. It was time. Akuma slipped down the ladder at the rear of the ship. The rest of Lance Corporal Jack Wilson's marines were perched right above him. "Go!" Nobunaga whispered, and Akuma slipped into the chilly saltwater. He swam hard to clear the next boat's track and let the *Day's* wake carry him through the gap in the breakwater. There'd be no stopping now. His navy blue marine armor, all wooden plates and repurposed plastics, made him buoyant. The wooden haft of his naginata helped keep the weapon looped over his shoulders afloat, despite the density of the business end. The dock didn't have a ladder, but the cabin cruiser tied up next to it did, so he hauled himself out of the water slowly to minimize the splash. He jumped down onto the dock, unslung his naginata, and knelt next to another old cruiser emblazoned *"Plan B."* He listened for signs they'd been detected as the rest of his marines swam in.

This was the worst part of the plan by far: the waiting. None of their little sailboats were large enough to carry more than a single lance at a time. They didn't have SCUBA gear, or wetsuits, or anything else that would let them gather their numbers and attack in a single wave, and any cabin cruiser large enough to haul them all had been out of diesel and out of service ages ago. They'd have to find a better way. He just didn't know what that would be yet.

Three full lances had joined him on the dock by the time sunshine first touched the marina. Akuma whispered to Wilson. "We're going ahead. The rest will have to catch up." They'd planned for this. Now all his troops had to do was follow the plan. The lance corporal tapped one of his PFCs on the shoulder. "Take point. We're holding the access. Go."

Private First Class Davidson crept forward, polearm at the ready. Wilson was second, with the remaining four on his heels. At Melissa Rainier's recommendation, Karisa Kesting had been offered an NCO slot in the marines, and her lance followed Wilson's. Rainier's lance was third. The dock branched out into seven jetties, and at a rough count, this one had well over two hundred berths. Fewer than half were occupied by intact hulls. Half of *those* didn't even have masts, and Akuma wrote them off immediately. His first twelve Marines guarded the single ramp, blocking access. Lance Corporal Hong's fourth lance was close behind, and they followed Rainier to the north end. Akuma was pleased. Everyone was doing as ordered; no one had fucked up. He almost felt superfluous.

Rainier's lance took the north-most jetty, and Hong's took the second. They divided their teams in half, and each trio methodically boarded and searched each boat in line. Akuma paced impatiently up and down the jetty connecting them. He was on pins and needles; they didn't know what to expect—how many fighters the Victorians might be able to rally in a short period, how they might be armed— they just didn't know. All they knew was that roughly one raid in ten was stealthy, like the one on Deer Harbor, but the rest were executed by violent marauders and crazed maniacs. As the half lances searched each boat, they tore down curtains, cushions, paper, and anything else flammable and took them up to the top deck and laid them out. Rainier splashed a seat cushion with the contents of a canteen on her belt, then she moved on to the next one.

A squawking, spluttering, angry voice came from the next boat. Rainier and Terry Cobb emerged from below decks, dragging an occupant with them.

"It's mine!" he wailed. Rainier adjusted her grip on the scrawny man, took a big handful of his hair, and punched him in the mouth.

"*Never was,*" she hissed and punched him again. They threw the man overboard, and his arms and legs flailed until he belly-flopped into the harbor. He scrambled up the adjacent boat's ladder and stormed back down the jetty, indignant, but drew up short when met with bared steel.

"You can sit there, silently, or you can be shark chum, asshole," Akuma said. He brandished his naginata and barred the unarmed man's way. "Makes no difference to me." Now he could read the rear of the ship and understood Melissa's temper. It was the *Buoyancé*, stolen from *her* marina, under *her* watch, all those weeks ago.

The squatter retreated to the far end of the jetty, beyond the area they'd searched already, and stewed there, glaring. Rainier, Cobb, and Bradley tossed the storage chests, sail bags, and cabin for ropes and sails. The lance corporal appeared at the rear of the ship and reported in. "We're good. It's a disgusting pigsty inside, but it's functional. They haven't fucked her up *too* badly."

"Good. Carry on then, Lance."

"Oorah."

More shouting followed by more splashes from elsewhere in the marina drew his attention. Hong shouted from his jetty—they'd found the *Carpe Piscium*, stolen in another raid on San Juan a year earlier. It was still functional too. Many of the boats seemed to be little more than floating housing, and the one or two sleeping onboard were rudely awakened and tossed into the bay. Lances five and six finally joined them, and Akuma rolled his eyes as Sam Alvarez used his naginata to cross-check an occupant over a cabin cruiser's bow railing.

"*What's the meaning of this?*" a voice bellowed. Akuma searched the waterfront for the source of the voice and spied a man in his thirties on the small peninsula to their south. He wore a tattered bathrobe, but the men at his heels wore something like a uniform: blue and green shirts and faded black pants, and they carried rough chopping blades. The man stormed down the beach, flanked by his guards, and Akuma went to meet him.

The man who'd shouted drew up short when he realized armored men and women carrying polearms were causing the disturbance on the Yacht Club's docks. Akuma waited for him, leaning on his naginata, backstopped by Wilson and Kesting's troops.

"Morning," Akuma began, supremely unimpressed by the Victorian's striped robe and slippers. "You own these boats?"

"Yes, I'm Baron—"

"WRONG!" Akuma thundered, and the man took a step back. "For twenty years, you people have raided our islands, stolen our boats, and killed my brothers and sisters. For twenty years, the shogun has refused to pay you back in kind for the piracy and theft. Well, *no more*. We're taking our ships *back*. Be glad you're still breathing."

"Stop them!" the 'baron' squealed. The guards, wearing what Akuma now recognized as hockey jerseys, drew their swords, which were mostly rough leaf-blade machetes. The baron's hands fell to the terrycloth belt holding his robe shut like he expected a weapon to be hanging there, but the fool had confronted them in pajamas and was therefore helpless. Kesting and Wilson were decidedly not. Jack marched his marines forward, and they formed a line at the base of the dock just behind him and held their gleaming polearm blades high in the air, ready to chop down at any guard foolish enough to rush them. Kesting's lance formed a second wall of armored bodies and lethal blades.

Akuma eyed the mansion atop the peninsula, where he'd first spied the man. It was a sprawling, multi-story affair with a private beach and a surprisingly well-manicured garden. "That your digs? Seems nice. Be a shame if something happened to it."

"What—" the man started, but Lance Corporal Isaac Hong interrupted.

"Search is complete, Samurai! We have five functional boats."

"*Five?*" That was fewer than he'd expected. Far fewer. For a marina that could berth hundreds, he'd hoped for far more than *five*. It would have to do. "Mount up, Onamazu! We're leaving!" Wilson's lance parted smoothly to let Akuma pass, but he paused and turned back to address Mister High And Mighty. "You might want to evacuate that swank house of yours, Baron. Oh, and get your people off the docks, too." He pointed to the last of the jetties where his troops were just finishing. "That's distilled alcohol we're pouring all over those flammables. About eighty percent, by volume. And this," he produced a long, red tube from his belt pouch, "is a marine flare."

One foolish guard rushed forward to stop Akuma from leaving, but Jack Wilson brought his naginata sweeping down. The guard skidded to a halt, and the blade split the man's foot. He howled and collapsed, then the rest of them dragged him clear.

Wilson and Kesting fell back, leapfrogging to cover each other. The marine flares were a finite resource, but they'd salvaged hundreds of them from all the boats throughout the shogun's islands, so bringing half a dozen wasn't going to break the bank. Akuma splashed some accelerant on the wooden dock, touched off a flare, and ignited the puddle. The alcohol flared, and the dock ignited. All across the jetties, marines lit alcohol-soaked cushions and set the boats aflame before racing for their rides. Akuma jumped aboard the *Buoyancé*, and they paddled for all they were worth to get away from the burning jetties, using the broad blades of the naginatas on their polearms as paddles. The marines hoisted sails, reefed down ropes, and sailed for the sunrise.

Akuma signaled for the *Aquaholic*, where his seventh and last lance of marines had waited out the raid. Lance Corporal Kobalynski had been stoic, but unhappy, at being left out of the strike, but Akuma needed one boat of archers to remain as fire support in case of disaster. Rainier brought the *Buoyancé* in close, and he pointed to the mansion on the peninsula.

"Ten volleys, flame arrows," he said. "That's their grand poobah's place. If he isn't the one who ordered the raids, he's the one who kept the boats afterward. Torch it."

"Hai, Samurai!"

* * *

Samurai Akuma's elation at their first triumphant raid faded before the smell of burning fiberglass and wood did. Their newly reinforced squadron was making, well, maybe not good time, but they were pointed in the right direction, and nobody had broken down. Given the state these sailboats had been in, that right there was more luck than skill. The dawn's light revealed how poorly the ships had been maintained—not at all—and that all five needed repairs. The *More Pacifically* needed a new ship's steering wheel since its original one had cracked. The *SoFishticated*'s rudder needed some TLC; it turned to starboard just fine, but straightening out or turning to port was a physical struggle.

Of all the recovered sailboats, the *Buoyancé* was in the best state, but how that angry mouthpiece had trashed the interior that quickly was a mystery. Staying out on the deck in the chill spring air, despite his wet clothes, was vastly preferable to descending into the stink below. Staying on deck is what allowed him to notice a distinctive white bit of flotsam bobbing on the waves. He pointed it out, and Melissa's face darkened.

"Is that…?"

"I think so."

"Bring us about," Akuma ordered quietly. He looped a safety line around his shoulders, made sure there was plenty of rope to spare, and when the *Buoyancé* heeled around, he gritted his teeth against the shock of the cold water, *again*, and jumped. He swam a few swift strokes and grasped the object, then held on tight as the Onamazu on the ship heaved him back aboard.

"Yeah. No one else had armor like this before Gaunt attacked," he said bitterly. The flotsam he'd spotted was one of his *suneate* plates—greaves, in English. Each piece of wood had a foam backing and then a thin sheet of aluminum. It bore the intricate carvings his daimyo had painstakingly etched onto each plate, but it was stained with dried blood, despite floating in the ocean for nearly a week, and it had a score of nicks, scars, and chips. One of the leather calf straps was torn, and its partner was missing.

"You gonna tell Aya?" Rainier asked.

"How can I not?" he asked. He pointed to the island at their port side, where Friday Harbor was just barely visible. "I'm amazed it's floated this far. We're almost to the channel."

"I can find somewhere for you to hide at Deer Harbor if you want," Rainier offered. "Leave you there, 'accidentally,' and buy you a day or two's reprieve." Akuma couldn't tell whether she was being serious, then her mask slipped a bit. "I shouldn't joke."

"Not necessary, but if I come up with any other bodies that need hiding, warm or cold, I'll let you know."

* * *

That evening after dinner, Akuma rather regretted not taking Melissa up on her offer. His former superior from the Satori had always been calm and collected, a natural-born spook who was utterly unflappable.

Now, she was *unhinged*. When he somberly presented her with that single armor plate, she'd frozen, poleaxed. She rushed to him, tore it from his hands, and stared down at the battered thing. Her eyes took in every chip and every gouge, and they shone with tears for an instant until rage replaced them. The *suneate* plate whistled when she threw it across the Ops hangar like a Frisbee, and she'd not been "calm" when she added the first half dozen dents to the aluminum overhead door.

"AYA!" Mikael shouted. Or tried to. In truth, he gasped, because the hole in his lung was still healing, and it was all he could do to hobble around on their only pair of wooden crutches.

"I'LL! KILL! THEM! ALL!" she shrieked, punching hardened fists through the thin metal sheets.

"Akuma, get me the elephant trank gun," Grimstaadt rasped as if he was asking for a bowl of rice. Akuma had no idea what he was talking about, but before he could question the senior Specialist, Ayame rounded on him.

"DON'T YOU DARE!"

"Then calm the hell down," he replied, calmly. "One, I'm still too messed up to put you in a sleeper hold, and two, we don't *have* a tranquilizer gun, but nothing else was getting through. So get a fucking grip."

She burst into tears of fury and anguish and slid down the dented door. Mikael limped over next to her and slid down too. She tucked her head in against his shoulder and sobbed.

"I miss him too," he said to the top of her head.

"Damn Gaunt, damn Obsidian, and damn Teledyne," she whispered. "*They* did this."

"They did," Mikael agreed and craned his neck to survey the dents she'd pounded into the sheet aluminum. "But what did the door ever do to you?"

She smirked a bit, then giggled, then cut loose with a hysterical laugh.

"How are your hands?" he asked, and she dutifully held them up for inspection. Her knuckles bled freely. Hardened bones, redoubled muscles, and ultra-tough ligaments were one thing, but she wasn't a Geno-freak with 'gator hide.

"I'll be fine tomorrow. I just…I needed to get my mad out. Where did you find it?"

Akuma swallowed hard. "Below Shaw Island, just east of Friday Harbor. It was bobbing on the waves."

"So…he could have floated that far, then?"

"Aya," Mikael said, as gently as he could. "Don't you think if he had, he would have tried to get back to us? If he'd washed up anywhere in the islands, we'd know. But if you want to do something about warding off the impending depression, you could go with Akuma. Gaunt and his army of raiders might be gone, but there are plenty of Victorians to kill."

"I can't swim," she complained. "Don't want to wind up like…" and then she dissolved into quiet tears again.

"We're hitting Sidney next, Aya," Akuma said. "I've checked the charts. Two marinas, one just north of the pier, and a second one further up that is way, way bigger, and the water is only a couple fathoms deep at both. Literally hundreds of berths, in four separate docks, all in the same bay. If it's even the slightest bit protected, it'll be a bitch to raid, even with fifty marines. It's shallow enough so you could go overboard and walk in or even jump to the breakwater and then to the jetty."

She reached out a hand, and it was an electric shock when Ajay took it to help her to her feet.

"You want me to come too? I'm not going to steal your thunder, Samurai?"

"Hundred percent."

"And you don't mind if I get my mad out, killing scumbags and burning shit, even if it screws with your plans?"

"Not in the slightest."

The way she looked him up and down made him feel like she was a jungle cat, sizing up her next meal. It was a little terrifying, but the anger and tears had been replaced by something different.

"Then I think maybe you and I ought to retire to my room, so we can...strategize."

She grabbed him by the collar and dragged him from the hangar.

* * *

Sergeant Major (retired) Claudia Radcliffe stood unnoticed near the entrance to the Ops hangar. She joined her husband and clucked her tongue disapprovingly as the other two departed.

"If she screws him to death, you're going to have a helluva time finding a new leader for the Marines, Mikael. That'd be awkward as hell."

Grimstaadt laughed, then coughed when his chest seized up. Claudia shook her head and held her man until he recovered, then they headed for home. "What? You think I'm joking? Darling, there is only one person on this island familiar with the high risk/high reward perils of intensely emotional sex with one of you superhuman warrior badasses. I am she. That girl's pined after Rikimaru for twenty years and hasn't gotten spread *that entire time.* Now that Rick's gone, she's going to rebound like a rabid minx. I hope she doesn't break him, for all our sakes."

* * * * *

.

Chapter Thirteen

Duke Miles Horton had a problem.

"Everything?"

"Yes, milord." Baron Joyce bowed his head in shame. "Everything. The raiders came armed with accelerants and torched the whole dock, my estate, the boats, everything."

"The estate, too?" Horton *liked* that estate. It had been his until the late Duke Tremblay went and got himself shot by that Howell thug. Irreplaceable solar panels on the roof had provided a bit of power, but they'd been slowly failing over the years, providing less and less juice. Just having reading lamps was nice. There was a pool, servant's quarters, and the sunrises in the morning had to be seen to be believed. The docks were right there, meaning he got first pick of anything being unloaded by the few fishermen they had. As far as post-apocalyptic digs were concerned, it was grand.

Castle Craigdarroch, less so.

The great stone structure was ancient, almost two centuries old. It had originally been a mansion, then a military hospital, a college, a conservatory, and a museum, and now it had come full circle and was a mansion again. A drafty, cold mansion on an all too breezy hill, where he couldn't even hang plywood to close the ruined stained-glass windows because the exterior was stone. The museum curators had glued or mortared or bolted down brass plaques everywhere, dutifully informing any visitors who came by that he lived in a drafty-ass two-hundred-year-old stone castle on a hill. It had a beautiful porch, two turrets, seven fireplaces, and the insulation quality of a shrubbery. Maybe even less, since dirt didn't drain him of heat the way stone did. He was miserable.

Clearly, he needed to spend more time downtown. Victoria's bedroom was plenty warm.

"Yes. And they didn't kill anybody. I mean, if they *had* killed some of the residents, I'd have fewer starving mouths fighting over food, which would have been a pretty shitty silver lining, but such are the times we live in. I have one guard injured. Doc Tyson is trying to save his foot, but you know his track record. They threw everyone in the boats into the water, doused everything with alcohol, torched them, and hit the estate with fire arrows on their way out as a final 'fuck you.'"

Horton snarled, gripped the table in front of him, and heaved it over, sending battered pots and dishes scattering across the floor. Not satisfied, he punted one of the pots through a mostly-broken window as Joyce retreated.

"This is...intolerable," Horton said. "We will have to see her majesty and give her the update. And be prepared for more of Robitaille's ilk to throw down over this. Howell wasn't the first, nor will he be the last."

"Court is tomorrow. We'll have to talk to her then. See if she will...I don't know. *Do* something. They've got more boats, right? In the inner harbor?"

"They do, but she doesn't like to share." Horton paused. "Well, worst she can say is 'no.'" His momentary ire had dissipated.

"You know it can be a lot worse than that," Joyce said. "I have two other ideas if you want to hear them."

Horton didn't, not really; he was pretty sure he was screwed no matter what, so he raised an eyebrow, inviting Joyce to continue.

"One, we could leave the capital. There must be some farmer or fisherman out in Sooke, or Jordan River, or Port Renfrew who needs help. Let the empress figure out who's going to be in charge of this train wreck, and let them worry about how to feed their guards."

"*'Fuck it, I'm out'* isn't a great first choice, Ronald. We've never been quitters. What's the second?"

Joyce gulped, and in a quiet voice, he said, "Sail east."

It took a moment for Horton to clue in. "*East?*"

"You had to see the...I don't even like to call them *raiders*...in action. Raiders are, I don't know, a disorganized mob of hooligans and thugs. These men *and women* wore uniforms, carried standardized equipment, and wore standardized armor. They were fit, and the armor had rank chevrons on the shoulders. A dozen of them, with great big chopping spear things with hooks, kept us from getting on the dock. The rest were in teams of three, going from boat to boat. One called the leader "samurai." He called the rest of them—I don't know the word: oh-nah-something-something—when they left. They were methodical, used tactics, and covered each other, and their archers remained offshore in another sailboat. They worked as a team. Does that sound like the actions of a bunch of savage monsters? Or does that sound...civilized?"

Baron Joyce was making a lot of sense. And that worried him. Horton was, first and foremost, a survivor, and if war with the Shogunate was coming, he wanted to be on the winning side. "You know Sledge would execute you for sedition if anyone heard you talk that way."

"I do."

"I'll have to think upon it. We will have to see what court brings tomorrow."

* * *

Rikimaru jolted awake the next morning, and was out of bed, filleting knife in hand, before he could identify the noise.

It was loud and high pitched and...brassy?

Once it became clear that no one was beating down his door to murder him, he pocketed the knife and scooped up the rifle he'd taken from Thor. From his balcony, he spied four riders on horseback below. One held the offending trumpet, and they had a fifth horse, saddled, but without a rider. The other three wore swords on their hips, medieval helmets, and armor like the previous occupant's.

"You're not Marchand," the lead rider called up.

"He ain't here," Rikimaru said, "on account of a serious case of terminal deceleration. Who are you?"

"I am your duke," the speaker said. "Come down here at once, knave!"

Rikimaru paused for just a moment. He'd been healing, steadily, since washing up on the beach, but he suspected his hearing was still a little off. He stuck a finger in one ear, wiggled it around, and worked his jaw for a moment.

"Can you repeat that? Did you call me a *knave?*"

"I did! Now come down here at once!"

"Now I know where that Marchand idiot got it from. Knave? Really?"

Duke Whoever He Was kicked one leg over the saddle, landed gracefully, and dropped the visor on his helm. He drew the sword on his hip and strode purposefully into the building, followed by two of the others. The trumpeter remained behind, holding the reins of all five mounts. Rikimaru threw the door to his suite open and bellowed down the emergency stairway adjacent to the non-functional elevator shaft.

"Axton! Thor! Incoming! Get up here, but let them through. It seems we need to have a chat."

Both top sergeants dashed up the stairs.

"Shit," Axton swore. "Look, I'm really sorry, Baron Ronin, sir, I totally forgot. Today's court, in downtown proper. Happens once a month on the day of the full moon."

"You ever been?" Rikimaru asked.

"No," Thor replied. Axton shook his head as well. "You're going to be gone most of the day. It's about an hour, hour and a half's ride there. You schmooze and wine and dine and politick all day, meet any other new nobles who've won their titles, then ride back in time for dinner."

"I will, will I?"

Rikimaru was not interested in that in the slightest. He had more important things to do. Like teach his people to operate a sailboat, and how to fish, starting with 'tying fishing nets' and ending with 'chow.'

He passed the rifle to Thor. "Hang on to this. I don't expect there will be a problem, but if it looks bad, shoot them. In the back, ideally."

"Uh...yessir," Thor said and swallowed hard. Rikimaru drew the deceased Baron's sword—a functional and gorgeously decorated cavalry saber with *Perseverance* etched on the blade—and placed himself just inside the door. Thor and Axton retreated deeper into his suite, and they waited.

One of the Duke's sidekicks led the way up the stairs. Rikimaru heard the clinking and clanking as their armored forms jogged up, but they were losing steam after six flights of stairs. The door burst open, the first of the three took one step inside, and Rikimaru kicked his legs out from under him. He dropped like a wet sack of rice, and the chin of his helmet *clunked* when it bounced off the marble floor. His sword skittered loose, and Rikimaru scooped it up. He tossed it underhand out the balcony door where it plummeted from view. The trumpeteer below cried out in alarm, but Rikimaru ignored him.

The second armored "knight" tripped trying to clamber over his dazed comrade. Rikimaru knocked his blade aside, conked him on the helmet with his sword's pommel, and wrenched him aside with a handful of tunic. The knight, already off-balance, took three or four steps, trying to catch himself, and then he blundered into one of the support beams and fell on his back. His sword went over the balcony too, to the trumpeteer's further dismay.

The so-called duke was behind the other two, further back in the stairwell. After seeing both his men go down, he was somewhat less enthusiastic about charging in. Rikimaru sat on the second knight, pinning him to the floor beneath him, and rested his sword on his knees.

"You can come out now, your Duke-ness," Rikimaru said. "Welcome to my humble abode."

The armored knight edged around the corner. He sounded like he was right on the edge of panicking—Rikimaru could hear his rasping breath behind the full-face helm.

"Drop your sword," the Duke challenged.

"No."

Rikimaru got to his feet, slowly, making no sudden moves. He planted one foot on the back of the mailed figure at his feet and let the tip of his sword rest in one of the chainmail links.

"You can take off that silly helmet, put down *your* sword, and talk to me like a rational human being, or I can pin your friend here to the floor like a cockroach."

"You wouldn't dare!"

"Uh, Duke Robitaille?" Thor interrupted. The Duke's armored head snapped around, and he finally saw the skinny young man through his visor's slits. He took a step back when he observed the rifle held at the low ready. "This is, um, Baron Ronin. He defeated Marchand in a duel two nights ago. He very much *would* dare."

"I was there, milord," Axton added. "I saw it. Challenge was issued, challenge was accepted, and Lord Ronin put him over the balcony with a single strike. It was all according to protocol, Your Grace. Half a dozen more from the guard challenged him after, and he defeated them all, unarmed, one after the other, without pause or break. He's the best fighter I've ever seen, sir."

Robitaille slipped his fingers under his helmet, unbuckled the chinstrap, and pulled his helmet off. He was younger than Rikimaru but older than Axton or Thor. There was an angry red scar bisecting his face from above his right eye to his left cheek. He kept his brown hair short and affected a bushy mustache, with waxed tips curled up at the ends. He scowled at Rikimaru, and twitched his moustache left and right. "Is this true?"

"It is. And then we got to work cleaning up the death cult bullshit. Cut down all the dead people hanging from lampposts, had a proper funeral pyre, former Baron Marchand included, and today, I was going to hold classes on sailing because, apparently, none of you Victorians know the first thing about keeping your people fed. Your rude intrusion prompted Sergeants Axton and Thor here to advise me there's "court" in Victoria or some nonsense."

"'Tis not nonsense," the Duke objected. Rikimaru took the point of his sword out of the man's hauberk and tucked a toe under the man's arm to gently prod him into turning over. When he did, Rikimaru offered him a hand and hauled him to his feet.

"Yeah, it's nonsense. Is this seriously how you people have been organizing yourselves? Dukedom by deathmatch? Brawling for baronies? And how you guys talk? No wonder things are so fucked up."

"How else would we determine who among us are the mightiest?"

"Why would that be relevant?" Rikimaru asked in return. "Does being a mighty warrior mean you know how to tend crops? How to sail? How to fish? How to blacksmith or weave or tan leather or make *anything* useful at all?"

"No, but—"

"No. Alone, all a sword does is make sure there are fewer mouths to feed. It gives you the power, but not the authority, to shake down everyone for whatever they've got until someone puts a knife in your kidneys and dumps your body in a gutter. You're welcome, by the way," he said to the two knights he'd disarmed. "I *could* have done that to you two, but sometimes not killing someone is harder." He held out his hand in greeting to Robitaille. "I'm Rick Hanzo, but the kids from the beach call me Ronin, and it stuck."

"Jean-Luc Robitaille, Duke of Land's End." The Duke shook his hand in return. "My barons, Darius Lakonis of Deep Cove and Aleksander Orlov of Mount Newton. And yes, we enforce our rule with violence, when necessary, because the peasants will shank us any chance they get."

"They shank you any chance they get because you've set this entire disaster up as an us versus them thing. You hoard all the food and weapons and let them starve to death. Of course, they're going to come after you. Why wouldn't they? They've got nothing left to lose."

"This is as Empress Victoria dictates," Orlov spat. "Who are you to question her wisdom?"

"I'm the guy who…" Rick caught himself. He was, to be brutally honest, probably number two on Victoria's hit list. These warlords were willing to give him some sense of respect, at this point, because he was good in a fight and better to have on their side than not. But he'd already said too much about where he'd washed up. Better to downplay it, for now. "…who thinks, maybe, the peasants wouldn't shank people as often if they weren't starving to death. You were, what, a kid when the bombs fell?"

"I was three," Orlov corrected. "This is how it has been for as long as I can remember."

"Well, maybe the Duke here will remember a time when people didn't just go around slaughtering each other over tomatoes, potatoes, and fishkabobs. Do you *like* hacking down people for the crime of being hungry? Or would you rather just see everyone get enough to eat?"

"You make it sound so simple," Baron Lakonis objected. "I'd like to see you try."

"Let's get this ridiculous court thing over with, and you can watch me."

* * * * *

Chapter Fourteen

The trumpeteer gave Rikimaru a dirty look when he led the others out of the six-story building and pointedly returned Lakonis' and Orlov's swords to them. The duke quickly introduced Baron Ronin, and their "herald," Leonard, looked him up and down.

"Methinks he needs some armor and a proper tabard for court, Milord."

"Marchand's crap was useless costume junk," Rikimaru said. He looked a little closer at the duke's. "So's yours, for that matter."

"I'll have you know I spent *hours* making each piece." Leonard sniffed. "Days, in fact."

"You ever been hit by someone?" Rikimaru asked. "Like, with a proper blade?"

"No, but—"

"THOR!" Rikimaru bellowed. The skinny young sergeant ran out to the fifth-floor balcony, high above them. At his baron's instruction, he went inside for a moment and returned with the late Baron Marchand's armor. He tossed it over the edge, where it fell to the lawn in a heap.

"You are literally betting your life and limbs that this cosplay crap will save your life. Observe," Rikimaru said. He draped the mail over an old, bent street sign and hacked at it with three quick slashes. Links popped, chunks flew free, and it fell to the ground. When he held it up, they could see that the three quick strikes had rent the

241

chain apart so severely, they couldn't tell what had been the original neck hole and what was fresh damage. He took hold of one of the baron's chain shirts and yanked the man over to the duke to hold the mail up for closer inspection. "This chainmail is all butt-ended together, just mostly closed loops with no structural integrity! I could hit you with a *butter knife,* and those links would pop. All you're wearing is a false sense of security. Decent chainmail requires rivets for every single one of those links, tripling the production time. It's a huge pain in the ass to do well." He released Orlov, who was unhappy after being manhandled. Leonard was mute, shocked at how easily the chain shirt had come apart. "Now, can we go? I'll address your armor's failings after I've addressed the food issue. And apparently I can't address the food issue until this court foolishness is over with."

"If your lordship is in such a rush, his lordship can mount up, and we can leave," Leonard said. His tone was icy and as politely hostile as he could manage. Rikimaru eyed the sad animal. Its ribs were visible, it was scarred, and it had what looked like a nasty eye infection.

"How far are we going?"

"It's twenty-five kilometers to the waterfront," Leonard replied. "Why?"

Rikimaru did the math in his head. Fifteen miles, give or take.

"No thanks. I'll jog."

"You'll *what?*" Robitaille asked, incredulous.

"If I try to ride that nag, I'll break her in half. I don't look it, but I weigh close to a hundred and sixty kilos."

"You weigh three hundred and fifty pounds?!" Orlov spluttered.

"You frickin' Canadians, pick a measurement and stick with it already! Yes, I'm about three-fifty. If you had a Clydesdale or a Percheron, maybe. But this poor gal? No thanks, I'll kill her before we're halfway there. I can keep up; let's go."

"There's no way he weighs that much, but enough of this foolishness, milord," Orlov declared and mounted his horse. "If the braggart says he can keep up, let him try."

Duke Robitaille agreed. He mounted his horse and kneed it forward into a canter down Beacon Avenue to the Pat Bay Highway and turned south.

* * *

Robitaille was impressed that Rikimaru had kept pace to the end of Beacon Ave.

He was more than a little worried when they trotted past Elk Lake, half an hour later, and he saw that Rikimaru had only fallen behind by perhaps thirty or forty meters.

By the time the empress' palace on the waterfront came into view, he was downright terrified.

* * *

The inner harbor had that refreshing, salty tinge to the air that reminded Rikimaru of so many of the fishing villages back home. Friday Harbor, in particular, had the same ancient stonework, the same small-town feel, and the same patchwork of floating jetties lined with fishing boats. He counted a couple dozen boats that appeared functional and crewed. He winced as a novice captain brought his ship in a bit too fast. His crew backpaddled hard and threw bumpers over the side to minimize the damage, but it was a rough docking nonetheless.

The morning's catch was being gutted and cleaned on the dock, adding to the smells and odors wafting through the waterfront. One team of four had even hauled in a harbor seal, no doubt lured to the docks by the guts and offal being shoveled back into the water. He was pleased to note they had harvested the skin cleanly; sealskins had been a valuable commodity for thousands of years.

He learned "The Empress" was both a person and a place. He'd never spent any time on Vancouver Island before the fall; he'd always been away on some op or another. The Empress, the building, was a former luxury hotel that looked like an anachronistic palace from the Victorian era.

He hit himself mentally in the forehead. *Of course it was.* For that matter, he rather doubted "Empress Victoria" had been born with that name.

Of course she's the empress, she lives in the Empress Hotel!

Of course this is her city, that's her name, isn't it?

The audacity of it struck him, and he couldn't help but smile. Whoever she was, Victoria was smart. She was branding.

Robitaille spent a few minutes asking some basic questions—he'd need to "introduce him" to the court, and Rikimaru gave the duke some random answers that satisfied him and would have to do as his "biography." Then, they headed inside.

A short platoon of workers scoured every visible surface with something that smelled like apple cider vinegar to drown out the fish smell from outside, but it gave everything a vaguely sour, fruity scent. He couldn't help noticing that none of the empress' staff appeared to be starving or even hard done by, especially by Sidney standards. Lakonis hadn't said a word to him when they arrived. If anything, he looked shaken. Orlov seemed positively terrified and gave him plenty of space.

A braggart, am I?

No, merely improved. It's not arrogant if you can do what you say you can do.

Robitaille led his trio of barons past a gallery of folding chairs to luxurious, cushioned seats fanned out in front of a central dais. Other nobles occupied eight of the twelve chairs, and the duke quietly pointed out his counterparts for Lower Saanich and Goldstream. The lighting was low, save for a pair of windows that allowed sunlight to stream in like a spotlight. He looked carefully at the apparent throne and suppressed a knowing smirk. The dais was portable. No doubt it was moved from place to place across the hall's floor for maximum effect, depending on the month and the season. More branding.

Robitaille guided them to their seats and not ten seconds later, a well-muscled kid in his mid-twenties came out from a side door. He had some kind of pump shotgun slung over his back, and he carried a full-sized sledgehammer in his hands, with a black business end and a yellow handle. His polo shirt was clean, and a size or two too small, which showed off his shoulders, chest, abs, and biceps. Even before the fall, the kid would have been in great shape. Now, Rikimaru wondered what his secret was—did Victoria have access to pre-fall body mod tech or was he the honest product of healthy eating and pumping iron?

The guy reached the dais at the front of the cavernous hall and rapped the head of his hammer twice on the marble floor. "All rise."

Rikimaru could monkey see, monkey do with the best of them, so he stood and assumed a position of parade rest. The door opened again, and his heart caught in his chest.

She'd braided the glossy raven-black hair at her temples into a halo and accented it with a pearls-in-silver barrette. The rest of her hair fell to her mid-back, kept tidy with more white beads. She wore a sky blue, satin Mandarin dress, accented with silver dragons that caught and reflected the few beams of sunlight allowed into the hall. Her makeup was subdued—but he was impressed she'd gotten her hands on some. She'd always been resourceful. She'd always been beautiful. Twenty-five years later, "Victoria" hadn't aged a day. Ashley Roisin Connelly, his ex- from Teledyne's marketing department, remained just as gorgeous as the day they'd met.

* * *

The spotlight effect made Victoria's jewelry glitter, and tiny sparkles of rainbow light bounced all over the chamber. Her dress shone like a bright summer day, and her hair had an iridescent, almost blue gleam to it. The effect was dazzling—she'd always known how to make an entrance. Rikimaru glanced around the room and confirmed his suspicions—every "noble" was male, and she was playing every single one of them, and their hormones, for maximum effect.

"We are pleased to welcome all to this court of May 2085, in the twentieth year of our reign. You may be seated," she said, and her court of twelve did as ordered. "Lord Goldstream, you have a new member among your entourage. Stand and be recognized, sir."

"*That's Duke Armstrong,*" Robitaille whispered as the man stood, approached the dais, and bowed deeply.

"Your Imperial Majesty, I regret to inform you, Baron Daniel Fields of Rocky Point suffered a catastrophic injury at Albert Head and was not found for several days. A landslide trapped his leg between boulders, and he expired. With your permission, I wish to introduce Baron Arthur Knight to the court."

"Please."

Duke Armstrong recited a brief biography of his nomination for the position. When he finished, Baron Knight, whose name was sure to be a matter of some confusion, approached the dais and knelt. Her Imperial Majesty offered her hand, and the new noble kissed a ring she wore, rose, and bowed again before returning to his seat. Rikimaru was still having trouble believing Empress Victoria was his pre-collapse ex, Ash.

When it was clear Armstrong had no further official business, she gestured for the Duke to sit and turned to the next Duke in line. "Lord Horton of Lower Saanich, what news from our southeastern shores?"

"Your Majesty, I wish I bore glad tidings, but the news is…grave. We have suffered an insult from the accursed Shogunate."

"We beg your pardon?" Victoria replied. Horton swallowed visibly and stammered before continuing.

"Not two days ago, approximately fifty armed raiders, marines, soldiers—I'm not sure what the appropriate term would be— attacked. Your Majesty will recall, at last court, the late Duke Tremblay's report. Their raid had only been successful in the mildest sense. One ship stolen…uh, rather, *claimed*, but this has provoked the Shogunate into retaliatory attacks. They seized the only four functional fishing boats we possessed and burned the rest."

"The rest?" she asked, eyes narrowed to dangerous slits.

248 | JAMIE IBSON

"The dock, the jetties, all the houseboats, and Baron Joyce's estate, Your Imperial Majesty."

"We see." She pursed her lips and appeared to be weighing the matter.

Oh, shit, Rikimaru thought. *That complicates things.*

"I'm reluctant to ask for additional ships—" Horton began, but she cut him off.

"Of course you are, Miles. Because you already know what We will say—*no*, a most emphatic *no*. Our fishing fleet is essential to maintaining the Inner Harbor. Even if We had ships to spare, which We do not, We simply cannot entrust them to one who cannot guarantee their absolute safety."

"I understand, Your Majesty."

"How many casualties did your valiant troops suffer in this heinous raid, Lord Joyce?"

The noble next to Horton mumbled something Rikimaru couldn't hear.

"One?" Victoria shrieked. "ONE? How could this have happened with a mere single casualty, Joyce? *Explain yourself!*"

"Your Majesty...by the time the sun came up, all fifty of the attackers had occupied the dock. They wore armor and carried polearms and alcohol to use as an incendiary. Their polearms gave them far more reach than our blades. My sole casualty, your Majesty, was my sergeant, whose foot they cut in half from six feet away. My medic was unable to save it and had to amputate."

"Sledge, take Mister Joyce into custody. We will need some time to consider the extent of his negligence before We pronounce sentence."

Joyce was crestfallen but didn't resist. The hunk at Victoria's side produced a length of colored fabric—an old cargo strap, if Rikimaru had to guess—and wrapped the fabric around one of Joyces's wrists, then the other, and secured them with a knot. He led the man away and shoved him through another side door. He closed it, and secured it with a padlock. *A closet-turned-jail-cell, then.*

"Duke Horton, We realize you have only held your present office for a month, so We are willing to overlook a certain amount of ineptitude, but Lower Saanich is *your* responsibility. We have no idea where you will source a new fishing fleet, nor how you'll repair the infrastructure at Our Royal Yacht Club, but if you can't, one of your Barons will find themselves abruptly promoted. *Do We make ourselves clear?*"

"Yes, Your Majesty," Horton replied glumly. "May…may I have your permission to besiege the savages at Brentwood Bay?"

Victoria pursed her lips and regarded him through narrow eyelids. "Make your case."

"The belligerents at that…hole have never bowed the knee to Your Majesty, as they should. They maintain a fleet of their own and raid Saltspring, Pender, and the rest of the Strait of Georgia, using their location in Your Majesty's territory to make themselves safe from attack. For years, they have hidden behind Your Majesty's shield, without ever paying Your Majesty's due tribute. I fear the situation in Lower Saanich is becoming dire. I could marshal my household's entire force and bring them into compliance. We would restore our fleet, the Baron Mount Newton would gain access to the marinas there, and it would put a stop to this thorn in Your side once and for all."

She considered it for a moment. "You have Our blessing, Lord Horton. I trust that if you fail, you won't return."

It wasn't a question.

She blew out a breath and composed herself. "Be seated, Horton. Lord Robitaille, what does the Duke of Land's End have for Us today?"

"Your Imperial Majesty, the seat of Sidney has changed twice since our last court appearance. You'll recall, I'm sure, Baron Howell committed a murder while dueling Lord Tremblay and was executed by the Champion. Baron Kevin Marchand was Lord of Sidney until bested in righteous combat two nights ago. I give you Baron Ronin of Sidney."

Rikimaru stood, but there was no recognition on her face. The spotlight effect of the sunbeams might have blinded her so she couldn't see into the stark shadows.

"The Baron washed up on our shores one week past after an accident swept him off his vessel north of Pender Island. He is a fit and capable warrior, and he has pledged to address the chronic food shortages that have plagued the Sidney region since Howell's reign."

Here goes.

Rikimaru approached the dais as he'd seen Baron Knight do earlier, kept his head low, and knelt. She presented her ring—on the index finger—to kiss, but instead of kissing the gaudy thing, he kissed her ring finger, where she'd once worn his engagement band.

She snatched her hand away, and he looked up, finally meeting her eyes.

Recognition.

Shock.

"Rick? Where—?"

Anger.

CRACK!

The slap was like a gunshot, shattering the quiet calm of the hall.

Rikimaru had fought JalCom Juggernauts, Obsidian special forces, hundreds of raiders on the Deception Pass bridges, and Stephen bloody Gaunt. *None* of them hit him as hard as Ash Connelly did.

Totally worth it.

* * * * *

Chapter Fifteen

"**O**ut! Everyone out, *now*! Begone! Robitaille, wait for your man outside by the waterfront. Baron Ronin remains."

Ten nobles, half a dozen randoms in the gallery, and every servant fled the great hall. Only "Sledge" stayed put. She rounded on him and pointed to the entrance. "What part of *everyone* was unclear? Go! *Run!*" she yelled, and the young man glared at Rikimaru before sullenly departing. When the room was finally clear, Rikimaru got to his feet and massaged his cheek where she'd smacked him.

"How ya been, Ash?"

"I haven't been Ashley Connelly in twenty years, Rick! I'm Victoria now. And the answer is, surviving, barely."

"*Just* Victoria? Or Her Royal Imperial Majesty, Empress Victoria the Second?" he teased and opened his arms to offer a hug. "I've missed you."

"I—" she paused, then she threw herself into his grasp. "It would have been a lot easier with you at my side. God, Rick, I thought you'd bought it when Seattle went up in a cloud of angry plutonium!"

"I nearly did. What happened to the SoCal transfer?"

"I went. They were assholes, it didn't work out. They transferred me back, with a promotion, just to get me out of their hair. I landed in Victoria, to visit mom, and I was going to surprise you. Then the

254 | JAMIE IBSON

world ended, and everything went to hell," she said. The bitterness in her tone was palpable.

"I thought your folks had died?" Rikimaru asked, confused.

She looked away for a second. "Dad did, yeah. But that doesn't matter. Mom was in Sooke, but she's gone now, too. Where have you been all these years? Don't tell me you fell off a boat in Saltspring."

"That's a helluva question," Rikimaru said. He cleared his throat, checked his feet for dust, and swallowed hard. "But lying wouldn't make things any easier, so I'll tell you right now, and you'll probably hate me for the answer. Those were *my* troops that just torched your yacht club."

He expected another slap. What he didn't expect was for her to recoil in horror.

"What? How? Why?"

"Do you want an explanation? If you ask a question you don't want an answer to, expect an answer you don't want to hear."

The hurt in her eyes made his heart ache, but she nodded for him to proceed. So he explained, from the beginning. The *very* beginning. The race from the Seattle core against inbound missiles. EMPs cooking their vehicles' electronics and fleeing by sailboat. Establishing control over the San Juan Islands. How Operations Vice President Akihiro Kojima wound up as shogun, and how Specialist Rick Hanzo became the daimyo of their little island kingdom. The raids, blamed on the ever-present, but poorly understood, Victorians, and Shogun Kojima's shift in policy. Gaunt's horde. Blowing the bridges and waking up, much to his surprise, on the beach south of Sidney.

"...and things went from there. A couple of assholes started smacking the kids around. I stood up for them, and the assholes came at me with spears. Then *their* asshole friends came at me the next day. Then the *Baron's* asshole friends came at me, and once Baron Marchand explained how your little promotions process works, I punted him off the balcony. Robitaille showed up this morning, wondering who the fuck I was and what had happened to the previous guy. Things are pretty screwed up there; it's going to take a lot to fix it."

"Back up a bit. You said *we're* the bad guys?" Victoria objected. "Who told us to fuck off and starve back in May of sixty-five? Teledyne operated here, too, Rick. Teledyne owned everything from Anchorage to San Diego, Edmonton to Tucson! We were on the same team!"

"Wasn't us," Rikimaru said. "We had our hands full, getting everyone on board, but hell, if you'd asked for help, you'd have gotten it."

"Bullshit," she countered. "All the senior Teledyne staff for Vancouver Island were in Seattle for a conference the weekend the bombs dropped. On Monday, I checked in with the local office, and it turned out I was senior to every surviving rep. I sent *three* envoys on sailboats. I remember each one like it was yesterday—the *Dirty Oar*, the *Ships n Giggles*, and the *Sea Sea Sea Señora*. No one ever came back."

She was obviously bitter, and if it had gone down as she claimed, she had every right to be. Rikimaru chewed on that for a moment.

"I don't have an answer for you. Mikael took point as field trainer, Ayame was intel, and I was overall in charge of operations. We never, to my knowledge, saw those boats." She glared at him, disbelieving, but he went on. "I can definitively say, the punitive raid on the yacht club was a retaliatory strike after the raid on Deer Harbor a month ago, but that's the very first one we've launched in twenty years. Kojima forbid it before then. *Shit.*" He jammed his eyes shut and massaged his temples for a moment.

"I'm going to need to sail home and wave them off. There were more raids planned. A lot more. Once I've stopped them, I'll set you up to meet Kojima, and we'll work it out. Can I use one of those ships in the harbor?"

"No," she said. He opened his mouth to object, but she held up a single finger to shush him before he interrupted. It was comforting; that single finger reminded him of one of their old agreements, from when they were engaged, where one of their etched-in-stone rules of the relationship was that they wouldn't interrupt each other. "Look at it from my point of view. I just imprisoned Ronald for letting *your* people torch his boats, not that anyone else knows that, and then I denied Miles access to mine. Some new random shows up, the empress slaps him in front of God and everyone, and she sends everyone away for a super-secret talk with the new guy. Now, new guy's sailing away in one of those same boats on a mystery errand? I'll have a revolution on my hands before you get home. You must have boats of your own now that you're Baron of Sidney?"

"We do, yeah, but they're in terrible shape. It'll delay me, but if it's not politick, well, you always understood that kind of thing better. That's fine; this is a long term problem. I was going to hold classes for everyone on fishing and sailing. We can bodge together new, functional ships from old ones and new ropes from our hemp farms. Our Komainu conscripts are part defensive militia, part infrastructure labor force. With Kojima's blessing, I can get a company or three here to get some proper large-scale farming and gardening going. Seeing the conditions here...I'm gutted. I had no idea how close to the ragged edge you are. Maybe blowing up that bridge was the best thing I've done."

"Can I count on your discretion?" she asked. "I'm going to have a hard enough time explaining this away. If word gets around about their Empress's ex-boyfriend—"

"Ex-fiancé," he corrected.

"Ex-*fiancé* just showed up, the rabble will talk."

"Would that be so bad?" he asked. "If not for your SoCal transfer..."

"Rick, look at me. I don't dress in slinky satin dresses and pearls for my health. The only thing keeping these guys under some kind of control is that they think they might get laid. Everyone's got their eyes on the prize. Even after an apocalypse, men still think with their balls. *Especially* after an apocalypse."

"Nobody's ever...tried to...force you...?"

"Jesus, Rick, of course they have! Do you know how many would-be rapists I've killed over the years? Start at "a couple of times a year," times twenty years, then scale up from there. For that matter, it was an issue *before* the nukes! I have ways and means of dealing with them, including siccing the occasional would-be suitor on the occasional rapist-in-waiting. Sledge isn't my first Champion." She eyed him, from head to toe to head again. "But, if this all works out...maybe he'll be the last."

"I'd like that. As far as anyone's concerned, you were my boss before the fall."

She kissed him on the cheek. "That will do. It's been a long time, Rikimaru Hanzo; I've missed you. Get me that meeting with the shogun, and we can put all this behind us. Now go."

* * * * *

Chapter Sixteen

"Y"ou were in there a long time, Ronin," Robitaille observed when Rikimaru finally made his way down the steps outside the Empress.

"We had a lot to talk about," he replied. "She was my boss in Teledyne before the fall."

"And?"

"And nothing. She's given me a priority tasking, meaning I need to get home and get on a sailboat. And if all goes according to plan, I can tell you more once all's said and done."

"Are you planning to *jog* home? Your little display this morning was a bit much, mister. *What are you?*"

Rikimaru rolled his eyes. "Someone on your side." Robitaille crossed his arms and glared. Orlov and Lakonis were there too, silent but suspicious. He'd never been a very good liar, and he'd forgotten they'd already seen some of his capabilities. "Alright. I worked for Teledyne Operations Directorate. We had different cover names for it, depending on location, phase of the moon, and whatever disinformation campaign they were running. I'm sure, if you asked Victoria, she'd just say we were in marketing. I'm a Specialist."

Lakonis broke into a huge grin and punched Orlov in the shoulder. Wordlessly, Orlov rolled his eyes and handed over a small stack of chits.

"And you just happened to wash up on our beach last week? Where the hell have you been this whole time?" Robitaille demanded.

"I can't tell you," he said. "I have given the Empress an honest explanation, which she accepted, rather than executing me on the spot. You'll have to content yourself with that. Now, as I said, I need to get home and get a sailboat. Beyond that, all you need to know is now that I'm here, I'm going to help."

With that, he turned and broke into the same ground-eating lope as before and sped away northbound, knowing they'd eventually catch up on their horses.

* * *

Rikimaru was breathing hard when he finally reached territory he recognized. He spotted the sports field vegetable garden on his left and turned off the highway to grab a bite there. Then he caught a whiff of something on the wind that worried him and glanced through the trees to the north. Thick smoke blackened the sky.

"No...No no no..."

He was nearing physical exhaustion—he'd burned several thousand calories today, and he needed to rehydrate, but with what he'd just heard at court, he knew what the smoke meant. The Onamazu were moving quickly, far too quickly. He sped up, raced down Beacon Avenue—and collapsed when he reached the lawn of his new abode.

He breathed in heaving gasps of toxic smoke. The marina and all the fiberglass hulls still present were wholly engulfed.

"Baron!" Thor shouted and came running, rifle in hand. Katie, Dyson, Waylan, and more of her kids ran out to meet him on the lawn.

"Water," Rikimaru gasped.

"It's too far gone, milord," Thor said. "We can't put it out."

"For him to drink, Sergeant!" Darius Lakonis corrected. "And I daresay, if you can get him some dried fruits or any salmon jerky you might have, he needs to refuel."

"Of course, milord," Thor replied, chastened, and he dashed off to the main building.

"Where is everyone else?" Robitaille asked Waylan. "Where are the guardsmen?"

She pointed to the conflagration. "Milord Baron, Sergeant Axton, and most of Sergeant Thor's squads were in there when it went up."

"No," Rikimaru protested. "No, damn them!" Thor returned with food and drink. Rikimaru took several swigs of water and regained his feet. "What about Roberts and his squad?"

Thor shook his head. "They...the raiders hit the north marina first. It's the bigger one, like, a lot bigger, and it took them longer. That's what let everyone here get ready."

Though he feared the answer, Rikimaru had to ask. "Did we kill any of them?"

Thor pointed to the water. Rikimaru leaned on the railing and retched. One of Akuma's Onamazu marines floated there on his back. Sam Alvarez's face stared up at him, eyes wide to the sky and unblinking, empty. The dead marine's armor was similar to Rikimaru's white plates, but they'd been painted navy blue. There was a visible bullet strike in his upper chest, where the navy paint had chipped away, exposing unpainted plywood beneath.

"Get him out of there before some bloody shark eats him," he said. He felt sick, and it wasn't just a lack of calories.

"What? Why?" Thor asked, then gulped when he realized he'd questioned his Baron's order.

"BECAUSE HE'S—" Rikimaru barked, then caught himself. They didn't know yet. "Because it's the right thing to do. And, we can salvage that armor. Show you how to make a proper kit for fighting people with swords and spears."

Thor nodded and went in search of a hook or gaffe to reel the body into shore. Katie tugged on his leg.

"You said you'd protect us, Mister Ronin," she whimpered. "What happened?"

"I…I had to go meet the Empress, young one. And they attacked while I was gone."

The malnourished nine-year-old's eyes welled with tears, and she rubbed them away. "Why?"

"Because…because adults aren't very good at talking. Or sharing. And they were mad because of something one of the other dukes did. So, they came here to punish us because they think we're all the same."

"I *hate* you!" she wailed. "You were supposed to *stop them!* You were supposed to be different! You *promised!*"

"Katie, I—"

The little girl fled, tears streaking her face. Sid and Dyson chased after her, and Waylan followed.

Duke Robitaille joined him at the railing and observed as Rikimaru's sole surviving guardsman pulled the marine to shore and dragged him out.

"What was his name?"

Robitaille knew. Rikimaru exhaled a deep breath he hadn't realized he was holding.

"Samuel Raphael Alvarez. He was nineteen, about to be released from the Komainu, our guardians, when the guys down at the Royal Yacht Club stole a ship from Orcas Island. That was the straw that broke the camel's back, and we got new orders from the shogun: Form a new, kickass unit, and go sort out those dastardly Victorians who raided us for boats and killed our people one time too many. So he signed up for another hitch."

The duke nodded in understanding.

"His name will be etched into the surface of the *kami* stone at Memorial Park, next to Ryu Doraku, probably Mikael Grimstaadt's, and probably *mine,* and the hundreds of others who've died over the years. They'll celebrate his life, mourn his loss, tell tall tales about his bravery and badassitude and service to the Onamazu, and then a dozen more kids will sign up."

"Unless?"

"Unless I can stop my best friend and her top lieutenant from coming back here with more blood on their minds and fire in their hearts. They think I'm dead, which is awkward, and my best friend just killed all my people and torched my ride home." He laughed, a harsh, bitter snort. "You wouldn't happen to know where I could steal a boat, would you? Seems I'm fresh out."

Robitaille looked thoughtful.

"Actually, I do."

* * * * *

Chapter Seventeen

Of all his enhancements, Rikimaru was currently most thankful for the shine job he'd gotten on his eyes. He could see deeper into the darkness, if not as well as a cat, then pretty close. It made them appear to glow, like a cat's out on a nighttime patrol when the light caught them just right. Night was his friend. It made his enemies blind or sleepy or put them in the mood for partying. Sometimes all three, and all three gave him a tactical advantage.

He'd spent the day perched on Willis Point, southwest of Brentwood Bay, noting hardpoints, observation towers, patrols, sailboats, and the extent of these "pirates'" fortifications, with Robitaille and the others. Getting out of Sidney was for the best, for the time being.

These savage pirates' rubble walls were extensive, made possible by an armored bulldozer currently parked at the east end of town. Orlov's knowledge of the region and advice had proven invaluable. From the roof of the ancient fire hall, he'd pointed out the continuous wall of destruction. It defined the compound's borders, from the ferry terminal in the east to West Saanich Road in the south, then west again to the more southern marina. The bulldozer crew had battered down nearly every house on the perimeter, creating near impassable fortifications.

They'd cannibalized more houses to make observation platforms and, to Rikimaru's shock, *shooting* platforms. Every one of those platforms was manned by someone wearing what looked suspiciously like tac gear and carrying what looked suspiciously like pre-fall assault rifles. Any of Victoria's forces approaching by land, expecting a battle with sword or spear, would blunder into kill zones extending hundreds of meters beyond the crude walls. It would be a slaughter.

The only positive was, despite its size, it didn't look like the town was all that populated. From his observation point, he'd only seen tiny groups of people out on foot and maybe a dozen armed guards on the various observation posts. Robitaille had said he knew where to steal a boat, not that it would be easy.

The busiest place had been the docks, where half a dozen sailboats cruised back into their slips as the sun disappeared beyond Mount Malahat. The crews dragged the fifteen prisoners off and collected them on a sprawling beachfront property. There was a little ceremony with their grand poohbah—and then the captives' throats were cut.

Rikimaru retched quietly over the side of the hull when he realized they were being *dressed*, like hogs for a pig roast. A bonfire burned down until it was a bed of coals, shimmering with heat, then the savages set up rotisserie stands for the night's beachfront roast. As night fell, the pirate cannibals gathered on the waterfront, celebrating their hunt with booze, music, and food. That music drifted over the water to their distant hide, and the coals glowed a malevolent red.

"You wished to know when night had fully fallen, Specialist?" Robitaille asked. "I believe it is dark enough."

"Good. Take your men back down the hill and make your way to the fields by the old butterfly gardens. You'll be able to see my flare from there."

"You're sure you can do this?" Orlov asked suddenly. "By yourself, I mean?"

"Don't tell me you're concerned, Aleks," Rikimaru chuckled. "Yesterday, you hated my guts."

"I didn't *hate*—"

"Watch for my flare. Red for 'Oh shit;' white for 'Clear.'"

And then he slipped away, down the steep hillside behind the firehall. He rustled leaves but avoided branches as best he could until he emerged from below the canopy, barely feet from the shore. He slipped Robitaille's loaned rucksack from his shoulders and checked that the sail/tarp was still tied tightly, giving it some degree of buoyancy and waterproofness.

And here's where we hope Sam's armor is as buoyant as mine.

He took a deep breath, slipped into the water, and found that the navy blue armor kept his head above water, if only barely. He was thankful for Robitaille's ruck—with the contents wrapped in the tarp, he could carry his saber, rifle, and ammunition with him. No doubt, if he'd had to carry the equipment on his person, he'd have gone straight to the bottom and had to walk the whole way. He paddled quietly across the inlet, then hugged tightly to the shore, and steadily breast stroked as silently as he could manage. If he remembered correctly, it got deep in the inlet, fast.

The chill of the water sapped his strength, but he kept paddling, mentally berating himself for every splash he made. The beach party was obnoxiously loud, and music, the first synthetically reproduced music he'd heard in decades, carried over the water. For a time, a short, rocky island occluded the party.

Halfway there.

The booming music of the party allowed him to relax his noise discipline a bit, and he swam faster. After what might have been an hour, he finally reached the south marina. The hardest part was having to wait and listen for anyone who might detect him. He saw no one, and he heard no one, so he kept going. He swam under the jetty until his feet finally touched the bottom.

He rose, slowly, to allow his clothes and armor to drain without too much splashing. He advanced, slowly, ears and eyes open, until he finally had dry land under his feet.

This corner of the cannibals' turf was thick with growth, and much of it seemed abandoned. He didn't waste any more time. He took Perseverance from the ruck, belted it onto one hip, and slung the battered rifle over a shoulder. He then put the ruck and tarp under a tree in some tall grass, to be retrieved later.

Infiltration complete.

If he'd had any reluctance before, he didn't now. The cannibalistic display meant the Steiner protocols were a go.

The first guard tower was maybe a hundred meters ahead. All he had to do was follow the wall of bulldozed debris to a house they hadn't demolished. An aluminum ladder provided easy access to the already-flat roof, two stories up. He leaped the distance vertically, caught the roof's edge, and hauled himself up with an explosive chin-up. The sole guard turned at the scraping noise, but Rikimaru closed the distance in two strides and drove three feet of steel straight through the man's sternum. Rikimaru's hand clamped over the dying cannibal's mouth, just in case, but barely more than a wheeze escaped the man's lips before he collapsed. Rikimaru was correct, the black clothing they wore was pre-fall tac gear. This one had a helmet, starlight goggles, a load-bearing vest, mag pouches, and a blocky, suppressed pistol in a drop holster.

For the first time in decades, he heard an electronic *beep* and a quiet whirring. His eyes locked on the device to his left, which was camouflaged with carefully constructed junk. He'd disregarded the massive black shadow in the immediate rush, but now a shiver ran up his spine.

No wonder these cannibalistic brutes had remained independent for so long, they had *machineguns.*

Beneath the corrugated tin shelter, an MG3A6 medium machinegun rested in a modular auto-turret cradle. The cradle made the whirring sound and the electronic tone. The gun had a long, blocky shroud protecting the barrel, and the turret cradle concealed the trigger mech. Disintegrating link ammo locked into the feed tray from a can to its left. The boxy thing slowly traversed, left to right, right to left, scanning the fields south of them like a silent sentry. A thick power cable exited the blocky lower half, draped over the edge of the platform, and disappeared in the grasses below. A second chirp drew his attention to a dim LED screen at the rear of the turret.

29...28...27...

A red warning indicator on the screen began blinking.

RESET? Y/N

Rikimaru thumbed the *Yes* button and deeply sighed with relief when the counter changed to five minutes. Teledyne troops had had such a thing at some of their forward facilities. If the gun needed to be reset every five minutes, the turret acted like a babysitter, preventing the crew from screwing around or dozing off. If the assigned team got whacked by a well-placed rifle round, the MG would go to automatic and engage anything it 'saw.'

Technology!

He went back to the dead guy in tac gear. The helmet was a bit small, but it was in decent shape. His hands shook, a little, because after all this time, he had his hands on some real modern tech. It didn't seem real. He quelled the flutter in his chest and slipped the goggles down.

He cursed.

The upgraded eyeballs Teledyne paid for did a lot of things, but they didn't allow him to see in infrared. One such beam, now visible thanks to the electronic aid, lanced out from the turret base and swept back and forth across the fields beyond their bulldozed fortifi-

270 | JAMIE IBSON

cations. That was how it 'saw' its targets. Rikimaru looked east and saw two more beams sweeping the night. If he couldn't do something about the five-minute timer, his 'stealth' mission would get far more complicated.

He hadn't thought he'd ever see this kind of equipment again. He was pleasantly surprised to learn there wasn't any kind of lockout on the turret's interface. Whether that was complacency or illiteracy, he didn't know, nor did he care. By tapping on a few menus, he quickly found the timer settings and deactivated them. For now, the gun wouldn't betray him.

* * *

After looting the dead man's rifle (bullpup, select-fire, unknown make) and pistol (sixth-gen Maxim 9, integrally suppressed but not remotely silent), and filling his pockets with ammunition, the Specialist silently dropped to the ground behind the tower and ran for the next. He felt faintly ridiculous, racing down the dark bulldozed zone, sword in hand, but it was the quietest option. Perhaps fifty meters short of the next machinegun nest, a man and woman strode out from between a pair of houses. The man shuffled after the woman, his pants around his ankles, and she giggled, playing hard to get and staying just out of his reach. He slashed through the man's neck with Perseverance, sending his head spinning off in one direction and his body toppling in another. The woman drew a deep breath to scream. Rikimaru still had some semblance of chivalry deep in his core, so it was with a modicum of regret that he decapitated her on the backstroke.

They eat people. Stealth mission: no witnesses, no survivors.

He roughly shoved the bodies down the alley between the houses and kept going.

The second machinegun nest was on another intact house, this one with a balcony. He reached the roof in two fast jumps. This nest held two targets, but the couple below had served as a dress rehearsal. Forehand, backhand, and two more bodies collapsed. A bottle of rotgut suggested they'd been having a celebration, despite being on duty. He flicked the saber to clean some of the blood off and checked the second gun's control panel.

This one had a lockout, and the timer was just passing *ten* minutes. Not good.

The first person wore the same light gear as the previous guard, but the second wore more than a simple mesh vest. He had armored pauldrons and level IV plates—front, back, and sides—all backed by a heavy Kevlar weave. Was this one of their leaders? Rikimaru popped the side clips, slipped the armor free of the decapitated body, and searched it. There were more rifle magazines in the pouches, and one zippered vest pocket hid something plastic, thin, and rectangular. He slipped it out and nearly dropped it.

It was a Teledyne RFID card, with *Ashley Roisin Connelly*'s face and name on it.

Why in the nine hells was something like Ash's corporate ID card here?

He gingerly held the card out to the reader plate on the turret's side, and the LED panel blinked green.

Shit.

What isn't she telling me? What didn't she tell that duke, Horton?

He shut off the automated reset timer on the gun and stared accusingly at the ID card. She really had spectacular genetics. The date on the card indicated it was her initial issue. The photo was twenty-five, twenty-seven years old, but she hadn't aged a day.

For now, it didn't matter; mysteries would wait. The dead NCO's plate armor was much more functional than the mesh crap, and on land, much more functional than the navy blue plywood, for that matter. He upgraded his kit again, then he was on to the third tower.

* * *

Forty minutes later, the last gun tower crew lay dead. Half an hour after that, he'd set five of the six guns they'd had to activate, looking *inwards,* with a delay. They created overlapping fields of fire that would make approaching them lethal from any direction but one, and it was not an obvious route. He lugged the first gun down to where he'd stashed his ruck by the southern marina, dragging the thick power cable the whole way.

Have to check that later. Where are they drawing power from?

He cut down more drunken wanderers along the way, wanderers who didn't recognize him in the dark with his helmet and armor disguise until it was too late. He laid in the last gun's left and right arcs, breathed deep, and centered himself. He and Death were old comrades. Taking lives didn't trouble him, but he didn't engage in the wholesale slaughter of an entire people very often.

He didn't come across murderous cannibal pirates often either, so there was that.

To the northeast, a burp of machinegun fire echoed through the houses like the faint rumble of thunder. Then another.

The revelers on the beach didn't react, deafened by liquor, laughter, and music, but the rest of the compound would figure it out pretty quickly. He mashed the *Active* indicator on the LED panel and shouldered his rifle.

Tracers scythed out from the MG3, traversing back and forth, grazing the entire beach with waist-high machinegun fire. Glowing machinegun rounds caromed wildly into the night when they hit something and bounced, but otherwise, the partiers collapsed, and the automated gun belched more fire. The MG and screams of those panicking on the beach drowned out the staccato cracks of his rifle. He allowed himself twenty seconds of slaughter, but then the shock of the ambush was over, and survivors would be trying to encircle him and counterattack.

Time to move.

He retreated to the first, now-empty gun tower and covered the turret's spot on the beach from up high. As he suspected, several human BBQ beachgoers emerged from a side alley between houses and crept forward to try to flank the turret and shut it down. He let them get onto the cleared path behind the rubble wall, where they were exposed, and ambushed them again. Six more died.

Reload.

Move.

He dropped off the platform and melted into the shadows by the mouth of the alley. Feet pounded up the alley toward him, but Rikimaru clotheslined the savage with his saber, neatly parting his head from shoulders. If he blundered into the machineguns' kill zones, they'd kill him just as dead as anyone else, despite the modern ballistic plate, and his raid would be over, unfortunately early. He crept down the path, keeping his mental map firmly in place.

* * *

The sun was coming up, bathing the compound in beautiful rays of red sunshine, despite the carnage inside. Four of the six guns had run dry overnight, and it had been half an hour since the last one fired. Everyone had either gone to ground or died. Perseverance was bent, but not broken, from a misjudged swing where he'd smashed the venerable blade into a pirate wearing modern armor like the plates he'd looted at the first machinegun nest. It was a great sword, and with a forge, he could repair it. Three times, he'd returned to the dead riflemen on the compound walls to swap empty mags for full ones.

In his initial reconnaissance, he had counted ninety-six people through his binoculars. The dead numbered twice that in reality. *A good night's work.*

He disabled the last two active turrets and fired a white flare into the air. He threaded his way through the abattoir to the southeast tower to link up with Robitaille and his troops. The duke was pale and anxious when he led his troops out of the forest.

"That was the most horrific night I can imagine," he said without preamble. "I have *never* heard that much gunfire in a single night."

"Could have been worse," Rikimaru said. "You could have been here, with me."

He pointed to a hidden gap in the rubble a short distance away. "It's camouflaged, but you can come in through there, single file."

Inside, the short company of Robitaille's household guards formed up in four ranks.

"Listen up, troops! There are *eight* roads running east-to-west in here," Rikimaru began. "Just *two*, north-to-south, but walking paths and alleys cut through this place like worms in rotten apples. I want ten troops per road, one supervisor per. Check every single house, every single room. Take your time. Be slow, be methodical. Survivors may have guns or pre-fall armor or both. They'll probably have booby traps and who knows what else. Sweep as a cordon, and don't let anyone slip through. Use Hagan Road to dress your lines before you push for the beach. Who has shooting experience?"

A dozen men put their hands up.

"Not bad, assuming none of you are lying. You will take point for each search. Rifles and vests are there." He pointed to a pile of bloody equipment he'd laid out. "If anyone has a negligent discharge, their shooting rights will be suspended immediately. If anyone hurts or shoots a friendly, you will face summary field execution. If you think I'm joking, take a good look around."

"You can't just—" Robitaille began, but Rikimaru cut him off.

"I can, I will, and I did. I've just slaughtered two hundred armed cannibals, solo. If you think I'll cry over some fudd who doesn't know how to stay safe with modern weapons, you're wrong. I will meet you on the beach when the sweep is done. Until then, I have something to take care of."

* * *

He found a forty-five-foot sailboat by the ferry terminal and stripped it of its mainsail and ropes. He hauled the armload of canvas to the beach and laid the sail out flat. There were plenty of corpses available, so he dragged over one that wasn't too stiff yet.

Waste not, want not.

Lacking paint, or time, he hacked off the dead savage's arm with Perseverance and used the oldest stain known to man.

In strokes five feet high, he painted a trio of symbols on the sail with the dead man's blood. He stepped back and surveyed his work. His Japanese was rusty, but it would do.

Once the symbols were dark enough for his liking, he dragged the sail and ropes to the ferry and climbed the boom atop the ancient *MV Kahloke*. The ferry once carried cars to the terminal north of Mount Malahat, but more importantly, it was the largest ship present and had a boom above the bridge. He lashed the sail to the top of the boom, returned to the deck, and tied down the sail's corners with more ropes. He took a moment to appreciate his work.

That should do.

* * * * *

Chapter Eighteen

Ayame gasped in orgasmic bliss, and Ajay collapsed onto the sheets next to her. When she'd caught her breath, she rolled over and kissed him deeply. "Remind me to thank Kael when we get back," she said. "His suggestion to hitch a ride with you on these expeditions was a *great* idea. Turns out, killing raiders and torching boats is one *hell* of an aphrodisiac."

"I will." Kumar smiled and kissed her back. It was probably time, though. She reached for her bra and zipped it shut. Good athletic bras were hard to come by; she didn't even like risking them in combat. What if they got damaged?

But Ajay liked them, especially when she only half unzipped the front to tease him and drive him crazy. It had been a *long* time, so to hell with the fraternization rules. Even if one of these missions went horribly wrong, getting laid 'one last time' before going into battle had a certain sense of tradition to it. Keeping it a secret (not that it really was, but Nobunaga hadn't said a word) and sneaking these moments of intimacy in the *Seas The Days'* front cabin made it that much more exciting. She felt like a teenager again.

When they emerged, young Derek Frost suppressed an embarrassed grin and turned away. Nobunaga leaned over and whispered in her ear.

"Your shirt's on backwards and inside out, Samurai. Please hurry, we've already passed Henderson Point. The docks should be just past that forest."

277

"Shit." She darted back below decks and re-emerged moments later with her top properly adjusted. She threw her armor over her shoulders, and Ajay tied her laces tight. "What in the hell is that?" Ajay asked a moment later, pointing to the old ferry terminal ahead of them. The instant she saw it, Ayame's legs gave out, and she hit the cockpit's bench, hard.

"What's wrong?" Ajay asked. "Can you read it?"

"It's *kanji*," she whispered.

Dan Nobunaga was staring at her, eyes wide. He could read Japanese too. "It says, *Rikimaru lives.*"

"*What?*" Akuma gasped. "What the hell does that mean? Is it some kind of trick?"

"I don't know," Ayame replied. "Are they...could they be holding him captive somewhere?"

Nobunaga produced a set of binoculars from his storage chest and swept the beachfront. "I don't think so. Captors don't typically dress their prisoners in ballistic armor or arm them with swords. Or bullpup carbines." A broad smile crossed his face, and he passed the binos to Ayame.

Sure enough, her boss, mentor, friend, and would-be partner stood at the end of the next dock past the ferry. A silver blade rode on his left hip, a carbine hung on a sling at his right, and matte-black ballistic plates covered his torso. Blood splattered his face, but otherwise, he looked intact.

So why did he look so grim?

* * * * *

Part Three: Shogun

Chapter Nineteen

It was a gamble, but Rikimaru liked to think he knew his core team pretty well. No matter who was leading these marine incursions, the odds were pretty good Dan Nobunaga would be driving the lead boat. He painted the enormous Japanese characters—characters only he, Dan, Ayame, and a handful of others could read—to let his team know he was alive. And they were encoded so hardly anyone else would understand.

His gamble paid off. The *Seas The Day* was, indeed, the first ship to round the point. His troops, his people, had come to whisk him away home at last.

So why did he feel like this was a betrayal?

Derek Frost, Ayame, and Akuma lined the rail of the *Seas the Day*. Derek waved his hands so hard he looked like he'd take flight, and Rikimaru inclined his head in a subdued bow. Ayame wore her wooden samurai plate, and even Akuma had gotten into the act, except his armor was navy blue like poor Sam Alvarez's. Rikimaru backed up to allow the other two onto the dock, but Ayame didn't wait. She jumped, hard, and landed in a three-point stance at the edge of the wooden platform before launching forward into a bone-crushing hug. She was laughing and crying at the same time, and Rikimaru reluctantly embraced her. Akuma crossed to the dock and wrapped both of them in a hug too.

"What—how—but—*you're alive!*" Ayame stuttered.

"Seems that way," Rikimaru agreed. He caught sight of a shorter figure behind her and shot a glance to Nobunaga as his boat sailed away, missing its second crewmember. Nobunaga spread his hands as if to say, *As if I could stop him.*

Rikimaru finally allowed a smile to cross his lips, and the thirteen-year-old dashed forward to get a hug of his own. "It's good to see you, young man."

"I'm glad to see you're alive, Daimyo."

"Likewise." Rikimaru released the boy, and he gestured toward the fleet bearing down on them. "I see you brought the whole crew? You might want to wave them off. I'd rather you didn't torch this joint just yet."

"Of course!" Akuma agreed and went back to the edge of the dock to signal orders with a pair of semaphore flags. Ayame caught his meaning, though, and followed him onto solid ground.

"How do you know about that?" she asked. "And, what's with the gear? You look like you're ready to go to war with Obsidian again."

"Do you want the short version?" he asked. Aya nodded.

"I washed up on the beach in Sidney and saved some kids from the adults here. They're pretty much all starving to death. One thing led to another, and in four days, I went from 'barely conscious flotsam' to local warlord. They're big on personal combat for promotion points. Then I met the Empress. Victoria, it turns out, is my ex-fiancé from Teledyne. She's nursed a hatred for the Shogunate for twenty years because we keep seizing her boats and killing her people."

Ayame interrupted. "We what?"

"I'm getting to that. These folks haven't got a clue about farming, cooperation is approximately zero, and might very much makes right around here. It's not so bad that it can't be unfucked, but it's close. They only hold court once a month. When Duke Horton of Lower Saanich reported that marines raided his Yacht club, it was obviously Onamazu handiwork. That had been the plan, before Gaunt came along and fucked everything up. Punitive raids, cutting-out expeditions; we wrote the textbook. You got inside their decision cycle and hit us faster than we could react. News travels slowly around these parts, and while I was at court in Victoria proper, you hit Sidney."

"Oh no..." Ayame whispered. The marines had disembarked, and the fastest of them were forming up on the beach. Rikimaru was pleased they'd left their weapons on the boats. Derek looked like he wanted to cry, so the daimyo wrapped an arm around the teenager's shoulders and gave him another squeeze. Akuma rejoined them, and though he was a little lost in the discussion, he didn't interrupt. Rikimaru continued. "Yeah. Of my thirty-one guardsmen, you killed all but one. Of the bare half-dozen fishing boats they used to drag nets and collect crab pots, you took or burned them all. The big marina to the north? Housing. You have left me one slightly-trained guard, no food, no way to get more in the too-short term, and a bunch of homeless peasants who hate the Shogunate. None of them know the shogun's general is now their Baron, either. *Awkward* doesn't begin to cover it!"

"We didn't know..."

"This isn't your fault. We've been angry with the Victorians' raids, violence, and theft for decades. *They* have been angry with *us* for the very same reasons. I think I've finally figured out why."

* * *

"Who's that?" Akuma interrupted.

Rikimaru turned and beckoned to Robitaille, Orlov, Lakonis, and Thor. The hostility on their faces was visible. Thor cradled his faux-wood rifle, much more confidently this time. The others only carried their swords, but their hands rested on the pommels.

"Duke Robitaille, Barons Orlov and Lakonis, meet Derek Frost, Samurai Kato, Samurai Akuma, and the Shogunate's new Onamazu Marine Raider Corps. Aya, Ajay, this is Jean-Luc, Aleksander, and Darius. According to local custom, Duke Robitaille is my boss. The young man with the rifle is Thor. He's my sole surviving NCO after the Sidney marina burned."

"What is the meaning of this?" Orlov snarled. "Who are these people?"

"They burned the marina," Rikimaru said bluntly.

"What?" Thor shouted and snapped his rifle up. Rikimaru had expected it, and he got one vice-like hand on the barrel and the other on the stock, then slowly wrenched the gun away.

"Calm, Thor," Rikimaru urged. "Intelligence is a survival trait. Don't make an idiot of yourself now. Do you trust me?"

"I thought I did!" Hot tears of rage streaked his face as he tried to wrestle the gun away, but he had neither the strength nor the leverage to fight his Baron's grasp, so he released his hold on the weapon. "Right up until thirty seconds ago!"

"Listen for sixty more. If, at the end of that minute, you're not satisfied, I'll give you the rifle back, and you can challenge me for the Baron's title. The Duke can witness."

Robitaille raised an eyebrow but didn't object. Rikimaru pointed out into the bay.

"Aya, do you recognize that boat?"

She blanched. "The *Moor Often Than Knot.* It was seized a couple years ago, while fishing south of Friday Harbor."

"How about that one, Jean-Luc?"

"The *Dirty Oar.*"

"And next to it?"

"*Ships and Giggles.*"

"Derek, the one to the left of the *Seas the Day.* Do you see it?" The boy stumbled over the name, but he'd been getting better with his letters. "The...*Ladies First?*"

Ayame didn't remember it, but Akuma cursed and explained. "Carlos Rodrigues, the private who joined in Govnar's scheme to join the Victorians? His dad was skipper of the *Ladies First.* His dad and the ship disappeared when he was a fresh recruit. That was part of why he was so angry and joined the plot against the shogun."

Rikimaru nodded. "Exactly. The previous occupants of this compound had the strongest fleet I've seen yet. The Victorians are starving. We kept blaming them for stealing our ships. Their most recent raid, the one on Deer Harbor, was inept and poorly timed. They didn't get any fishing equipment, and the only ship they got was the *Buoyancé.* Melissa Rainier's lance pincushioned them with arrows as they sailed away, and per the new Duke's report, their arrows managed to kill a handful as they escaped. Does that sound like the actions of a hardened, veteran crew of corsairs?"

"No," Akuma admitted. Rikimaru turned to Thor and the Victorians.

"You've seen me fight. You heard the shooting last night. Ayame is just as skilled, just as enhanced as I am, and there's a third Specialist back home. Do you have *any* doubt that the three of us could conquer Victoria, from Lands' End to the Empress Hotel, were we so inclined?"

"There are *three* of you?" Robitaille gasped. Carnage still littered the beach from the night before. One of the wrought iron spits lay in the sand, and Aya picked up the length of rebar and bent it into a U. She kept going, and in twenty seconds, she handed the spit to Robitaille, except it was now a twisted pretzel. Robitaille dropped it and paled, while Darius grinned widely and punched Orlov in the shoulder. Another stack of chits changed hands.

Rikimaru faced the bay and opened his arms wide.

"Behold the *true* Victorian raiders. These cannibalistic savages have preyed on both our people for decades and played us against each other. Without our two leaders communicating, nobody knew there was fuckery afoot."

At the phrase "cannibalistic savages," Ayame blanched and looked down at the pretzeled roasting spit in the sand. "You keep alluding to what happened here, but you still haven't explained your kit, Rick."

"Plan A was to sail home and try to reach you guys. To wave you off and explain the whole cluster and get the shogun to talk to Victoria. But you burned the marina and killed my people. Plan B was to steal a boat from here and do the same. But recon revealed these monsters had modern tech, and I'd get blasted before I got out of range. I couldn't *not* intervene because you had a schedule. Attack, recover, attack, recover. If you stuck to your schedule, which, thankfully, you did, you'd assault their beach today. And you'd all be dead instead of them." He popped the quick release on the carbine sling and threw it at her. She caught it and stared down at the grey polymer and steel dumbly. He drew his pistol, dropped the mag, locked the slide back, and handed it to Akuma for him to inspect. "They have *dozens* of carbines here, Aya. Just as many pistols. Six, count 'em, *six* MG3s, in powered auto-turrets! They have *electricity*! We had blades and plywood."

He reloaded, holstered up, and pointed to their southwest.

"From our perch up on that hill, we watched the *actual* raiders slaughter, butcher, and *cook* fifteen captives in an all-you-can-eat, beachfront barbecue. Once it got dark, I came down here, and I killed them all." Rick pointed to the carnage along the beach behind him, and Ayame was speechless. The bodies, the scorched sand, and the black iron spits hadn't registered. Now they did. "Because there was a chance—a very slim chance—Aya, that I could seize the marina before you got here. If I hadn't, then you would all be dead. It has been one hell of a week!"

Rikimaru was angry, but he didn't know at whom. Maybe he was angry with everybody or with nobody but himself, because he'd replayed everything over and over in his head and couldn't think of a single thing he'd do differently, but it had all gone to shit regardless. Maybe it wasn't all bad news. Then again, maybe it was?

"Did Kael make it?"

Ayame jerked out of her thoughts and nodded. "Yeah. He's pretty messed up, though. Lost most of one lung, but he's out of bed and hobbling around, grouching at everyone. Claudia's not taking any of his shit, though."

"Good. Did we lose anyone else?"

"Alvarez—but maybe you knew that?"

Rikimaru nodded, his expression blank.

☩ ☩ ☩

288 | JAMIE IBSON

Akuma slipped away to explain the situation to the marines as best he could before Rikimaru addressed them formally.

"How did clearing the compound go, Jean-Luc?"

"Twelve more savages dead, four of ours wounded, one dead. No negligent discharges, thank goodness. And a mystery."

"Do tell."

"The power conduits from the guns all run to a single building. Three of the savages were holding out in the basement. There's a door down there with some kind of electric lock. We can't get in."

"I think I can solve that one in a minute. Standby." He left the Victorian nobles and greeted the marines next. "Oorah, marines!"

They bellowed back in unison. "*Oorah!*"

He was glad to see more marines than they'd originally started with. Karisa Kesting hadn't been in the original selection, but there she was, leading a lance. Rainier looked ready and eager to kick some ass too. The fight on the bridge could have broken some, but those young women were right up front, ready for more. There were more faces he didn't recognize, but he'd get to know them in time. "It's good to see you; it's been too long. You came here to cut out ships, did you not?"

Akuma nodded. "Yessir."

"Problem. These are mine now, so you can't have 'em." Rikimaru smiled, and the marines chuckled. "But I could use a hand. I've got a thing I need to look into in the compound. Divide the bay and the marinas up into sectors and make me a master list of every boat name you see, functional or not. Even ones that have sunk, if you can."

"Can do, Daimyo," Akuma said. "Permission to dispatch a messenger to Whidbey? The shogun will want to know you're alive, soonest."

"True and granted. Get those names to Baron Orlov. This is his turf now."

* * *

The compound looked different in the sunlight, not nearly as sinister. The ruined houses turned walls looked like wreckage after a tornado. Rikimaru noticed an absence of bones, totems, skulls, and so on, but then he remembered the waterfront sat over a two-hundred-foot-deep precipice, which made garbage disposal somewhat less of a burden.

Robitaille led Rikimaru and Thor along the cleared path until they reached a community baseball field. One of the MG towers was directly adjacent, and the black, snake-like conduit feeding the gun power was plainly visible in the daylight. The cables arrived together at the same building, a square, single-story structure. The logo looked anachronistic—virtually everything in this part of the world had belonged to one subsidiary of Teledyne or another, and he had no idea what a 'Helios House' was.

"We found this place almost immediately, but the troops got held up trying to force their way inside. Everything we tried bounced, including shooting it. That's where one of our casualties came from."

Rikimaru gestured to the logo, a stylized sunrise done in red and orange flames. "That familiar to anyone?" he asked.

"No, sir." The guards shook their heads. Thor looked blank, and Robitaille shrugged so he opened the front door.

The interior of the building was a drab, corporate office. One featureless desk, one plain chair, a half rack of vague promotional material full of buzzwords that gave no specifics. Rikimaru couldn't tell what services this 'Helios House' even provided, the brochures' text was so opaque. Strangely, compared to many of the other structures, this one seemed intact. The light fixtures had bulbs. The windows had scratches, but were otherwise undamaged. He examined them. They were thicker than usual, there was a slight distortion to them, and they had a glossy sheen.

"I think that's aliglass," he said. "Aluminum oxy-something. Bulletproof, armored, and transparent. Someone wanted this building armored to the gills." He flipped a light switch, and the bulbs came on. "And they've maintained it all this time."

"Three of the savages ambushed us below, sir. Everything about this place screams 'bunker,' but it's just two empty rooms and a door we can't open."

"So you said. Show me."

Robitaille led the way to the rear of the building, then down a long set of stairs. More electric lights illuminated the passage. They reached a landing, turned, and kept descending. By the time they left the stairs, Rikimaru was pretty sure they were two or three stories below the surface.

One of the savages lay in a heap at the bottom. The dead man wore one of the black mesh vests and had a holster on his hip. The pistol lay just beyond his grasp. He'd been shot in the chest twice and had a superficial wound in his arm. Around the corner, two more men lay in puddles of blood, with more gunshot wounds. A black security bulb hung in one corner of the room, and the wall opposite the stairs was featureless except for a door and a swipe pad next to it. Rikimaru pointed to the bodies. "Have you searched them?"

"Yes, sir." Robitaille was having trouble keeping track of whether Rikimaru was his subordinate or not. "Pistols and magazines. Nothing else of note."

Thor pointed to the holster and pistol. "May I?"

"Sure," Rikimaru said. "Keep it holstered, for now, the area's pretty damn secure." He turned to Robitaille. "Any of your men down here?"

"No."

"Did they find anything like this?"

He passed over the RFID card.

Robitaille's eyes bulged, and he passed it to Thor.

"*Ashley Connelly?*" the guardsman asked.

Robitaille processed that for a moment. "You *did* know her from before."

"I'm beginning to suspect I didn't, even then. See if it opens the door."

The Duke placed the card against the reader, which chirped and blinked green.

* * * * *

Chapter Twenty

The door slipped aside silently into a recess. Rikimaru led the way with his pistol out, aggressively checking corners and clearing the room before he took in the details. When he found no threats, he holstered his pistol and slowed down.

The area looked like a small warehouse. A trio of steel racks divided the open area into two alleys. The left-most rack contained empty rifle racks, surmounted by pegs that would hold his new Gen VI Maxim 9. Opposite the rifle racks, he saw stacked crates and ammo cans, the whole way down.

"My…god…" Robitaille said. He made his way down the row of weapons, examining every detail. Thor followed.

"And now we know where those cannibalistic monsters were getting their arms from."

At the rear of the room, a complex piece of machinery with pipes, valves, control runs, and more dominated the wall. The pipes descended through the floor. Rikimaru followed them, noting how many weapon racks were empty, and how many crates of ammo appeared untouched. All of them and *lots*. He looked over the machinery. The RADIOACTIVE sticker was the big clue, as were the turret conduits attached at the base of a heavy-duty circuit breaker.

"A micro hybrid geo-nuclear powerplant, at a guess. The fissiles are buried deep enough the radiation won't leak, and they're built to be low-to-no maintenance, so long as there's a source of saltwater. We're right next to the inlet, so seawater gets piped in for the system, add in a geothermal supplement, and boom. Low yield, but long-term electricity. I wish we had more systems like these."

Down the right-hand row, opposite the ammunition, were a dozen clothing racks with dresses, women's business suits, women's combat fatigues, and footwear of all types. On a hunch, Rikimaru checked three pairs of boots. They were all the same size. The clothes were not, but that didn't mean anything. Despite all the technological advances leading up to the fall, women's fashion still hadn't figured out how to standardize sizing. The central row featured a work terminal on a plain desk with a couple of drawers at the closest end. The work terminal had a keyboard, a display, and a card reader. He swiped the RFID card. An indicator light on the screen blinked, and the system woke up. Some sunny, coastal village, where a couple in white toasted each other with martinis in front of an azure sea, replaced the black screen He swiped the screen, and the image darkened.

Welcome, Ashley. It has been 7329 days since your last visit. Use Biometrics or Draw Pattern to log in.

The date, May 24th, 2085, glowed in the corner. Rikimaru hadn't known what day it was in years. He leaned back.

"How's your math?" he asked Robitaille.

"Passable," the Duke replied.

"Seven thousand, three hundred thirty, divided by thirty?"

Robitaille abandoned the weapons and joined him at the screen. He pondered for a moment.

"Two hundred forty-four and change."

"Divide by twelve…twenty years," Rikimaru whispered. "Give or take." He opened the upper desk drawer and found a crumbling pad of paper and a pencil. He did some rough figuring.

"That's bizarre. Ashley last logged in a couple of days into May, *after* the bombs dropped. She abandoned all this stuff and left the arsenal to cannibals?"

Thor checked the other drawers, then looked up with a puzzled expression. "*Ashley?*"

"Connelly, yes."

He threw a stack of ID cards on the desk. One bore the iconic Teledyne 'T,' another had Obsidian's logo, another had JalCom's. Other Corporations were mixed in too. The names were all different, but the photo was the same.

Kassandra Kariadis

Cleopatrah Salah

Aoife Mahoney

Shakira Perez

"Who the *hell* is she?" Robitaille demanded.

"I don't know, but I intend to find out," Rikimaru answered. He tucked the ID cards into his armor's pocket. He'd deal with them later. Thor lost interest in the computer and wandered down the right-hand row, past the ladies' clothes. "Uh, Lord Ronin?"

Rikimaru led Robitaille down the right-hand aisle, and found Thor standing next to a rough, unfinished-looking Obsidian brand...tanning bed? Like the tablet, the control panel lit at Rikimaru's touch. He slipped the 'Aoife' Obsidian ID card into the card reader, and the menu opened. The GUI was rough and unfinished, and in a blocky black & white font, it listed skills programs by type.

"What is that?" Robitaille asked.

"How old were you when the bombs fell?"

"Nine."

"Thor?"

"I'm nineteen, sir. I think."

"Kids these days...This *looks* like a first-gen Obsidian imprinter. Maybe even a prototype."

"What does that mean?"

Rikimaru searched his memory, trying to find the best way to sum it up.

"Before the bombs fell, the new hotness was that Obsidian employees could start their shift on Monday, get their 'operating' personality imprint for the week, and put in their shifts. Once their week was over, the original person was imprinted back into the body for the weekend. They had a personality for whatever they needed. Corporate guard? Check. Corporate assassin? Checkety-check. Special Forces soldier, forensic detective, engineer, truck driver, tank driver, cargo pilot, fighter pilot—whatever they needed—they had a personality for it with the necessary skills. Plug the imprint into an enhanced body like mine, and off they went. They worked fine on unenhanced bodies too, but the enhanced warrior types were bad on toast."

Thor looked worried. "And...this bed thingy is one of those personality imprint machines?"

"An earlier, limited version." Rikimaru shook his head. "It's too old and too unfinished, and the menu lists skill packages, not names." He scrolled through the menu and read some of them aloud. "Biology—Marine. Biology—Research. Engineer—Combat. Engineer—Mechanical. Pilot. Soldier. There are a couple dozen here. Before they figured out the personality bit, all they could do was provide skill packages to people who already had a basic understanding of the subject matter. A fisherman would benefit from the marine biologist package, but not the pilot package. It has limitations.

The skill package fades with time, and it leaves the base personality intact. Full imprints are as permanent as if you'd been born that way. The old person is just gone until they put back the original."

"How do you know all this?" Robitaille asked, suspicious. "You worked for Teledyne."

"We tried to steal one," he answered. Robitaille cocked an eyebrow, not satisfied with the answer, so Rikimaru continued. "Corporate espionage was fast and furious back then. If I remember correctly, Competitor Relations 'accidentally' fed JalCom the location of the lab and watched them hit it from a distance, then we were going to hit JalCom when they went to extract it. It turned out they'd already figured out the imprint tech. Half a dozen prototype Agents supported their security on base. Five guys and one woman, versus two juggernauts and a battalion of troops. No contest."

" JalCom won?"

"Not even close. Final score was Obsidian five hundred and two, JalCom zero. They blew the base as they left and were northbound before we could set up a secondary ambush. I gotta be honest, having seen those Agents in action, I'm kinda glad the directorate called off the second hit. We would have been hamburger."

"And this is just the light version? Skills packages?"

"I think so. I mean, there's just one way to find out, and that's to imprint someone and hope they're still themselves when they come out again."

* * *

"**M**ilord Duke Robitaille?" one of the guards shouted down the stairs.
"Here!"

"It's Duke Horton, sir, outside the walls! You're needed!"

Rikimaru left everything as it was and chased Robitaille up the stairs. He kept track of his orientation as he ascended, and when they exited "Helios House," he confirmed that the enormous bunker was directly beneath the adjacent baseball field. That explained how it got there, and now he was going to be suspicious of sports fields for a long time.

One of Orlov's guards waved at them from an observation platform, and they climbed the ladder to it.

Horton stood at the head of his army in the field across from the rubble wall. Robitaille did a quick headcount. "Seventy-two? That's Lower Saanich's full military might, Miles?"

"Fuck off, Jean-Luc. It's a long walk, and these boots pinch my feet terribly. Your men say you've stolen my victory out from under me, though, so I'll thank you to keep your mockery to a dull roar."

Rikimaru eyed the dormant MG3 turret next to him and pointed west. "I'll meet you at the access. It's hidden."

Duke Horton was surprised to meet the mystery baron at the hidden path. The machinegun in his arms may have added to the shock value.

"What's the meaning of this?"

"You guys do like that phrase." He offered the machinegun to the duke. "This is a belt-fed, air-cooled MG3A6, capable of firing fourteen hundred rounds of seven-six-two a minute. It interfaces seamlessly with half a dozen commercially manufactured smart turrets. For most folks, the problem with a gun like this is keeping it fed. At that rate of fire, it can empty a standard ammo can in ten seconds flat."

Horton tested the heft of the gun and let out an *oof* when Rikima-ru released its full 25lbs of weight.

"That's beastly," he said and handed it back. "Why are you telling me this?"

"Six of those guns were guarding the grounds outside the compound yesterday afternoon. Where you stood not three minutes ago was covered by two of them with interlocking fields of fire. Had I not rendered this compound's occupants combat ineffective last night, the guns would have turned your seventy-two troops into barbecue. No joke."

Horton had the good grace to look chastised.

"What now?"

"Join the party. We were about to hash this out down on the beachfront. You're gonna find the political situation has gotten a tich more complicated."

* * *

"You're braver than I thought, Miles," Robitaille said. "You marched all this way wearing those?"

Horton looked at his pointy-toed black leather cowboy boots and grimaced. "They're the only decent leather footwear that fits, and I feared I was going to get into a field battle where having protective leather footwear might be relevant."

"And instead, you learned you were going to march right into an ambush, huh?" Ayame asked. She stuck her hand out in greeting. "Lot of that going around this morning. I'm Ayame. Friend of Rick's."

Horton looked at the offered hand suspiciously but shook it. "And what brings you to Brentwood Bay, Miss?"

300 | JAMIE IBSON

"She was here to steal the boats and burn the rest," Rikimaru cut in. "Just like she did to your Royal Yacht Club. Just like she did to me."

Horton's hand went to his sword, but as with Thor, Rikimaru had expected the response and caught his wrist before the blade could clear the scabbard. Horton struggled against his vice-like grip, and his face flushed red with rage. Robitaille shook his head and offered Horton the pretzel-spit instead. The ludicrousness of the offering was enough to break Horton's concentration.

"Ayame, would you please?"

"Certainly."

In front of Horton's disbelieving eyes, she *un*bent the pretzel until it was more or less a straight but wobbly length of rebar again. She turned and, with a deep grunt of effort, hurled it into the bay like a javelin. It flew past the dock and the moored ships, its arc flattened, and eventually it splashed down far enough out that they had lost all sense of distance. Horton reluctantly sheathed his sword. "You'd best start talking."

And they did. The nobles, the marine leaders, and Rikimaru sat at a beachfront picnic table and brought Horton up to date. In a twisted sense, that Ayame had torched the Sidney marinas eased the sting, somewhat. It would be tacky to lose one's temper over such a minor thing as one soldier with an injured foot, when 'Baron Ronin' remained calm, despite losing his entire guard contingent. Further, he wasn't the only one who had wandered into the death trap. The marine commander was frank about how thoroughly those machineguns would have killed them too. When Rikimaru explained his plan for the savages' fleet, Horton was on board.

Rikimaru got the names of the functional boats from the marines and assigned twenty-three crews to them from Horton's and Robitaille's respective entourages. They still had boats left, so he divided up the Onamazu lances until each lance had a half-crew too. "We'll have to come back. That's fine. Still lots of functional boats to go around and some we can get back into working order with the right salvage or the right ropes from the right place. Now, gentlemen, dukes and barons, samurai, and marines, it's time to opt-in or opt-out. To be honest, my Shogunate troops don't have a choice in the matter, I'm their commander. But Victoria forces-wise, I have exactly one guardsman under my direct command. So, this is an *ask*, not a tell or a make. I will bring Victoria before the shogun, by force if necessary. I'm hoping she sees reason and will accept—I think *vassalization* is the right term. Anyone who sails with me gets a seat at the table as we reorganize this grabasstic clusterfuck of starvation and misery. It needs to be fixed *now*, because the Baron of Oak Bay and I will start to see deaths through starvation in, like, a week. I have my reasons for confronting Victoria, Ashley, or whatever the hell her name is, but personal shit is not what's important here. We can work that out afterward."

"How, exactly, do you intend to force Empress Victoria to do anything?" Horton asked. There was a dangerous edge to his voice. "She tends to do as is her wont, and she is a master at turning allies against each other."

"And you were doing so well, not speaking in Ye Olde English, Billy Shakespeare. To answer your question, three things. One, Me. Two, Ayame. And three, fifty marines who will be armed, armored, and imprinted to know how to use pre-fall modern firearms."

"*What?*" Horton shouted and jumped to his feet. "You can't do that!"

"Sit *down,* Miles," Robitaille said. "If there is one thing I have learned in my short acquaintance with Ronin, it is that when he says he will do a thing, he will give his utmost to do it. It is now clear that before she was empress, Victoria had a bunker here. She had weapons, ammunition, racks of clothes, and stacks of IDs. I have seen them with my own eyes. Do you think, for an instant, she didn't know why nobody could conquer the Brentwood Bay savages? Do you think, for an instant, she didn't know when you begged permission to march up here that you were marching to certain death?"

The anger in Horton's eyes faded.

"You think she set me up?"

"Of course she did," Duke Robitaille said. "Unquestionably. You'd become inconvenient and your friendship with Joyce was a liability. An heroic death would let her save face since it was *your* idea. Then, she could force a hard reset on the rest of Lower Saanich and continue the game."

The blood fled Horton's face. It was one thing to march into potential danger. It was another to learn one's sovereign had knowingly sent him to his doom.

"That *bitch.*"

Rikimaru laughed. "I propose we replace her with a council of the peninsula. There's been too much destruction and death. We have a host of master sergeants in our militia, the Komainu, who are experts in all manner of skills. They can teach if people will learn. How to build gardening implements. How to garden. Ropes and sails. Clothing. Cooking. The works. Anyone who is willing can study. The Komainu can teach construction and other crafts, and they can get to work prepping fields for crops. You folks have *way* more urban sprawl than we do, so shelter isn't an issue, and we've got forty or fifty more 'houseboats' here in the bay that can supplement housing. *I* have an enormous decommissioned airport with acres and acres of fallow fields that no one has put to use. I don't know the first thing about large-scale farming, but I know some people who do. To get through the short term, we will share our food stores with you until the crops come in. But to do all this, Victoria has to go."

"You certainly aren't asking for much," Horton mused. Robitaille lifted a hand.

"You said you'd be arming your marines. I thought your troops need training first?"

"Correct. To further supplement our skill base, people who show promise will come to this bunker and get a skill package imprint to supplement their knowledge until their genuine knowledge is sufficient. I'm going to take the squad leaders for the marines and run them through the tactical imprint. With only one quasi-imprinter, that will take a bit of time. The skill imprints won't last, but we only need them for the one day. We won't have time to imprint everyone, so the rest of the troops are just going to have to bluff." He looked around the beach, puzzled. The marines and most of the guardsmen had gotten down to the foul task of cleaning up the battlefield, but his skinny, blond sergeant with the battered rifle was nowhere in sight. "Speaking of which, has anyone seen Thor?"

* * *

The access pad beeped, and the door slid silently into the wall.

"*Wow*," Ayame said. "That is a *lot* of ammunition."

Rikimaru led the way. The leadership, which included each of the Onamazu lance corporals, followed behind him. Sure enough, his lone NCO lay inside the tanning-bed-like-device. Ten seconds passed, then it chirped, and the upper half of the clamshell hissed open. Thor's eyes snapped open.

"Ohhhhh hohoho this Is Ah-MAZING!" With a manic giggle, he jumped out of the imprinter and tapped the menu. Rikimaru put a hand on his shoulder.

"Thor! what are you doing?"

"First, I updated my literacy with the basic education program. Then I took the imprinter operator download, and I can take six more programs before I exceed the maximum daily recommendation, and I'm all the way to the Ds already!" He blurted it all out in one quick breath, took another breath, and kept going. "I can see why Obsidian made this tech! It is *incredible!* My brain is on *fire* with everything I've just learned! Did you know sharks don't have bones they have cartilage? And that killer whales are properly called orcas and they don't actually kill people and Friday Harbor is like RIGHT THERE and it used to be one of the killer whale research capitals of the world!"

He plunked his butt down on the imprinter again and leaned up to press the button, but Rikimaru slipped his hand over the control pad. Thor pouted in protest.

"Thor, did you take the tactical skill set while you were in there?"

A slow, mischievous grin like that of a child who knows a secret spread across his face.

"Mmaaaayyyybbeeeeeee."

"Okay. You're done, for now. I don't need you to be a special forces marine biologist chef pilot tanker. I need you to get your head on straight."

"Just six more!" he pleaded and tried to slip his fingers under Rikimaru's. "C'mon, please? Six? Five. Five? Boss? Boss. You don't unnerstan what this is *like;* this is *awesome!* You keep saying intelligence is a survival trait and I am getting *smarter and smarter and smarter!*

"Intelligence is knowing a tomato's a fruit," Rikimaru said. He took hold of Thor's wrist, the one trying to pry at the control panel, then grabbed the other. He yanked the young sergeant off the imprinter and threw him up against the wall. "Wisdom is knowing it doesn't belong in a fruit salad," he gently admonished. He wrenched Thor's hands behind his back and held him there. "Ties? Cuffs? Something?"

"No, no, no no, no no no!" Thor squealed, getting more and more panicked. "NononoNONO!!!

Melissa Rainier darted forward through the crowd and slipped a cargo strap with a grommet around one wrist. In a moment, she'd cinched it tight and used the grommet as a tie-off point. Rikimaru drew the pistol off Thor's belt, passed it to Aya, and spun the young man around, forcing him back to the bare room at the base of the stairs.

"Duke Robitaille, would you please secure my guardsman upstairs? I haven't enough security of my own to keep him in custody. *Fucking Obsidian tech,*" he cursed.

"I'll see to it," Robitaille said.

"NO! NO! NOOO!" Thor screamed as Robitaille and Lakonis each took an arm and dragged him toward the surface.

"New rule!" Rikimaru announced. "No one uses the imprinter alone. No one uses it more than once per month. No one takes more than one skill program at a time. *I* will keep the access cards for the time being. Poor kid's tweaking like a Turbo addict."

Horton looked out the door, horrified. "And you want to subject your marines to that?"

"Fair question," Rikimaru allowed. He swiped through the menu for a moment. "The marines will be getting a single skill package though, not the nine Thor just pounded through. Correction, eleven, he said he did the literacy and the operator courses too. I won't order anyone, though."

"I'll go," Rainier volunteered. "I'm not afraid."

"Next," Kesting said. Behind her, each of the marine NCOs indicated their willingness to proceed.

Rainier lay down on the imprinter surface, and Rikimaru swiped through the menus until he found the soldier imprint. He tapped it, and with a quiet hiss, the clamshell closed.

For a moment, everyone held their breath. The timer on the control panel counted down. *9...8...7...*

"How long does an imprint take?" Akuma asked and then the clamshell hissed open. Melissa's eyes were wide.

"Holy shit," she gasped. "No wonder blondie was all fucked up. That's a trip."

"Did it work?" Ayame asked. Melissa held out a hand to ask for Rikimaru's carbine. He handed it to her. She dropped the mag, cleared the action, inspected the chamber, and announced, "Clear!" She popped a retaining pin at the rear of the receiver and hinged it open. In ten more seconds, she had disassembled the carbine for field maintenance. She closed her eyes, and in fifteen seconds, she put the carbine back together again. She reseated the magazine, racked the bolt, and put it on safe. Every movement was mechanically precise.

"Oh yeah." Rainier let a feral smile cross her lips, and she rolled her shoulders. "It worked."

* * * * *

Chapter Twenty-One

As far as celebrations went, Sergeant Carey thought it was a bit much. As every soldier knows, the only thing faster than the speed of light is a rumor, and rumor had it Daimyo Hanzo was *not* dead. Depending on which story one believed, he'd ridden an orca to Vancouver Island. Or he'd conquered the entire island, single-handedly. Or he'd wooed the empress and would return with her as his queen. Or they'd found him, but he'd lost his memory to amnesia. Or he'd been horribly scarred and had defeated the *marines* single-handedly until they'd finally recognized him. The stories were as wild as they were varied. The sole thing they agreed on was that he was alive and on Vancouver Island.

There was dancing in the streets, music, and drinking. You'd think, from the way people were carrying on, it was the second coming of the Lord Jesus Christ. Carey had known Rikimaru, but he'd known him as a *man*, not as Teledyne's brand of superhero. Judging by the partying, Rikimaru had quite the accidental cult of personality going. It was madness.

"Sergeant! *Sergeant!*"

Private Ian White came running up the roadway. Ian was the excitable type, so Carey sipped his tea until he got closer than shouting distance.

"Yes, Private, what is it?"

"There's been a murder, Sergeant!"

"A what?"

"Someone's been killed on Goldfinch Street!"

"Blast it." Carey dumped the rest of his tea—half a thermos worth—and clipped the thermos to a biner on his belt kit. "Lead the way!"

They walked a few blocks, then cut through the trails leading to Goldfinch. Private Scott Blackthorne stood outside a house, looking green. There was a bit of vomit on his uniform shirt, and more stained the grass.

"Jesus, Thorny, you'd think you'd never seen a body before! What's wrong, man?"

"I've seen bodies, aye," Scott replied. "But I've not seen one butchered before. This was no murder, Sergeant. It was butchery."

Carey paused. Sensational details like that would need to be locked down quickly. "Right. Ian, check the neighbors across the street. Get us some information, find witnesses. Scott, clean yourself up a bit and do likewise on this side of the road."

Carey drew his truncheon, the preferred sidearm of Komainu guardians working the urban footbeat, and used it to push the door open. Immediately, a miasma of coppery blood assaulted his nose. Private Blackthorne hadn't been kidding, but Carey was made of sterner stuff and entered the home. He only made it to the living room before the carpet *squished* beneath his boots.

My God.

It was butchery in a very literal sense. The parts arrayed across the living room wall were all identifiable.

Bladder.

Heart.

A loop of intestines.

Kidneys, liver, lungs, and stomach.

The *butcher* had pinned the organs to the wall with steak knives. He'd seen quite enough and squelched back outside. Thorny's reaction was a bit more understandable. Ian returned with an older woman in tow.

"Sergeant, you recall that shark attack victim we spoke of?"

"I do," Carey replied.

"This is Iris Hoffman. Please tell the sergeant what you told me."

Hoffman looked a bit bewildered. She looked like she was in her late fifties or early sixties, perhaps, and she had silver hair, glasses missing one lens, and a knit shawl wrapped around her shoulders.

"Well, I was telling the young man here, my bridge partner Margaret Ward lives there. She never had no kin, but she kept cats. Not for long, mind you, but there's a feral momma what lives in the neighborhood who adopted Maggie as her preferred babysitter. She would look after the cat's litter whenever she had kittens."

"I'm not sure how—" Carey began, but Ian waved him off, indicating he should let Mrs. Hoffman proceed.

"Anyways, you can imagine my surprise when, instead of looking after kittens, she decided she's going to help this poor fisherman who got bitten by that nasty shark. It was *very* odd. He'd lost the whole arm below the elbow and tied his necktie around his, what do you call it? Upper arm, anyway, and staggered into town. No one knew him, so Maggie, she's always lonely for company, so she helped him. She's a fair hand with a needle and thread, darned more than a few socks. So she sewed up the stump pretty good."

"He didn't go to the hospital?" Carey asked. "That's odd."

"It seemed to me, too," Hoffman agreed. "I saw him just yesterday, down at the market. Bought himself an old knife. You know the curved ones, with the ring at the bottom? I guess he's worried with only one hand he'll drop it. I was just surprised he was up and around. I would have thought a shark bite like that would need a lot more care, but the bandages were off, and his stump healed up nice already. What's this all about, anyways? Is Maggie in trouble?"

"I'm afraid she might be. She's been hurt, badly, and might not make it," Carey lied. "I'd like to talk to this fisherman. Or can I get his name? Would you recognize him?"

"Oh yes," Hoffman replied. "It's awful what people do to each other in this Fallen World, just awful, sometimes. He's a tall, skinny lad—lean face. Thirties, I think. He wore a white collared shirt, when I saw him, with short sleeves, and I guess he kept the tie after he didn't need it for his arm anymore because he was wearing one. Honestly, who still wears a tie these days? Oh, and he had short brown hair, scars on his forehead, and, of course, he was missing half an arm. British accent. What was his name? Oh, I forget."

* * * * *

Chapter Twenty-Two

The marine NCOs all came out of the prototype imprinter, reporting an endorphin rush to go with their soldier package. Rikimaru worried about the psychological impact. Kesting made an observation when the clamshell hissed open, and Hong, the last marine in line, rose from the machine.

"Theory," she began, "on what went wrong with Thor."

"Go."

"You know the afterglow of sex, sir?"

"That's a bit personal, Karisa. The woman we're about to go capture was my fiancé once upon a time. So, yes, despite my ascetic lifestyle these last few decades, I'm aware that sex is a thing most people enjoy." He chuckled, and she blushed a bit before continuing.

"I don't know about you, but sex, fighting, a running high, or any adrenaline dump in general, gives me a warm, yummy buzz afterward. That machine just injected months of combat training directly into my veins, more or less. I bet, if you took some random sheeple and fed them the same program, they'd come out sick to their stomachs."

"An interesting theory. Explain Thor, then."

"Starved for education. Brain, desperate for knowledge, responds to stimulation with a straight dopamine rush. And, as a poor, starving Victorian, there hasn't *been* a lot of dopamine in his life before now."

"What do your parents do, Karisa?"

"They raise alpacas, sir."

"Is that what you plan to do when you retire from the marines?"

"Retire, sir?" Kesting cocked an eyebrow, and Rikimaru suppressed a grin.

"As *oorah* as all this is right now, especially with our new equipment, people with your kind of insight are who will start putting civilization back together. Don't limit yourself."

"Oorah, Daimyo."

Rikimaru pulled the Obsidian ID card from the imprinter's reader and secured it in his pocket. Everyone scooped up a crate of ammunition or a pair of ammo cans and headed upstairs. He silently prayed that Thor hadn't damaged himself permanently. His lone surviving guard and two assigned custodians waited upstairs. Even with his hands bound, he jumped and bounced and jittered while muttering random factoids to himself.

"Alright, mister, time to go."

Thor's head snapped up, crestfallen.

"But, there's, but—"

"Time to go." He pointed out the door, with a stern look etched on his face. "If you want to put that big brain of yours to use, you can return with us to the Shogunate. We have a handful of bookstores and even a couple of libraries. You can earn your knowledge the hard way, so it'll stick."

Ayame pitied the young man and chimed in. "I have a bunch of books, Thor. I can lend you some."

"Promise?"

"Promise."

* * *

The pyre at the beach was high and hot. There were a lot of dead to burn, and Baron Orlov's men were busy working.

"Sorry I made such a mess, Aleks," Rikimaru said, offering the baron his hand to shake. Orlov grasped it and pulled him in for a hug.

"Why should you be sorry? You do realize you've just made me one of the most...I was going to say powerful, but maybe it's *influential* men around, yes? The marina, the boats, the fortified compound, *electricity*. For years, this little town has been a canker sore that wept pus and misery on the Saanich Peninsula's backside. No more, and it's thanks to you."

"Tell me," Rikimaru said. "You and Darius keep betting on something, and you keep handing over stacks of chits and credits. What's up with that?"

"Darius was...I believe the term is a *fanboy*. He was eleven when the bombs fell, old enough that he'd already purchased dozens of Teledyne comics. They were little more than propaganda put out by their marketing department."

"And?"

"And he has worshipped Specialists as real-life superheroes since he was a child. He had you and Ayame both pegged as Specialists from the moment he laid eyes on you. One of the comic book characters even looked like you. Did you not say your ladyfriend, now empress, worked in marketing?"

"You've got to be shitting me."

"Hah! Today truly is a day for revelations. When you see her, you should ask her about the *Specialist Yojimbo* comics. But not the gritty reboot." Orlov picked up an arm, blown off at the elbow, and heaved it into the center of the bonfire. "Darius found it too gory for his taste."

Orlov and his men fed the funeral pyre more parts, and Rikimaru made his way to the dinghy where Derek waited to paddle him out to the *Seas the Day.*

* * *

Three hours later, Rikimaru climbed from the cabin into the cockpit of the *Day* as they tacked past the Swartz Bay ferry terminal and flopped onto one of the benches.

"How was your nap, stranger?" Nobunaga asked.

"I'm getting too old for this shit," Rikimaru answered. He rolled his shoulders and worked his neck. "I can't even use body armor as a pillow anymore."

"Oh no!" Nobunaga chuckled in mock horror. "Not that! Time to hang up the spurs then, no question."

"Maybe it's time," Rikimaru agreed absently. He knew Dan had been joking, but he had a point. Very few Specialists died in bed. There'd come a time where the nanites and the training and luck just weren't enough. Mikael's close call with Gaunt, Aya's near-certain death at Brentwood, had he not gotten there first, even a couple of times during that long night of running and gunning...

"I didn't get to apologize with the rest on shore, Rick," Nobunaga said a few minutes later. They'd sliced through the narrow channel northeast of the more extensive marina, and now the one next to 'his' scraper was coming into view. Rikimaru stood up to take one more look at the pier and the scars where the dock had burned.

"No need. Funny how easily we write off anyone not in our tribe, huh?"

"Funny or awful. Who's going to run things now that their baron is gone?"

"They can manage for a day or three. They might even do better without the 'nobility' taking all the choice cuts of meat and veg. Long term, I'm hoping Thor recovers enough to run the show. He isn't a bad kid." Rikimaru caught a glimpse of motion on a small stretch of beach and swore. "Cut in! There! Sorry, unscheduled stop. Get as close to the shore as you can manage and drop anchor. I'll need a minute."

Dan didn't question him, but he did bellow, "Tacking!" before throwing the wheel over to the right. The rudder bit, the ship leaned sharply, and the boom snapped overhead. They got in close enough to shore to see the sandy bottom, and Dan wheeled back to the left, so the bow was parallel to the shoreline again.

Rikimaru threw open some of the chests and collected some fishing equipment in a scuffed, clear plastic bucket. Then he jumped overboard.

"What's he doing?" Derek asked.

"I have no idea," Dan replied. "You'd think I'd have figured him out by now."

* * *

"Katie, look!"

Katie wasn't interested in whatever game Dyson was playing. She'd spotted another gooey, but it had retracted its siphon, making it harder to find. Her digging stick had rotted through too, and the new stick wasn't as good as her old one. The head wasn't very wide, and the sand kept smooshing back down when she tried to clear it out of the way.

"Don't care, Dyson!" she snapped. "I've got another gooey. If you get over here and help me, I'll even share."

"How very *un*selfish of you, young lady."

She whirled, stick up, ready to defend herself. Baron Ronin stood a short distance away, waist-deep in water and soaked.

"Go 'way," she pouted and turned back to her digging. "I don't wanna talk to you."

"I'm not surprised," Ronin said. "But I promised to take care of you as best I could."

"For you to take care of us, you'd have to *be* here," Sid spat.

"Also true," Ronin agreed. "Or you could come with me."

"Where?" Katie asked suspiciously. She turned back to face him and noticed, for the first time, the lots and lots and *lots* of sailboats sailing in the direction of the palace. More sailboats than she had fingers, easy.

"That would be up to you." Ronin held out a bucket. A *clear* bucket. "If you really like it here, if you really don't want to go, then all I can do is give you the best tools I have and wish you luck. But that wouldn't be my first choice."

Katie carefully reached out and snatched the bucket from him. He didn't react, he didn't try to grab her arm, he just let it go. She looked through the contents—kids' size goggles, a fish bat, a keen filleting knife, a reel of fishing line, a waterproof plastic package of hooks, and…carrot seeds?

"I'm not well suited for parenting," Ronin said. "A man has to know his limitations, and I know I'm not. I *do* know some people who are brilliant at raising kids, even if they're not his blood. The man sailing that boat out there is one of them. You wouldn't be hungry anymore, but you might have to do some chores. You'd have proper clothes and shoes, but you'd probably have a bedtime. You could probably teach him a thing or three about how to prepare gooeys, to be honest. It could be a little scary, at first, because you've never been to the island where I'm from, but you're three brave little kids, and now that I can honestly make that offer, I have to try."

Katie eyed her new bucket of treasures and then looked back at Mister Ronin. "What if I want to stay with *you*?"

Ronin's eyes got really shiny, and he looked away for a moment. When he looked back, he was crying. "I'm sorry, Katie, but you can't. My job is dangerous, and I've almost died a couple of times just this week. I should have been dead the day I washed up here. I'm not going to adopt three children just to orphan them. You'd have a safe home to live in, no adults would hurt you, and you could visit me any time. But if that's a deal-breaker...I understand."

Katie bit her lip. She'd never even gone to Victoria, never mind another island. It sounded *scary*. She looked at the other two. Dyson gave her a quick nod, but Sid was hesitant.

"Can...can we hunt gooeys together sometimes? You have gooeys, right?"

Ronin laughed and nodded. "Yes, child, we have gooeys. Beaches full of them. And cages for crabs, and nets for fish, horses and cows and llamas and alpacas, goats and sheep... All the animals you care to name."

"Okay," she said, shyly, and she waded out to hug his leg.

"Okay," he agreed. He sounded sad, but happy at the same time. "Gentlemen?"

Dyson nodded. "Yes, please!" He seemed happy to be going—he was going to be out of Miz Waylan's this summer anyway. Sid agreed too.

A little rowboat came up behind Ronin. A *boy* was paddling. He had blond hair and tanned skin like a sailor's, and even though he was a kid like them, he looked super strong and *way* bigger than even Dyson.

"Captain Nobunaga figured you'd need a ride back, Daimyo?"

"Do you have room for my plus-three?" Ronin asked. Katie didn't know what a dye-mee-oh was, but the way the boy said it, it was probably something like a baron or a duke.

"Sure," the boy said and beached the boat. "He did ask us to be quick; we're falling behind the rest."

"No problem. Kids, this is Derek. Derek, this is Katie, Sid, and Dyson. They're coming with us."

"Cool!" The boy smiled and offered Katie a hand into the boat. Derek had a friendly smile. Maybe this wouldn't be so scary after all.

* * * * *

Chapter Twenty-Three

"**V**ictoria? *Victoria!*"

Ashley Connelly was used to Sledge crying out her name, but it was usually in private, and it didn't usually have an edge of panic to it.

"Here! What is it?" She strode down the hall from the dining room and entered her current champion's quarters. They were up on the third floor, looking out over the inner harbor.

"When you sent that new baron whatsisname off to bring his master back here for negotiations—did he say anything about an invasion fleet?"

"What? No, of course not." She cut in front of him to look out the ornate window, one of the few still intact in the entire palace, and gasped.

"Shit. What the hell is he doing?"

The inner harbor was positively *choked* with sails. Most of her sad, little fleet was moored at the seven main jetties directly in front of the palace. The intruders, all thirty or forty or fifty of them, were lowering their sails and dropping anchors a short distance out, save one. A few dinghies were already being rowed to the waterfront where their passengers could debark.

The lone ship had lowered its sail and was gliding in on momentum. It coasted along the more northern edge of the harbor, with a handful of passengers lined up on the portside rail. It crossed the T of the center float, and two by two, the passengers stepped off as smoothly as though they weren't moving at all. The ship's captain wheeled hard to starboard and pointed the ship's bow back out into the harbor in an instant. Whoever he was, he was very, very good. The passengers worried her, though. They marched with military precision, and although they were still a good distance away, she could see they were wearing uniforms.

"Baron Ronin and I go way back. We loved each other once. I can't imagine he means me harm. Gather the guards and have them meet me out front. Move up one floor to the old library with the broken window. You'll have the best vantage point with your scattergun from there, in case things go horribly wrong. I doubt they will, though."

"You're sure?" Sledge asked. She didn't like that about him one bit. Familiarity had bred complacency, and he was challenging her orders more and more frequently lately. She backhanded him, *hard.* He slammed against the wall and knocked his head against the window frame.

"I'm sure, *Tristan,*" she hissed. "Do as you're told. I will await my entourage at the doors."

Today's garb was comfortable, rather than dazzling, because court had just passed, and she hadn't anticipated meeting anyone of consequence. Today, she wore a high-slitted, ankle-length strappy black skirt she could wear decent boots with, instead of those godforsaken heels, and her favorite sky blue blouse. Rikimaru wasn't likely to be dazzled either way, so it would do. She returned to her quarters and slipped her P365 into her boot holster. Aside from Rikimaru, whose reflexes were quite literally inhuman, she could probably draw and shoot faster than anyone could pull out a blade. Her hair was a mess—she'd thrown it up into a messy half-bun, ponytail thing, but the chopstick hair needles were coming loose, so she gathered it all in a scrunchie and threaded the ten-inch pins through it again. There. Nobody would suspect they were titanium alloy and an entirely lethal weapon in her capable hands. Hiding in plain sight came second nature to her. It had for years.

Tristan sent down the regular house patrol, four guardsmen who were good for little except acting as a speed bump, but they'd do. Two opened the door for her—terrible practice, that—and she strode out onto the veranda flanked by the others.

Yes, the welcoming party was wearing uniforms. In fact—

Oh, shit.

Boy, that is awkward.

Shut up. I don't need the color commentary.

She ignored the quiet voice that rode on her shoulder and scanned the group. Her stomach dropped, when she recognized the armor they wore. It was from the bunker. *Her* bunker. Or what used to be hers, once upon a time. Rikimaru and his entourage carried carbines, too. One of them even hefted an MG3, with two feet of linked ammo hanging out the feed tray. Rikimaru, that little bitch trainee sidekick of his, whatever her name was, and a half-dozen hard-looking sorts, men and women both, marched straight up to her, bold as could be. From the other side of the wharf, Duke Robitaille, Duke Horton, and assorted hangers-on had landed in those dinghies and joined them.

This is bad.

Very bad.

I said, spare me the commentary!

She'd talked her way through the end of the world, though, and if Rikimaru wanted her dead, he could have picked her off from the pier. That would have been awkward. Best to play it calmly. Her ex and his entourage halted at the bottom of the steps, well out of arms' reach.

"Rick, this doesn't look like the negotiating party you promised me. Did something go wrong?"

"You could say that, Ash," he replied, and from a pocket, he produced a card. He flicked it through the air, and it bounced off one of her guard's chests. "You mind explaining why that opened an arsenal hidden beneath the sports diamond at Brentwood Bay?"

The guard reflexively bent to pick it up and passed it to her. It was her old Teledyne ID from before those monsters seized Helios, and the town around it.

"Rick, I—"

"Don't *Rick* me, Ashley. Or is it Aoife? Shakira? Kassandra?" He threw more cards. All her old, bogus IDs. All her old covers. "*Who are you?*"

This is bad on garlic toast.

"Begone," she spat. Her guards looked at her quizzically, and she grabbed one by the throat and *threw* him back inside. "GO!"

The other three scurried inside, and a gunshot shattered the evening calm. Victoria ducked, covering her ears, and when she turned back, the redheaded woman at Rikimaru's five o'clock lowered her rifle.

"Sniper down. Fourth floor, open window."

Despite her orders for them to go, her guardsmen rushed right back out again, knives in hand. Rikimaru's soldiers were ready. The troops to his left and right dropped to one knee simultaneously, and opened fire. The fusillade was deafening but precise. Her men tumbled down the stairs in a heap, cut down by carbines that, by rights, should have been hers, but she remained untouched.

"Sniper?" Rikimaru asked her. There was fury, and devastation, and emptiness in that single word. He thought she'd meant to assassinate him.

"Sledge. Overprotective to the end, the fool. Judging by your armor and weapons, I take it you found Helios House?"

"Yes. And your workstation. And your imprinter. And your *arsenal*. What I can't figure out, is why you'd abandon all that stuff just days after the bombs dropped."

"I didn't, I—"

Rikimaru had always been a quick draw too. Age hadn't slowed him one bit. One moment she was protesting, the next, she was staring down the barrel of one of those blocky Maxim 9s.

That hurt, he isn't supposed to interrupt!

She raised her hands in meek submission and remained silent.

"Don't lie to me anymore," he snarled. "There's been quite enough of that already. Your workstation kept track of how long it's been—seven thousand, three hundred, twenty-nine days since you last logged in. By my count, that would be May third."

"Rick, I swear, I didn't access that pad after April 30th. Do you honestly think, if I'd had access to that equipment, I'd be down here schmoozing with ferals?"

"No, at this point, I'm almost convinced you *equipped* the savages squatting on Brentwood Bay. Sicced them on *everyone* to cause as much chaos as possible."

"Oh my god, Rick, absolutely not!"

How do I tell him the truth?

You cannot.

He didn't look very convinced.

* * *

She wasn't very convincing.

"Then explain this to me. You said you sent, and I quote, The *Dirty Oar*, The *Señora*, and the *Ships and Giggles* as envoys to us after the fall."

"Yes!"

"Then how is it those boats wound up in Brentwood Bay, next to seven of *our* boats, in the hands of cannibal savages, with half a dozen of *your* ID cards?"

"I don't know! Yes, I was at the bunker on April 30th—"

"Bullshit."

"No! It was Saturday!"

"We counted, Ash! Twenty years, times three-sixty-five, plus the days up to May 24th!"

She frowned, and scrunched her eyes shut as though in pain. When she opened them, the pain was gone. "Did you account for leap years?"

Oh, for god's sake…stupid, stupid error. Does that mean…could she be telling the truth?

She must have read his face because she continued. "I'd just flown in from SoCal. It was Saturday. I'd planned to call you Sunday afternoon, surprise you, and meet you at the ferry terminal. The world ended, instead. That's the god's honest truth, Rick! I rode out the destruction at Helios, and then I raced out to Sooke to check on my mom. I must have dropped my ID card somewhere then. I couldn't find the ID after, I had all the kit I could carry already, and the traffic and the panic and the emergency services shutting down travel meant getting to Sooke was near impossible! By the time I finally made it back, those… *monsters* had already bulldozed the town and fortified it. What the hell were they called, the animal-spliced beast things?"

"Geno-freaks," Ayame supplied. Her tone was cold, and her arms were crossed, clearly hostile.

"Yes! One was a bear, one was a mountain lion. The few survivors around town said they'd gone full cannibal, and their followers had to, too, or else they'd be the next main course. Of course, the 'freaks don't live too long after splicing, so I figured I'd bide my time, give it a couple years, and go back once those terrors were fish bait. But no, whoever was in charge kept the guns readied at all times. Eventually, I gave up."

"That would have been bloody useful information to know two days ago, *Empress*," Horton snarled.

At least she had the decency to look ashamed. Rikimaru holstered up. "We're taking you to the shogun. You can negotiate with him for the future of your island, but I think you'll find cleavage and skin doesn't work as well with the old geezer as it does with these gentlemen. And once that's over, you and I are going to have a long chat."

Rikimaru pulled a length of cargo strap from his pocket and slipped the first loop over Victoria's left wrist. "Starting with, whether the woman I fell in love with ever existed at all." He pulled both wrists behind her back and secured a second loop around her right. He tied a knot in the center between the loops, and pulled on it to snug it as tight as he could manage. He patted her down, thoroughly and professionally and raised an eyebrow when he found the holdout P365. He passed it to Ayame, who gave it to Rainier. Once his prisoner was secure, he turned to Horton and Robitaille. "Gentlemen, I trust you can take care of informing Lord Goldstream there's been a change in management?"

Robitaille flashed him a thumbs up. "We can. We'll be parting out the boats to each Barony's marina, and we look forward to the results of the…" He glared at Victoria. "…negotiations."

* * *

"*I betcha she is,*" Dyson whispered.

"*I betcha she isn't,*" Sid whispered back.

"What are you two whispering about?" Rikimaru asked. Despite the cacophony of the gunfire lately, it seemed his hearing had finally returned to normal. Even over the crash of the surf against the *Day's* hull, he could hear the two boys whispering to each other.

"*I* think that's the Empress," Dyson said.

"And I think she's not," Sid supplied.

Rikimaru looked at his ex, who refused to meet his eyes.

"Yes," he said at the same instant she said, "No."

"Still telling fibs, *Victoria?*"

She looked at him, finally, and glared. "No matter how things go today, I think it's safe to say the reign of Empress Victoria the Second has come to an end. If the child had asked me if I were the empress, say, at lunchtime, I would have agreed with you."

Rikimaru leaned back against the seat and conceded the point.

"Fair."

"Were you really engaged?" Dyson asked, but Sid smacked him on the arm.

"Yes," Victoria whispered, looking away.

"But, that was a long time ago," Rikimaru said. "Things have changed since then."

"*I* think you're pretty," Katie said, shyly. "It's sad you and Ronin didn't get married."

Rikimaru got up without a word and walked out of the cabin to the cockpit with Dan. But not before he heard Ashley whisper, "I think so too."

Just when I'm glad to get my hearing back…

* * *

The marine squadron was well past the southern tip of Lopez Island when a red flare blossomed against the blood-red sky.

"Are you kidding me?" Rikimaru gasped. "*Another* one?"

"Derek!" Nobunaga shouted. "Get the jib up!"

"I don't know why you don't sail with it all the time," Rikimaru complained. "If you've got more speed, why don't you use it?"

"That's why I'm the skipper, and you're the brute. The sail's starting to fray in some spots, too much pressure on it will tear the thing to shreds. Better to have it, and not need it, than need it, and not have it. So we save it for when we need it, like right now. Get up there and help the boy."

Rikimaru followed Dan's apprentice to the forward deck over the front cabin. Derek slipped the jib sheet from its sack, and Rikimaru passed him the halyard to raise the sail. He remembered that much, at least. When the top of the sail was clipped, he shouted back to Dan, and the sail slowly unfurled. The moment the leading corner was free, Derek passed it to Rikimaru and pointed to where the sail

330 | JAMIE IBSON

clipped on. By the time the bow point was attached, Derek had already run both lines back to the cockpit.

"Very smooth," Rikimaru congratulated him.

"Don't encourage him!" Nobunaga laughed. "It'll go straight to his head!"

"Everyone needs a little positive reinforcement, now and then," Rikimaru countered. "How long?"

"Couple minutes. With you and Aya both here, I'm going to aim for the sand right there by Intruder Street and beach it. You can push me off the sand later."

"And if we need to race back out again?" Rikimaru asked.

"You'll have to push harder!"

Ayame and Akuma joined them on the deck. Dyson wanted to see too, but Rikimaru shook his head. Derek invited the other boy below, to keep them entertained and distracted until they hit the beach.

The minutes seemed to drag, but as they got closer to the beach, Rikimaru could make out the white foam of the waves where they swept up a sandy beach, a klick south of their regular dock. Dan fired a flare to signal the base they were coming. "Hold onto something!" Dan warned, and the ground rushed up to meet them.

Katie screamed at the impact, then the boat ground to a halt. The keel dug into the sand, and rode up it until the whole sailboat rested at a cockeyed angle, the port side down low and the starboard high in the air. "Katie's fine!" Derek called up.

"Stay with them!" Rikimaru ordered, and vaulted over the railing. Akuma jumped down, but Ayame paused.

"What about the prisoner?" she asked.

Shit.

"She comes too! I'm not leaving her here with Dan and the kids!" Ayame snarled an order, and Ashley came to the railing. The high cut skirt concealed sensible boots, not stilettos or something foolish, and she stepped across the cables that lined the boat's edge. Even with her wrists bound behind her back, the former empress jumped down to the beach gracefully.

"Samurai?" a voice shouted. "That you?"

"Here!" Rikimaru bellowed. They made their way up the beach, where Master Sergeant Ericksen greeted them.

"We gotta stop meeting like this, sir," Eriksen said. "We have a real problem."

"Details, Marcus," Ayame snapped.

"Gaunt's back. He's at the inn, he's taken the shogun hostage in the *honden*, and he is demanding we bring him the Daimyo."

* * * * *

Chapter Twenty-Four

"Gaunt's back?" Ayame snapped. "That's impossible! He was…on the bridge."

"Just across from me, yeah," Rikimaru said. "And here I am, much better after being only mostly dead. No more of this uncertain doom bullshit, we don't count him out until he's leaking grey matter."

Ashley rolled onto her back, slipped her hands below her feet, and brought her hands in front of her. "I trust you won't begrudge me my hands if Stephen fucking Gaunt is here?"

Rikimaru nodded his assent and racked the handle on the carbine. He took off in a ground-eating run, Eriksen by his side, Ashley behind them, with Ayame and Akuma covering their six.

"The rest of the marines are on the other boats; I don't know how far behind. They're coming, though. I trust you've got, well, it's Gaunt, so maybe not containment, but scouts watching? In case he moves?" Rikimaru asked.

"Yessir. I'm afraid he killed five of the homeguard on his way in, and three more when the rest of the platoon responded. He's made it adamantly clear he's not going anywhere until you show up."

"What does he want?"

"He won't say. Just that if you aren't there in twenty-four hours, he'll kill the shogun and go to work on everyone else. He's been quite explicit about that part."

They rounded the corner onto Saratoga, and the inn came into view.

"No change, Master Sergeant!" Sergeant DiPaulo reported from the door. "It's good to see you, Lord Hanzo."

"And you, Mario. Congratulations on your promotion. Is Mikael here?"

"No, sir. He's been in rough shape since the bridge, sir, and is down at Fort Casey doing rehab with the new class."

"I see. They're in the *honden*?"

"Yes, sir."

"Very well. Ayame, you cover me. Akuma, Victoria's your responsibility. Aya, if you get the shot, take it."

"Will do." She nodded.

"Move."

Rikimaru entered the inn at a near sprint, sweeping the barrel of his carbine left and right with absolute precision until he reached the sanctuary. They stacked on the right hand side of the double doors, and when Aya squeezed his shoulder, he sprang out into the open, cleared the doorway, and kept going. Gaunt was hunched low behind the shogun, who was kneeling behind the *kami* stone. Rikimaru found a wall's edge and moved up, while Ayame moved up the far wall.

"Stop now, or he dies!" Gaunt shouted. Rikimaru froze—Gaunt held a karambit to the shogun's throat, and he was tight enough to the octogenarian's body that neither of them had a clear angle.

"I told you they'd come, Akihiro." Gaunt chuckled. "Rikimaru can't help but throw himself on any grenade that comes his way."

"You shouldn't have," Kojima said, "I seem to recall ordering you to call in an airstrike on Gaunt, and damn the collateral."

"*Reeaaally?*" Gaunt asked. "An airstrike? For little old me?"

"It was that or nuke you from orbit," Rikimaru said.

"And even then, you couldn't be sure." Gaunt snickered. "Obsidian would just print another me, and the game would continue. No, it seems the rumors of both our deaths were greatly exaggerated. Let us finish what we've started now. I'm impressed you managed to source some guns, but they're too little, too late. Unload them and throw them over here. Now, Rikimaru, or so help me the last thing I will do is end this geezer's life."

"Don't do it," the shogun pleaded. "Shoot him!"

Rikimaru couldn't. Akihiro Kojima had been his mentor for decades. To kill Gaunt, he'd be killing his lord and master. He cursed to himself, and lowered the carbine.

"Good. Magazine out. You too, faithful sidekick."

Ayame followed Rikimaru's lead, dropped the magazine from her carbine, and racked the bolt to eject her round.

"Toss them in the corner. Do it now."

The guns clattered when they hit the floor.

"Pistols, too. Don't think I don't see them, Rikimaru." Gaunt squeezed the shogun even tighter, eliciting a gasp, and pricked his neck with the tip of the wickedly sharp karambit.

Rikimaru drew, slowly, and cleared that gun too. He tossed it in the corner.

"Perfect."

Gaunt slashed the shogun's throat and blood fountained, then he kicked the body away.

"*NO!*" Rikimaru screamed. He dove for his weapon, but Gaunt was there too. He flung the karambit at Rikimaru, and the Specialist dodged away. The knife's handle bounced off his ballistic plate and skidded aside. Gaunt followed with a roundhouse that launched Rikimaru backward, and he skidded across the floor. Rikimaru got his first good look at Gaunt and realized he had lost an arm below the elbow, but it didn't seem to have affected his deadliness. Rikimaru sprang to his feet to tackle him, but Gaunt pirouetted like a matador and helped Rikimaru along, bashing his face into the wall. Rick stumbled back, stunned, and felt a hand clutch his vest. He warded the hand away, but he had blood in his eyes and couldn't see.

Rikimaru heard a series of pops to his right, and he ducked low, trying to clear his vision. When he could see again, Gaunt was halfway across the sanctuary, slipping a magazine into the Maxim 9, as Ayame raced to reload her pistol too. Time slowed. Gaunt had the handgun jammed under his armpit, and he was faster on the reload. He smoothly gripped the gun in one hand, extended it, and fired.

Ayame fell.

Gaunt chuckled, spotted Rikimaru regaining his feet, and skipped over to deliver another bone-crushing snap kick to his vest. Rikimaru flew backward, cracked his head against the wall, and slumped to the floor again, dazed. Gaunt kicked the carbine away, took hold of Rikimaru's topknot, and bashed his head into the wall, once, twice, a third time, and the Specialist blacked out.

* * *

Gaunt stood and returned to the gut shot Specialist in the corner.

"Oh, Ayame," he sighed. "Always the bridesmaid, never the bride, eh? Standing there in big, bad Rikimaru's shadow?"

The sidekick groaned and clutched at her stomach, just below the armor. There was too much blood to be certain, but he might have clipped one of her kidneys. He didn't want her dead. He wanted her to *suffer* as he had these last twenty years.

"I'm sure you've heard of the Mozambique drill?" he continued. "Two to the body, one to the head?"

He stepped on one foot, pinning it to the ground, and she cried out in pain. He appreciated that.

"I like to think I've improved the drill. I call it the Provo Three-way. One to the body," he said. He aimed carefully, fired another shot, and she shrieked in agony. Then he fired a third time, this time into the leg he'd trapped. "Two to the knees."

"You bastard!"

Gaunt rolled his eyes. It was like it was a *surprise* to these people. Stephen bloody Gaunt wasn't just a bastard. He was *the* bastard. The Indian kid who'd arrived with the Specialists planted himself in the doorway and opened fire. Gaunt spun aside and moved into a series of one-handed somersaults and dives until the tagalong's magazine ran empty. Gaunt popped up, tisk-tisked him with his remaining hand, and mimed looking at a watch as the kid hurried to reload. The kid panicked and bobbled the magazine. It fell to the sanctuary floor, and when the kid reached for it, Gaunt pistol-whipped him. The kid collapsed, out like a light. Gaunt picked up the carbine and popped the retaining pin. He pulled the bolt one-handed and flung the pieces across the sanctuary floor.

"You know guns sap the fun right out of a good tussle." He popped the magazine free and *bent* the barrel, ruining the gun completely. He addressed Rikimaru, still prone up against the far wall. "Our fight on the bridge was far superior to this. Much more personal." He picked the karambit up again, spun it off his pinky once, and smiled as the curved handle slapped against his palm. "Where were we? Oh, right. You wouldn't *share*, you and your precious Shogunate, while I starved in Seattle. And now your sidekick plaything is crippled, your precious Shogun Kojima is dead, the new guy is down with a traumatic brain injury, and now it's your turn. There's no bridge to drop, no danger-close airstrikes, just you and me. The bridge was a nice touch, though. Very sneaky. You almost had me."

* * *

Are you sure?
Sure as I have been about anything.
This is a terrible idea.

Ashley stepped past the unconscious Akuma, raced forward, and delivered a vicious flying kick to the base of Gaunt's skull. It didn't break his neck as she'd hoped, but he did stagger forward a few steps before turning to face his newest attacker. She dropped back into a light, bouncing Tae Kwon Do stance since her hands were still tied.

"Dost mine eyes deceive me?" Gaunt held the karambit low in front of him, keeping it loose and mobile. "Is that Miss Aoife Mahoney? What are *you* doing here, with these Teledyne fools?"

Ashley snapped a short front kick at Gaunt's lead knee, but he was too quick and danced back out of reach.

"I haven't been Aoife Mahoney for a long time," she said. "I almost didn't recognize you. It's so much easier for an Agent to wear a different face."

"You haven't aged a day, my dear. What's your secret?" Gaunt lashed out with his knife in a flurry of slashes, but Ashley bobbed, ducked, and weaved out of the way of the flashing blade. "Don't tell me, you bathe in the blood of virgins too? It's done wonders for *my* complexion."

Gaunt circled left, and she moved with him. He was judging her, searching for some clue about what she was up to. "You're an enigma, aren't you? Lab assistant, if memory serves? But that was twenty-seven years ago! Yet here you are, not a day older, and quick enough to go boot-to-knife with yours truly. What are you?"

"*Angry.*"

Ashley aimed a roundhouse kick at Gaunt's knife hand, flew into the air and twisted to bring her other foot around for a followup. She didn't expect to *hit* the hand holding the blade, but anyone armed with a weapon tended to focus on it first. Gaunt obliged, snatched his hand back out of the way, and as he darted forward to cut her, her second boot smashed into his jaw. He spun away, and she dropped lithely to her feet. She let a brief smile cross her face and danced back out of reach again.

Great. You pissed him off.

That's the plan.

Gaunt recovered and worked his jaw for a moment. There was an audible pop as it snapped back into its socket.

"You're going to pay for that, Mahoney."

Gaunt charged forward like a bull, unafraid. As she'd hoped, he led with the karambit. She feigned panic, and as he slashed down, she brought her left arm up defensively. Pain exploded in her brain, and she collapsed to the floor, less one hand, which flopped to the ground just in front of her. Gaunt turned away. She slipped her now-handless wrist from the loops binding them, and scooped up the amputated appendage that belonged there, cradling it close.

Was that part of the plan too?

Yes. Now shut up and hit me with a stim. That hurt.

* * *

Rikimaru's gaze was unfocused. He knew he'd been out for a few seconds, and the pounding dizziness in his head screamed concussion. In the other corner of the *honden*, Ayame twitched and moaned as she slowly bled out. Akuma was down, and now Ashley was too. Gaunt had sliced cleanly through her wrist in one stroke, and the hand fell next to her.

That should have been him.

His place was between his people and those who threatened to harm them. That was his duty. He couldn't back down, or allow Gaunt to run amok, no matter the cost. He should have shot Gaunt when he had the chance. But he hadn't.

He climbed up the *kami* stone, inches from the engravings, until he got his legs under him. The stone had a new name, etched near the bottom of a too-long list: Rikimaru Hanzo.

I'm not dead yet.

His sword still sat on his hip, bent and warped from Brentwood Bay. It was out of its scabbard because it no longer fit, so he had tucked it through his belt, in its place. He drew Perseverance and held it out in front of him.

Gaunt laughed.

"You're a fool, Rikimaru. Your death won't accomplish a thing. You're a relic in this Fallen World. There aren't any heroes here, just winners and victims."

"There are monsters, too, Gaunt," he gasped.

Ashley stirred behind him. He urged her silently to go, but if he said anything, Gaunt would hurt her solely because she was important to him. His legs grew weak, and he stumbled away from the *kami* stone. The blade became heavy, and the point wavered and dipped.

Gaunt moved closer.

* * *

Rikimaru lost his balance, and his sword clattered to the floor.

It's now or never, Ashley.

Hit me again.

Another stim slammed into her heart, redlining her pulse, until she vibrated. Her hand wasn't strong enough yet, but she had exactly no time left. She pulled one of the titanium hairpins from her bun with her right hand, and she surged to her feet. Two steps and she jumped the void between her and the murderous Agent. She clamped onto Gaunt's back in a parody of a piggyback. Her left hand barely had the strength to grab hold of his tie, but it would do.

She screamed, and stabbed down with the hairpin. Bone crunched.

Ashley buried eight inches of titanium in Gaunt's ear canal, and the psychotic assassin dropped, like a puppet with its strings cut. She fell with him, but she had time to recover. She levered his head over with the hairpin, and buried her second one deep in an eye.

He did say "leaking grey matter," but I doubt he meant it quite that literally.

Quiet.

* * *

Rikimaru had no strength left. His vision was tunneling, and he could feel his pulse in his temples and the front of his head. It felt like his brain was trapped in a vice, and each heartbeat tightened it one more notch. He placed his hands on his knees to steady himself and was vaguely surprised to see his sword hand was empty.

I'm not dead yet!

He hit the floor, and the sanctuary marble was blessedly cool.

Then Ashley had him in her arms, and she sat there on the floor, hugging him close. He could smell her hair, and it reminded him of a long time ago before the world fell. It made him feel like everything would be alright. He cracked his eyelids to look up at her one last time.

She had *both* hands!

How did she have both hands?

"What…what *are* you?" he whispered.

"*Sorry,* my love. I am so very, very sorry."

* * * * *

Epilogue

"How are they doing, doc?"

Master Sergeant Eriksen passed Doc Marcum a mug of tea in the clinic's reception area. Marcum looked exhausted, but hours of high-pressure trauma surgery tended to be draining.

"To be bluntly honest, varying degrees of messed up from 'badly concussed, but he'll be fine,' to 'crippled for the rest of her life.'"

"I thought Specialists could bounce back from anything?" Rainier asked. "They always seemed invincible to me."

"I thought so, too, until they brought Mikael down from the fight on the bridge. He's lost a good chunk of his lungs, and he isn't going to get better. Ayame won't ever walk again. Maybe, before the fall, we could have reconstructed her knees, but not now, not a chance. They haven't had a nanite update in twenty years, maybe they're finally failing? I don't really know. All I could tell Mikael was, some injuries just don't get better." He took a long sip of tea, and when he lowered the mug, he wore a confused expression. "That woman they brought with them hasn't left the daimyo's side. Does anyone know who she is? She just said she was Ashley, an old friend."

"It's…complicated," Kesting supplied. "She's kinda our prisoner. She's also kinda Empress Victoria. And she's kinda Rikimaru's ex-fiancé, too."

343

Marcum threw his hands up. "I don't want to know, thanks. Leave me out of it. Just bring me the broken and damaged, and I'll do what I can. Rick's awake; you can go see him, if you want."

Eriksen thanked the doctor and filed into the recovery room with the marines on his heels. Rikimaru smiled weakly when they came in.

"Well, if it isn't trouble on six legs. Come in."

"Thank you, Daimyo," Eriksen replied. "Or is it Shogun now?" He looked at the woman by his bedside, then grimaced as a wave of nausea hit.

"No. Rick's fine, for now. We were just talking about that."

Rainier eyed him suspiciously. "Do tell?"

"You have nothing to fear from the Victorians," Ashley said. "You have friendlies there and open communication. The reign of Empress Victoria is over, and those people need your help."

"The bridge to the mainland is gone," Rikimaru continued. "The Komainu and the Onamazu are competent and fit, and they have a professional officer corps with folks like Master Sergeant Eriksen, Lieutenant Moon, and Captain Hayes. It's time we enhanced types took a back seat and stopped handling problems with violence just because it's the most convenient. I'm comfortable saying that because, most importantly, Gaunt is dead. Ashley leaked the ever-loving hell out of his grey matter. No uncertain doom this time."

The silence hung in the air for a moment.

"So…what then?" Rainier asked.

"Oh, I'm sure you guys will figure something out. Write up a charter and a constitution. Rebuild the kind of citizen-based republic we had before the Corporations seized control. If they could manage it three hundred years ago, you can figure it out now."

Eriksen looked at him suspiciously. "*You guys?* What's this, *you guys?* Where are you going to be in all this?"

Rikimaru sat up a bit straighter in bed and covered his eyes as nausea clobbered him again.

"Mikael is crippled. Aya's never going to walk again. I'm *hoping* Thor is going to recover from his bout with that prototype imprinter, but it's going to be weeks before we'll have any real idea."

"There's another bunker," Ashley said. "One like Helios House, east of the SoCal Sprawl." Ashley went rigid, clenched her jaw, and grimaced as though in pain. The moment passed, and she was fine again. "There were a lot of corporations pre-fall working on…consumer health products. Very advanced consumer health products, and some corporations were more successful than others. I think I know where to find some pre-fall tech that could help Aya, and Mikael, and other people with crippling injuries like theirs."

Rikimaru nodded. "I owe it to them to try. That said, we're going to need some time to plan and prepare because that's a hell of a long trip in this Fallen World."

# # # # #

ABOUT THE AUTHOR

Jamie Ibson is from the frozen wastelands of Canuckistan, where moose, bears, and geese battle for domination among the hockey rinks, igloos, and Tim Hortons. After joining the Canadian army reserves in high school, he spent half of 2001 in Bosnia as a peace-keeper and came home shortly after 9/11 with a deep sense of fore-boding.

After graduating college, he landed a job in law enforcement and has been posted to the left coast since 2007. He published a number of short stories in 2018 and 2019, and his first novel came out in January 2020. He's pretty much been making it up as he goes along, although he has numerous writer friends who serve as excellent role-models, mentors, and, occasionally, cautionary tales. "We Dare: Semper Paratus" is the second anthology he's edited, and he will probably keep doing annual, themed anthologies as long as Chris will let him.

His website can be found at https://ibsonwrites.ca/. He lives in Abbotsford, British Columbia, is married to the lovely Michelle, and they have cats.

* * * * *

The following is an
Excerpt from Book One of The Devil's Gunman:

The Devil's Gunman

Philip Bolger

Available Now from Blood Moon Press

eBook, Audio, and Paperback

Excerpt from "The Devil's Gunman:"

I eased the door open and braced for gunfire or a fireball.

I got neither. I swept the entryway with my rifle's sights. Nothing more offensive than some high school photos glared back at me, and I didn't hear anything running down the hallway or readying a weapon. There were no shouts from police or federal agents, either.

What I did hear, from the living room, was incessant chatter underscored by the occasional interjection of a laugh track. The chatter was accompanied by the soft peripheral glow of my television. Whoever had broken into my house was watching a sitcom.

"I'm unarmed," a man's voice rang out. "So put down the rifle, and let's have a talk."

"The fuck we will," I shouted back. "You broke into my home!"

I moved down the hallway, keeping my rifle on the opening to the living room.

"That's part of what we have to talk about," the voice said. I peered around the corner and saw a young Caucasian man. His pale features and dyed blue hair did little to mask the malicious smirk on his face. He was dressed in an oxford shirt and slacks with a skinny tie, as though he couldn't figure out if he wanted to look like he'd just joined a band or an investment firm. He wore a silver tie clip with a red blood drop on it.

I stood there with my rifle sights on his head.

"I'm here as a messenger," he said and flashed his teeth. I saw pointed incisors. That was enough for me. "This is peaceful, Nicholas. No need to be violent."

I lowered the rifle. I didn't like the prick's condescending tone; he sounded like he enjoyed the sound of his own voice. Those types were always eager to give up information.

351

"Okay, let's talk. Who's the message from?" I asked.

"I hold the honored post of Emissary of the Lyndale Coven," he said politely, examining his nails. "We've taken a professional interest in you, and Coven leadership sent me."

"Oh yeah?" I asked. "What for?"

"To dictate the terms of your surrender," he said, locking eyes with me. His hands twitched, then curled slightly. I imagined him leaping off the couch and knocking me down. I fought the urge to bring the rifle to bear, keeping it at the low ready.

"Thought your kind needed an invite," I said.

The man snarled.

"We both know who built this house. I have a standing invite. The coven master says that the Duke no longer wants you, so you're fair game. Our agreement, which I have right here, has the details."

He pulled a no-shit scroll out of his suit jacket and put it down on my coffee table. I glanced at it. The Lyndale Coven seemed to be under the impression that I belonged to them. I read the word "slave" once, and that was enough for me to decide I wasn't interested.

"No dice," I said.

"These terms are much more charitable than those the Coven Master wanted," he said, warning in his voice. "Oath breakers aren't normally given this kind of clemency."

I didn't have much idea what he meant about oath breakers, but I wasn't going to play ball with this pompous fuck.

"Not charitable enough," I said. "Why do you guys want me? Running out of blood from young clubgoers and runaways?"

The young vampire smiled again, flashing his teeth with what I'm sure he thought was menace.

"It'll certainly improve our coven's standings with the Duke if we prove we can clean up his loose ends. I'm sure you'll make an excellent blood thrall. We'll be taking a pint of blood every month, as—" I raised the rifle and sighted in on his head. He sighed, and rolled his eyes.

"Look, you primitive ape, guns won't—" I fired three times, the rounds earth-shatteringly loud in such a tight place. He screamed in pain and terror as the holy rifle's bullets tore through him, the wounds leaving bright blue caverns of light.

His screaming echoed in my head, so I kept shooting. I fired the rest of the magazine until there was nothing left but a corpse, riddled with holes and glowing softly, and me, standing there in my gunpowder-fueled catharsis.

I dropped the mag and slapped in a fresh one, savoring the sound of the bolt sliding forward and knowing that if the emissary had any friends, they too, would be introduced to the kinetic light of St. Joseph.

"Anyone else here? I got more."

* * * * *

Get "The Devil's Gunman" now at:
https://www.amazon.com/dp/B07N1QF4MD.

Find out more about Philip S. Bolger and "The Devil's Gunman" at:
https://chriskennedypublishing.com/philip-s-bolger/.

* * * * *

The following is an
Excerpt from Book One of The Shadow Lands:

Shadow Lands

Lloyd Behm, II

Available Now from Blood Moon Press

eBook and Paperback

Excerpt from "Shadow Lands:"

The combatants, for lack of a better term, were both resting at the edges of the dance floor. To the left was a very butch-looking blonde in what looked to be purple leather, along with her entourage, while to the right, a petite, dark-skinned Hispanic in a princess outfit stood, surrounded by meat popsicles wrapped in leather. Vampire fashions make no damn sense to me, for what it's worth. There were a few 'normals' huddled against the far wall, which showed signs of someone's face being run along it, repeatedly. Sure enough, the London 'Special' was in the DJ booth. He killed the sound as soon as he realized we were standing there.

"Ladies and gentlemen, may I introduce the final players in our little drama, the Reinhumation Specialists of the Quinton Morris Group!" the Special said into the mike.

"Fuck me running," I said.

"With a rusty chainsaw," Jed finished.

The two groups of vampires turned to face us.

"Remind me to kick Michael in his balls when we get back to the office," I said.

"You're going to have to get in line behind me to do it," Jed replied.

"You can leave now, mortals," the blonde said with a slight German accent. She had occult patterns tattooed around her eyes, which had to be a bitch, because she would have had to have them redone every six months or so. Vampires heal.

"Like, fershure, this totally doesn't involve you," the Hispanic said, her accent pure San Fernando Valley.

"Jed, did I ever tell you how I feel about Valley Girls?" I asked, raising my voice.

"No…"

"Can't live with 'em, can't kill 'em," I replied, swinging my UMP
up and cratering the Valley vampire's chest with three rounds into
the fragile set of blood vessels above the heart. Sure, the pump still
works, but there's nothing connected to it for what passes as blood
in a vampire to spread. On top of that, company-issue bullets are
frangible silver, to which vampires have an adverse reaction.

With that, the dance was on. The damn Special in the DJ booth
at least had the good sense to put on Rammstein. *Mien Teil* came
thundering out of the speakers as we started killing vampires. Gunny
ran his M1897 Trench Gun dry in five shots, dropped it to hang by a
patrol sling, and switched to his ancient, family 1911. I ran my UMP
dry on Valley Vamp's minions, then dropped the magazine and reloaded in time to dump the second full magazine into the Butch
Vampire as she leaped toward the ceiling to clear the tables between
us and the dance floor. As soon as Butch Vamp went down, the remaining vampires froze.

"Glamour," the Special called, stepping out of the booth. "I can
control a lot of lesser vampires, but not until you got those two
randy cunts thinking about how much they hurt."

"You. Fucking. Asshole," I panted.

Combat is cardio, I don't care what anyone else says.

"Yes?" he replied.

I looked him over. He was wearing a red zoot suit—red-pegged
trousers and a long red jacket with wide shoulders over the ubiqui-
tous white peasant shirt, topped with a red, wide-brimmed hat. He
even had on red-tinted glacier glasses.

I felt his mind try to probe mine, then beamed as he bounced
off.

"My that hurt," he replied.

"You know, we don't work with Michelangelo for nothing," Jed
replied. Apparently the mind probe had been general, not specific.

I went through the messy side of the business—staking and be-heading—assisted by Capdepon. Crash helped Jed sort out the normal survivors, followed by prepping the live lesser vampires for transport. The Special leaned against a wall, maintaining control of the lesser vampires until we could move them out. Once all the work was done so the cleaners could move in, and the lesser vampires were moved out of Eyelash, I stepped wearily to the Special.

"What's your name?" I asked.

"You can call me," he paused dramatically, "Tim."

I kicked him in the nuts with a steel-toed boot. Even in the undead, it's a sensitive spot.

* * * * *

Get "Shadow Lands" now at:

https://www.amazon.com/dp/B07KX8GHYX/.

Find out more about Lloyd Behm, II and "Shadow Lands" at: https://chriskennedypublishing.com/imprints-authors/lloyd-behm-ii/.

* * * *

The following is an

Excerpt from Book One of The Darkness War:

Psi-Mechs, Inc.

Eric S. Brown

Available Now from Blood Moon Press

eBook and Paperback

Excerpt from "Psi-Mechs, Inc.:"

Ringer reached the bottom of the stairs and came straight at him. "Mr. Dubin?" Ringer asked.

Frank rose to his feet, offering his hand. "Ah, Detective Ringer, I must say it's a pleasure to finally meet you."

Ringer didn't accept his proffered hand. Instead, he stared at Frank with appraising eyes.

"I'm told you're with the Feds. If this is about the Hangman killer case…" Ringer said.

Frank quickly shook his head. "No, nothing like that, Detective. I merely need a few moments of your time."

"You picked a bad night for it, Mr. Dubin," Ringer told him. "It's a full moon out there this evening, and the crazies are coming out of the woodwork."

"Crazies?" Frank asked.

"I just locked up a guy who thinks he's a werewolf." Ringer sighed. "We get a couple of them every year."

"And is he?" Frank asked with a grin.

Ringer gave Frank a careful look as he said, "What do you mean is he? Of course not. There's no such thing as werewolves, Mr. Dubin."

"Anything's possible, Detective Ringer." Frank smirked.

"Look, I really don't have time for this." Ringer shook his head. "Either get on with what you've come to see me about, or go back to wherever you came from. I've got enough on my hands tonight without you."

"Is there somewhere a touch more private we could talk?" Frank asked.

"Yeah, sure," Ringer answered reluctantly. "This way."

Ringer led Frank into a nearby office and shut the door behind them. He walked around the room's desk and plopped into the chair there.

"Have a seat," Ringer instructed him, gesturing at the chair in front of the desk.

Frank took it. He stared across the desk at Ringer.

"Well?" Ringer urged.

"Detective Ringer, I work for an organization that has reason to believe you have the capacity to be much more than the mere street detective you are now," Frank started.

"Hold on a sec." Ringer leaned forward where he sat. "You're here to offer me a job?"

"Something like that." Frank grinned.

"I'm not interested," Ringer said gruffly and started to get up. Frank's next words knocked him off his feet, causing him to collapse back into his chair as if he'd been gut-punched.

"We know about your power, Detective Ringer."

"I have no idea what you're talking about," Ringer said, though it was clear he was lying.

"There's no reason to be ashamed of your abilities, Detective," Frank assured him, "and what the two of us are about to discuss will never leave this room."

"I think it's time you left now, Mr. Dubin," Ringer growled.

"Far from it," Frank said. "We're just getting started, Detective Ringer."

Ringer sprung from his seat and started for the office's door. "You can either show yourself out, or I can have one of the officers out there help you back to the street."

Frank left his own seat and moved to block Ringer's path. "I have a gift myself, Detective Ringer."

Shaking his head, Ringer started to shove Frank aside. Frank took him by the arm.

"My gift is that I can sense the powers of people like yourself, Detective," Frank told him. "You can't deny your power to me. I can see it in my mind, glowing like a bright, shining star in an otherwise dark void."

"You're crazy," Ringer snapped, shaking free of Frank's hold.

"You need to listen to me," Frank warned. "I know about what happened to your parents. I mean what really happened, and how you survived."

Frank's declaration stopped Ringer in his tracks.

"You don't know crap!" Ringer shouted as Frank continued to stare at him.

"Vampires are very real, Detective Ringer." Frank cocked his head to look up at Ringer as he spoke. "The organization I work for…We deal with them, and other monsters, every day."

Ringer stabbed a finger into Frank's chest. It hurt, as Ringer thumped it repeatedly against him. "I don't know who you are, Mr. Dubin, but I've had enough of your crap. Now take your crazy and get the hell out of my life. Do I make myself clear?"

The pictures on the wall of the office vibrated as Ringer raged at Frank. Frank's smile grew wider.

"You're a TK, aren't you?" Frank asked.

"I don't even know what that is!" Ringer bellowed at him.

"You can move objects with your mind, Detective Ringer. We call that TK. It's a term that denotes you have telekinetic abilities. They're how you saved yourself from the vampire who murdered your family when you were thirteen."

Ringer said nothing. He stood, shaking with fear and rage.

"You're not alone, Detective Ringer," Frank told him. "There are many others in this world with powers like your own. As I've said, I have one myself, though it's not as powerful or as physical in nature, as your own. I urge you to have a seat, so we can talk about this a little more. I highly doubt your captain would be as understanding of your gift as I and my employer are if it should, say, become public knowledge."

"Is that a threat?" Ringer snarled.

Frank shook his head. "Certainly not. Now if you would…?" Frank gestured for Ringer to return to the chair behind the desk.

Ringer did so, though he clearly wasn't happy about it.

"There's so much to tell you, Detective Ringer; I'm afraid I don't even know where to begin," Frank said.

"Then why don't you start at the beginning, and let's get this over with," Ringer said with a frown.

"Right then." Frank chuckled. "Let's do just that."

* * * * *

Get "Psi-Mechs, Inc." now at:
https://www.amazon.com/dp/B07DKCCQJZ.

Find out more about Eric S. Brown and "The Darkness War" at:
https://chriskennedypublishing.com/imprints-authors/eric-s-brown/.

* * * *

Manufactured by Amazon.ca
Bolton, ON

16429032R00201